Killa Kounty

Khufu

Lock Down Publications and Ca$h Presents

Killa Kounty

A Novel by _Khufu_

Khufu

Lock Down Publications
P.O. Box 944
Stockbridge, Ga 30281

Visit our website @
www.lockdownpublications.com

Copyright 2021 by Khufu
Killa Kounty

Lock Down Publications
Like our page on Facebook: Lock Down Publications @
www.facebook.com/lockdownpublications.ldp

Book interior design by: **Shawn Walker**
Edited by: **Lashonda Johnson**

Stay Connected with Us!

Text **LOCKDOWN** to 22828 to stay up-to-date with new
releases, sneak peaks, contests and more…
Thank you.

Submission Guideline.

Submit the first three chapters of your completed manuscript to ldpsubmissions@gmail.com, subject line: Your book's title. The manuscript must be in a .doc file and sent as an attachment. Document should be in Times New Roman, double spaced and in size 12 font. Also, provide your synopsis and full contact information. If sending multiple submissions, they must each be in a separate email.

Have a story but no way to send it electronically? You can still submit to LDP/Ca$h Presents. Send in the first three chapters, written or typed, of your completed manuscript to:

LDP: Submissions Dept
P.O. Box 944
Stockbridge, Ga 30281

DO NOT send original manuscript. Must be a duplicate.

Provide your synopsis and a cover letter containing your full contact information.

Thanks for considering LDP and Ca$h Presents.

Acknowledgments

First and foremost, *The Almighty* for giving me the world as my canvas, and for allowing me to paint whatever picture I desire. A special shoutout to Ca$h and the entire Lock Down Publications camp! I appreciate this opportunity to share my thoughts and life experiences with the world under the most prolific and authentic publishing company in existence.

To everybody who turned their backs on me, I would like to thank y'all the most! Your betrayal powered me up. To my mother, Patty. Thank you for never forcing anything on me. I love you! You allowed me to choose my own path at an early age, helping me become the man I am. To the whole Fort Pierce—stand up!

Killa Kounty we here!

Dedication

This book is dedicated to my son A.J., and three important people that I lost to gun fire. Stacy, Tayda, and Tela. May y'all Rest In Power. I love y'all 4eva!

~All is but change and transformation~
First the caterpillar, then the chrysalis, then the beautiful butterfly.
Likewise, first the physical man, then the mighty mind, and at last the mighty soul!

About The Author

Born September 27, 1985, raised in Fort Pierce, Florida. I was born a premature baby at six-months old. The doctor told my mother I wouldn't make it, but I prevailed. My mother raised me the best way she knew how, but the streets was so captivating and alluring I fell victim to them. I've watched countless friends and loved ones die. I've sold drugs, been on both sides of the gun, and I've been behind enemy lines most of my life.

As soon as I changed my life and tried to fly straight, I let some peasants trick me out into the streets and the feds did a sweep! My only regret is leaving my son out there in this cold world. In my city I'm a *Rap God*! I figured If I can write music and paint a picture, then I can write a book. I refuse to be stagnant because of my present situation, after all, you can't see a star without darkness! Ride with me and picture my life!

Khufu

Chapter 1

Retaliation in the Evening

"Aye, bra, fix me a cup," Mundo asked Baby G who was smokin' a dirty.

"Nigga, who da fuck I look like, Amilia Badilia?"

"Come on, bra, I'm driving. I woulda did it for you. Why you always think a nigga trying you?"

Blowin' lace that's all Baby G needed to hear to take flight. "See nigga, if you overstood how da universe worked you would know that it moves through vibration. So, when you feel disrespected the universe gon let'chu know through that natural vibration we all born with."

"Baby G, bra, stop smokin' dirties da shit ain't that deep."

Before Baby G could continue, his phone blared the ring tone, *Help me Rhonda* from *Pastor Troy's 'Face Off'* album. It was Shenida, Baby G's ride or die childhood friend who did whateva for him. "What it is, what it ain't, ma?"

"Baby G, where you at, boo?"

"Shid, I'm in route, what da play is?"

"I just wanted to lace you up on dat nigga who hit'chu up. He on thirteenth street right na in front of Adnewz."

"Say less, ma, I owe you one."

"No sweat, daddy. Just come put dat dick on me later you know how we play."

"Already! I'll be dat way in a few," replied Baby G.

Click!

"Aye Mundo swang through da tray it's dinner time," said Baby G cockin' his Ruger wit' Steph Curry hangin' out' em.

Steph Curry was street slang for a 30-round clip since the NBA guard wore #30.

"Who momma we finna front row now?" asked Mundo.

"Dat nigga Cee in front of Adnewz right now!" replied Baby G.

Mundo made a left on 13th and D creepin' until they got in front of the hole in the wall club. Clear as day the nigga Cee was up there bustin' plays. Mundo backed into the club's small parking lot and left the car running. Behind tint Baby G fired up another dirty, and watched Cee make sale after sale, on his beach cruiser oblivious to the fact that death was only ten feet away.

Pulling out a Garcia Vega tube, Cee dumped all the stones in his hand, counting what he had left before he called it a night.

Dropping the passenger window smoke began to leak out of the minivan they rented from a smoker. Baby G had so much coke in the blunt Cee couldn't help but smell it. Looking to see where it was coming from, he looked directly at a van he didn't realize was there until it was too late. When the smoke cleared all he saw was fire jumpin' out of a Glock, bullets hittin' all chest and stomach sending his dope flying in the streets where he lay stretched out.

Mundo pulled off and got in the wind, bending a few corners until they reached a bando' on 17th Street, where they switched cars and swung back through 13th. To their surprise, Cee was gone. They had no idea the club owner ran outside after hearing the shots. He saw Cee bleeding in the streets and pulled him into the building until help arrived. Cee was gone but one thing Baby G knew for certain was that he'd hit his man.

"Aye, bra, drop me off at Shenida's spot. I'ma kick it over there for a few," said Baby G.

"Alright, just hit me up when you ready to go back cross town," replied Mundo.

Pulling up and hoping out at Shenida's spot all Baby G could think to himself was, *That a nigga shot me but I'm still breathin' it's killin' season retaliation comes in the evening.*

Chapter 2

Shenida's Spot

Shenida was an eighteen-year-old, single mother, living on low income. She came a long way from the trenches with no father figure. Her mother was a prostitute before catching a ten-year bid for conspiracy to commit murder, and on top of that her brother was serving a life sentence for first-degree murder. Going through all this made Shenida a real solid bitch. She was a real one who did whatever to make sure her daughter was straight.

Baby G knew all this, and that's what made her so attractive to him—the struggle, and the fact that she was a true Dominican Goddess with almond-skin and a cute mole on the left side of her face that accentuated her beauty. Baby G also loved that her shoulder-length hair was natural. As she sat on her couch, rolling up a few joints in a lace panty and bra set, she heard her back door open and close. She already knew who it was, being that there was only one other person with a key.

"What's good, baby girl?"

"What dey do, daddy?" replied Shenida as she stood to embrace her male best friend with a hug and a kiss.

Grabbin' both cheeks, Baby G whispered in her ear, "Damn, you gotta ol' soft ass nerf booty."

"You already know this all you. Anytime you got it on your mind, daddy." Shenida hit the joint then passed it to Baby G. "Did you handle that lil' problem?"

"You already know I put my demo down. But what's overstood don't need to be discussed, ma."

Having no more words to say, Shenida pulled Baby G's dick out and gave him slow, decent treatment until he was on the verge of skeeting. She then got up and straddled Baby G's nine inches and rode him into submission. Baby G loved the way she fucked because she was always so turnt whenever they did. He wanted what they had forever—best friends who made it do what it do. Still, slumped from the power of that pussy, Baby G laid strecthed out with Shenida on his chest. She started stroking his dick hoping for another round when Baby G's phone vibrated. Now woke, he opened the message and saw that it was Shantel asking if he was coming home tonight.

Shantel was twenty-six-years old making her seven-years older than Baby G who was only nineteen. *Fresh out of prison he met her in the parking lot of Wal-Mart as she was putting away her groceries. Seeing all that ass he slid up on her and offered to help put her food away. Off rip, Shantel was attracted to the young man who had a glow to him as if he'd just did a bid. Baby G had on some Jordan gym shorts that showed his dick print, which Shantel couldn't stop eyeing. Jordan slides, and a tank top that showed he worked out a lot.*

"Damn, miss lady! Yo man let chu come out alone knowing it's niggas like me out 'chere?"

"First off, I don't have a man and my name is not miss lady, it's Shantel."

"No disrespect intended, beautiful. I'm just shootin' my shot."

"I guess," said Shantel.

"Everybody calls me, Baby G. It's nice to meet 'chu."

"Nice to meet you too, Baby G," said Shantel.

Ever since that day they were inseparable.

Baby G dialed Mundo's number and he picked up on the first ring. "Yo!"

"Aye, nigga, get up and swang through. I need a ride to my slider," said Baby G, referring to his whip.

"Give me fifteen minutes, I'll be there," said Mundo.

"Already!"

Click!

"Nooo! I wanted you to stay the night with me," cried Shenida.

"You know I fuck wit' cha, but I gotta go home to my bitch. You know what it is."

"Damn, man, I swear I'm jealous of that loyalty you show her."

"How is dat loyalty when I just pulled my dick outta you?"

"But still doe, you go home to her every night. I wish I had what she got fa real!"

Baby G got a text from Mundo saying he was outside. "A'ight,

14

Shenida I'm gone. Hit me up later."

"Okay, Baby G, I love you. Be safe out there."

"You mean off safety?" said Baby G.

"Boy, bye!"

"I love you too, ma," said Baby G as he left Shenida's spot.

Khufu

Chapter 3

What's Da Wordz

As he walked to the car Baby G looked both ways with his Glock out ready for whatever may await until he was in the car with Mundo.

"What's hood, lil' bra?"

"Ain't shit, just koolin'. You been on Facebook yet?" asked Mundo.

"Nall, I been laid in Shenida for a few. Why what's da word?"

"They saying that Cee is in the ICU, and he lookin' to pull through."

"Damn, dat pussy nigga lucky! I knew I flipped his ass doe. As soon as his ass recovers, we gon' throw his ass a party. I'm talkin' 'bout *big decorations!*

"You already know!" replied Mundo. "While you was in there laid up and shit. I ran into Scrab."

Scrab was another one of Baby G's childhood friends who took guns from one party and sold them to the next.

"He sold me a SK, two nines and a vest for six hunnid."

"Damn, I wonder who he savaged dat shit from this time?" said Baby G wit' a light chuckle. "Fuck all dat, we got it now," replied Mundo.

"I'm, wit' cha when you're right, nigga. Matter of fact, make this right on Dunbar, so I can pick my slider up from Off Top's spot."

Off Top was the big homie, and also Baby G, and Mundo's brother-in-law. He was a boss nigga who was hood rich just off selling weed. Niggas was always robbin' him, but not in the physical sense. They'd hit his stash spots when he left, and he'd just order a bigger shipment. If they hit for a 100 pounds, he would just grab 500 more. When they pulled up to the spot, Off Top was already outside smokin' one.

"A'ight, lil' bra, I'ma fuck wit' cha later."

"Already," said Mundo.

Khufu

"Baby G, boy what's happenin'?" asked Off Top.
"Ain't shit, bra, just pickin' up my slider finna take it in."
"Come see me in the morning, bra."
"Already," replied Baby G.

18

Killa Kounty

Chapter 4

Have You Killed Before

After hollin' at Off Top, Baby G hopped in his O6' Monte' Carlo and headed to Shantel's apartment playing his new mixtape, titled *DNA Klone Muzik.*

Part of an agenda/genocide niggaz live to die/ niggaz is uncivil/silver .4-O keep 'em civilized/ Sworn oath swag/I'm da truth I can't live dem lies/ Married to dem bandz/So, no fuck what I give dem guys—

Baby G turned the music down as he pulled into Shantel's complex, turned the car off and got out. He then walked across the street to a canal called Taylor's Creek and threw the Glock he hit Cee with in it.

Taylor's Creek was legendary for all the bodies, guns, and cars that were put in it. A lot of people drowned in Taylor's Creek, running from the police. Legend had it that the creek had weeds that wrap around a person's legs when they tried to cross it. If the weeds didn't get 'em, the gators or the police would. The police killed countless people claiming they were shooting at the gators, but that's Fort Pierce for ya ass!

Baby G headed back to the apartment, stuck his key in the door and entered to the smell of loud. Shantel was koolin' on her plush leather sofa, blowin' power packs and sippin' straight Remy. She was light-skinned with hazel eyes, standing 5'5, sporting a mohawk and thicker than a pot of grits. She had on a T-shirt with no panties. Looking at all that thigh meat, Baby G found his manhood rising to attention and instantly remembered he'd just fucked Shenida. He headed to the shower and got in. Once in the shower, he heard the door open and close. Shantel had come in and sat on the toilet while still smokin' her joint.

"Baby G, where you been?"

"You already know, I was in the studio, bae."

"I went there, you wasn't there."

"I didn't go to my brother's studio. I went to C-Major's. We

19

shot a video and all."

C-Major, was Baby G's white homie that he'd known for years. He shot the best videos in town.

"I was worried 'bout you, bae, cuz somebody got shot today. They say some dude named Cee got shot and almost died. Do you know him?"

"Nall, I don't know dat nigga, bae. You know my circle small."

"It's funny you say that, because I was in the salon gettin' my hair done, and overheard talk about how that dude Cee shot you a few years ago."

"Don't be listening to dem hoez in dat shop. I don't know who shot me, I didn't see the shooter."

"Baby G, have you ever killed someone?"

"Damn, baby, why you pressin' a nigga like dat?"

"I just wanna know who I'm lying next to at night, bae, that's all. If you out here shootin' and killin' people. Don't have me in the blind, baby. I love you regardless, bae."

"I love you, too, bae."

After hearing those words Shantel took her shirt off and got in the shower with Baby G dropping to her knees. Hissing like a snake, Baby G grabbed the back of her head as she sucked him up viciously. Looking into her hazel eyes was too much for him and caused him to skeet prematurely. Shantel sucked him back to attention, then bent over. She was so wet that Baby G slid right in and fucked the air out of her. Baby G still had another round in him so he picked Shantel up, carried her to the room and did the same until they were both slumped and fell asleep.

Fifteen minutes later, Shantel was unable to sleep due to the fact that Baby G's daily activities kept her stressed out. As she laid beside him rubbing his chest looking in his face full of street art.

She thought, *How did I get caught up with this young man deep in the streets, yet so full of life?*

She loved everything about Baby G, especially his music. He had a promising career waiting on him, but he couldn't stay out of trouble long enough to see the fruits of his talent ripe. Shantel knew that the odds were stacked against him being black in Amerikkka, let alone in Killa Kounty. On top of all that, she was pregnant and waiting for the perfect time to tell him. Before Shantel knew it, it was morning. She put Baby G's dick in her mouth, waking him up the way a young king should be. The heat from her mouth raised him from the dead, causing him to squirm.

"Damn, bae, you savage life dis mornin'?"

"Umm—yes, daddy! Now shut up and feed me." Baby G, came in her mouth and was halfway slumped again until his phone started ringing. "Bae, pass me my phone please."

Shantel eyed the phone before passing it to him.

"Yo'!"

"Top of the morning, nigga. What's hood? You up?"

Taking the phone from his ear, Baby G looked to see who was calling. It was Off Top.

"Yeah, bra, I'm up. I'm finna head to you now."

"Aye, Baby G, make sho' you brang Mundo wit' cha."

"Already!" After ending the call, Baby G dialed Mundo's number and got dressed to hit the streets.

Khufu

Chapter 5

Mundo's Spot

"Who was on the phone?" asked Yana.

"Mind yo bidness and fix me some shit to eat."

"Damn, that's how you ask for shit you want?"

"Why is it so hard for you to do what the fuck I tell you? Don't I cut a check when a check is needed?"

"That don't mean you can talk to a bitch like that, Mundo!"

"Yeah, a'ight, have my shit ready by the time I get out the shower."

"Damn, nigga, I can't get no quickie or nothin'?"

"Duty calls! I'll knock ya lil' socks off later," said Mundo, closing the door to the shower.

"I swear, this nigga be doing the most," said Yana but got up to make breakfast, she knew Mundo was looney for real.

Stepping out of the shower, Mundo heard a knock at the door. "Aye, Yana, get da doe!"

Yana got up to open the door for Baby G. "Hey, Baby G."

"What's good, sis? Where crazy man at?"

"He in here gettin' dressed. You thirsty or anything?"

"Nall sis but thank you, doe."

"Alright, Mundo should be out in a minute."

Walkin' in, Baby G stopped and looked at all the club pictures of him and Mundo on the wall.

He thought, *Damn, we be hangin' the fuck out.*

While Baby G was taking a trip down memory lane, Mundo walked up strappin' on his vest and tucking his Glock 9 with an extention.

"What's good, bra? What da play is?" asked Mundo. "I got a call from Off Top this morning. He wanna holla at us 'bout somethin'."

"Shid, if Top wanna holla at us it gotta be about dat bag!" said Mundo.

Yana came into the living room with her hands on her thick,

curvy hips, and stood parrot toed. She had a red complexion, with low cut hair.

"Mundo, yo' food done, come and eat before it gets cold."

"Bag dat shit up and put it in the oven, I'm gone." Mundo peeled off three hunnid and threw it on the coffee table. "Baby G, bra, let's slide."

"Shid, say no more, we out."

Both brothers left to hit the streetz of Killa Kounty, while Yana just stood there looking crazy and hurt. All she wanted was for Mundo to stay home and spend time with her, but he was too far gone—he was all in.

Chapter 6

Such A Shame How Friendships Change

Once in the car, Baby G lit a dirty, and took a shot of Remy. "Damn, my nigga, it's too early for dat shit, bra. You geekin' fa real."

"My nigga, spare me dat!" said Baby G. "The world fucked up, so I'm fucked up too." Mundo just shook his head, and turnt up the music.

Sliding through the hood, Baby G stopped at a red light on 29th Avenue D. Mundo hopped out and ran toward the car that was behind them and put the whole thirty clip in the driver's side.

"Lilly pad ass nigga!" Mundo yelled and jumped back in the whip with Baby G. "Take me to Granny's Kitchen, a nigga kinda hungry," said Mundo.

"Nigga, next time give me a headz up. Da fuck wrong wit' cha?"

"My bad, but aye—you gotta get it when you can."

"Who was dat you put to sleep?"

"Oh, dat waz da lil' nigga Billy Da Kid. He was in Yana's inbox talkin' 'bout what he wanna do to her pussy and what he'll do to me. I guess, he thought dat waz gon' get him da pussy, but instead it got' em thirty on his mind."

"Damn, my nigga, I thought y'all waz kool. Such a shame how friendships change," said Baby G.

Chapter 7

Granny's Kitchen

Pulling into *Granny's Kitchen*, Mundo hopped out to go order. "Aye, Mundo, grab me a corn beef hash breakfast with a half and half drink of lemonade, and tea."

"Nigga, where ya money at?" asked Mundo.

"I got chu when you come out, don't trip," replied Baby G.

When Mundo walked in the building, Baby G noticed Shenida coming out, and got out to approach her. "What's good, daddy? I been meaning to scream at chu 'bout something, Baby G."

"Talk to me, baby girl, what's hood?"

"Okay, so I was at the hospital with my homegirl Nene kuz she just had a baby."

"Damn, I ain't know Nene was pregnant. Tell her I said congratz!"

"Yeah, yeah, nigga anyway like I was saying. I went to the parking lot to get my phone so I could take pictures of the baby an I saw that nigga Cee rollin' out in a wheelchair with his sister. I guess he was checkin' out."

"Good lookin', baby girl, I owe you once again."

"No problem, daddy, It's anythang fa my nigga!"

Baby G peeled off a few hunnid dollar bills and handed them to Shenida, but she refused to accept it. "I'm good, Baby G, this personal for me too. Dat pussy nigga killed my kuzin."

"Say less, baby girl, you already know I got chu. Don't even trip on dat."

"I know what it is wit chu. Datz why it's *whateva* for you." Mundo walked out and got in the whip with their food. "Alright, baby girl, get at me later?" said Baby G. He hugged Shenida then hopped in the car.

"What was ol' girl hollin' 'bout?"

"She just laced me up on some shit. Ain't nothin' I'll scream at chu later 'bout it. Let's go holla at Top."

"Already," said Mundo.

Chapter 8

What It Iz What It Ain't

Baby G made a right on 29th and Dunbar then pulled in Off Top's trap. He let the AC run while they finished their food.

"What chu think Top got on his mind?" asked Mundo.

"At this point, bra, it don't even matter. My bag gettin' kinda low so I'm all in regardless."

"I'm feelin' dat, shit, let's go in and see what da play iz."

Baby G killed the engine, and they got out to knock on the door, but it opened before they could.

"What's good y'all, boyz?" asked Top.

"Same shit, different toilet," said Baby G.

"Y'all boyz come in and talk a lil' bidness."

Both brothers walked in and saw that Top had poundz of weed everywhere.

"You hangin' da fuck out in dis bitch?" said Baby G.

Before Top could respond a pretty, redbone with dreadz came out the back room. "Hey, big brudi and lil' brudi!" It was Baby G's and Mundo's sister . She and Top had kids together named Machi and Hezron.

"What's good, sis?" asked Baby G. "Busy as alwayz. What brings you two fools on this side of town?"

"They just came to talk a lil' bidness give us a minute, baby," Top interrupted.

"Okay, bae, I'm finna go get dinner started anyways." C.C. kissed Top and told him that she had counted two hunnid thousand. Top peeled off three bandz, hear, go get the kidz something I'll be there later."

"Okay, bae, bye y'all. Y'all be safe."

"You mean off safety?" said Baby G.

C.C. shook her head and left the trap.

"Listen, I already know how y'all get down. Da streetz talk. I got a play for y'all twenty-k a piece. Y'all ain't gotta give me an answer right now."

"Say less! We on dat," Baby G interrupted.

Top slid Baby G the envelope with the hit in it. After viewing its contents he passed it to Mundo, who smiled once he saw who the victim was. "Y'all boyz get ten now, and ten later," said Top.

"Just stay by the TV shid you know we keep it on da newz," said Baby G.

Mundo grabbed a half bottle of Patron off the living room table and took a shot. After putting the bottle back down, he rose to leave, and told Top, "Don't worry 'about paying us ten up front, bra. We gon' get paid in full when the drill is done. Baby G, let's slide."

Both brothers left the trap with murder on their minds.

Chapter 9

Da Big Bad Wolves

Baby G took Mundo back by his spot to grab the other vest, the SK, and his other Glock with extra clips. After strapping up, they headed to the vic that was in the envelope. It was a young, hot-headed nigga named Piggy; a red nigga with a big azz pig nose. Piggy and Mundo used to be crime partners until Piggy started robbing and shooting at people Mundo was kool with. Instead of killing Piggy, Mundo just fell back from him. But now that he had a ticket on his head, Mundo was all in.

"Baby G, bra, swang through da plaza. Dat nigga Piggy baby momma stays in da Island."

The Island was a hood surrounded by two canals called Taylor's Creek which gave it its name, *The Island*. The Island had a bunch of young niggaz running around with blue flagz calling themselves I.B.C, *Island Boy Crips*. Baby G had been red flagging for years but grew up with most of the Island Boyz, so his face was good in the hood.

"Pull up in dat gas station and park, bra," Mundo said. "What da play iz, lil bra?"

"The nigga Piggy baby momma stay four houses down from the gas station, bra. She alwayz leave the slidin' door open for Piggy in case of emergencies. Bra we slide right in there."

Without saying anything Baby G grabbed a gym bag with a hoodie in it, put it on, folded the SK and put it in the gym bag. Mundo grabbed both of his Glocks and tucked them in his front two pockets, then looked at Baby G like lets ride. Both brothers got out and Mundo led the way through the dirt trail that ended in the back of Jazzmine's house. It was a gate with a hold in it, they went through it and was now in her backyard.

"Sssshhh," Mundo told Baby G, as they crept through the yard straight up to the sliding door.

Just like Mundo said, it was open. Once inside, Mundo upped both Glocks as Baby G took the stick out of the gym bag and held it like a guitar. As they tiptoed through the kitchen, a woman's voice could be heard singing *K. Michelle's Hard to Do*. Mundo held up two fingers to let Baby G know that it was two bedrooms. Baby G shook his head and swung his stick in the room to the left. He found a baby sound asleep in its crib. The other room was clear, so Mundo opened the bathroom door slowly, and crept up to the shower curtain.

All in one motion, Mundo snatched the curtain open and slapped Jazzmine in the face, knocking her out cold in the shower. Mundo put both Glocks in his front pockets and picked Jazzmine up, taking her to the room that was clear.

Baby G walked in and saw Mundo putting Jazzmine in the bed. "Damn, bra, you done knocked da hoe out? We need her woke to get lil' Piggy over here."

"Well, wake the bitch up then," said Mundo.

"Give me one of yo Glocks," Baby G told Mundo.

Mundo handed Baby G a Glock, and what he saw Baby G do next was unforgettable. Baby G opened Jazzmine's legs and started fucking her with the barrel of the Glock.

"Wake da fuck up, bitch!"

Jazzmine started squirming and moaning until she opened her eyes and saw two niggaz in her house. She recognized one of them and screamed, "Mundo! What da fuck you doing in my house?"

Mundo pointed his pistol in her face. "Bitch, shut da fuck up. You know what it iz. Now, this how dis shit finna go." Mundo grabbed her phone off the dresser and threw it at her. "Call dat nigga Piggy and tell him his son ain't feeling well. Tell him you finna take him to the hospital, and you want him to ride with you."

"Nigga, y'all got me fucked—" Before she could finish her refusal, Baby G left and came back with the sleeping baby, putting the same Glock he used to fuck Jazzmine with to the baby's head. "Okay, please nooooo! Give me my baby!"

"Make the call, this is my last time saying it," said Mundo.

Jazzmine fumbled with the phone, dropping it a few times before gaining control over it. Finally, she dialed Piggy's number with a shaky hand.

Mundo put his Glock in Jazzmine's face. "Put it on speaker phone and act normal. And we'll let the baby live."

"Hello," said Piggy.

"Piggy, baby, where you at?"

"I'm, where I'm at. Why what's up, Jazz?"

"Your son is runnin' a fever. I need you to come home so you can take us to the hospital."

"Okay, Jazz, I'm on the way. Be ready when I get there."

"A'ight, Piggy, I love you—"

Click!

As soon as Jazzmine hung up the phone, Mundo put two holes in her face, spraying fragments all over the wall and headboard.

"Damn, bra, you done Picasoed da hoe's brainz everywhere in dis bitch. You a ill nigga for dat," said Baby G, laughing hysterically while passing the baby to Mundo.

Seconds later, a car door could be heard closing. Baby G picked up the SK and hid in the closet, while Mundo stood next to the bed with the baby in his arms. The front door opened, and Piggy could be heard walking through the house.

"Jazz, baby, where you at? I told you to be ready when I cam—" Piggy's words were cut short when he saw Jazzmine's head busted, and his old crime partner with his son in his arms.

"What dey do, Pig?" asked Mundo. "Onk onk, pussy nigga! You ain't never seen a wolf as bad as me, huh?"

Piggy upped his Glock 40. "Nigga, put my son down."

"Nall nigga, you put dat shit down fa I fuck 'round and kill dis lil' nigga."

Piggy inched his way forward, thinking he'd get a shot off if he got close enough, but he was wrong.

Baby G stepped out of the closet and put the tip of the SK to the back of Piggy's head. "Drop dat shit bitch azz nigga! This my first and last time saying it, swine."

Piggy tightened his jaw and dropped his pistol. "What da fuck you niggaz want man? Ain't shit here."

"See, dats where you wrong, swine," said Mundo. "We came to take soulz, nigga. I was supposed to front row yo momma yearz ago, but Jazzmine begged me to spare you. Yeah, I fucked da hoe, nigga, straight in yo face up. You knew dat hoe wasn't shit but we ain't here for all dat. You done pissed da wrong nigga off and it's a ticket on ya head, swine." Mundo walked past Piggy with his son in his hands. "Follow me, pig."

Baby G pushed Piggy in Mundo's direction as he headed toward the bathroom. Mundo lifted the toilet seat and put the newborn in it head-first, then closed the lid and flushed it repeatedly. Mundo then walked past Piggy, who ran to try and save his son, but was chopped in half when Baby G let the S-K loose. Half of Piggy's body laid in the tub while the other laid on the side of the toilet.

"Damn, I know somebody heard dat stick let's be out, bra," said Mundo.

"Nall, my nigga, fuck dat," said Baby G, who headed to the kitchen and came back with a knife and a ziplock bag.

"Baby G, bra, let's get da fuck!"

Baby G ignored Mundo and rolled Piggy's top half of his body over, cut his nose off and put it in the ziplock bag. "Nigga, now we can leave!" said Baby G.

Since they both wore gloves, they didn't wipe anything down. They left the same way they came—unnoticed.

Chapter 10

Gots To Be More Careful

"Baby G, baby, wake up!" said Shantel.

"I'm up—shit! Damit, man, what'z up?"

"I'm headed to work, baby. I love you and don't forget to take the trash out kuz the garbage man run early this morning."

"A'ight, ma, I got it."

"Give me a kiss, daddy."

"You gotta come get it if you want it," said Baby G.

Shantel crawled across the bed and kissed Baby G, then left for work.

Five minutes later, Baby G got up, brushed his teeth, and took a shower, then got dressed. He grabbed the keys off the dresser, pulled the drawer open and saw that he still had an eight ball and a few bags of weed, but he needed blunts.

"I gotta stop by the store," Baby G said to himself as he lifted the mat and grabbed his 40 with the lemon squeeze on it. Headed out the door he grabbed the trash and locked up the house.

He walked to the end of the road, where he dumped the trash. An undercover cop pulled up, rolled down his window and threw a starbucks cup in Baby G's garbage can. It was Detective Peer, a real racist, gung ho type motherfucka. He was always fucking with Baby G and Mundo because he knew how they rocked but could never make anything stick. Realizing he had a gun and an eight ball on his person, all he could do was laugh.

"What's so fuckin' funny, Mr. Moss?" he called Baby G, by his Government name.

All in one motion, Baby G spun around and yelled over his shoulder, "Nothin'!"

The Detective pulled off as Baby G got in his whip, heart beating like a mothafucka. "Damn, dat pussy caught me slippin' I'm trippin' hard." Baby G started the car and headed to One Stop Shop to get a box of cigars and a newspaper.

Khufu

Chapter 11

Dem 36s

Baby G pulled up and hopped out with his swag on *God* and headed in the store. "What'z good, Mike?"

Mike was an Arab who owned a couple stores around the city.

"Hey, Baby G, what's going on, man?"

"Shit, just koolin', shid let me get four natural leaves and a newspaper."

"That'll be seven-seventy-five."

Baby G handed him ten dollars. "Keep da change, my nigga."

"Thank you, my friend," said Mike.

Baby G read the paper not paying attention to what was in front of him. Baby G bumped into a stallion. She was 5'11, with long hair, almond colored skin, a beautiful face, and a body so righteous as if she'd just stepped out of a cocoon.

"Damn, lil' baby, you just gon' run a nigga over, huh?"

"I am so sorry, Uhh—"

"Baby G! My name is Baby G, beautiful. And you?"

"Baby G? Dats a cute name, my name is Rina. Nice to meet you and again I am so sorry."

"It's all good, Rina. Maybe we can talk about it over dinner. That's if you're not spoken for."

"I'm—it's complicated. Right now, it's like we're pullin' in two different directions. For some reason he can't seem to leave them streetz alone. He just got out of the hospital kuz somebody shot him up real bad, I mean it's just to much."

"Damn, I'm sorry to hear dat, ma. Seemz to me like you kud use a night out to enjoy yourself. You should let me take you out and eat chu—I mean feed you," Baby G said with a light chuckle.

"Yeah, I bet," said Rina with her eyebrows raised, smiling.

When Baby G saw her smile he knew he had her. "Put cha number in my phone," said Baby G, handing her his phone.

Rina took the phone and did as she was told.

"How's tomorrow, ma?"

"Tomorrow is good, Baby G,"

"A'ight beautiful, see you then." Baby G went in his pocket and gave Mike a hunnid dollars. "Whateva she gettin' on me."

"You didn't have to do that, Baby G," said Rina.

"Don't sweat it," said Baby G as he left the store.

Back in the car Baby G read the headliner. *Newborn Drowned While Parents Slain!* Then it went on about how the young black male's body was chopped in half with his nose missing. *No suspects have been found at this time.*

After reading the paper, Baby G called Mundo on speaker phone while building a dirty joint.

"Yo, what it do?" asked Mundo.

"Aye, meet me at the spot in twenty minutes."

"Already!" replied Mundo.

Baby G put flame to his spliff and headed back to his house to grab a bag out of the freezer, then headed to the spot to meet Mundo. When Baby G pulled up, Mundo was already sitting in his whip, he hopped out when he saw Baby G pull in. Baby G grabbed the bag off the passenger seat and hopped out to embrace his lil' brother.

"How you livin'?" asked Baby G.

"Off safety," replied Mundo.

"As you should," replied Baby G. You seen the paper dis morning?"

"Nall, but the shit we handled all over Facebook. We good doe, ain't nobody saying shit."

While they were politicking the door to the trap opened, and Off Top came out blowin' a joint of loud. "Baby G and Mundo, what'z good?"

"Money and pussy," replied Baby G.

"I hear dat, y'all boyz come in."

As soon as they got in the spot, Top let it be known what he had seen and heard. "I see y'all handled dat wet work, but damn shawty, and the lil' one?"

"Shid, all is fair in money and murder," said Mundo.

"Yeah, I left all dem sensitive feelins in my momma's pussy, my G. Ain't no room for feelins out chere in deez streetz, that shit will get chu killed," said Baby G.

"It's all good, I ain't trippin'," said Top.

Baby G handed Top the bag that he brought out of the freezer. "What da fuck is dis?" asked Top. Top dumped its contents out on the livin' room table. *"What the fuck!"* yelled Top.

"Yeaahhh! Onk, Onk, huh," said Baby G. "That's dat bitch azz nigga Piggy's nose."

"Come on, man, get dis shit da fuck out my spot," said Top.

"Ease up, my nigga, I got it," said Baby G, laughing crazy-like as Baby G picked Piggy's nose up with a paper towel and headed out back where King and Queen were located.

King and Queen were two trained German Shepherds that'll fuck you over if you show any signs of fear. Top had them trained by the best.

As soon as Baby G walked out the door, they rushed him.

"Sit!" said Baby G.

Both dogs sat wagging their tails with anticipation. Baby G threw Piggy's nose in front of both dogs, they just stared at the man's nose waiting for the command.

Baby G walked back to the door and screamed, *"At ease!"* Both dogz went in for the kill, scaring themselves in the process. Back inside, Mundo and Top were pouring up shots of eighteen hunnid.

"I see y'all started communion with outta nigga, huh?"

"Nall, fam you got perfect timing," said Top. "I was just tellin' Mundo I got some shit y'all might be interested in."

"Oh, yeah? Let's get to it then," said Baby G.

"Sit tight, my nigga, give me a minute." Top got up and disappeared in the back of the trap.

Baby G poured him a shot and downed it ASAP.

"Aye, my nigga, What da fuck King and Queen was ape shit about?" asked Mundo.

"Oh, dat ain't 'bout nothin'. I just fed dem a lil' pork."

"You's a silly nigga, fa real," said Mundo.

Top came back with two envelopes and a Wal-Mart bag. He sat everything down on the table, took a moment to fire his joint up, inhaled and exhaled before speaking, "In dem dare envelopes is twenty-K a piece. Since y'all boyz had to put in a lil' extra work, I threw in a lil' somethin' for you boyz."

Baby G grabbed the contents out of the bag which was wrapped in duct tape and sat it on the table. "Nigga, I know dem ain't dem 36s?" said Baby G.

"Datz exactly what it is, my G," said Off Top. "Y'all boyz know I'm da king of da city when it comes to dis weed shit. I don't fuck wit coke, but my plug dropped dis on me kuz he don't fuck wit coke either. So, now, I'm droppin' it on y'all, dat's if y'all want it."

"No disrepect, Top, but we don't sell dope. We kill niggaz you know, front row niggaz mommas and shit," said Mundo.

"Hold up, bra!" said Baby G. "How much you want for dis?"

"I told y'all datz on me, my nigga. Consider it a bonus," said Top.

"Dat'z love, my G, we'll take it," said Baby G.

Chapter 12

What Now

Once outside, Mundo stopped Baby G, putting his hand on his chest. "What now, Pablo?" asked Mundo.

"Da fuck you mean? Now we get money!"

"Baby G, bra, we ain't dealerz, we hittaz."

"What chu mean?" said Baby G. "What chu think I went to prison for? For pitchin' muthafuckin' crack, nigga! I just ain't never seen dem 36s before. Now we got 'em, ain't no lookin' back only way is forward."

"So, when we move dis shit how da fuck we gon' re-up? Top said dis a one-time thang he don't fuck wit' coke remember," said Mundo.

"You know what, I think I gotta way we can jiggalate," said Baby G. "You wit' me or nall?"

Mundo rubbed his hands through his dreads. "Fuck it! Letz rock out."

Khufu

Chapter 13

Brother From Another Color

Ten minutes later, Baby G and Mundo were pullin' into a trailer park. It was C-Major's studio/trap. "Bra, what da fuck we doing at dis craka spot?" asked Mundo.

"Dat craka you refering to, been my nigga for ten yearz. Dat'z my brother from another color."

"Okay, I hear all dat shit, but why the fuck we here?" Mundo asked, frustrated.

"A'ight, my nigga, peep dis," said Baby G. "When I come here to record and shit, I watch C-Major go through a nine-piece gram fa gram at eighty a pop. He got all da rich white school kidz, my nigga, killin' em fa real."

"Okay, nigga, and?" asked Mundo.

"*And?*" asked Baby G. "Nigga, do the math! A nine-piece at eighty a gram. Nigga, dat'z over twenty band yandz in one day! In four hourz to be exact. If we drop the whole thirty-six on C—Major, nigga datz over eighty band yandz! If he puts a nine on it which I'm sho he will—dat's over a hunnid bandz easy! The precise number wud be one hunnid thousand, eight hunnid. We let C-Major keep twenty bandz while we each toughin' over forty each without touchin' nothin'."

"Dats a lil' nice play you set up, but why not just give'em bricks, then come back and lay his azz down for everythang he got?" said Mundo.

"Bekuz, I already told you C-Major is my nigga. Now get cha azz out da car."

Baby G grabbed the bag and they headed to the front door. Baby G then knocked on the door, giving Mundo the eye, letting him know to straighten up his face.

"Yeah! Who is it?" yelled C-Major.

"What up, Major, dis Baby G. Open dis shit up, my nigga."

Major swung the door open. "What's up, bro? You come to record and hang out or what?"

"Nall, not today, bra. I came to talk bidness wit' cha."

"Come on in, bro, you want something to drink or anything?"

"Nall, bra, I'm on straight bidness today."

"What about you, Mundo? You want anything?"

"I'm good."

"Okay, so what's in the bag bro?"

"Dis for you, my guy, if you willin' to play ball."

"Talk to me, bro."

"Dis here, is a brick and I'm willin' to leave dis here wit' chu, but when I double back, I want eighty thousand, eight hunnid."

"Come on, bro, you shittin' me, right? I'll give you sixty thousand, right now for it, man."

"I can't do dat, Major. I know what yo gramz go for out here. You got Vero Beach and this trailer park on smash. I know you gon' make over a hunnid easy after you rerock dat shit, plus I'm frontin' dis hoe."

"I don't know, bro, let me think about it," said Major.

"Yeah, a'ight!" Baby G said as he put the bag on the kitchen counter. "I'll be back in four days for dem eighty. Mundo let's slide."

Chapter 14

No Plug

Back in the car, Mundo looked at Baby G with a smirk on his face.

"Nigga, what chu smirkin' fa?"

"I thought you said dat waz yo nigga? Yo' brother from another color?"

"He is. What chu mean?"

"Then why you chargin him like a out of town nigga?"

"Shid, an outta town nigga ain't gon' make what Major gon' make off dat one brick, I'm really lookin' out."

"We still ain't got no plug, bra. So, what'z next?" said Mundo.

"I'm already on dat, my nigga, just chill. In four dayz you'll have forty bandz to go with da twenty from Off Top. I gotta handle some shit, bra. So, I'm finna drop you off to yo whip. You good?" asked Baby G.

"Yeah, just keep me posted," replied Mundo.

Khufu

Chapter 15

Prison Or Death

Baby G put his key in the door and walked in on Shantel, coming fresh out of the shower, ass and thighs everywhere. She had a golden skin-tone that Baby G loved.

"What'z good, bae, how was work?"

"It was alright?" replied Shantel who walked in the bedroom and started putting cocoa butter on. Baby G grabbed the bottle of lotion and started rubbing it on her soft skin.

"Baby G, baby, I gotta talk to you about something."

"Dat's what I'm here for. Now turn over so I can get cha back."

Shantel turned and laid on her stomach, then Baby G started massaging the lottion on her back. "So, what' cha wanna talk about, baby? I'm all earz."

"Well, I don't know how to say it or how you gon' take it bu—"

"Man, spit dat shit out!" Baby G interrupted.

"Okay, baby, I'm pregnant."

"Don't play wit' me like dat, Shantel. You fa real?"

"Yez, I took the test four timez. Baby you mad at me?"

Baby G put the lotion down and started kissing the back of her neck. "Mad at chu?" He placed more kisses down her lower back. "How far you gon' baby?"

"I'm, eight weeks in, ooohh shit, daddy!" Shantel said between kisses.

"Shid, let me show you how mad I am." Baby G spread both of her ass cheeks and ran his tongue down the crack of her ass, blowin' softly afterwards.

"Oh my gawd! Baby, what chu shh—ssshhhiitttt boy damn!"

Baby G put his whole tongue in her ass in and out, while playing with her clit at the same time.

"O—okay—ssss—ooookkaayyyy!" Shantel tried to run up the bed but Baby G crawled right behind her.

When it was nowhere else to go, he pinned her in the corner, and sucked her pussy from the back until she came. Baby G then placed passison marks on her ass cheeks, then slid in her from behind. After flipping Shantel for two hours, Baby G laid there and enjoyed the after effect of a nice slice of pussy and thought about how he would be a great father. He also knew that being in the streets he could be separated from his child at any given moment. Prison, or death.

Chapter 16

Put Dat Up

The next morning, Baby G was up early doing his hygeine thing and showered. Once he got out of the shower, he got dressed in a pair of red joggers, a red fitted V-neck, and a pair of red Air Max 90s. His head full of waves complimented his baby face. A lot of women told him he favored Lil' Scrappy the rapper.

"Where you going, bae? It's eight-thirty in the morning," said Shantel.

Baby G went under the mattress and pulled out his .40 cal and the twenty bandz he got from Off Top. "Dis why I'm up so early," said Baby G, spreading the bills to show her that it was all hunnids. Baby G threw ten bands on the bed. "Put dat up for my son."

"Boy, we don't even know what we having yet. You talkin' 'bout yo son."

"I know it's gon' be a boy so kill all dat. And why the fuck you ain't get dressed for work yet?"

"Baby G, I'm off today, boy. I been told you my schedule. See you don't ever listen to nothing!"

"Shid, dat can't be true, kuz I'm listening to yo azz nag right now. Matter fact I'm gone, I'll catch you later."

"Baby G, be careful out there, I love you."

"Yeah, a nigga loves you, too," Baby G stated as he left out the door.

Khufu

Chapter 17

Calling Rina

"Hello!"

"Good morning, beautiful."

"Good morning, who is this?" asked Rina.

"Oh, I'm, just da nigga you assaulted in the store."

"OMG, Baby G, don't do that to me. I didn't mean it, and what took you so long to call me?"

"You been thinkin' 'bout a nigga, huh?"

"Maybe. You kinda got this unforgettable aura about 'chu that's so captivating."

"Oh, yeah?"

"Yeah!"

"Okay, I'm feelin' dat, but peep dis—a nigga feelin' you a lil' more, Rina."

"Baby G, boy you don't even know me, boy stop."

"True enough, I don't know you, but you are someone who I wish to learn. I got to be feeling you if I'm willing to take the time to learn you."

"I guess," said Rina.

"You guess what?" replied Baby G.

"I guess we'll see."

"So, where yo nigga at?"

"Oh, he at his sister's house. We don't stay together no more, he got too much going on."

"I hear dat," said Baby G. "What time we hangin' out, ma?"

"You can come get me around six-thirty or seven o'clock, I'm in Grand Savana apartment number three-o-four."

"Okay, beautiful, I'll be there."

"Bye, Baby G."

"Aight, ma."

Khufu

Chapter 18

All White Party

Baby G was slidin' down 23rd blowin' a joint listening to a rapper outta Texas, by the name of Skeet Taste when his phone started ringing. He turned down the music and answered the phone, "Yo'!"

"What'z good, daddy?"

Baby G knew the voice on the other end by the sound. "Shendia, what'z good, baby?"

"Daddy, I'm callin' to invite you to a party."

"Is dat right? What type of party we talkin', ma?"

"It's an all-white party," stated Shenida.

"What time dis party start?"

"In one hour, daddy."

"Anybody else know 'bout dis party?"

"No, daddy, you the only one I told."

"Aight, ma, thanks for the invite. Text me the address and I'll swang through there wit' a few decorations."

"Okay, daddy, I love you!"

"A nigga loves you, too.

Khufu

Chapter 19

Brang Da Toolz

Mundo was playin' Call of Duty when his phone started ringing. "What dey do?" asked Mundo.

"What'z good, family?" replied Baby G. "Listen, you gotta extra pair of wheels?"

"Yeah, why, what'z hood?"

"My car broke down, brang da toolz," said Baby G.

"I'm on it. What'z da location?"

"I'm up here at Chucky Ducky's."

"Say less, I'm on da way. Order me one of dem burgerz wit da Texas toast."

"Nigga, just brang yo greedy azz on!"

Mundo left the game on pause, got dressed and grabbed the latest weaponry he'd bought from Scrab. He caught Scrab at the brown store on 25th and gave him $200 for two judges. They were hand guns that shot 410 shells.

"Please be careful," said Yana.

"Don't worry 'bout me, I'm alwayz good," replied Mundo. "But if some shit do happen—" said Mundo walking up on Yana, kissing her on the lips. "—da money in the meat patty box in da freezer. Cold Cash," clowned Mundo.

Mundo grabbed the duffle bag out of the hallway closet and left.

Khufu

Chapter 20

What Da Play Iz

Baby G was backed in Chucky Ducky's when Mundo pulled in next to his '06 Monte Carlo. Baby G grabbed the food he bought for Mundo and got in the car with him.

"Here, greedy azz nigga!" said Baby G. "Everytime we run a drill, you get the munchies and shit."

"Whateva, nigga. What I brought da toolz fa?"

"Shenida invited us to an all-white party, I'm waitin' on da location now. What kinda toolz you workin' wit?"

"Oh, da nigga Scrab came through wit two cannons he took from some niggaz from da other side. They in da duffle bag on da back seat."

Baby G grabbed the bag to examine the heat. "Oh, shit my nigga, you got da *judges!*"

"Dis shit gone blow a nigga like da hood hoe." Baby G's phone vibrated letting him know that he had a message. "Okay, my nigga, we got action. Datz da invite let's roll out."

"Where we at wit it?" asked Mundo, starting the car. "Head out to Bethany's Court."

"*Bethany's Court?* Hold on," said Mundo poppin' the trunk. He got out and grabbed three hoodiez, then hopped back in. "Here, nigga, put dis on."

"Whatz da extra hoodie for?" asked Baby G.

"Dats fa Shenida."

Khufu

Chapter 21

You Freaky Bitch

As they pulled into the low-income complex, Baby G told Mundo to head to the back.

"Bra, you seen all dem niggaz in da front posted up?" asked Mundo.

"Yeah, we good doe. We in da back, pull in right here, bra." Both brothers strapped up then Baby G grabbed the duffle bag. "Let's rock!" said Baby G.

They got out with their hands in their hoodies, clutching, because they knew they were violating being on the wrong side of town. Baby G walked right up to door #21 and turned the knob. It was open just like Shenida said it would be. They entered the apartment, drew both cannons, and heard a male's voice making the weirdest noises ever.

Mundo swung left and saw that the first room was clear. Baby G swung right where the noise was coming from.

"Aahhh—ssshiittt bitch do that shit!"

Baby G turned the knob, pushed the door open, and couldn't believe his eyes. Shenida had this nigga in the buck, killin' him wit' the strap on. The shit that really fucked Baby G up was that he recognized the nigga. It was a nigga name Yada a supposed to be all around street nigga. Come to find out he was just an all-around faggot azz nigga.

"A'ight fagget azz nigga! Playtime is over," said Baby G.

Mundo walked in right behind him, gun aimed at Yada. "Damn, it smells like straight shit in dis bitch! Da fuck going on in dis— aahhh lawd Shenida in here rippin' dis nigga's azz apart, gay azz fuck nigga!" yelled Mundo.

Shenida pulled out of the nigga. "Damn, daddy, what took you so fuckin' long? Dis pussy nigga stank as fuck dog!" yelled Shenida.

"What da fuck you niggaz doing in my baby momma's shit? Get da fuck out nigga you know who you fuckin' wit'? Nigga, dis

Yada!"

"First of all, playboy," said Baby G. "You ain't in no position to be talkin' dat gangsta shit. Oh, girl just pulled out cha azz. On top of dat nigga, we strapped, which meanz you'z a fuckin' dead man, silly nigga. Now where it at pussy nigga?" asked Baby G.

"Daddy, the money is in a shoe box in the closet, and the work in them cereal boxes on top of the fridge."

"Mundo, go check it out," said Baby G.

"Bitch, you set me up! Hoe you gon' get yours," said Yada.

"I'm, wit' cha when you right," said Shenida. "I am gon' get it right out cha pocket." Shenida picked up Yada's pants and took a small bankroll, and his phone.

Baby G moved in and put the cannon to Yada's head. "Night-night, nigga!"

"Daddy, no!" said Shenida. "Dats too loud, I got em, just chill." Shenida left the room while Mundo was coming in.

"Jackpot, bra! Da nigga had a thirty-six in each cereal box, and a hunnid and twenty faces in da shoe box we good."

Shenida came back in with some zip ties and a box cutter. "Turn yo' gay azz over," said Shenida.

"Bitch, fuck you, I ain't doing shit."

Baby G snapped and pistol whipped both of Yada's eyes closed. "Aaahhh! A'ight please, lil' homie don't kill me please!"

Baby G spit in Yada's face. Nigga, I ain't yo' fuckin' homie!" yelled Baby G breakin' Yada's jaw.

Mundo stood there laughing' while Shenida zipped tied Yada's hands and feet. Shenida then straddled his back, lifted his head, and slit his throat.

"See, nice and quiet. I told you I got 'chu," said Shenida walking up on Baby G grabbing his dick through his joggers. "Damn, daddy, dis murder shit got dis pussy wet."

"You freaky, bitch!" said Mundo, throwing her a hoodie. "Later for dat shit, put dat hoodie on so we can get da fuck!"

"Yeah, ma, I got chu later, tighten up," said Baby G.

Mundo looked out the window checking the air. "Big bra, we got company. It's like eight niggaz standing by the whip."

"Oh, word? Give Shenida the keyz letz go. Shenida, baby, stay behind us."

Mundo grabbed the duffle bag with one hand and clutched his cannon with the other. Baby G opened the door, and they formed a wall in front of Shenida as they walked toward the whip with gunz out.

"Whatz up with all dat red!" screamed one of the eight niggaz who stood there."

"You niggaz ain't never heard of Santa Clause? Merry Christmas, y'all boyz!" yelled Baby G as he and Mundo upped their guns, giving it to the whole crowd.

Doom! Doom! Doom! Doom!

Everybody got low and ran behind another set of apartments except for the nigga who was asking Baby G about all the red he had on. He laid there holding his stomach, moaning and screaming for somebody to help him but nobody came. Baby G walked up on him and stood over him.

"You wanted to know what all dis red like, huh? When you get to the other side remember dis face stood over you and told you to *remind our enemiez of bloodshed*!"

Doom! Doom! Doom!

Baby G left the youngin's face open and hopped in the whip where Shenida and Mundo were waiting. Shenida drove out of the complex when shots rang out dropping' the back window of the stolen car.

"Oh, shit!" yelled Shenida.

Mundo hung out the back window lettin' loose his last two shots.

Doom! Doom!

"Mash out, baby girl, we got 'em," said Baby G.

"Damn, dis pussy just nutted everywhere," said Shenida.

Mundo shook his head. "You freaky bitch!"

Khufu

Chapter 22

Bust Down

Back at Shenida's spot, they sat at the kitchen table and divided the money. Baby G counted out twenty bandz and handed it to Shenida, while he and Mundo took fifty a piece.

"So, what we gon' do wit deez four bricks?" asked Mundo.

"Shid, when we go see C-Major tomorrow, we gon' drop two on him and sit on two."

"I don't mean to get in y'all bidness, but why y'all just won't move da work y'all selves?" asked Shenida.

"Yeah, I said da same shit," said Baby G. "But after thinkin' 'bout it, I figured why risk gettin' caught up in a drug conspiracy when we can just take it and drop it off, then pick up the money in a few days. It's hard to beat conspiracy, but murder can be beat all day in Amerikkka."

"Oh, datz what y'all doing?" asked Shenida. "I'm feelin' dat. I want in, daddy. Let me rock out with y'all."

"Every now and then we'll let chu ride," said Baby G.

"Speakin' of ridin' wit us. What da fuck was up wit' you and dat nigga Yada?" asked Mundo.

"I'ma keep it real wit chu, I was feeling the nigga at first, until he asked me to get on dat funny shit. I did it to him once before, and I made up my mind right then that he had to be got for makin' me catch feelings for his gay azz. The nigga was flexin', showing me where he keeps his money and work. A stupid nigga, fa real."

"You one freaky bitch!" Mundo chuckled. He turned to Baby G. "A'ight, bra, keep me posted."

"A'ight nigga, love!" said Baby G. "Make sho you burn dat car or put da bitch in Taylor's Creek."

"I'm on it," said Mundo as he left Shenida's spot.

As soon as Mundo left, Baby G spreaded all the money out on the table and then beat her pussy backwards.

"Ooohhh sssshhhittt! Nigga, throw dat dick!"

Hearing Shenida talk that shit, caused Baby G to stand on his toes and give her everything he had. "Paint dis dick, bitch!" Baby G grabbed both of her cheeks and spread them, then applied more pressure. "Bitch, I said paint it!"

"Ooohhh ssshit, daddy, pussy skeetin'!" Shenida grabbed a hand full of money as she skeeted all over Baby G. "Ooohhh, boy fuck!" Shenida's pussy muscles contracted around Baby G and got wetter with each stroke.

"Damn, dis pussy butta!" said Baby G.

Between watching her lil' soft azz jiggle with every stroke and glancing at the four bricks caused Baby G to skeet all in Shenida. "Aaggghhh—*damn it, man!*"

"Take dat wit cha," said Baby G, referring to his seeds.

"Damn, daddy," said Shenida as she dropped to her knees and cleaned Baby G with her mouth. "Ummm—I love you, daddy."

"You know a nigga loves you, too, girl." Baby G's phone started ringing. "Yo!"

"Baby G, what's going on, bro?"

"Major?"

"Yeah, bro, this me. I'm calling to let you know it's all good."

"Oh, word?" said Baby G. "I'll be through there in a few."

"Alright bro, I'm here."

"Already," Baby G ended the call. "Shenida, baby, get dressed and drop me off to my slider." Baby G grabbed his share of the money and work. "Tighten up, baby girl, let's go."

****

In Deez Streetz

"C-Major, I'ma need three hunnid twenty-three thousand, and two hunnid this time and you keep eighty bandz. I know I'm trippin' wit' da price, but if you knew what I had to go through to get deez bitches you wud overstand."

"It's kool, bro. The police never even come out here. I'd rather move it for you anyway then to have you get caught up, bro. We got to start dumping this money into your music, bro and fast."

62

"I hear you, and I'm wit dat but I'm in deez streetz right now. Give me a minute, fam, then we gon' handle up."

"Okay, bro, just let me know," replied Major.

"I'm out," said Baby G, grabbing the eighty bandz and leaving the four bricks.

****

Put Up 4 A Rainy One

Baby G pulled in front of Mundo's spot, and dialed his number.

"Yo!" said Mundo.

"Nigga, step outside for a few," said Baby G.

Mundo grabbed his banga and stepped outside. "What's up?" asked Mundo.

"Nigga, get in, let me scream at' cha for a sec."

Once in the car Baby G reached under his seat and grabbed forty thousand, and four hunnid, handing it to Mundo. "Don't run through dat shit, my nigga, put some up for a rainy one."

"You ain't gotta lace me up, I'm on point, bra," replied Mundo.

"Aight, I hear ya, but dig dis. I gave Major all four, that put us at three hunnid twenty-three, and two hunnid which is one hunnid sixty-one thousand, and six hunnid a piece. Major gets eighty bandz off dis one."

"I ain't doing no trippin'," Mundo said, "just keep me posted."

"A'ight, my nigga, love! I gotta lil' date so I'ma get at cha later," said Baby G.

"Damn, my nigga, where da sister at? Put me in da car. What'z up?"

"I just met her, bra, but I'ma see what'z up."

"A'ight, fuck wit me," said Mundo.

Khufu

Chapter 23

Bitch I'm Patty Son

Baby G went home and to his surprise Shantel was gone. He put the money he got from Off Top and Yada under the mattress, which put him at sixty bandz, after giving Shantel ten.

Her azz betta not be spendin' my unborn child'z money, Baby G said to himself, grabbing' his pistol.

Once back in the car, Baby G dialed Rina's number as he headed to Urban Appeal to get a suit for his date in a few hours.

"Hello!" said Rina.

"How you doing, beauty queen?"

"You ready for me, or what?"

"Yes, I'm ready, handsome. I was just thinking about you actually."

"Oh, yea? What were you thinkin'?"

"I was thinking—I hope I can keep deez pantyz on kuz you just too much, I don't know."

"Just be kool and let da universe do what it do best."

"Oh, yeah? And what is dat?" asked Rina.

"Reveal! The universe always reveals in due time. If you really want thug passion and you put forth the right effort, the universe will conspire with you and I'll be makin' love to you in no time."

"Baby G, boy, you crazy, but I guess."

Driving past the Chink's Rice Hut on 25th Street, Baby G saw a familiar face and made a U-Turn.

"A'ight, beauty queen, I'ma meet up wit chu later. I gotta handle some shit."

"Okay, handsome, don't stand me up. Where we going, anyway?"

"Meet me at da jetty round eight-thirty."

"Okay," said Rina.

Hanging up the phone from Rina, Baby G pulled in the Rice Hut next to an old friend by the name of Black. Black let down his window and told Baby G to smoke one with him. Baby G smirked at Black as he got out and hopped in with him.

Once in the car, Black passed Baby G the joint that was already lit. "Baby G, what'z good, homie? Listen, man, dat shit dat happin' a few weeks ago, datz dead, homie. I'm coming to you as a man to let you know dat I don't want no smoke wit'chu. I was drunk homie, dat wasn't me."

Baby G hit a joint and exhaled. "It's all good, my G! We all make mistakes, I ain't trippin' on dat."

"See, datz why I fuck wit chu. You'z a real one," said Black.

Baby G hit the joint and passed it to Black dropping it on the floor of the car. "Damn, my bad," said Baby G.

"It's all good," said Black reaching for the joint.

Blocka! Blocka! Blocka!

"Bitch azz nigga!" Baby G went in Black's pockets taking a hunnid and forty-two dollars. "Nigga, dis all you—" *Blocka!* "Nigga, dis all you had?" *Blocka! Blocka!* "Broke azz fuck nigga!"

Baby G wiped the door handle off, got out and left Black slumped under the steering wheel with the joint still clutched tight in his fingers.

A couple of weeks ago Baby G was in the club doing him, when Black came through on some hatin' shit, and snuck Baby G, knocking him down. Mundo being on point knocked Black down in return, causing the bouncers to rush to the altercation. They knew Black well, so they put Baby G and Mundo out of the club. Mundo and Baby G laid on Black in the parking lot, but the police who normally posted up when the club was over pulled up causing them to abort the mission. Baby G vowed to get Black, and now he'd finally got him.

Back in the car, Baby G was laughing and talking to his self liked he'd lost his damn mind. "Pussy nigga won't put his handz on nobody else! I told you. *Bitch, I'm Patty's son!*"

Chapter 24

Don't Mind If I Do

Pullin' up to Urban Appeal, Baby G hopped out and went in.

"Heeyyy, Baby G, baby! How you been doing? said Crissy.

Crissy was 5'5, mixed with Black and Mexican and fine as hell. Baby G had met her through his sister a while ago. Every now and again, they would rendezvous and have a fuck session.

"I'm above ground so I'm kool," said Baby G. "What chu got in here not too flashy but new?"

"What's the occasion?" asked Crissy. "I'm just hangin' out wit' a friend."

"A friend, huh?" Crissy asked with a raised eyebrow. Right this way."

Baby G followed her to the far right of the store, watching her ass the whole way over. "Damn, Crissy, I see you been eating cornstarch straight out da box ? Dat stuff back dare lookin' real weefy!"

"Cornstarch? No, baby, this all squats no shots," said Crissy. "Yeah, I got something you can squat on alright."

"I hear you," said Crissy, grabbing an Armani t-shirt and held it up to Baby G's chest. "This fits you but what is that red stuff, splattered on your shirt?"

"What cha talkin' 'bout?" said Baby G, looking' down at his shirt. "Oh, dis? Dis ain't 'bout nothin'."

"Nothing my azz!" replied Crissy. "Wait right there." Crissy went and turned the *Open* sign to *Sorry We're Closed*, then went to the back where Baby G was. "Take that shirt off, and come in the back." Crissy took the shirt from him and put it in a garbage bag. "I'll get rid of this because I know exactly what that is on this shirt."

"I told you, dat ain't 'bout nothin'," lied Baby G, walking up on Crissy, kissing her with pure passion.

"I don't want anything to happen to you, Baby G." He ignored her and planted kisses on her neck. "Damn, baby—I—I just want you to be safe," moaned Crissy.

Baby G took her shirt off and planted more kisses on her forehead, cheeks, and chin while removing her bra.

"I miss you, Baby G!"

"I know," said Baby G while now kissing on her perfect size breasts and removing her panties. Baby G bent down and put his arms under her thighs, lifting her and putting her back against the wall.

Crissy couldn't believe it. Baby G was sucking her pussy in the air. "Daammnnn! Baby, please stop! I can't take it no more!"

Baby G braced himself using the wall and used one hand to pull his dick out. Once he had his pole out, he went back to tongue kissing her clit.

"I'mmm—fuck—daddy—ssssss—suck this pussy, nigga!"

Hearing Crissy talk that freaky shit, caused Baby G to go animalistic, sucking, kissing, and licking like it was a do or die situation. Crissy's legs began to shake uncontrollably, as she nutted nonstop.

"Oh, my gawddd! Boy, damn!"

Baby G zoned out, and started rubbing his face in her pussy, wiping her juices all over his face like lotion.

"Damn, boy, you freaky as hell!"

"Shut up and take this dick!" Baby G lowered Crissy down on his dick slowly until all nine inches were in her. "Fuck this pussy, daddy!" Baby G started lifting her up and down at a steady pace, until Crissy came. Her wetness caused Baby G to speed up bouncing her on his dick violently.

"Yes, nigga shit! Aaahhh datz it, kill this pussy! Ssss—fuck!" Crissy could no longer hold her arms around Baby G's neck. She came so powerfully that it caused her body to go limp with the top part of her body dangling. Baby G still held her legs and continued to fuck the shit out of Crissy until he came.

"Ggrrrr—aaahhhh—shit, *bitch*! Damn it, man!" Baby G came and laid on her catching his breath, kissing her on her lips, and cheeks. "Get up, and lock the door, ma, I gotta go."

"Okay, baby, give me a minute, shit." Crissy laid there and fell asleep.

Baby G got dressed, grabbed the bag with the bloody shirt in it and headed to the front of the store. "Shid, I don't mind if I do," said Baby G as he grabbed a whole Armani outfit, and left the store.

****

"Hello!" Baby G answered his phone.
"Hey, Baby G, this Rina."
"What'z up, baby girl? I was just headed to you."
"I'm headed there too, handsome."
"Yeah, how close you iz?"
"I was at a friendz at the Steven Store Apartment, but right now I'm at the light on Highway US, by the McDonald's."
"A'ight, ma, I'll be in yo' chest in no time."
"Okay, Mr. Baby G. I'm in a peach Lexus, see you then."
"A'ight, beautiful."

Khufu

Chapter 25

Bake Zetti

Baby G pulled right behind Rina, killed his engine, and wondered if he should leave his banga in the car. True enough the Jetty is a nice relaxing place on the beach, but sometimes the wrong people run into each other from opposite sides of town, which often ended in shootouts.

"Fuck dat," said Baby G and tucked his banga in his Armani sweats.

He got out and approached Rina. Standing in front of her car door, smiling.

Rina exited her car, and stood there, looking like a horse. "I thought that was you behind me," said Rina. "What took you so long to get out the car? You having second thoughts or what?"

Baby G grabbed her by the hand and spun her around slowly. "Any man that second guesses heaven on earth gots to be outta his rabbit azz mind! *Damn it, man!* Rina, baby you lookin' magically delicious fa real," said Baby G, pulling her closer and sneaking a kiss on her neck."

"Boy—don't—do—dat," whined Rina, sounding like a little child.

"Come on, beautiful, letz get some food in ya."

"Dat's what I'm talkin' 'bout. Let a sister get her grub on." Rina walked in front of Baby G as if she was on a runway for America's Next Top Model. She had on a Fendi dress that looked as if it was painted on. Every step she took her azz cheeks moved with a delayed reaction.

"Yezz lawd."

"I'm finna hang da fuck out," Baby G whispered to himself. "Let me get dat for you." Baby G opened the door for Rina.

"Why thank you, handsome," uttered Rina, as she stepped into the Bar-N-Grill known as Hurricanes.

"Let's grab dis table, right here," said Baby G pulling out a chair for Rina.

"Well, aren't you the perfect gentlemen slash gangsta."

Baby G sat across from her and looked into her eyes.

"*Gangsta?* What gives you the impression dat I'ma gangsta?"

"People talk, and I do have ears."

"First off, I'm not a gangsta! I am what I am."

"Oh, yeah, and what is dat?"

"I'm Baby G, Patty's son. Second of all, people gon' talk, baby girl. Dat's what dey do."

"I guess," said Rina. "So, why you gotta bring a gun in a place of bidness if you're not thuggin', Patty's son? Yeah, when you snuck yo lil' kiss in earlier I felt it on ur waist."

Baby G chuckled lightly. "Dat still don't make me a gangsta. It just meanz dat I'm prepared for the unexpected."

Before Rina could respond the waitress approached. "Hello, my name is Candice. I'll be waiting on you tonight. Are you guys ready to order?"

"Yes, we are. Rina, baby, what do you have a taste for?"

"I don't know, whateva you chose for me is fine."

"Okay, then, we'll have the fifty-piece Parmesan wings and eight shots of seventeen-thirty-eight."

"Will that be all, sir?"

"Yeah, dat will be all for now, Candice."

"Thank you, your food will be here shortly."

As soon as Candice walked off, Baby G's phone started ringing. "Excuse me for a minute, Rina."

"Yo, C-Major, what'z good, fam? You gotta holla at me 'bout what? Why can't you tell me over the phone? A'ight then I'll get at' chu tomorrow. Yeah, bet."

"Is everythang okay, Baby G?" asked Rina.

"Yeah, everythang's everythang, beautiful."

"Your drinks are here," said the waitress. "Your food will be here shortly."

"Thank you," said Rina.

Baby G downed two shots of Remy before the waiter could even sit all the shots on the table.

"Slow down, baby. Ain't nobody gon' take it from you, I

promise," Rina joked.

"Shid, ain't no use in playin' wit' it. Gon' head and take a shot."

"Dat's probably not a good idea, baby. You'll end up wit' a whole lotta pussy on yo face."

Baby G laughed. "Shid in dat case, take two shots. I'm tryin' to see if it tastes as good as it looks."

Rina downed two shots with no problem. If you like how air taste then you gon' love dis," said Rina.

Before Baby G could indulge in what was turning into sex talk, the waitress came with their wings. "May I help you with anything else tonight?"

"No, we're good, Candice. Thank you so much," stated Baby G.

Rina wasted no time digging into the wingz. "Um—um, boy, these parmesan wings like dat fa real."

"Damn, you sho' know how to put it away, huh?" Baby G teased.

"Boy, ain't nothin' bougie 'bout me! Ain't no shame here, I'm gon' eat, I don't care how fine you iz," said Rina with a mouth full of chicken.

"Gon' head and finish dem off. Dat'z all you, baby girl." said Baby G, downing two more shots of 1738.

"No, you didn't!" said Rina. "See now, I feel like you being funny."

"Nall, not at all, baby. I love a beautiful woman wit' an appetite. Come here." Baby G motioned for her to lean across the table.

Once they were face to face, Baby G licked the sauce off the corner of her mouth.

"Um—you do taste good," he savored her taste.

"Dat's just the outside, wait till you taste the inside," replied Rina kissing and sucking on Baby G's bottom lip.

The waitress cleared her throat. "May I help you with anything else?"

"Yes. Can I have a takeout bag and the check, please?" Rina asked politely.

"Sure thing, I'll be back in a minute," said Candice.

Baby G downed the last two shots as a familiar face walked through the door of Hurricanes. Baby G thought he was trippin' from the six shots of Remy, but the familiar face was one he would never forget. It was the nigga Cee.

"Ain't this some shit?" Baby G said in his mind, gripping his banga.

"Here's your takeout bag. Will that be all?" asked Candice.

"Yes, that will be all," Rina replied.

Baby G couldn't even hear them. He was focused on that nigga Cee. Cee and some girl grabbed a table on the far side of the place, never noticing Baby G and Rina.

"Baby G, pay the ticket," said Rina.

Baby G brought his focus back to her. "You ready to get outta here, beautiful?" He gave her a little smile and sat the money on the table.

"Yeah, we can do dat," Rina agreed.

Baby G and Rina got up and headed towards the door. Before Baby G walked out, he took one last look at Cee, who still didn't notice him, and thought, *Boy, ya azz baked zetti.*

Chapter 26

Dis Shit Krazy

Back at Rina's apartment, Baby G had her running from the head he was giving her. "Oh, my Gawd! Ssssss—ooowww what you doin' to me, daddy, shit!"

"Uh-uh—come here," said Baby G pinning her up in the corner of her bed. He then spread her pussy, licked her clit and blew on it softly.

"Yeesss, blow on dat shit just like dat!"

Baby G put two fingers in her as he licked, and sucked on her.

"Damn, dis pussy cummin', daddy!" Rina's legs started shaking as she nutted all over Baby G's mouth and chin. "Damn, baby, please put dat dick in me," cried Rina.

"Nall, just chill and don't move," said Baby G as he got up to rinse his mouth out.

After rinsing his mouth out, he went in his pants pockets, and pulled out a cigar and some loud, then rolled a blunt.

"Boy, you just gon' eat da pussy and don't give me no dick?"

"Be kool, baby, I gotcha." When Baby G finished rollin' up, he opened Rina's legs and rubbed her pussy juices all over the blunt, then fired it up.

"Boy you'z a whole freak out chere in deez city streetz," said Rina.

"Shut up, and turn over," said Baby G.

"Okay, Zaddy!"

Rina turned over and put a mean arch in her back, face down, and ass up. Baby G rubbed his dick on her clit, and pushed in her halfway, then pulled out again, and spanked her clit with his massive dick, teasing her.

"Come on, daddy, stop playin' wit' me," Rina cried.

Baby G then slid in her slow while blowin' the joint at the same time.

"Get dis pussy, don't play wit' it!" moaned Rina.

Baby G put the joint between his lips, spread her ass cheeks, then gave her everything he had. "Aaaaggghhh—sssss—tha-ooowww—thank you-ooowwww—good-dick!" Baby G was applying so much pressure, that Rina started reaching and grabbing for shit that wasn't even there.

Smack!

Baby G slapped her azz dropping ashes all over him and her azz cheeks. "Take dis dick bitch!" Rina bit down on her pillow hard, wetting' the sheets and Baby G's stomach. Baby G pulled out of her, flipped her on her back, then put the joint on the table that was next to the bed. He grabbed his dick and played with her clit before sliding in her. "Damn dis pussy wet!" said Baby G, slow stroking her deep.

"Ooowww, daddy I feel you! Ssss—*shit you deep!*"

Baby G lifted Rina's right leg, and planted kisses on it while stroking her long and deep. For some reason, watching Baby G kiss her on her legs while he slow grinded in her like a Jamaican, caused her to skeet automatically.

"Damn, nigga! Ssssss—stop!" Baby G got him another stroke in. "Boy, stop moving!" Rina started shaking and couldn't stop. "Hold! Hold on! Give me a min—sssss—give me a minute *please!*"

Baby G laughed and pulled out of her, while she laid there shaking from an orgasm. Baby G grabbed the half blunt, fired it up and went to the bathroom to wipe off. After wiping off with some baby wipes, he brought a few of them out with him. Not to his surprise Rina was snoring when he came out.

"Damn, I got dat dope dick!" Baby G said laughing.

He got in the bed and cleaned Rina up causing her to jump from the wetness of the wipes.

"Was I sleep long?" asked Rina.

"Not at all, baby girl."

"It's been a while since I had some real pressure like dat," said Rina.

"Oh, yeah?" asked Baby G lying next to her. "So, what's good wit you and yo' dude, y'all ain't active?"

"I mean, I tried, but dat bag turns me off. I just can't do it."

"Bag? What chu mean *bag*?" asked Baby G. "Remember I told

you somebody shot him up real bad?"

"Yeah, I remember dat."

"Well, because of dat he gotta wear a shit bag and it's just a major turn off."

"Damn, so you just been sexually frustrated?"

"Yesss—I have. It's been hard for a sister out chere in deez streetz, but I gotta drawer full of batteries, so I'll be aight."

"You got me, too, babygirl," said Baby G. "You gotta nice lil' slice on ya so I'm most definitely gon' be on yo trail. Just make sho me and yo' dude don't bump headz, kuz I ain't on dat sucka shit."

"You don't have to worry about that," said Rina. "You probably know him, everybody knows him." Rina reached over and pulled a picture out of her dresser. "See dis is him, right here."

Baby G examined the photo, and thought to himself ain't dis a bitch? It was the nigga Cee.

"Do you know him?"

Baby G handed the picture back. "Nall, I don't know da nigga."

"Dats surprising because I know you deep in the streetz. Anybody dats really in the streetz knows or at least heard of him," stressed Rina.

"I don't know, babygirl, I move different. Plus, I don't be checkin' for niggaz, that ain't me, but I guarantee you he heard of me," said Baby G with a light chuckle.

"Anyways, I had a good time wit' chu tonight, Baby G. I hope me giving you dis coochie on our first date don't make you look at me differently and run you off."

"Not at all, beautiful! We grown, so it is what it's gon' be."

"Oh, yeah, and what iz dat?" asked Rina.

"The beginning of something beautiful," said Baby G as he gave her a forehead kiss.

"The beginning of something beautiful—I like dat," said Rina.

She snuggled up under Baby G and fell asleep. All Baby G Baby G could do was gaze at the roof and think to himself.

Damn this shit krazy!

Khufu

Chapter 27

Keep Ya Wife Safe

The next morning, Baby G headed to C-Major's spot to see why he had called him so early. "What dey do, my G," said Baby G. "What was so important you couldn't tell me over the phone?"

"Here, bro." Major handed Baby G a bag of money. "Hell yeah, shid, What dis is three-twenty-three?"

"Nall, bro, that's one-sixty, eight hundred," said C-Major.

"Okay, so you ain't move the other two yet? Why you ain't call me when you got done with all four bricks?" asked Baby G.

"That's why I called you early, bro." I moved two of them, but yesterday I took the wife out to eat. I came back home, and my shit is broken into, bro."

Baby G pulled his banga out and held it by his side. "Run dat by me again, My G."

"Baby G, bro, be kool!"

"Be kool?"

Click! Clat!

Baby G cocked his banga. "Explain to me why a nigga takes two bricks but leave over two hunnid bandz!"

"Bro, I had the money in my safe, it's bolted to the floor, ain't no way in hell they coulda removed it, bro. I knew you wouldn't believe me. That's why I'm glad I have cameras."

"So, you mean to tell me dat you have the fucks who took my shit on camera?" asked Baby G.

"I do bro, but I'm not sure if I should show you this. I don't need you getting into trouble, bro. We can always get it back," said Major.

"My nigga, quit talkin' crazy, and run da camera back." Major exhaled then ran the camera back.

The intruder could be seen clear as day, knocking on the door before kicking it in. Baby G did his signature chuckle to hide how heated he really was.

"Oh, yeah," said Baby G. Shit just got real. "How many people seen this shit, my G?"

"Nobody, bro," replied Major.

"Did you tell or show your wife?"

"She knows someone broke in but doesn't know about the footage."

"Did you call da police?"

"Fuck no, bro!"

"Good!" said Baby G. "Get rid of the footage, and we never had dis conversation." Baby G grabbed the bag of money and headed toward the door.

"So, what now, bro?" asked C-Major.

"I'ma hit cha when I'm good, my G. Keep ya wife safe."

Chapter 28

Free Bandz

Later that day, Baby G pulled into J&J's and grabbed some Remy, and back in the cut. Between losing two bricks and having a baby on the way and fucking the same girl as his enemie had Baby G a lil' frustrated. He got out of his car and broke the seal on the bottle of Remy, and took several shots to the head.

"What dey do, my dog?" Baby G looked up and saw his childhood friend coming his way.

"Mango, my nigga, what'z good homie?"

Mango was a street nigga who sold some of everythang from dope to DVDs and shit. This nigga was a tall ass, Bob Marley lookin' ass nigga. Mango was also legally carrying and trigga happy fa real. He alwayz stated that he couldn't wait for a nigga to get his time wrong. So, he could pull out and get his shine on.

"I'm backed up over there. I just saw you pull in, so I came to fuck wit cha," said Mango. "You smokin'?"

"Hell yeah. Pass dat shit." Baby G hit the joint and started coughing hard.

"Yeah, straight pressure," said Mango.

"Yeah, dis shit smokin," Baby G agreed. "I see you slidin' real decent like. What dat is dat new Audi truck? asked Baby G.

"Hell yeah, you know I gotta give it to deez niggaz every chance I get. Bitch, you straight?" asked Mango. "I gotta few plays lined up if you trying to touch a few band yanz," said Mango.

"Nigga, I'm alwayz down wit free bandz, plug me in," replied Baby G. "Just swang by my spot tomorrow, 'round twelve noon. I'ma fuck wit' cha doe, my dog. I got dis lil' baby in da truck. Make sho you swang through, my nigga."

"Say none, my nigga, I'm there," replied Baby G.

Khufu

Chapter 29

He Don't Want No Smoke

Baby G pulled up to Mundo's spot, and to his surprise his lil sister was outside having a drink with Yana. He grabbed the empty Remy box, put sixty bandz in it and got out of the car.

"Heyyy, big brudi!" said C.C., hugging Baby G's neck.

"What's good, lil' sis? I see y'all out chere turnin' up. Everythang good?"

"Yeah, we just kickin' it, but let me holla at chu for a minute," said C.C., pulling Baby G to the side. "What da lick read?" asked Baby G.

"Okay, so the other day I went to Miranda's to get me a sub, and guess who walks in?"

"Come on, sis, get to da point!"

"Man, dat nigga Cee walked right in dat bitch, bra!" Baby G gripped his banga. "Dat nigga put his hands on you' sis?"

"Nall, bra as soon as I seen da nigga. I put my hand in my purse. You know I keep dat toolie on me, boy!"

"So, what da nigga was hollin' 'bout, sis?"

"Bra, how 'bout da nigga told me to tell you dat he ain't the one who shot you. He told me to tell you dat he don't want no smoke wit chu."

"Oh, yeah? What chu told da pussy nigga?"

"I told him dat I don't know what he's talkin 'bout and leave me outta dat shit. He didn't even order any food, he just left."

"I know dat niggaz M.O. he trying to rock me to sleep," said Baby G. "I don't like how he got so close to you, sis. I gotta gon' knock him off."

"Do what you do best, just calculate yo steps, big bra."

"Already!" said Baby G.

"What dat iz, you sippin' on Remy?" asked C.C.

"Nall, dis for Mundo. I just brought him a lil' something. Excuse me for a minute, sis."

"Alright, bra, just holla at me before you leave."

"I gotcha, sis. What dey do, Yana?" asked Baby G.

"What'z good, bra? You a'ight?"

"Yeah, his crayz azz in there," said Yana.

"A'ight bet," replied Baby G.

Baby G walked in and could hear Mundo in the studio going ham. "Forty on me/ dat's two twenties extended clip on dat bitch/it holds two twenties steady aim/but it moves my wrist when I'm shootin'/ Call of Duty shit/ I be on the roof wit shooterz—"

Baby G walked in the garage where the studio was located. "Damn, my nigga, you going in! You got room on dat track for me?" asked Baby G.

"What'z good, bro?" asked Mundo. "Hell yeah, you can get on dis bitch, I ain't trippin."

"I'm just fuckin' wit cha, my nigga, but here dis you. Dat's sixty bandz from C—Major, you get the rest when he finishes."

"Gotcha."

"Fuck all dat for now. What'z good?" asked Baby G.

"What chu mean?" replied Mundo.

"Let's bend a few cornas."

"Shid, letz do it," said Mundo grabbing' his banga.

Chapter 30

Where's Piggy's Nose

Slidin' through the streetz of Killa Kounty Baby G pulled up to the pool hall on 11th Avenue D.

"Let's go in and have a few drinks," he said.

"I'm wit it," replied Mundo. As soon as they got out of the car, a Crown Vic pulled up, causing Mundo to clutch his banga. "Who da fuck dat iz?"

"Look like dem people, my nigga, be kool," Baby G cautioned.

Detective Peer casually exited his vehicle approaching the brothers. "How's it hangin' gentlemen?"

"About nine inches to da right," Baby G clowned.

"I see somebody's in a joking mood today?" said Detective Peer. "Why is he looking suspect?" Peer nodded his head toward Mundo. "I bet my last dollar if I pat you boys down you would come up dirty. You gang banging pieces of shit!"

"Da police is da biggest gang in da world. Da fuck is you talkin' 'bout?" remarked Baby G.

"Yeah, and I'm not lookin' suspect. I just don't fuck wit' pigz!" added Mundo.

"It's funny you say that because I was just about to ask you fucks. What did you do with lil' Piggy's nose?"

"What da fuck you hollin' 'bout?" questioned Baby G.

"What the fuck am I talking about? I'm talking about Mundo's and Piggy's beef being all over Facebook. Then, *coincidentally*, Piggy, his girl, and their infant child are murdered. I'm talking about a triple homicide, you fucks!"

"I don't know what you're referring to, detective. Me and the Pig was good friendz before his passing. If you ain't here to cuff me, then fuck ya!" spat Mundo.

"Okay, tough guy! Just make sure you keep that same attitude when we bump heads again, and that's Detective Peer to you. You fucking jigga boo! See you boys later."

As Peer pulled off, Baby G thought about the hunnid bandz

under his front seat.

"Fuck dat pig, he ain't got shit," said Mundo.

"Yeah, I hear you. Letz get da fuck from up here, doe." Baby G was ready to bounce.

Chapter 31

He Die's Today

Thirty minutes later, Baby G and Mundo were backed in at Rina's apartment.

"What we doing out here in Grand Savana?" asked Mundo,

"This where da lil baby Rina stays at. Just chill, I'm finna see if she gotta friend for you."

"Hell yeah! Dat's what I'm talking 'bout," Mundo replied excitedly.

Baby G dialed Rina's number. *"You have reached a voicemail box of Rina!"* Baby G called again and got the same results. "Aahh—haaa! Looks like Tank Top Tony, got cha girl in da Nestle Crunch," teased Mundo.

"Shid nigga, dat ain't my hoe, we just kickin' it."

"Dat'z what ya mouth says!"

"Fuck it, we out," said Baby G.

As soon as Baby G started the car someone could be seen coming down the steps of Rina's apartment.

"Bra, you see dis shit?" asked Mundo.

"Do I? It'z amazin' how da universe be settin' shit in place for you, dis bitch ain't shit!" exclaimed Baby G.

Mundo gripped his banga and reached for the door handle.

"Hold up!" Baby G said. "Not right here, bra, they got cameras out here. Be kool, we got him."

Just a few feet away, Cee got in his car, and left. Baby G trailed Cee making sure he stayed a few cars behind.

"Bra, make sho' you don't lose dis nigga, he dies today! Matter of fact, pull up on him at da next light," Mundo commanded.

"Nall bra, I'ma kill him where he lays his head."

"What if this nigga takes us somewhere dat's to his advantage?"

"Then we deal wit' it or get dealt wit'," replied Baby G.

Ten minutes later, Cee pulled into a house that was in Sunland Gardens, where an old lady could be seen tending to her garden.

"Hey, grandma! You need some help out here?" Cee asked.

"No baby, I got it."

Click! Clack!

Both brothers cocked their bangaz.

"What dey do, my dog? You hard to kill ana?" asked Baby G.

Cee's eyes got big as if he'd just hit a dime rock.

"Come on, man, spare me. I'm at my grandma'z house.

"You know what? You're right, where are my manners? How you doing, grandma?" asked Baby G.

"Young man, I command you to put that gun down in the name of Jesus!"

"In da name of Jesus, huh? Let me ask you something gramz. Do you believe dat everything is written?"

"Without a doubt, young man, I do."

"So, then without a doubt if I kill you and yo punk azz grandson, right now. That wud mean God used me to send y'all home, correct?"

"Well, I guess you can look at it like that—"

Blocka! Blocka! Blocka! Grandma's words were cut short.

"Tell Jesus I said He's taking too long. Shit's still fucked up down here!" snorted Baby G.

"Oh, my gawd! Grandma nooo!" Cee bent down and cradled her as tears fell rapidly down his face. "My nigga, I swear to God dat wasn't me who shot you!" cried Cee.

"Then who da fuck was it?" asked Baby G.

"It was—"

Blocka! Blocka! Blocka! Blocka!

Mundo put four shots in Cee's head and neck.

"Damn, my nigga, he was finna tell me some shit!" screamed Baby G.

"Man, fuck dat nigga! A nigga will say anythang when he's finna die," responded Mundo. "Let's get da fuck before them people get here.

As they left, the sirens could be heard in the distance. Baby G stayed calm as a lake as he made a clean getaway.

"Boy, I see you don't respect yo elderz. You wet gramz da fuck up, kid." Mundo laughed hysterically.

"Yeah, my nigga, bullets is like Chicken Pox, my nigga, everybody get 'em," answered Baby G in a nonchalant way.

As Mundo continued to tell Baby G how cold-blooded he was, Baby G's mind was on Cee's last words. He really wanted to hear what Cee had to say but his trigga happy azz brother couldn't wait five more secondz.

"You heard me?" asked Mundo.

Snapping Baby G out of a trance like state. "Nall, I ain't hear you. What'z good?"

"Damn nigga, where yo mind at? I said you ain't got no plays set up?"

"I might have something tomorrow. Just be ready in case I hit cha," said Baby G pulling into Mundo's spot.

"A'ight, my G, stay off safety," replied Mundo.

"All da time," added Baby G.

Khufu

Chapter 32

Two Hunnid Bandz Up

Baby G walked into the house and found Shantel on her phone. "What's good, bae?" questioned Baby G.

"Nothing much, I'm just looking online at some baby stuff."

"You find anythang you like?"

"Yeah, I found a lot of stuff. I'm just waiting to find out the sex of the baby."

"I already told you, we having a lil' Baby G."

"Anywayz! What'z really good wit' chu, Baby G? Like fa real doe!"

"State yo issue."

"Okay, why you just been in and outta here not answering yo' phone and shit? I mean, is this the type of father you gon' be?"

Baby G walked into the room to grab the money he had under the mat, then went to the kitchen table.

"So, you don't hear me talking to you, Baby G?"

"You know a nigga hear you, my nigga, ease up!"

"Well, say something then, nigga, *fuck*! A bitch pregnant and shit. My hormones and emotions all over the fuckin' place. I really need you to be here, Baby G."

Baby G dumped all the money on the table and started counting until Shantel placed her hand on the money.

"You still don t hear me talking?" asked Shantel.

Baby G grabbed Shantel, picked her up and put her on the money.

"Boy, what is you doing?"

"Shut da fuck up!" ordered Baby G, ripping her panties clean off all dat azz and pussy."

"Nigga, you can't just come up in here, fuck me and think shit sweet!"

Baby G started sucking on her inner thighs leaving passion marks everywhere.

"Boy stop! No! Ssss—stop I said nooo—ssss! Ooohhh, shit boy!

Oh-my-gawd!"

Baby G latched on her clit, and Shantel went crazy.

"Uh-huh, what chu was saying now?" asked Baby G.

"Daddy, please don t stop!"

"Yeah, I know," said Baby G as he proceeded to mash the gas on her.

After sucking the life out of Shantel, Baby G fucked her for a good forty minutes all over the blood money. Shantel was so wet, Baby G had to pick her up and take her to the bedroom because she was wetting up all the money. He fucked her again for another hard fifteen minutes until she was slumped, leaving her snoring while he finished counting the money.

When he was done counting, he was two hunnid bandz up.

****

"Aye, Shantel! Get cha azz up."

"What's up, bae, *daammmnnn!*" Shantel rubbed her eye boogers off.

"I need you to call in and tell dem folks you can't make it to work today."

"Boy, I just can't do that, I run a bidness I gotta be there".

"You'll think of something. Shid, call Mercedes and tell her to fill in fa ya."

Mercedes was Shantel's best friend, and assistant manager.

"What exactly am I calling in for, Baby G?"

Baby G threw ten bandz on the bed. "Dat's ten bandz, go get my car sprayed ASAP."

"What chu mean ASAP?" asked Shantel. "Boy what the hell you done did in dat car?"

"I ain't do shit, it's just time for a change."

"Well, why the hell you ain't take it to get sprayed while I go to work."

"Because I gotta take care of something. Now get cha azz up and do what da fuck I told you to do. Da fuck iz up wit' all deez questions and shit? I gave you more than enough money. Go shopping or some shit when you get there."

"Damn, man, you just—you just got out of prison."

"Why is it so hard for you to sit ya azz down somewhere?"

"Why is it so hard for you to shut da fuck up and listen? I gotta go, just do like I said." Baby G grabbed ten more bands then put the rest under the mat. "Shantel, you seen my bangaz?" he asked.

"Yeah, I put them in the dresser."

"My nigga, don't be touching my shit, straight up!"

"Boy, whateva, I ain't sleeping on top of those guns, so I put them in the dresser drawer."

"You heard what I said," replied Baby G. He grabbed both of his guns and kissed Shantel, then headed out.

"Baby G, I love you, please be safe."

"I love you too, ma."

Khufu

Chapter 33

A New Slider

Baby G stood across the street from Shantel's apartment on Taylor's Creek ditch bank and threw the .40 that he used to kill Cee's grandma. This was just one of many pistols he'd thrown in the canal over the years. Baby G just stood there in a daze until his phone started ringing.

"Yo!" yelled Baby G.

"What's good, daddy? What chu got going on?" asked Shenida.

"Damn, Shenida, I was just finna call you. Listen, I need you to swang through Avenue T, and scoop me up. I gotta handle some shit."

"Say no moe, daddy, I'm on my way right now."

"Bet!"

Fifteen minutes later, Shenida pulled up in a new Lexus Truck and Baby G hopped in.

"Damn, lil' baby, you lookin' good as dis new truck you pushin'! Who da new nigga iz?"

"Boy, please, dis truck ain't got shit on me. And ain't no new nigga, I'm just doing me."

"Iz dat right? Well, I'm trying to do me, too. Dat's why I called you. I need you to take me to get a new slider."

"What dealership you had in mind, daddy?"

"Fuck a dealership, right now, I ain't on dat flashy. I want one of dem old schools. One of dem old crackas done put on the side of da highway and shit."

"I just seen some on Oleander and Sunrise the other day. You wanna go see bout 'em, daddy?" Shrines offered.

"Yeah, let's ride."

"Hold up, first pull dat dick out." Shenida's voice dripped with lust.

"Man, you trippin'! My girl spot right dere, and she 'bout to leave, man. She might pull up on us."

"Nigga, fuck dat! I ain't moving till you let me taste dat dick."

"Maannn, tightin' up!" said Baby G pulling his dick out.

Baby G looked around nervously as Shenida's head bobbed up and down on his dick.

"Ahhh—ssshhhiittt—daammnnn! You eatin' dat up girl."

"Um!" Shenida, moaned as she sucked and slurped curling Baby G's toez.

"Ssss—fuck! You taste dat dick?"

"Yeezzz, daddy!"

"What dat dick taste like?"

"Um—taste like real nigga dick, daddy."

"Well, get it up out of me then. Goddamnit eat it!"

Shenida went animalistic causing Baby G to run from her head. "Uh-uh, come here," said Shenida, putting every inch in her mouth.

"I'm finna skee—ssss—shit!"

Shenida gave Baby G everythang she had until he came.

"Uuuggghhh—shit, man!" yelled Baby G. "You gon' get a nigga caught up out 'chere, man, let's go."

After swallowing everything, Shenida put the car in drive.

"Nigga, shut da fuck up! You love livin' on the edge so miss me wit dat," Shenida pulled his card as she drove off.

Ten minutes later, Shenida pulled up on Sunrise. Baby G saw exactly what he was looking for. It was an all white Parasian with cocaine insides, everything was original. After calling the number the owner left on the car, they met up and did business. The car was owned by an old, white guy just as Baby G had assumed and in mint condition. Baby G gave the guy thirty-five hundred, and Shenida a thousand for bringing him.

"You didn't have to pay me for branging you here," said Shenida.

"Oh, dat wasn't for the ride, baby girl. Dat was for dat performance you gave me." Baby G chuckled lightly.

"Boy, you so stupid! I told you it's anythang for my nigga."

"Listen, I gotta go handle some shit, babygirl, I'ma fuck wit' chu later."

"A'ight, just call me if you need me. Oh, yeah, I meant to ask you, did you hear what happened to yo boy Cee?" asked Shenida.

"Nall, shid I ain't heard nothin'. What dey talkin' 'bout?"

"Boy, I ain't stupid."

"I said I ain't heard nothing, baby girl. I'ma holla at cha later."

"Yeah, a'ight, Baby G, be safe."

"You mean off safety," replied Baby G.

Khufu

Chapter 34

Da B.G.s

Baby G took his new slider through the city, enjoying the butter soft seats, and the smell of the fresh leather. He was rolling glass house, so he was noticed by haters and a few eaters he ran through. People were flagging him down, but he just blew the horn and kept it pushing. After sliding down 29th, he pulled into an apartment complex called Bookers Garden, or the B.G.'s. A Lot of people get killed in this area over beef that started way before their time. As a matter of fact, the whole city is cursed with blood from senseless murders. Literally every street you turn down, has blood on it. Baby G's face was good anywhere, but he still hopped out with his banga in hand, as he walked up the stairs. Before Baby G could knock on the door it opened.

"What dey do, my dog?" asked Mango. "I saw you when you pulled in, bih come in and put dat shit up nigga. You straight over here."

Baby G tucked his banga, dapped Mango up, then slid in.

"What'z good, bih? You want some liquor or something?" asked Mango.

"I really came to see 'bout dat bidness we dicussed at da liquor store, but I'll sip something. What chu sippin' on?"

"Shid, I got some 1738. Dat bitch India and her lil' friendz drunk all my Raynal."

"Y'all still together?" asked Baby G. "Hell yeah! You know she ain't gon' let a nigga be wit' nobody else."

"Ol' Mango, in love and shit." Baby G laughed.

"Whateva, nigga, I love money!" Mango poured two shots of Remy.

"Speaking of money, let's get to it," said Baby G.

"Oh, yeah, bih come in da kitchen," replied Mango.

When they walked in, Baby G saw little blocks of duct tape, and a machine. "Damn, nigga, you gotta compresser in dis bitch?"

"Yeah, nigga, just chill. You know what dis is?" Mango pointed to a white powdery substance.

"I know it ain't coke?" said Baby G.

"You right, it ain't. Dis dat shit dey cut boi wit', nigga dis Fentanyl."

"I'ma keep it gangsta, I ain't never heard of it. You know I only fuck wit' coke," admitted Baby G.

"Dis a whole other level, my dog," Mango boasted. "This dat shit dat put elephants down. Tranquiliser type shit."

"Okay, so where da Heroin at?" questioned Baby G.

"Nigga, ain't none! All deez blocks is Fentanyl. You see this?" asked Mango, picking up a big ass can of Nestle Quick. "I mix this with the Fentanyl to give it dat brown color, then I press dem shits and flip 'em ninety bandz a piece."

"Keep it real wit' cha self, somebody gon' bust yo head for playin' like dat."

"Nall, bra, dat Fentanyl stronger than dat boi. Dem zapps been bangin' dis shit. So, niggaz been coppin' like crayz. They don't know what I'm serving them. They just know dat they phone doing numbers off dis shit."

"If this shit doing numbers like you say it is. Why the fuck you still in da B.G.'s?" questioned Baby G.

"Oh, don't get it twisted, dis just where I perform at. Nigga I gotta big azz house on Indian River Drive."

"Nall!" said Baby G.

"My nigga, let me show you something," said Mango bending down and opening a cabinet under the kitchen sink.

What Baby G saw next made him clutch his banga. It was a duffle bag full of blue faces.

"Nigga, you see dis shit?" asked Mango holding the bag open with his back turnt to Baby G.

"Hell yeah, I see it!" Baby G took a second to make a decision. *Damn, my nigga, I can't fuck Mango over like dat. We grew up in da trenches together,* thought Baby G as he released the grip on his banga.

"Nigga, dis three-hunnid-k!" said Mango.

"Okay, I'm feelin' dat, but what's da next step?" asked Baby G.

"What chu mean?" replied Mango. "You said you had something for me, my nigga, dat's why I'm here."

"Just chill, and rest easy, my dog. I'on play no games. You know I get money, dis shit ain't nothing to me. Here, my nigga," said Mango handing Baby G twenty bandz and a Nestle Quick brick. "Look, my nigga, I don' gave you da game. I don't know who you gon' run it on, but when you do, I'll sell you a brick of Fentanyl for thirty racks. This shit hard to get, my nigga, but I'ma look out fa ya."

"I respect dat, my nigga. Dis ain't really my lane, but I'ma see what it's hittin' for. I gotta make a move so I'ma scream at cha later, my nigga. I appreciate dis shit," said Baby G tuckin' the brick in his pants.

"You already know, my dog! Now go get money," replied Mango.

"Already!"

Khufu

Chapter 35

What a Fuckin' Day

Baby G was walking to his car when he saw a youngster he knew named Poppa from the Tree Top Pirus coming up on a beach cruiser. As soon as Baby G was finna acknowledge him, he hopped off the cruiser.

Blocka! Blocka! Blocka! Blocka!

Poppa dropped another youngin' who was standing there talking to some girl. Seeing this, Baby G snatched his banga out just in case Poppa felt like he had to clean everything on sight. Poppa got back on the cruiser, and rode right past Baby G.

"You might wanna put dat up, dis ain't for you, homie," advised Poppa.

Baby G ignored him and kept his finger on the trigga until Poppa was out of sight.

"*Aaaagggghhhh!* Some—somebody help me please!"

Baby G looked and saw the girl on the ground holding her stomach next to the dead youngin', fighting to stay alive. Baby G wanted to put her in his car and take her to Lawnwood Medical, but the thought of detectives lurking around the hospital changed that. Baby G peeled out, and dialed 911, blocking his number.

"Hello, nine-one-one, state your emergency!"

Yeah, it's two white boyz shot up real bad in Bookers Garden off twenty ninth, you need to hurry!"

Baby G knew that they would take their time if he didn't lie. "What a fuckin' day!"

****

Baby G pulled up to Shenida's spot and dialed her number.

"Hello, what'z up, daddy?"

"Step outside for a minute, baby girl."

"Damn, why you just ain't use yo' key to come in?"

"I really ain't got da energy to be jumpin' up and down in you, right now, my nigga, just come check it out right quick."

"Nigga, please! You sound real stupid, right now. Kuz all a bitch gotta do is come right out there and take da dick. I'll come right out there and put dis pussy all over yo' new white leather seats. Now nigga, say some shit I'on like!"

"Just brang yo' silly azz out da doe."

Two minutes later, Shenida came out in a sports bra, and boy shorts that left little to the imagination, her pussy was everywhere. Shenida got in the car and immediately started playing with Baby G's dick.

"What da fuck is dis?" asked Shenida, referring to the package that Baby G had tucked in his pants.

"Dat's what I came to see you 'bout. You don't know nobody who be fuckin' wit' dat dog food?" questioned Baby G.

"You talkin' 'bout heroin, right?"

"Yeah!"

"Um—matter of fact, I do. This dude I used to fuck wit', he used to fuck off wit' dat food, but it's been a while since we talked."

"You still got da nigga number?"

"Yeah, I got it."

"Hit him and see if he good. If da play go through, I gotcha."

Shenida dialed the number as she continued fondling Baby G through his pants.

"Yo! Who is this?" Swope answered nonchalantly.

"Damn, nigga, you ain't got my number logged in no moe?" asked Shenida.

"I ain't look at the phone to be honest wit' cha, but I know that voice anywhere."

"What's good, Shenida?"

"What dey do, Swope? I was callin' to see if you still be buying food for all dem damn dogs you got."

"Hell yeah! You know dem dogs greedy as shit, they alwayz need food."

"Well, you ain't gotta go to Wal-Mart, I gotta few bagz over here."

"Shid, what da ticket is?" asked Swope.

Baby G held up nine fingers, and a zero to let her know the price to tell Swope.

"Well, you know, dat dog food cost a hunnid in da store, but you can get it for ninety."

"No problem. Where you at? I'm finna pull up," said Swope.

"Just meet me at da car wash on twenty-nineth," replied Shenida.

"A'ight, give me twenty minutes, I'll be there."

"Already!" said Shenida as she ended the call. "Head to the carwash, daddy, he gon' meet us there."

Ten minutes later, Baby G was backed in at the car wash getting ate up by Shenida. "Sssss—shit! We came to handle bidness and shit, and all you wanna do is eat da meat off da bone."

Shenida took Baby G out of her mouth long enough to say a few wordz, "Nigga, dis just a lil' motivation."

"Well, at least tell me what da nigga driving."

"He drives a green Audi, boy, damn."

Three minutes later Shenida got everything that she was gon' get outta him and swallowed it all.

"Damn, my nigga, I gotta stay focused and here you is draining all a nigga's energy."

"You good, daddy. Dis nigga ain't cut like dat."

"I hear you, ma, but a nigga like me don't trust nobody. Matter of fact, get in the driver seat," said Baby G climbing in the back seat.

"There he go right there." Shenida started flashing the lights.

"Make da nigga get in the front seat," said Baby G cockin' his banga.

As Swope approached the car, Shenida opened the passenger's door. "Get in, nigga."

Swope peeked in the car, saw Baby G and hesitated.

"Nigga, get cha big, scary azz in, you good," said Shenida.

"Who this is you got wit' chu? I don't do bidness like this."

"Nigga, chill, this my kuzin Baby G. He the one wit' da food. Swope, Baby G—Baby G, Swope."

"What's good, my nigga?" said Swope, holding out his hand for some dap.

Baby G reached out and dapped Swope with his left hand. It wasn't due to disrespect or nothing, it's just that his right hand was clutchin' his banga behind the passenger seat.

"What'z happenin'? You got dat Lucciano?" asked Baby G.

"No doubt, you got dat food?" replied Swope.

"Shenida, baby, grab dat from under the front seat."

Swope saw that everything was okay and pulled a bag out of the front of his pants. "All blue face hunnids," said Swope, handing the money to Shenida in return for work.

"Bust it open and check it out," instructed Baby G.

"Nall, my nigga, I trust baby girl. So, all that ain't necessary."

"I'm feeling dat," said Baby G. "Anytime you need food just hit my kuzin' up and we'll get 'er done."

"Respect," said Swope as he tucked the pack back in his pants and got out of the car.

"Here, daddy," said Shenida, passing Baby G the money.

"Let's slide, ma, head back to yo' spot." Baby G thumbed through the money and smirked at the thought of making ninety bandz in less than thirty minutes. "I'm fuckin' wit dis," said Baby G as his phone rang. Seeing that it was Rina, he was hesitant due to the fact he'd just murdered her so-called ex, and his grandma. "Hello," answered Baby G.

"How you been doing?" asked Rina.

"You know a nigga just been moving and grooving. What's good wit' cha?"

"How come I haven't been hearing from you, Baby G?"

"Shid, I been trying to put shit in order. You feel me? Gettin' to da bag. What's wit' all da third degree?" asked Baby G.

"I'm sorry, I don't mean to sound like I'm drilling you or anything. It's just that I've been going through a lot these past forty-eight hours. I really need you to come hold me."

"Talk to me, baby girl, What seemz to be da problem?"

"I'll tell you when you come over. Can you please come over, Baby G?" The way Rina was talking led Baby G to believe that she really didn't know anything and just really wanted to be held.

"I gotcha, baby, I'll be through there in a few. When I get done makin' a move."

"Okay, I ll be waiting. The door will be open."

"A'ight, ma, see you then."

"Who was dat, G baby?" asked Shenida. "Dat was nothin.' Here," said Baby G, handing her ten bandz.

"Thanks, daddy."

"Yeah, just hit me when dat nigga Swope want some moe food."

"Why you just won't come in and relax? All dis moving around you been doing. You just need to sit yo azz down for a few dayz."

"Shenida, you already know I'm too much of a street nigga to be a stagnant. Now get cha azz out da car I'ma fuck wit' cha later."

"Yo' direspectful azz better be lucky I love you. Bye, boy. Make sho' you call me."

"A'ight," replied Baby G, getting in the front seat and pulling off.

Khufu

Chapter 36

Nothing Personal

Back at the apartment, Baby G was thumbing through everythang he'd accumulated. He was now two hunnid and sixty bandz up.

I need to invest dis shit, Baby G was thinking until a knock at the door interrupted him. Baby G grabbed his banga and peeked out the window. "Yo!" yelled Baby G after seeing who it was.

"Open da door, nigga, dis me, Mundo!"

"Hold up!" said Baby G as he headed back to the table to put the money up. After securing the bag, he opened the door.

"Damn, dude, what took you so long to open da doe?" asked Mundo.

"I had to put some clothes on, my nigga, What'z up?"

"I just came to check on my big bra. I can do dat, right?"

"Yeah, nigga, come in."

"Who white Parasian out there?" asked Mundo.

"Dat's my shit, I just got it."

"Dat bitch nice, I'm fuckin' wit' it. Listen bra, I talked to Top he got a job for us," said Mundo.

"Who and when?" replied Baby G. "He said he'd get back at me, I'm just lacing you up."

"Well, you know I'm on dat, just keep me posted."

"I ain't da smartest man in da world, but I'd say you was kickin' me out."

"And I say dat ur politically correct! It ain't nothin' personal, my nigga, it's just dat I gotta be somewhere."

"A'ight then, bra, say none. I'ma hit chu if something changes."

"Yeah, yeah," said Baby G as he closed the door behind Mundo.

****

Who Shot Chu

Fresh out the shower, Baby G got dressed, grabbed his banga, and left, headed to Rina's apartment.

"Damn, I hope I don't have to kill dis pretty muthafucka," muttered Baby G. "Dat wud sho'll be a waste of good pussy."

Ten minutes later he was parked outside of Rina's apartment dialing her number.

"Hello," answered Rina.

"Yeah, ma, I'm outside."

"Why did you call me? I told you the door was unlocked, baby."

"You know I had to call in case you had company. It's about respect, baby girl."

"Can you please just come up here? I been waiting on you all day, Baby G."

"A'ight, ma, I'm in ya chest in a few minutes."

Baby G grabbed his banga and headed up the stairs. Once he reached Rina's apartment, he used his shirt to open the door and locked it. "Yo!"

"Yeah, baby, I'm back here," said Rina.

Baby G walked in Rina's room and found her completely naked, spread out across Egyptian Cotton. *"Damnit, man!* All dat for me?" Rina opened her legs, and played with her clit.

"Come get dis pussy, daddy, please."

Baby G pulled out his banga and placed it on the dresser next to the bed. He then removed his shirt, showing his well-built frame with Pharaohs, and Nefertities tattooed everywhere.

"Ohhh, shit hurry, daddy, she wet," moaned Rina.

After removing his pants and briefs, Baby G dove in head-first, latching onto her clit, sending chills all throughout her body. Baby G considered himself to be a master at eating pussy. He enjoyed it more than his partner; it was just the thrill of pleasing a woman that drove him over the edge.

"Sssss—damn, daddy, ohhh. Pussy skeetin' already, boy. Fuck, I'm—ssshh—ssshhhitttt!" Rina gripped the sheets and creamed all over Baby G's face. "Put it in, daddy, I can't take it no moe!"

Baby G bent her legs to her chest and gave her everything he had until they both came multiple times a piece.

"Damn, Baby G, it's like you gotta personal connection with

my hoo hoo. I think I love you, boy."

"On some real shit, ma. Stop playin' wit' me. You gotta keep it real wit' cha self, Rina. You ain't even known me a full month yet."

"Trust me, Baby G, I know it sounds crazy, but I can't help what I feel."

"Yeah? Tell me—what exactly is it dat you feel?"

"Baby G, I feel like when I'm with you my world is complete. It's like my mind, body, and soul are one with your being. I feel we bumped into each other in that store for a reason, Baby G. Maybe you know—I was brought into your life to slow you down from all this madness in deez streetz," stated Rina.

"First off, Rina, I'ma street nigga at heart! Ain't no slowing me down from dat, it's all I know. Second of all, I don't feel the same way you feel, baby. I don't love you. I enjoy yo' company, but ain't no love there, baby."

"That's kool, Baby G, I understand. You'll learn to love me once you realize that I am the one for you."

"Look, Rina, you talkin' real krazy right now."

"Baby G, can I tell you something, without you getting mad at me?"

"Yeah, what'z up?"

"Say you promise!"

"A nigga ain't on dat, my nigga. What's up?"

"Promise me, Baby G."

"I promise, Rina, now what's up?"

"Why did you lie about not knowing my ex?"

This question grabbed Baby G's full attention. "What makes you feel like I lied 'bout dat?"

"Remember, I called you to come over but you never came?"

"Yeah, I remember—and?"

"My ex ended up poppin' up on me, and we had a talk. He told me that he saw us that day in Hurricanes, but he acted like he didn't. He said most likely you had a gun on you. He told me to tell you that he wasn't the one who shot you. Baby G, he told me that it was your own brother who shot you."

Hearing that, caused Baby G to stand up and grab his banga. He pointed it directly at Rina's face. "So, you really gon' make me kill you in dis bitch for talkin' stupid, huh?"

"Baby G, you promised me you wouldn't get upset. Before you pull that trigga, you really need to listen to me, then we can go from there."

"Bitch, I think I done heard enough."

"Not yet, baby, just please listen to me. You see my ex- Cee was fuckin' Yana, Mundo's girl, right? Yana told Cee everything about you and your brother. She told him how Mundo thought you was fuckin' her because one day he came home, and I guess she had let you in without callin' him to let him know. She said that he made her strip naked to smell her pussy, then beat her even though she didn't smell of sex. He also went in her phone and found back and forth messages between her and Cee. Mundo wanted Cee dead. Baby, think about it, who told you that Cee shot you? Now I'm not taking Cee's side, but he was with me the whole night that you got shot."

Baby G took a moment to consider everything Rina had just dropped on him. He thought back to that day he went to Mundo's house to give him half of a lick he'd just hit. *Yana answered the door in a tight, form-fitting, bodysuit that accentuated her curvy figure.*

"Hey, Baby G. How you doing?" She smiled.

"What up, sis? Where Mundo at?" asked Baby G.

"Oh, he ran to the store real quick."

"Aight, I'll come back in a few." Baby G turned to leave, but Yana quickly stopped him.

"Nall, don't leave," she said. "He's coming right back. You can come inside and wait for him, boy."

"Aight," replied Baby G against his better judgement.

After he stepped inside, Yana closed the door behind him. "Are you thirsty?" she asked.

"Nall, I'm good. It smells good up in here." Baby G sniffed the air.

"That's my sweet cornbread." Yana blushed.

Looking at her hair, Baby G remarked, "Damn, sis, what chu got in ya head?"

"Boy, don't play." She giggled as she ran a hand through her hair. "This is all natural."

"You lying! That shit look like possum hair or some hyena shit." Baby G cracked up, causing Rina to double over in laughter.

A second later, their clowning was interrupted by Mundo's entrance. He glared at both of them with suspicion.

"What's good, fam?" asked Baby G.

"Aye, bra, I gotta handle something. Come back later." Mundo's tone was dry as fuck, but Baby G brushed it off.

"Cool. I'll get with you later." Baby G dipped, and decided to just keep the whole lick himself.

Now, what Rina had just said made perfect sense.

Baby G then thought back to that rainy night on 23rd Street, between E and G. Money was swanging, but troll was patrolling hard, so Baby G didn't keep his banga on him. He saw somebody coming up the street that looked like a smoker, so he met him halfway askin', *"What you need"*

Before Baby G knew it, he was hit two times in the chest and shoulder, laid out in the rain. If it wasn't for April, Baby G woulda just laid there and bled to death. April was a girl that Baby G was dating at the time. She knew Baby G was outside hustling when she heard the shots and ran outside. She found Baby G bleeding everywhere and called 911. Baby G found it odd that the shooter didn't even rob him, he had a whole thirty-five hunnid on him. He also found it odd that once he was stable, which was two hours after arriving at the hospital, Mundo showed up and told him that some nigga name Cee from the other side was the gunman.

How da fuck kud he know who shot me in such a short notice? thought Baby G. Rina was making too much sense to Baby G for it to be not true. Baby G walked to the room's window, gun still pointed at Rina and looked to see if the parking lot was crawling with cops.

"I didn't call the police on you, baby," Rina stated. "I told you, I love you, nigga, What about dat, you don't get? Me and Cee weren't together when he died. I knew his number was up sooner or later. He was doing too much. I know for a fact he didn't shoot you, but I know dudes that he actually killed. My apartment was invaded, and I was duct taped and raped by some dudes he crossed. To be honest with you, he got exactly what he deserved. I just felt like you deserved the truth. Baby G, I love you," Rina's tears flowed freely down her face.

"Did you tell anyone else 'bout dis?" asked Baby G.

"No, G baby, I promise."

Baby G lowered his gun, feeling like he was going to regret not killing her.

"Come here, baby, I'm sorry for puttin' dis pistol in yo face, but I'm sure you overstand."

"It's okay, bae," said Rina putting her head in Baby G's chest.

"Listen, Rina, I like you alot, but I'm not gon' sit here and tell you I love you because I don't, not yet. However, I can learn to love you. Can you let me do that?"

Rina laughed while still crying. "Yes, daddy."

Baby G leaned Rina's head back and kissed her passionately.

"I'm sorry," said Baby G.

Blocka! Baby G shot her under her chin killing her instantly. She laid there with a hole in her head, and eyes open.

"I kud never love you."

Baby G closed her eyes, then hopped in the shower to rinse the blood and other fragments off. After cleaning himself, he bleached the bathtub, took her phone, and left the room. He then wiped down everything he saw. Once dressed he left without a single trace.

Chapter 37

Get Rid of Dis Nigga

He can't know I broke into C-Major's shit and took the work, kuz he still gave me a cut. He most definitely can't know I shot him kuz I'm still breathing. You know what, fuck dat shit! How he gon' cut somebody else in on what we got going on? A white boy, at dat? He supposed to be my fuckin' blood. How he gon' fuck my Yana like dat? He lucky I ain't kill his azz. Mundo's phone rang interrupting his rage rant. It was Baby G.

Ain't dis some shit? thought Mundo.

"Yo' what's good, big bra?"

"What's good wit' dat play Top was hollin' 'bout?" questioned Baby G.

"He still ain't hit me back, fam. I got'cha when he do," replied Mundo.

"Yeah, you do dat," said Baby G.

"A'ight, big—"

Click!

Baby G hung up in Mundo's ear.

"Damn, dis nigga been rude as shit lately. I might have to finish dat nigga off. Yeah, I gotta get rid of dis nigga." Mundo turned the music up, let his seat back, and bent through the city of no pity.

****

I Used to Fuck His Bitch

Baby G dialed Mango's number for the third time, and just like the first two times, he got sent to the voicemail.

"Fuck it, I'ma just pull up," muttered Baby G as he made a right on 29th. As Baby G was creeping up the block, he saw a familiar face. "Damn dat looks like my nigga Billy Boy," Baby G said, as he rolled down his window. *"Billy Boy Smith!* Nigga, what da fuck iz up!" yelled Baby G.

Seeing that it was Baby G, Billy took his hand off his banga, "Oh, boy, I almost blew in dis bitch. I ain't know who da fuck you was," said Billy. "You know some nigga and a chick just got hit up out dis bitch. So, niggaz is noid, and shit."

"Yeah, I heard. So, you was just gon' kill me?"

"I told you, I ain't know who you was," repeated Billy.

Baby G snatched his banga out of his right pocket. "So, you was just gon' leave my lil' brainz all over da white leather, huh? You was gon' front row my momma, huh?"

"My nigga chill out, you trippin', Baby G, fa real. It ain't like dat."

Baby G laughed. "Nigga, I'm just fuckin' wit' cha. What's good, doe? What chu doing for it?"

"Shid, I wanna go get a bottle, you wit' it?" questioned Billy.

"I was finna go holla at Mango."

"How you gon' do dat?"

"What chu mean?" asked Baby G.

"Nigga, you ain't heard? Dem people kicked Mango doe in earlier."

"Jack boyz? Or dem people?"

"Nigga, dem people—nigga da alphabet boyz—Da Fedz!"

"Man, gon' head on wit' dat bullshit," said Baby G.

"Fa real bra, but he wasn't there when they came. They got his bitch, doe. And you know how dem people play."

"What, he served an agent or some shit?"

"Nall, bra, they say he served one of his zapp's dat Fetanyl shit, and he overdosed. They got his zapp's phone and saw dat him and Mango had been texting. You already know dem jump out boyz know Mango like a muthafucka."

"Damn, dat shit just fucked up my play," complained Baby G. "Fuck it, hop in let's go get dat bottle."

After going through J&J's and grabbing a bottle of 1738, Baby G bent through the projects known as Vietnam, or V-Side.

"My nigga, you still on dat music shit?" asked Billy.

"Yeah, I do a lil' something but dat shit secondary. Right now,

116

I'm chasing illegal tender."

"What da fuck iz tender?" questioned Billy.

Baby G laughed. "Money, my nigga—dat fetti."

"Well, why you ain't just say dat?"

"Man, fuck all dat!" said Baby G. "You ain't got no plug on dat food?"

"What kinda food?" asked Billy.

"Man, heroin!"

"Why da fuck you keep talkin' in code and shit?" asked Billy.

"Billy, dog, quit acting like you two sandwiches short of a picnic all da time."

"What da fuck dat's suppose to mean?"

"Never mind, Billy, *damnit, man!*"

"I ain't got no plug on no heroin, but I know who got poundz of weed."

"Who got it?"

"You trying to cop or, you trying to take some shit?" asked Billy.

"My nigga, you know how I get down. I'm trying to take some shit."

"Shid, my nigga, I'm wit' cha!" stated Billy. "You know a nigga named Big Gene?"

Baby G chuckled. "Yeah, I know dat fool."

"Why you laughing?" asked Billy.

"Kuz, I used to fuck his bitch. She used to give me da nigga shit. You know a pound here, a pound there. I never laid his azz down on da strength of her, but he gon' get it now."

"Shid, I know da nigga whole set up. We can hit dat nigga's azz tonight," stated Billy.

"Say no more," replied Baby G.

Khufu

Chapter 38

You A Gangsta Now?

Four hours later, Baby G, Shenida, and Billy were backed in two houses down from Big Gene's trap in a Baser rental,that Baby G had fogged up with dirty smoke.

"Damn, my nigga, put dat stank azz shit out!" requested Billy.

"Nigga, fuck ya!" replied Baby G.

"I don't see how you sprinkle powder on yo' weed. Nigga, you might as well smoke crack."

Baby G hit the joint, then blew smoke in Billy's face. "Nigga, if you keep talkin' stupid, I might as well shoot yo azz in da face."

"Y'all niggaz kill dat. We ain't here for all dat. Now, what da play is?" Shenida asked.

"My nigga, why did you even brang her?" asked Billy.

"Kuz pussy makes a nigga weak, silly nigga!" answered Baby G.

"Whateva, my nigga. Anyway, dis nigga got cameras in da front of da trap. Ain't none in the back. In da backyard it's a hole in the fence, we can slide through there and lay on 'em til' he come out," explained Billy.

"Who all be trappin' in there wit' him. asked Baby G.

"He be in there dolo," stated Billy.

"Shid, fuck l aying on him, we gon' make him come out." Baby G went in his pocket and gave Shenida three hunnid dollars. "I want chu to pull up to the trap and buy an ounce of loud from da nigga. After you do dat, get back in the car and act like it won't start, pop da hood then mess around wit' the battery. If he got cameras, he gon' see you, and come out to help. When he do dat, his ass baked zetti. Just make sho' you got dem shorts pulled up in dat lil' fat pussy, down there, and we good."

"I gotcha, G baby," said Shenida.

"Billy let's go, grab da gloves and shit."

"Let's do it,."

They got out, jumped the fence, and went through a hole in

another fence, putting them right behind Big Gene's trap.

"Put cha mask on, we here now. Let's eat, baby." Baby G was amped.

"Already!" replied Billy.

Seconds later, Shenida could be heard getting out of the car.

"Come on," whispered Baby G as he crept on the side of the house.

Shenida knocked until Gene opened the door. "Damn, ma, why you bangin' on my shit like you crazy!"

"My bad, big daddy, but you got dat music so loud up in there. I'm trying to blow something. You straight?"

"What chu lookin' for, ma?"

"Let me get an O of loud."

"You know dat's three hunnid, shawdy."

"Yeah, I know," said Shenida.

"Gon' 'head and come in, ma. I got chu."

Shenida walked past Gene with the most provocative strut she could muster.

"*Damn!*" said Gene, closing the door behind them.

"Damn, what?" replied Shenida.

"Dat azz looks so soft."

"You should see how it looks when you get behind it," flirted Shenida, turning around and making her ass clap.

"I'm trying to see what it's hittin' fa, shid. What da ticket is?" asked Gene.

"Well, you kinda cute, so this one is on me. The thing about it doe is dat I gotta girlfriend and we fuck together, so it's both of us, or it ain't nothin'."

"I'm most def down wit' dat, shid. Where she at?"

"Here." Shenida handed him the money for the ounce. "I gotta go get her and come back."

"Nall, ma, you keep dat," said Gene with a big ass Kool-Aid smile. "You just make sho you swang back through."

"Fasho, big daddy, walk me to da car."

"A'ight, baby, hold up," said Gene, grabbing a big ass .357, and tucking it in his jeans. "Let's go. Shawty lead da way."

120

Once outside, Shenida made sure she dropped the keys, then bent all the way over showing all camel toe.

"Damn, dat shit sittin' like a pinecone," Big Gene gawked.

"It's all yours in 'bout ten minutes, big daddy." Shenida smiled as she got into the car.

"Hurry da fuck back, ma, fa real."

Shenida half turned the key a few times, then hit the steering wheel. *"Fuck!"*

"Pop da hood, ma, I got chu."

Shenida popped the hood, then got out and watched Big Gene get under the hood and check the battery.

"Baby, you gotta stay in the car to see if it will start."

Click! Clack!

Baby G put the banga to the back of Gene's head. "Nigga you move, I'ma mash yo' shit out here."

"Fuck!" screamed Big Gene. "Nigga you know who you fuckin' wit'?"

"Hold up, daddy," said Shenida, grabbing the .357 off Gene's waist.

"Oh, nigga, you strapped, huh?" asked Billy slappin' Gene in the back of his head wit' his banga.

Crack!

"Aaaahhh—shit! Please don't kill me, my nigga!" cried Gene with his hands in the air.

Baby G snatched Gene by the collar. "Nigga get cha stank azz in here, and brake it off." Baby G kicked Gene in his ass.

Billy and Shenida followed suit, went in the trap behind them and closed the door.

"Lay yo' bitch azz down," ordered Baby G.

Gene followed orders and laid down, while Baby G searched his pockets, and found a bank roll in the process.

"Y'all tear dis bitch up!" screamed Baby G.

"The shit in da deep freezer," blurted Gene. "My nigga, don't kill me please!"

Baby G put the banga to Gene's nose. "My nigga, sssshhh! You a gangsta? Don't let dis situation change you, my nigga, keep it G!"

"Jackpot!" exhaled Billy. "Bra, dis shit loaded bih, we done hit."

"Where baby girl at? Baby girl, where you at?" yelled Baby G.

"Back here, daddy, I found something!"

"Billy put dat shit in dem Glade bags, so we can load dis shit up. Gene get dat azz up, and head to da back."

Once they reached the back room of the trap, Baby G found Shenida kneeling down by a safe.

"Look, G baby, it's bolted down to da floor."

"Ain't nothing in there, man," cried Big Gene.

"You got three secondz to spit dat combo out," threatened Baby G.

"One-two-nine-twenty-twenty-seven, my nigga don't shoot me. I got a daughter, *please!*"

"Open da safe, baby girl," instructed Baby G. "It's done, daddy, looks like about 30 gee'z."

"A'ight, grab da shit, let's be out."

Billy came into the room sweating. "I loaded all dat shit up, my nigga, it had to be at least a hunnid and fifty poundz of loud in dat bitch."

"Go start da car, we coming," Baby G instructed.

"Fasho, my nigga, tighten up doe," said Billy as he left out the room.

"I got it, daddy, let's go."

"Hold up, let me see the money."

Shenida gave Baby G the money. "She promised you the pussy, right?"

Big Gene just laid there sweating and looking stupid.

"Turn over, big boy," said Baby G. Gene did as he was told. "Baby girl, eat him up."

Shenida looked at Baby G like he was crazy, but all he did was nod his head affirming his command. Shenida got on her knees, pulled Gene's lil' dick out and went to work. Her head game was pure flame, so it was hard for Gene to just lay there silent. He made the weirdest noises, while looking up at Baby G scared to death.

"Nigga don't look at me, I'm not the one suckin' yo' dick."

Something in Gene made him say fuck it and grabbed Shenida's head as he got into it.

Blocka!

Baby G hit Big Gene right in the top of his head, killing him off the rip. The shit scared Shenida, causing her to bite down taking a piece of Gene's dick completely off.

After spitting it out, she yelled at Baby G, *"Damn, nigga, you scared da shit outta me!"*

"You gon' have to cut da rest of dat nigga dick off, and pour bleach on his shit. Kuz I'm almost positive you left DNA on his big azz. I'll be waitin' in da car," said Baby G.

Five minutes later, Shenida came out and jumped in the whip. They left the scene a hunnid fifty pounds and thirty bandz richer.

Khufu

Chapter 39

He In da Way

After splitting the money three ways, and the loud two ways, the trio departed with the promise of meeting up again. Baby G bent down Avenue T and was about to pull into Shantel's apartment but saw Detective Peer talking to his baby mama, and kept it moving.

"*Fuck!* Da hell his bitch azz want now?" Baby G thought about the seventy-five pounds he had in the trunk, and dialed Off Top's number.

Top picked up on the second ring. "Yo!" answered Top.

"What's good, Top, you at da spot?"

"Damn, baby boy, you been ghost for a minute. You a'ight?" asked Top. "Yeah, I'm a'ight, I just need to swang through, and check da air for a sec."

"I'm not at da spot. I'm home, come to da house."

"I'ma pull up on ya in a few."

Click!

Ten minutes later, Baby G was pulling into Top's driveway popping the trunk. Top was already outside, blowing loud as usual.

"Come on in, baby boy. What dat is you got wit' chu?"

"What dey do, bra? Dis her for you," said Baby G as he walked past Top with the lick.

"Boy, you smelling real good, and loud," said Top closing the door behind hm. Let's see it."

"Look, bra, I'm on something right now, so let's make dis quick as possible. Dat's seventy-five poundz of loud. Give me sixty bandz, dey yours."

"What dat is eight-hundred a pound?" asked Top. "Say no moe consider dem bought. Peep dis doe, I gotta job for ya. Now whether you brang Mundo in on it or not, it's on you, but da ticket's eighty bandz."

"Eighty ban yanz?" Yeah, I accept. Who da vic is?"

"You know a nigga name Swope?"

"Yeah, I done seen him around. What's good?"

"He in da way. You feel me? I need a path to be cleared."

125

"Normally, I wouldn't ask questions, but why Swope? I thought he fucked wit' dat food."

"He do, but he just opened a weed hole right across da street from my trap on Dunbar, and I can't have dat," said Top. "So, you telling me. I can run down on dis nigga on Dunbar right now?"

"Nall, he ain't gon' be there, but his lil' niggaz will." Listen, dis nigga just opened a pool hall on twenty-fifth, in da same plaza as J&J's. He be in there gambling till the sun comes up. I want chu to hit dis nigga in front of all dem niggaz to send a clear message."

"I gotcha but check it. I'ma need this one up front, big homie. I gotta handle some shit."

"No problem," said Top as he left and came back with a hunnid and forty thousand.

"You already know, my G. Just keep da tube on da newz, I'm out," said Baby G.

"Already!" chimed Top.

Baby G left three hunnid and ten bands up.

Chapter 40

Wanted For Questioning

Back in the car, Baby G's phone was vibrating crazy. He'd left his phone in the car and saw that he had seven missed calls from Shantel. Baby G called her back, and she picked up on the first ring.

"Hello," answered Shantel.

"Yeah, baby, talk to me," Baby G replied.

"Man, dis detective was here asking me all kinda shit about 'chu. Like do I know that I'm living wit' a killa? And what did you and Mundo do wit' Piggy's nose?"

"What did you tell 'em?"

"I asked him why he was coming to me wit' all dis bullshit. He replied that he was given a tip that you stay here wit' me. He said he was told that you keep gunz, and drugz in my apartment. Then asked if he could search my shit?"

"Did you let him in?"

"No, I told him not without a warrant. He just said he would be back wit' one. Baby G, baby, I'm scared!"

"First off, calm down and breathe. He ain't got shit on me, baby, he just fuckin' wit' you."

"Baby G, he said that you're wanted for questioning in a triple homicide."

"I don't know what he talkin' 'bout, baby. I didn't do shit. Listen, you remember what I told you in case shit ever got real?"

"Yez, daddy, I remember."

"Good, I need you to get on dat like right now!"

"Okay, Baby G. Baby, I love you."

"Yeah, yeah, a nigga loves you, too!"

Click!

As soon as Baby G hung up the phone, it started ringing again. It was Shenida.

"What da bidness is?" asked Baby G. "Baby G, listen! You remember ol' boy from da carwash, right?"

"Yeah, what about him?"

"He called me talkin' reckless saying dat shit wasn't right, and dat muthafuckas was dying off dat shit. He said he should fuck me up for introducing y'all and dat he got something for you."

"Is dat, right?" Baby G half-chuckled. "Check it, get suited. I'm on my way."

"Okay, daddy, I'm here."

"Shenida!"

"Yez!"

"Grab dat bag outta yo room closet."

Chapter 41

Might As Well Get Blood on My Handz

"So, what's da plan, daddy?"

"Shid—I gotta spot, I'm finna hit up. Then I'ma go tighten ol' boy up."

"When we get to da spot, just wait in da car. I'ma be in and out."

"Nigga, you got me fucked up! If we get caught, I'ma get the same amount of time as you. I might as well get blood on my handz too!" stated Shenida.

"That's deep!" said Baby G. "A'ight then, dis what it is. Drop me off on the street over from Dunbar. Then pull in the house directly across the street from Off Top's trap and buy some dank. You know what to do once you get in there. I'ma be right behind you."

"Okay, daddy I got chu." Baby G unzipped the bag he told her to bring, grabbed a baby compact 9mm and handed it to Shenida. He then pulled out extra clips for the banga he used to kill Big Gene and put on a red Chicago Bulls hat pullin' it as low as he could. "Pull in dat complex right there and drop me off."

Shenida pulled into the complex off 29th and D and let Baby G out. Baby G hopped out and mobbed through the complex until he came to a fence that was right behind the house, he was about to terrorize after jumping the fence. He pulled out his banga and put one in da head. Baby G crept to the back of the trap, and to his surprise the bathroom window was open. He slipped right in without a sound and wiped the window down regretting that he didn't bring any gloves. As he sat and waited, someone could be heard knocking on the door. Baby G knew it was Shenida but still waited.

Khufu

Chapter 42

I'ma Spare You I Promise

"Damn, lil' baby, you know you ain't gotta pay for shit, right?" said one of the lil' niggaz named Clambo.

"Lil' boy, what 'chu on?" asked Shenida. "Dis pussy to wild for you, youngin'!"

"I can show you, better than I can tell you. Lick you up, lick you down, baby."

"Shid, I ain't turning down no head. Where we at wit it?" asked Shenida. "Nigga, stop hollin' at every bitch dat come in the trap!" said another youngster by the name of Batman. "Dat's why yo' end alwayz coming up short trick azz nigga!"

"Look, here Batboy. *Fuck you!*" said Clambo. "Nigga, dis my dick! I can do what I wanna do wit' my dick!"

"Just serve da hoe and get her azz da fuck out. We got bidness to tend to fool. I'll be right back." Batman went to the restroom to take a shit. He'd been having the shits all day. "Ohhh shit!" screamed Batman as he entered the bathroom, pulling his pants down, barely making it to the toilet before lettin' it rip. "Aahhh—damn!"

Batman was farting loudly and spraying the whole toilet bowl with shit everywhere.

"This stupid azz nigga stay fuckin' up da pack. I gotta end up covering for his trickin' azz. I'm tired of dis shit, I'ma tell Swope dat's what I'ma do, fuck it."

Baby G stepped from behind the shower curtain, putting his finger to his lips lettin' Batman know to be the fuck quiet. Seeing this Batman shitted uncontrollably and pissed at the same time. Baby G snatched him by the collar and led him to the front room while he was still shittin' on himself.

"Dat's it young nigga, eat dis pussy!" screamed Shenida as she rotated her hips, throwing pussy all in Clambo's face.

She looked up and saw Baby G coming with Batman. Who now had tears flowing freely from his face with his pants down, and put her hand up letting Baby G know to wait a minute.

"Sssshit! Ooohhh—I'm finna cu—"
Blocka!
Baby G hit Clambo in the head spraying blood and fragments all over Shenida, and her pussy.
"*Damn, nigga!* You couldn't wait thirty moe seconds, *fuck!*"
"Fuck all dat!" said Baby G. Where it at lil' nigga? Tell me I ain't gon' kill ya."
"My nigga, say you promise you ain't gon' kill me," said Batman who turned around to get a look at his perpetrator's face. "Oh, shit, my nigga. Baby G, dat's you? My nigga, I fucks wit' yo' muzik hard, my nigga fa real! Dat video C-Major shot for you called Live or Die was deep. My nigga, you went in, fa real," said Batman wiping tears from his eyes.
"Dat's what's up, lil' homie. I'm feelin' dat. I tell you what, lil' nigga. Since you fuckin' wit' da movement. I'ma spare you, I promise. Just tell me where dat paper and work at."
"It's ten poundz in the backroom closet. I got ten on me, and Clambo should have close to five on him."
Shenida went in Clambo's pocket removing the bankroll while Baby G took the ten off Batman.
"Nigga, where da safe at?"
"Come on man, leave me something. I can't afford to lose all of Swope's shit, kuz then he gon' kill me," cried Batman.
"Last chance," said Baby G.
"A'ight shit, bra. Da safe in the same room as the weed. You gotta move the dresser and you'll see the safe in the wall."
"Code?" questioned Baby G.
"Five-thirty-one-seventeen," said Batman.
"Let's go, lead da way."
Batman took them to the safe and opened it immediately.
Baby G grabbed the money, while Shenida checked the closet. "Daddy, I don't see no weed. He lying, kill his azz!"
"No, wait!" screamed Batman. "The weed is in dem canz right there. You need a can opener to get it out."
"I got it, baby girl, hold dis nigga down."
Shenida put her baby nine in Batman's face. "I got him, daddy."

Baby G put the cans on the bed and used the sheet to tie them up. "Bet dat up, lil' homie. You've been very helpful, so I ain't gon' kill ya."

"Thank you, Baby G. Man, I knew you was a good nigga."

As soon as the praise left Batman's mouth, Shenida put a slug in his head.

Boc! It echoed loudly.

"I told ya I wasn't gon' kill you, lil nigga. And I didn't, but I didn't promise you shit about baby girl," Baby G said to Batman's corpse.

"Facts!" Shenida echoed.

Boc!

"Let's go, baby girl," said Baby G.

He figured someone probably heard the gunshots, but deep down he didn't give a fuck about much of anything no more.

Khufu

Chapter 43

God Please No

After dropping Shenida off with fifteen bands, Baby G headed straight to the pool hall on 25th. He didn't want word to get to Swope that his spot had been hit, so he had to be dealt with ASAP. Baby G pulled into the Elk's Lounge, a hood club that sat in between Vietnam and Duce Tray; two rival gangs that gave it to each other, every chance they got. Baby G hopped out of his Parasian after putting on a hoodie and walked over to the pool hall, which was no more than 25 yards away.

"Damn, Baby G, you just don't call a bitch no moe, and shit."

Baby G looked back and saw a lil' eater he used to crush, named Lexus. "What dey do, Lex? It ain't dat deep, Ma, don't trip."

"I'm trying to see you. What'z up?" asked Lexus. "I'ma kinda in the middle of something right now, Ma. But when the club let out, I'ma hit' cha line."

"Don't be lying, Baby G, kuz I'ma be waiting on yo' call, fa real,"

"I gotcha," said Baby G, as he slipped through a hole in a gate that led to J&J's plaza.

The poolhall was the first door on the left, and Baby G could hear a bunch of niggaz in there gambling and talking cash shit. Baby G swung the door open and walked straight up to his man while pulling his hood down. Seeing who it was, and the attire that Baby G had on. Swope knew it was game over.

Baby G lifted his banga while Swope cried out, *"God, please noooo!"*

God must have been busy because Swope's prayers went unanswered. Baby G planted four hot ones in Swope's face, neck, and chest. Baby G then looked around the room and recognized everybody there.

"Y'all boyz good?" asked Baby G.

Everybody screamed in unison, *"Yeah, man, we good!"*

A few of them even pushed their money toward Baby G, but he

declined.

"Fuck you niggaz money. You niggaz can push all the dope you want. But ain't no weed holes being opened up! I find out you moving weed, I'm coming to see ya. What's good, Rocky Boy, you a'ight?"

"Yeah, my nigga, I'm alwayz a'ight! You already know how I'm living."

Blocka!

Baby G slumped Rocky, then looked around the room. "Anybody else in dis bitch feel like I know how they living?" asked Baby G.

Everybody just held their heads low hoping they'd make it home to their loved ones.

"If I hear anythang 'bout dis, I'm coming! But you niggaz already know dat," said Baby G. "Enjoy da rest of your night, gentlemen, as you were." Baby G left and got in the wind.

Killa Kounty

Chapter 44

Ten Poundz of Loud

"Yo'!" said C-Major.

"What's good, my guy? This Baby G, step outside for a minute."

"Alright, bro, give me a minute. I'll be right out."

Baby G popped the truck and got out of the car when his phone started ringing. "Hello!" answered Baby G.

"Baby, where are you?" asked Shantel. "I got everythang set up for you out here. Baby you need to get out of dem streets."

"A'ight, Ma, I'm headed to you now. Don't worry yourself, I love you, a'ight."

"I love you too, boy."

"How my son doing?"

Shantel managed to smile even though she was stressing. "Boy, we don't know what we having yet!"

"Girl, I asked you how my son doing?"

"Oh, my gawd, boy, we doing okay, *damn*!"

"A'ight den, act like you know. I'll be there in a few."

"Okay, daddy, I'm up."

Baby G looked up and saw C-Major

"Awe, ain't that sweet!" teased C-Major.

"Whateva, dude," said Baby G.

"Bro, it's two-thirty in the morning. What the hell you got going on?" asked Major.

Baby G grabbed the ten canz and handed them to C-Major. "Deez fa you, my guy, dats ten poundz of loud."

"How much do you want for these, bro?"

"I don't want nothin', fam. Dats for da inconvenience. You saw da footage and you kept it gee, I respect dat, Major."

"It's all good, bro, you been family for ten years. I would never turn my back on you, bro."

"A'ight, my gee, enough of dis sensitive shit. Dat's you, you don't owe me shit, but I gotta go."

"Okay, bro, thanks for real. There's one more thing. You have a show booked at Lawnwood Stadium in two weeks."

"C-Major I got too much shit going on right now. I can't be rappin' and shit."

"Bro, it's five grand in it for you."

Baby G thought about it and five grand didn't seem worth risking getting caught. He was wanted for questioning and would be taking a chance going to Lawnwood. After thinking it over, he said fuck it, hell he had a baby on the way, so every dollar counted.

"How da fuck did you pull dis shit off?" questioned Baby G.

"I been promoting your music all over the internet. They fuckin' love you, bro! Me and a friend rented out the stadium. We're charging twenty dollars at the gate, and on top of that you're opening up for Kodak Black."

"Kodak? *Hell yeah!* Count me in."

"Alright, bro, be safe, and stay on post."

"Already!" said Baby G, as he got in his whip and peeled out.

Baby G grabbed Shantel and held her tight, kissing her forehead. "Girl, you know I'ma be a'ight regardless of whateva situation. But thank you for being so patient wit' a gangsta. I love you for dat."

"I love you too, boy."

"You know I'm a whole man out 'chere. Cut dat boy shit and getcha azz in dere and lay it down."

"Okay, daddy, you gon' give me some?"

"Yeah, I gotcha lil' baby, get in dare."

Once inside Baby G laid down and held Shantel in his arms, while she poured her heart out about her love and concerns. But five minutes into it she heard Baby G snoring. It had been a long day for them, so she just kissed him on his cheeks, and fell asleep in his arms.

Khufu

Chapter 45

Auntie Beverly

Baby G pulled up to the booth and waited for the officer to end his phone call. Baby G had told Shantel if he ever got in trouble she should clean her house and take all of his money to his aunt's place on the Indian Reservation.

He knew that the reservation had its own police and was not the jurisdiction of the local cops. He knew they could hide out there for a long time.

"Hello, sir, who are you here to see?" the female officer asked.

"My name is Baby G, and I'm here to see Beverly."

"Oh, yes, she informed me that you would be arriving soon. Have a nice morning."

"Same to you, beautiful," Baby G replied.

The officer blushed as she opened the entrance gate for him to enter.

On the way to his aunt's house, Baby G admired the mini mansions and foreign cars that he passed by. When he pulled up Shantel was waiting on the porch.

Parking the car and walking up on the porch, Baby G said, "Damn bae, what chu doing out here? You supposed to be asleep. If something happens to my baby I'ma kick your azz." He rubbed her stomach affectionately.

"Boy, you know I couldn't sleep without you by my side." She frowned.

Baby G hugged her and planted a kiss on her forehead.

"You know I'ma be a'ight regardless. But thank you for being patient with me. A nigga love you for dat."

"Love you too, boy," she said.

"I'ma whole man outchea. You can kill that boy shot and get'cha azz in there and lay it down."

"You gon' give me some?" she purred.

"Yeah, I got you, lil baby." He squeezed her ass.

Once inside the bedroom, Baby G laid next to Shantel and held her in his arms while she poured her heart out to him. She voiced her love for him and her concerns. Five minutes into her dialogue, she heard him snoring. She shook her head and smiled lovingly. It had been a long day, so she understood that he was exhausted. She planted a soft kiss on his cheek and fell asleep in his arms.

Chapter 46

Just Be Careful Please

"Baby G, baby, wake up." He heard Shantel, but just wanted to lay there and catch up on some rest. The streets had been draining him.

"Baby, wake up, yo auntie in there cooking breakfast. She told me to get' chu up." Shantel shook Baby G until he got up.

"Okay, bae, I'm up! I'm up! Shit!" Shantel tried to kiss him on his lips, but he turned his head. "Chill out, I gotta brush my shit, and get right, girl move."

"Boy, please! Give me dem stank kisses." Shantel grabbed Baby G's face and forced kisses on him.

Baby G pushed her off him, then got up to grab his towel, rag, and toothbrush.

Shantel slapped his ass. "Um dat's my booty!"

"A'ight now, I done told yo azz 'bout dat gay shit! I'ma fuck round and shoot yo azz in da leg!"

"Boy, bye! Go get right before I put dis coochie on yo nose."

Baby G laughed as he headed to the bathroom to brush up, and shower. Moments later, Baby G returned feeling like he'd just rinsed the filth from the streets off him.

"Aye, bae, whose Lexus truck dat was outside when I pulled up dis morning?"

"Baby, that's our new truck," said Shantel.

"What da hell you mean our new truck, baby?"

"Ain't it nice?"

"Shantel, you know I don't like payments and shit. I'ma give you the money to pay it off."

"That's fine, baby, I'll go to the dealership today."

"Listen, I got some money I want you to put up. I know shit finna get real, so I need you to hold me down."

"I got 'chu, daddy. You know I'm wit' chu."

"Time will tell," said Baby G. "I gotta run to the car real quick, I'll be back."

"Okay, baby," replied Shantel.

Baby G slid through the hallway, and saw his auntie cooking with her back turned to him, singing gospel. He slipped through the living room and went outside to get the money out of the car. It was now daylight out, so he could see the truck better.

"Damn, dat bitch clean!" said Baby G.

It was his favorite color red. After grabbing the money, he pulled out his phone and dialed Mundo's number. Mundo picked up on the third ring. "What's good, big bra?"

"Shid, I was callin' to see if you was ready for dat party."

"Which one you hollin' 'bout?"

"Top," replied Baby G.

"Oh, yeah! Already, I'm here."

"A'ight, I'll be through dare," said Baby G.

Baby G slid back inside and eased back past his auntie, then went into the room with Shantel. "Put dis money wit' da money we already got. It should put us a lil' bit over three hunnid bandz. I gotta go handle some shit real quick."

"Tsskkk." Shantel sighed, as she got up to put the money up.

"Wait, hand me two bandz outta dat money."

"Here, Baby G."

"Don't act like dat, Ma. This the last lil' thang I gotta do then I'm takin' a break from da streets, I promise."

"Just be careful, Baby G, please."

Baby G changed into an all-black jogging suit and grabbed the keys to the new truck.

"I'm taking the truck," said Baby G handing her the keys to the Parasian while kissing her on the forehead. "I love you, baby mama."

"I love you too, baby daddy."

Baby G tucked his banga as he slid into the hallway headed to the kitchen. "Auntie, what's good?"

"Hey, auntie's baby!"

Baby G hugged his aunt while she planted kisses all over his face. "How's my favorite nephew doing this morning?"

"I'm good, auntie."

"That's good, now sit down and eat your breakfast."

"I ain't got time, auntie, I gotta be somewhere."

"I said *sit yo azz down*!"

Baby G reached into his pocket and handed her a thousand dollars. "I'll be back, auntie."

"Okay, baby, I'll wrap it up for you. It will be here when you get back."

"Okay, auntie," said Baby G laughing at how money changed everything.

"I love you, nephew."

"I love you too, auntie Beverly."

Khufu

Chapter 47

Pop's House

Baby G pulled to his pop's house on 14th street, got out and knocked on the door.

"It's open," said Baby G's father, whose name was Jimmy Lee Johnson. Just like his son, Jimmy was a killer, except he didn't believe in guns. Jimmy preferred the knife because he said he liked getting close and personal with his vics, so that he could look 'em in the eyes as they died slowly.

When Baby G was five years old, his father was sent to prison for stabbing a man to death in Golden Corral. Jimmy worked in the dish room, where a guy pushed him and that was all she wrote. He chased the guy down, and gutted him like a fish, in front of all the customers. Jimmy took a plea and came home and stabbed another guy and did another bid. Now he was fresh out of prison.

"What's good, pops?"

"I'm good son, What brings you this way?"

"I need a favor, pops."

"Speak on it, son."

"You still got dem cuffs you used to cuff Rose to the bed wit'?"

"Yeah, why?"

"I need dem for something."

"You and Shantel into bondage?"

"Not really, but we figured we'd try some new shit."

"Go look in my room in the first draw."

Baby G went into the room and opened the draw. "Damn, pops you got paddles, anal beadz some moe shit in here."

"You got's to freak these whores, son."

Baby G grabbed six pairs of cuffs and left the room. "I gotta go, pops. You okay? You need anything?"

"Yeah, son, can you grab me a bottle of Vodka?"

Baby G went in his pocket and handed Jimmy five hundred dollars. "Here pops, I'ma swang through here later to check on you. I love you, pops."

"I love you too, son, be safe out there."
"Already, pops."

Chapter 48

I Wuda Died Bout' Chu

"Come outside, I'm here," Baby G told Mundo over the phone.

Moments later, Mundo came out in designer jeans, and a black fitted V-neck. He had a .40 wit' da extendo hanging out of his pocket.

"What's good, Baby G?" asked Mundo, hopping in the truck.

"What it iz, lil' bra?"

"Who truck dis is?"

"Shid, who sittin' in it?" replied Baby G with a light chuckle.

"Dis bitch sauced up! I might have to grab me one of deez."

"Shid, just let me know when you ready, I'll shoot you up there."

"Depends on what we hit for today. Shid, I might be ready tomorrow."

"I gotcha," assured Baby G.

"So, who we running down on today?" questioned Mundo.

"Some nigga name Swope."

"Swope? It can't be Swope because I heard he got hit up like two in da morning."

Yana had told Mundo that she had heard somebody named Swope had got killed. This raised suspicion in Mundo's mind, causing him to grip his banga. Baby G peeped it out of his peripheral but played it cool.

"Nall, dat's impossible kuz Shenida got him tied up on Avenue T at Carlos and Cheeseburger's old house."

"Oh yeah,?" asked Mundo, taking his hand off his banga.

"Yeah, bra, you remember da office building connected to the house dat we used to fuck dem hoez in?"

"Hell yeah, I remember!" said Mundo, getting hyped just thinking about the orgies they used to have. "You stayed brangin' Tina in dat bitch. She musta had a good slice on her. Damn, dem was da days, huh, bra?" asked Mundo.

"*Fuck yeah!* Dem was da dayz! But time changes everything.

Khufu

We here," said Baby G.

"How much Top kickin' out fa dis one?" asked Mundo.

"Oh, dis one here fa a hunnid bandz. He said dis one is personal. Dat's why I got him tied up. We gotta torture dis nigga."

"Wait a minute, how da hell Shenida tied dis nigga up by herself?" asked Mundo.

"Me and her kidnapped da nigga last night. I kuda killed da nigga last night, but nigga you gotta put yo' work in, ain't shit free."

"You ain't saying shit, let's rock out," said Mundo hopping out of the truck.

Baby G got out and followed behind Mundo who was hyped and turnt with his banga in hand. As soon as Mundo crossed the threshold.

Crack!

Baby G hit him in the back of the head with his banga, causing Mundo to drop his pistol and fall to his knees, holding his head. When Mundo turned around to see what was going on, Baby G gave him all the pressure he had, pistol whippin' Mundo relentlessly.

Crack!

"So, you like stealing from yo' flesh and blood, huh?" *Crack!* "Well, let me—" *Crack!* "—steal some of dis blood out 'cha." *Crack!* "Nigga, you think—" *Crack!* "—I'ma disloyal azz nigga?" *Crack!* "Dat I wud fuck yo' bitch?" *Crack!* "Nigga, you shudda killed me—" *Crack! Crack! Crack!*

Baby G beat Mundo unconscious, donating blood to the walls, floor and his clothes.

When Mundo came to; everything was a blur. Someone was bouncing up and down on his lap rapidly and couldn't make out who it was. He tried to get up but realized he couldn't move. His neck was cuffed to a pole, as he sat in a chair with his legs and arms cuffed as well.

"Oohhh shit! Give me dis dick, you Fetty Wap lookin' muthafucka! Sssshit, nigga, give it to me, daddy! Aahhh!"

When Mundo's vision cleared he could clearly see that it was Poola. Poola had full blown AIDS and everybody knew her. She even managed to get her a few hood stars, such as Poppa Duck and

Poppa Da Don from Mobb Squad. In the club, Poola would fool you due to the fact that she had a butta face, meaning everything looked good but her face. Poola was in her last stages, so she was looking like a creature, on top of Mundo, causing him to scream and squirm but to no avail. He could hear someone behind him laughing hysterically.

"What da fuck, man! Man, get da fuck off me, bitch!"

"Shut da fuck up and get dis pussy!" moaned Poola.

Poola was grinding, bouncing, and rotating her pussy on Mundo as if she was madly in love with him.

Baby G walked in front of Mundo and stood behind Poola.

"Get him, Poola!" barked Baby G, laughing crazily, because at this point Mundo was crying with boogers and snot running freely from his nose.

"Bro, please get her off me, man! I'm sorry, I fucked up!"

"I really feel like you crying kuz you hate the fact dat you enjoying dat shit," joked Baby G.

"Bro, you know how I am 'bout my Yana, man. I thought—I thought—I—"

"Nigga you thought I was a disloyal azz nigga!" said Baby G finishing Mundo's statement. "You shot me over some pussy dat I ain't even get. Then you stole from me when you didn't even have to. You gotta be dealt wit' accordingly."

"Ooohhh daddy dis pussy nuttin'!" screamed Poola.

Blocka!

Baby G put one in Poola's head, spraying blood and brains all over Mundo. Poola was still straddling Mundo with a half of head that laid on his chest.

"Bro, get dis hoe off me, *please!*" Mundo was shaking like a stripper at this point, panicking.

"Nigga, you ain't my fuckin' brother, and shut da fuck up fo' I kill yo' azz in dis bitch!"

"You might as well kill me, I'm dead anyway!" said Mundo.

Blocka!

Baby G shot Mundo in the leg.

"Aaahhh—shit, bra, don't kill me. *Please!*"

151

Baby G grabbed some duct tape that was on an upside-down bucket, and taped Mundo's mouth shut.

Blocka!

Baby G shot him in his other leg. "Nigga, I wuda died bout 'chu! I really had love fa you, but nah—nigga nah. You ain't nothin' nigga, kuz of you 'Rina is dead. I killed an old azz lady and for what? Pussy? Dat ain't no playa shit, homie. But then again, you ain't a playa type nigga. Nigga, you'z a *sucka*! Chill out wit' Poola for a while, I'll be back to check on you."

Baby G turned and walked out of the bando leaving Mundo screaming and pleading, but the duct tape muffled that. Baby G hopped in his truck thinking that he shoulda killed Mundo.

"I'll come back in a few weeks, with no water or food he shud be dead as fuck when I get back," Baby G said to himself as he drove through Killa Kounty.

Chapter 49

I See You Gotta Show Tonight

"Give me a kiss, baby, I gotta go. C-Major's outside."

Shantel gave Baby G a kiss. "Thank you, baby!"

"For what?" asked Baby G.

"For buying me this house."

"Shid, dis our house but you're welcome." Baby G found a nice house for a hunnid bandz, and had his stepfather D-Dog working on it for him. "I love you, girl."

"I love you, too, boy. Be careful, please."

"A'ight, ma, just make sho' you got my favorite meal cooked for me when I get home."

"I know, boy, brown sugar baked beans, mixed with ground beef, rice, and fried chicken."

"And some Kool-Aid!" added Baby G.

"Okay, bae, I got 'chu." Baby G stepped outside and saw that C-Major had rented a party bus.

"Come on, bro let's get it!" said C-Major, really excited.

"Damn, dis bitch nice, but where da hoez at?"

"Bro, we gon' bring the hoez back from the show," replied C-Major.

"Man, damn, Shan gon' kill me!" Baby G's phone started ringing, it was his sister C.C. "What's going on, big head?"

"I see you got a show tonight? It's all over Facebook."

"Yeah, I'ma do a lil' something. You gon' come support a nigga or nall?"

"I guess me and Yana gone come together."

"Yana?" asked Baby G.

"Yeah, she says she gon' come with me kuz she tired of being cooped up in da house. Mundo done left dis girl alone for two weeks now, and he won't even pick up his phone. Have you talked to or seen him lately, Baby G?"

"Nall, I was just finna swang through and see if he wanted to ride with me. I'm already running late. So, I'ma just gon' 'head out

dare. Call me if you get in contact wit' him."
"Okay, big brudi, see you out there."
"Already!" said Baby G.

Chapter 50

Showtime

Baby G hit the stage and couldn't believe the reaction he was getting. In the words of Beyonce, *"The crowd was going ape shit!"*

"Y'all already know what time it iz! It's *Baby G people!*"

"Please say da people! Live by die by/Dat's how shit goes in da field/Eagle on me like I'm Nick Foles in my city summers hot/but dey get cold/ It's Killa Kounty/so it's murder wit' dem kick doez/ What 'chu kno' 'bout being piss po' grab da fifth/like ya ex let da bitch go/ Take da sack to da kitchen/Water wrist flow trap bumpin' cookies like Nabisco/ When I'm in her/ pussy wetta den a slit throat/ My niggaz stupid/When dey sniff coke/ A lot of B's couple C's and dem pitch forks—"

The crowd continued to go ape shit, *"Baby G—Baby G—Baby G!"*

"Thank y'all for having me, my nigga. I love y'all! Killa Kounty Stand up!"

As Baby G was leaving the stage, he heard a familiar voice, *"Big, bra! Baby G, bra over here nigga dis yo' sister C.C.!"*

When he saw that it was his sister, he pulled her, and they left backstage together. "Damn, bra, you killed dat shit like fa real, fa real doe!"

"Yeah, I did do dat shit proper like!" said Baby G smiling from ear to ear.

"Hell yeah, bra, you on yo' way. Once you get da city behind you, it's to da roof, Batman! I'm proud of you, bro."

"Thanks, sis."

"Hey, Baby G, come on, bro! I got the girlz on the party bus," said C-Major. "All of them keep asking for you, bro."

"Aye, sis, how did you get here?" asked Baby G.

"My car parked out front. Why?"

"Where Yana?"

"She left with some dude she met, why?"

"C-Major, I think I'ma take a rain check on dis one, man. I'ma ride home wit' my sister."

"Baby G, bro, what am I supposed to do with all these girlz, bro?"

"Ride dey azz round da city, den drop dey azz off, shid." I'm going home dis time, my gee."

"Alright, bro, just get with me tomorrow. We'll go through the footage from the show and make a video," said C-Major.

"Dat's a bet, Major! I'ma see you tomorrow. Come on, sis, a nigga's hungry."

Chapter 51

You Had to Go

Back in the car, C.C. was playing one of Baby G's old mixtapes titled *Life After Prison*.

"Damn, sis, you still got dis shit?"

"Hell yeah, bra. I got a lot of yo' old music. When you gon' let lil' sis get on a track wit 'chu?"

"Shid, if you fa real, we can do some shit tomorrow."

"Don't be lying to me, bra."

"Nall fa real, sis, I gotcha."

"Wait! Hold up." C.C. turned down the music. "You feel dat?"

"Feel what?" asked Baby G.

"It feels like one of my tires wobbling."

"Sis, you trippin'!" C.C. pulled over, and got out of her car to check her tires with her brother right behind her. "Dis tire seem loose to you?" asked C.C.

Baby G bent down to inspect the tire. "Man, sis you trip—"

Blocka! Blocka! Blocka!

C.C. hit Baby G up and left him on the side of the road. "Sorry, big bra, but you had to go for what you did to Mundo."

C.C. got in her car and peeled out. She didn't know that Mundo had shot Baby G. All she knew was that some kidz found Mundo still alive with Poola dead in his lap and called 911. After Mundo told C.C. what happened she promised him that Baby G would get his.

The passenger of the car Mundo shot up was never hit and gave the detective's Mundo's name. They now had a corroborating witness.

While in recovery, detectives ran down on Mundo and placed him under arrest for the murder of Billy Da Kid.

"So, Mr. Mundo I'm sure you know why we're here," said Detective Peer. "You're going down for murder in the first, you piece of shit!"

Mundo just laid there as if Detective Peer was talking to the wall.

"If you haven't been informed, your brother Baby G was found on the side of Virginia Avenue with holes in his azz, but that's another story. What me and my partner want to know is, *what the fuck did you fucks do with Piggy's nose!*"

Chapter 52

Ask Piggy Bout da Big Bad Wolf

"Mundo, bra, they callin' you for mail," said Keedy.

Keedy was Mundo's cellmate and a close friend of the family. He'd been in St. Lucie County jail fighting a murder beef for four years now.

"Damn, how long I been sleep?" asked Mundo.

"Bra, you been down three dayz, my nigga. You need to eat something before you die in this bitch!"

"I can't eat that slop, shid—when they do canteen?"

"The cart comes by today, and you can order on the kiosk Thursday."

Mundo looked at his uniform and realized he was in a pumpkin suit. A pumpkin suit was jail slang for the orange uniforms inmates wore. It was for high-risk inmates only.

Damn, thought Mundo. "Do me a favor and hand me them crutches from over there, fam."

Keedy handed Mundo his crutches. "Damn, what happen to you, bra?"

"It's a long story, my nigga, I don't even wanna talk about it right now," said Mundo as he walked out on his crutches to get his mail. "Moss!"

"Yeah, right here."

"Moss, I know you heard me callin' you!" said the female C.O.

"My bad, I just woke up and I know you see I'm on crutches. Have a lil' compassion, you too cute to be uptight."

"Boy, get this mail and go lay yo' azz down, before I spray yo azz!"

Mundo smiled as he grabbed the letter from the C.O. and saw that it was Yana who had written to him. As he headed back to his cell, he noticed a few familiar faces from the streets. Two of them were members of Piggy's gang, The Hot Heads. They just stood there posted on the wall, nodding their heads at Mundo.

"Yeah, I'ma have to fuck one of deez niggaz up," Mundo said

to himself, as he headed to his cell.

"You a'ight, fam?" asked Keedy.

"Yeah, just watch the door while I read this letter. I saw some niggaz I got tension with."

"Read yo' mail, you good, fam. Deez niggaz know what time it is with me," said Keedy as he grabbed his shank made of pencils, jail house sheets, and multiple staples. He then stood in the threshold of the cell, ready to donate pressure. "Don't worry 'bout shit! You good, fam, do you," stated Keedy.

"Bet dat up, bra, I appreciate dat," replied Mundo as he tore open the letter from Yana.

Dear Mundo,

Why haven't you called anybody yet? Everybody's worried about you, baby. I hope you are holding up in there because Rock Road is truly a shit hole! Trust me I know. I feel like a lot of this is my fault. If I woulda never fooled around with Cee, none of this woulda happened. I'm so sorry, baby, I love you. Your sister put money on your books, and I used the money you left to get you a lawyer. He should be down there to see you sometime this week. I heard about the Poola situation too. Damn, that's like on some other shit fa real! I know what you did, and I know what he did. If you want my opinion, y'all both played it dirty. You need to get tested while you're in there, baby. No matter what the results are, I'm here for you regardless. I've been to the doctor, baby—I'm pregnant! I know—crazy timing, right? Hell, it's money on the phone, so call when you're ready.

I love you, Mundo.

Respectfully I Am, Yana

P.S. Baby G's still alive!

The only thing that captured Mundo's attention was the last line—Baby G's still alive! Flashbacks of Baby G standing behind Poola laughing as she killed him slowly played vividly in his mind.

"I'ma kill dis muthafucka!" yelled Mundo.

"Who you talkin' 'bout killin,' fam?" asked Keedy.

"Baby G!"

"Baby G? Why you speakin' on killin' yo' brother?"

"It's too much to get into right now. I don't even feel like talkin' bout dat shit anyway. Just know dat I'ma fuck him over!"

"Whateva it is, I'm sho you niggaz can work it out. After all, y'all family, and family comes first," stated Keedy.

"Blood don't make you family, my nigga, loyalty and love do," replied Mundo.

Something didn't feel right to Keedy because he knew Baby G thoroughly. He knew that Baby G brought chaos, only to those who snaked him, but he decided to keep his thoughts to himself.

"Chow! Hands off your jocks, and outta ya cotts! Come and get it while it's hot! Chow gentlemen!"

"It's chicken patty day, bra, let me get dat shit," said Keedy.

"You can get it, I ain't trippin'," said Mundo as he grabbed his crutches and headed out the cell with Keedy right behind him.

While standing in line, Mundo's thoughts were on the letter Yana had written, revealing that she was pregnant, when somebody bumped him. Coming back to reality from his day dream he turned around to see who was crazy enough to disrespect him. It was Tremendous, from the Hot Head Mafia, standing 6'2. He just smiled, while shaking his head up and down.

"Pussy nigga you tryin' to check in?" Keedy stated to Tremendous.

"Just chill, bra, that shit ain't nothin'," said Mundo as he grabbed his tray and found a table.

Seconds later, Keedy joined him at the table, with smoke coming out of his ears.

"My nigga, dat boy mash tayder's Idaho style—straight up!"

"Calm down, my nigga, get dis chicken patty. You want the rice and cookies too?" asked Mundo.

"Hell yeah! My nigga, dat's love. I gotta couple soups and chips in there for you, since you don't eat dis shit."

While Keedy was scraping Mundo's plate clean, Mundo saw Tremendous go into his cell and tie a sheet to the bars. Mundo had never done real time, but he was smart enough to know that Tremendous was taking a shit.

"Aye, I'll be back, I'm finna put dis tray up."

"A'ight, I'm right here," said Keedy.

Mundo leaned his crutches against the table, then got up to put his tray away. He limped towards Tremendous' cell with all kinds of torturous thoughts in mind. As soon as he reached the cell, he slid up under the sheet, and caught Tremendous on the shitter.

"Hey, man what da fu—"

Crack! "Shut da fuck up!"

Crack!

Mundo knocked Tremendous off the toilet, causing him to shit on the floor.

"Help!" cried Tremendous.

"Nall, don't holla now, nigga! I'm finna beat dat azz *tremendously* in dis bitch!"

Crack!

Mundo kept smashing his head in until he was unconscious. Another Hot Head named Bud came in to assist Tremendous, but Keedy had already peeped the play. Keedy came in right behind him and put his shank in the back of his neck repeatedly. Bud squealed like a pig being slaughtered, causing attention to be drawn to the cell. Keedy heard A.S.A.P. rushing in the dorm and flushed the shank down the toilet.

"Mundo, bra, dem people coming!"

"Man, fuck dis nigga, and dem krackers!" said Mundo as he whipped his dick out and pissed on Tremendous' unconscious body.

"Get the fuck down!" yelled A.S.A.P. as they came in spraying Keedy and Mundo.

Once they had Mundo on his feet in cuffs, he spit on Tremendous on his way out. "Ask Piggy 'bout da big bad wolf!"

Chapter 53

Suck My Entire Dick

Beep! Beep! Beep! The sound of Baby G's heart reverted from the cardiogram as he laid in the bed at Lawnwood Medical.

Baby G had been on bed rest for three months. He suffered from a gunshot wound to the back. The bullet went in and out without hitting any vital organs, and another one grazed him on the head. For eight weeks straight, Detective Peer and his partner Archie have been coming sporadically with contingencies of getting Baby G to rat on Mundo in exchange for a segment of time reduced. Day in and day out, they came with threats, but Baby G knew the evidence against him was circumstantial.

"Listen, you piece of shit! We have your prints all over Jazmine's house. There are multiple witnesses standing in line to testify that they saw you and Mundo leaving Piggy's house. We know you were front line with your brother in this Piggy beef! But guess what? Mundo already gave us a confession on your black ass! He cares nothing about you. After all the loyalty you've shown him. Just tell us who shot you and give us a confession on how Mundo brutally killed Piggy and his family, and you walk Scott free. So, what's it going to be, Baby G?"

"So, you say I walk Scott free?" asked Baby G.

"I give you my word," said Detective Peer.

"You need a recorder for the confession, right?"

"A written statement would be nice, but since you're in no shape to write anything, we'll just record it. Detective Peer pulled out his phone and started the recorder. You can start whenever you're ready, Mr. Moss."

"Come closer, so you can record everythang clearly."

"Go ahead, buddy, we're all set," said Detective Peer excitedly.

"Okay, first off, *suck my entire dick*! Right—then after you take care of dat, *call my fuckin' lawyer*!"

Baby G's cockiness caused detective Peer to turn beet red and utter all kinds of racial obscenities.

Baby G politely pressed a button that released morphine through his I.V., and sedated himself, leaving the detectives talking to themselves. This went on for weeks until one day, Baby G's attorney was present when they showed up. She ripped them both new assholes, and they haven't been back since.

"Good morning, Baby G. How are you feeling, baby?" asked Brittany.

Brittany was a nurse at Lawnwood Medical. She had been doing a little more than nursing Baby G back to health. In the process of getting him back to one hundred percent, she had fallen in love with him wholeheartedly. Standing five eleven, Brittany was a stallion with jet black hair and blue eyes. Her Marilyn Monroe beauty mark complimented her white completion. Baby G told her that she favored Khloe' Kardashian. They were from two different worlds, but that's what attracted her to Baby G. She knew he was a street nigga with a lot of potential and vowed to get him to direct that same potential towards something positive.

"I'm feeling a'ight, but I'll feel a lot better if you sit on something."

"Um—is that right?"

"Yes, ma'am."

"And what exactly is it you want me to sit on, Mr. Moss?"

Baby G pulled his dick out and played with it until it was at full attention. "I want 'chu to sit on dis soul pole and get real groovy wit' it," said Baby G looking Brittany right in her eyes while still stroking his beef stick.

"I believe I can help you with that one, sir," Brittany stated as she removed the bottom of her scrubs, straddled Baby G and wiggled down on all nine inches. "Ssss—wow! You feel so fucking good inside me this morning," moaned Brittany as she rocked back and forth like a rocking chair on Baby G.

"Fuuccckkk! Dat's it, ride dat dick bitch!" demanded Baby G, as he grabbed her waist, and met her halfway with every thrust.

"Aahhh—shit yesss—daddy fuck me hard you fucker! Ssss— sshit yeah!" Brittany was now bouncing up and down on Baby G like a mad woman, not caring if she got caught.

The thrill of it all caused Baby G to snap. He grabbed a handful of her hair with his left hand causing her head to lean back, while he choked her with his right hand, still meeting her thrust for thrust. Brittany had a fetish with sexual asphyxiation, so she reached her apex the moment Baby G put his hand around her neck.

"Holy—*fucking*—*ssshit*! I'm cumming, daddy! Aaahhh—ssshhit!" Brittany came and contracted her vagina muscles around Baby G, forcing him to cum simultaneously.

"*Fuuccckkk! Damnit, man!* Dat was a good one, bae," said Baby G catching his breath.

"Um—so I'm bae, now?" asked Brittany as she grinded slowly on Baby G trying to absorb everything he had in him.

"I don't remember us using a rubber since I been in dis bitch! You fuckin' right, you, bae now," Baby G stated as he grabbed two hands full of her succulent ass.

"So, what about your baby mother?"

"I'on know what's up. She hired me an attorney but haven't been up here to see me. I hope everythang a'ight with her and the baby, shid I check out tomorrow."

"If you'd like, I would be more than willing to assist you with whatever you need," said Brittany, still grinding on Baby G.

"*Ms. Ludwig!*" shouted doctor Zoloff. "What on God's green earth are you doing? Having sex with patients, clearly is unacceptable! I'm sorry, but I'm going to—"

"Don't waste your breath, doc, I quit! Baby G come on baby, you ready?" asked Brittany while removing the I.V. from his arm.

"You fuckin', right!" replied Baby G standing to leave with his new lover.

"I'm sorry, Mr. Moss, but I haven't released you yet. Get back in the bed now, please, sir."

"Come on, doc. Do it look like I follow orders? Get the fuck out my face before you get admitted in dis bitch!"

Doctor Zoloff stepped aside and watched as one of his best nurses gave up her career for temporary pleasure.

Khufu

Chapter 54

Make 'em Kill Ya

"Forty-eight—forty-nine—fifty." Mundo got up and paced his cell after doing his tenth set of push-ups.

He'd been in the hole twenty days since his altercation with Tremendous. Keedy was a cell over from him, they politicked occasionally.

"Aye, Mundo!" yelled Keedy.

"Yeah, what up?"

"Dem people talkin' 'bout givin' me added charges and shit," said Keedy with a light chuckle.

"Yeah, they talkin' dat same shit with me, bra. As long as dem niggaz keep it solid, we should be good."

"I hear dat! On some real shit doe, I done did all kinda fucked up shit to a lot of niggaz, but you a wild nigga fa real. Why you whipped ya dick out, and pissed on buddy like dat?"

"We gotta lil street beef, dat's all," said Mundo, cutting it short not wanting to get into details.

"I'm feelin' dat, shid—fuck dem niggaz!"

"Yeah, yeah! Bet dat up, for havin' my back, dat's love."

"You already know, Mundo, we family! We ain't blood related, but we grew up together, our mommas best friends."

"Already!" stated Mundo.

The sound of keys could be heard coming down the tier, letting them know a C.O. was coming. "Moss, get dressed!"

"Where I'm going?"

"You got a one-thirteen visit. You got five minutes to get ready," said the C.O. as he left the tier.

Mundo did a quick sink wash and brushed his teeth before he headed to one-thirteen. One-thirteen was a holding tank for inmates who had a public pretender, and paid attorney visits.

"Aye, where you headed, fam?" asked Keedy.

"One-thirteen, attorney visit."

"What dem crackaz got' chu on?"

"I gotta murder charge, bra! I'm finna see what dey hollin' 'bout."

"No prints, no face, no case, my nigga—*make em kill ya*!"

"You already know," Mundo said, laughing at the jail house saying.

"Moss, you ready?"

"Yeah, let's ride."

The C.O. opened the flap and took out his cuffs. "Moss, cuff up."

Mundo put his arms through the flap and cuffed up. Moments later, the C.O. opened the cell door and held Mundo by the arm so he could help him down the stairs.

"Moss, you got a brother named Baby G?"

"Yeah, why?"

"Shit, everybody knows Baby G! His name ringing all through this jail. Every time he comes, he shows his natural ass. I read about him getting shot up, how is he?"

"He a'ight, for now."

"What's that supposed to mean?"

"Nothin."

When the C.O. reached the bottom tier, he radioed central to pop the steel door. On the way out the door, Mundo heard Keedy yelling, *"Make em kill ya, my nigga!"*

Mundo just smiled and shook his head as he left out the door.

Chapter 55

One-Thirteen

When Mundo reached one-thirteen, the C.O. that was in the sally port checking inmates in told Mundo that his attorney was already here. This meant he didn't have to wait in the holding tank and listen to niggaz with petty charges cry about petty time.

"Moss, you're in room eight."

"A'ight," said Mundo as he headed to the room where his attorney was waiting.

As soon as Mundo entered the room, he didn't like who he saw. It was Mike Yolie, the same attorney that fucked Baby G out of five grand. The day that Baby G was supposed to be taking a deal for time served, and two years papers, he was sentenced to prison time instead.

"Mr. Moss, how are you today?"

"I'm good, man, what's up?"

"Okay, I'm going to get straight to the point. They have you by the balls, kid. They have a witness, but the good news is they have a deal for fifteen years. I think you should take it, you're still young."

"You really feel like dat's a good deal?"

"Yes, Mr. Moss I do."

"Well, craka you do it then! Fuck wrong wit 'chu? Give my bitch half of dat retainer back, craka, you fired!" yelled Mundo as he walked out of the room.

"Mr. Moss, you done?" asked the C.O. who was checking the inmates in

"Yeah!"

"Your ride is on its way, but you have to wait in one-thirteen," said the C.O. as he opened the holding tank for Mundo.

As Mundo walked in, he didn't recognize anybody, so he just took a seat on the concrete slab. While inmates sat and cried about the petty time they were facing, Mundo's mind was on the time he was facing.

If they offering me fifteen on a murder charge, they probably ain't got shit on me. Fuck it! I'm going to trial! Mundo said to himself.

The sounds of keys interrupted Mundo's thoughts, and the steel door opened. The C.O. had let an inmate in to use the toilet before seeing his attorney.

Damn, dis nigga look familiar, thought Mundo. He stood up and approached the guy to get a better view. "Ain't dis some shit," said Mundo as he recognized the dude using the toilet. It was another Hot Head named Cherry. "What kind of nigga would name himself Cherry?" asked Mundo as he crept up behind him.

Cherry felt someone approaching, but it was too late. Mundo put the cuffs around Cherry's head and put him in the yoke, street talk for the chokehold. "Yeah, fuck azz nigga! Caught cha wit cha pants down, huh?"

Cherry was now pissing on himself, farting and suffocating all at once.

"You gon' die today, bitch azz nigga!"

A white inmate that was in the holding tank started banging on the steel door. "Guard—C.O.!"

The C.O. opened the door and saw Mundo choking the life out of the inmate he'd let in to use the toilet. "Moss, let him go!" yelled the C.O. as he sprayed Mundo.

Mundo took his arms from around Cherry's neck, and kicked him in the back, causing him to fall over the toilet and lay in his own piss. After Mundo spit on Cherry, he surrendered to the C.O.

"You hot head niggaz all da same. When a nigga catch you by yourself, you pissin' and shittin' on ya self! Look at'cha dumb azz now!"

"Come on, Moss, that's enough," said the C.O.

"Man fuck dis nigga! You know what time it is, dis street shit! Mind yo' fuckin' bidness!"

The C.O. said nothing else, as he escorted Mundo back to the hole, with another assault over his head.

Chapter 56

You Know I'ma Street Nigga!

Once in the parking lot, Baby G followed behind Brittany as she sauntered toward a cocaine white S650 Maybach and unlocked the doors.

"Damn, baby girl rollin' pretty nice to be a nurse. This gotta be her husband, or a relative's car?" Baby G said to himself as he traversed to the passenger's side and got in. "Brittany, I need to holla at chu 'bout something, and I need you to keep it all da way one hunnid wit' me."

"Sure, babe, what is it?"

"Are you married?"

Brittany laughed before answering. "It's a little too late for questions of infidelity, don't you think?"

"You right, I probably shuda asked you dis shit weeks ago. But you ain't make it easy for me performing wit' dat mouth, and dat muscle between yo' thighs."

Brittany shook her head before replying. "To answer your question, no Baby G, I'm not married."

"Who car dis is?"

"Who's driving it, silly? Don't be weird, just because I'ma nurse—excuse me was a nurse, doesn't mean I'm not successful."

"Yeah, about yo' job. I'm sorry I played a role in you fuckin' up yo' medical career. That was not my intention, ma."

"Babe, don't worry about it, okay. I didn't need that job. I only did it to stay busy. We both just got caught up in the moment."

"What chu mean, you didn't need the job?"

"Baby G, babe, I'm twenty-eight years old with no kids. I have a M.B.A. I'm pretty successful. What is it that you do?"

"I survive."

"Doing?"

"You know, a lil dis, a lil dat. Come on, Brittany, you know I'ma street nigga!"

"Well, maybe we can change that."

"Yeah, I kud use a few changes in my life. Maybe you can show me a different route to da paper. You know, a change of scenery wouldn't be bad either, but dat ain't gon' take the streets outta me. I'ma always be a street nigga, ma."

"Baby, I know it's a process. I need you to know, that I'm here with you. I knew what I was getting myself into the moment you came in with bullet holes in your ass. It was your will to live that attracted me to you."

"Oh, yeah?"

"Of course."

"Well, it was dem blue eyes and dat fat azz dat attracted me to you."

"Wow! I mean, is that it?"

"Not at all, bae, ahh—you have great knees. You know, I'ma knee man!" said Baby G while laughing because he knew Brittany hated when he was comical in a serious moment.

"You know what, don't even worry about it," whined Brittany.

"I'm just fuckin' off, Britt, you know I love everythang about chu."

"Whatever, Baby G! Where am I taking you?"

"Take me to my baby mom's, she stays on ave Q."

"So, am I dropping you off, or am I waiting?"

"We'll see when we get there."

Chapter 57

Where My Bangaz?

"Pull in dat yard right there," instructed Baby G. "You mean the peach one?"

"Yeah, pull in behind dat truck."

"Your baby mother isn't one of those crazy ones, is she?"

"Nall, she kool."

"Baby G, don't have me sitting out here all day. Let me know if you're staying or coming with me. Now, I don't want any problems. So, please keep the situation under control."

"Relax, I wouldn't put you in dat type of situation, Ma. I'll be right out," said Baby G, as he got out of the car, and headed toward the front door.

Once he reached the front door, Shantel could be heard talking to someone.

Who the fuck is she talking to? thought Baby G, as he turned the doorknob and entered the house.

"Damn, my nigga, what up?" said Baby G with a smirk on his face.

"Mercedes, let me call you back. Girl, I'ma call you back! Baby G, what'chu doing here? Them people said, you wasn't gettin' released till tomorrow."

"Maan—*fuck all dat*! Why you ain't come visit me? I kuda died in dat shit, and you just up in here runnin' yo' fuckin' mouth 'bout nothin'!"

"Boy, I ain't wanna come see you laid up like dat! All dat mess woulda put stress on my baby. I did get chu a lawyer, so what's da problem?"

"You know what—you dead azz right! Where my bangaz at?"

"Where yo' bangaz at? Baby G, you just got out da hospital! You almost died! When you gon' stop runnin' da streets? You gotta fuckin' baby on da way!"

"You done yet? If so, you can tell me where da fuck my pistols at!"

Shantel turned her head to the side in disbelief as a single tear rolled down her cheek.

"In the closet, in the shoe box, on the top shelf," said Shantel in almost a whisper.

Baby G spun off to go change clothes, and retrieve his pistols, returning moments later. "Look, I'ma be out and about for a few dayz, you know, handlin' shit. When I get time, I'll come check on you and my baby." Baby G turned and headed toward the front door.

"Baby G, wait!" cried Shantel.

"Ain't nothin' to talk about at dis point. I'on even wanna rap! You left me for dead. Dat money I left, dat's all you." Baby G left with one thing on his mind. *Order out of chaos.*

Chapter 58

I'll Make Yo' Azz Famous

Back in the car, Baby G sat in the back of the S650 and just gazed out the window. He was feeling some type of way about Shantel's insensitive actions.

"Is everything okay, Baby G? Baby, why are you sitting in the back seat?"

"Yeah, I'm good. I just got a lot on my mind."

"Well, if you'd like, I have a condo down in Pompano. We could get away from Fort Pierce for a few days and just relax." It's whatever you decide, babe."

"Hold up! So, you tellin' me, you was drivin' from Pompano to Fort Pierce every day to work?"

"No, I have a house on Huthersons Island. I haven't been to my condo in a while. I just figured you would want to get out of the city for a while."

Damn, baby girl got her shit together, thought Baby G. "A'ight, check it, swang me by my momma house real quick. Then we'll go to Hutcherson's Island for now."

"That's fine. Where does your mother stay?"

"Back out, make dat right on twenty ninth, then make a left on avenue S. You'll see a blue and pink house, pull in and keep the car runnin'."

"Okay, baby."

Two minutes later, Brittany pulled into the driveway of Baby G's mother's house. When Baby G saw whose car was in the driveway he smiled wickedly. "What are you smiling about, hon?" asked Brittany.

"Nothin' new booty, I'll be right out," said Baby G kissing Brittany before getting out of the car.

Baby G's mother had her garage door removed and replaced with glass sliding doors. Instead of going to the front door he went through the sliding doors. In the garage there was a door that led to the kitchen, Baby G crossed the threshold, and could hear two women talking about heading out to the Crab Shack for snow crabs.

He walked through the kitchen and made a left causing his mother to stop talking and gasp for air.

"Oohhh—boy! When did they release you?" asked Patty, Baby G's mother.

CC turned around to see who her mother was talking to and farted once she saw Baby G standing there with a smirk on his face.

"I just got out today, momma. You know, I appreciate you coming to see me. I know how you hate missing days off work. That meant a lot to me."

"You're my son! You know I'ma come see 'bout you, boy!"

Baby G could tell by the way his mother was talking, she knew nothing about the discrepancies between her three kids.

"I love you too, momma. Damn sis, where da love?"

"Oh—he—hey, Baby G. It's good to see you."

"Is it?" asked Baby G, making a mental note that C.C. didn't have her purse with her, meaning she wasn't strapped.

"Baby G, you know they trying to give your brother fifteen years?" interrupted Patty.

"Nall, I ain't know dat, momma. What dey chargin' him wit'?"

"He facing murder charges. Mundo sent me his discovery and everythang," said Patty.

"Go get dat for me, momma, let me see it please."

"Okay, give me a minute to pull it out, hold on."

As soon as Patty went into her room to get the paperwork, Baby G pulled his .40 Cal and put it to C.C.'s head. "*Bitch!* If we was anywhere but here, I'd make yo' azz famous! How da fuck you gon' choose sides, and you don't even know da real? You shuda stayed neutral, kuz now—you got pressure on every corner."

C.C. just stood there glad that she was at their mother's house. She knew that if they were anywhere else, she was lunch meat.

"Here it go, Baby G," said Patty.

Baby G pushed the back of C.C's head with the .40, then concealed it before his mother came back in the living room.

"Here it is right here, everythang is in there."

"A'ight, momma, I'ma take dis wit' me. I'll be back in a few dayz."

"Who you out there with?" asked Patty.

"Touch your nose, I love you, momma. C.C.—I'ma see yo' azz later.

Khufu

Chapter 59

Cheese Eater

Back at Brittany's house on Huthersons Island, she and Baby G made love for hours on her Queen size mattress until she was jaded and fell asleep. Baby G, on the other hand, had too much on his mind. He tossed and turned until he decided fuck it, kissed Brittany on the forehead then headed to the kitchen with Mundo's discovery in hand.

The walls were covered with paintings by Thomas Morgan and the floor was laced with Tufenkian carpet that complimented the Serpentine sofas.

"Damn, dis shit laid," Baby G said to himself, as he headed to the kitchen. "All dat work I put in gotta nigga kinda parched," said Baby G, as he noticed that the refrigerator had Wi-Fi connectivity. It was the new Obsidian free standing with French doors.

He grabbed a peach tea then took a seat at the kitchen table that was custom made from Italy. After pulling the paperwork from the envelope, Baby G spread Mundo's discovery across the table and examined its contents. Baby G knew that Detective Peer was just blowing smoke about Mundo giving a statement to him. Mundo was a lot of things, but a rat wasn't one of them.

He'd found what he was looking for—a cheese eater. *A fuckin' rat!*

Khufu

Chapter 60

Come See Me Then

C.C. could barely put her key in the door to get in her house. She was still visibly shaking from the episode with Baby G. After finally getting the door open, she entered her house and secured all the locks, bolts, and chains.

"I wonder why momma ain't tell me Baby G was still alive?" said C.C. as she grabbed a shot glass and poured up some 1800. "I know I shot his azz in the head! Fuck! Now I gotta be lookin' over my shoulder and shit."

C.C. poured another shot, downed it, and headed to her bedroom.

"Dis nigga got me fucked up, talkin' 'bout he gon' see me!" C.C. reached under her mattress and grabbed her pink Nina. "Yeah, a'ight—come see me then!"

Khufu

Chapter 61

Niggaz Get Shot Everyday B

After going through Mundo's discovery, Baby G grabbed his tea and headed to the back patio. Once out back, he was impressed with the whole setup. It was a huge hut with a bar and 75-inch smart TV. The tables were laced with fruit that complimented the Mondrian sofas. He walked over to view the heated pool and jacuzzi when he heard a familiar voice.

"Man—I know dat ain't my nigga! Oh, hell—nawl. What dey do?"

Baby G looked over the fence next door and saw his tall azz homeboy smoking a fat ass blunt. "Mango? Nigga, what da fuck you doing out here? I thought you said yo' spot was on Indian River Drive?"

"It is, bih, I gotta couple spots all over dis bitch."

Baby G walked to the fence and dapped Mango up. "Damn, my Cee I went by yo' spot in da b. geez to come fuck wit' cha on dat money tip, but when I pulled up a nigga told me dem people kicked yo' spot in. What up wit' dat?" asked Baby G.

"Yeah, man dey on me and shit. Dey got my girl and all, bih. Everythang good, doe, I gotta attorney on both of our shit—I ain't trippin'. What's good wit' cha, doe? I heard you got shot all in da head, my nigga," said Mango passing Baby G the blunt.

Baby G was hesitant being that he hadn't smoked in three months. "I got caught slippin', but it ain't nothin'! Niggas get shot every day, B," said Baby G in his best impersonation of Cameron from the movie Paid In Full. He hit the blunt, then passed it back to Mango.

"I'm sayin', shid—you know who did it? Let me know, bih. You know me, I'm ready to get my shine on."

"Be easy, big homie, you hot right now. I got dat covered already. I might need you for something else, doe."

"Talk to me, bra, what 'cha need?" asked Mango, passing the blunt back to Baby G, who was now feeling the effect of the high grade chronic.

"I think I wanna get in da coke game, my nigga. You gotta line for me?"

"Come on, man, act like you know dis what I do. I gotta line down in Pompano—shid, I'll set some shit up. When you tryna grab?"

"I'll be ready in a few dayz, shoot me the math so I can hit' cha when I'm ready, doe."

"You know where I'm at when you ready, fam."

"Damn, bra, I can't get da math?"

"Ain't nothin' personal, my nigga. I told you I'm here."

"A'ight, my nigga, respect! I'ma pull up on ya when I'm ready. Let me get back in here, shid dis dank gotta nigga kinda 'noid."

"Aye, before you leave, my nigga tell me how you manage to pull dat baby, doe?"

"What 'cha mean?" asked Baby G high out of his mind.

"Brittany! I been tryin' to shoot my shot for a minute. Shid—I thought she ain't like niggaz!" replied Mango.

"You been tryin' to shoot 'cha shot, huh? Sound to me like you been using da wrong ammo. You can get da thought off ya mind. She off the market for good. Just be ready when I pull up."

Chapter 62

I Gotta Get da Fuck Outta Here

"Moss, you got mail!" yelled the female C.O. as she slid the envelope under the door. It had been two weeks since the altercation Mundo had with Cherry. He was given twenty more days in confinement for assault.

Before Mundo could bend down and pick up his mail, Keedy could be heard through the vent. "Aye, fam who wrote 'cha?"

All Mundo could do was laugh. "Damn, dis shit kray," Mundo said to himself. "Look like it's a letter from sis," replied Mundo.

"Sis? That's C.C.? When you shoot back, tell her lil' Keedy said what up!"

"A'ight, I gotcha," Mundo uttered while ripping the envelope open.

Mundo,

Hi, lil bra, what's been good wit 'cha? Why the fuck you don't call nobody? You need to stop being so stubborn and let us know what's going on witchu. The real reason I'm writing you is to let chu know Baby G is out of the hospital and he's pissed off way past pisstivity! He came by momma's house in a fuckin' Maybach!

How da fuck dis nigga pullin up in 650's? And on top of dat dis nigga pulled da tool on me! I'm talkin' 'bout put it right to my fuckin' head! If momma wasn't there da nigga wuda push my shit back. Something told me to bring my woolie dat day to. Anyway, momma gave Baby G yo' discovery. I'm not sure what he wanted with it. You need to call home. I need to talk to you. Keep yo' head up lil bra, they can't hold a real one.

With love, C.C.

Mundo put the letter on the top bunk, and laid on the bottom one. He gazed out of the small window and wondered why Baby G took his discovery.

"Dis nigga hoppin' outta 650's and shit. Dis nigga musta found a plug," Mundo said to himself. "*Fuck!* I gotta get the fuck outta

185

Khufu

here!"

Chapter 63

I Gotta Play for Us

"Babe, I'm stepping out for a few hours. I was going to ask you if you wanted to come with me? If you're feeling up to it," asked Brittany.

"Nawl, you gon' head and handle yours. I got some running around to do myself."

"Okay, babe, I'll just call you when I'm on my way home. Here's a key to the house, and there's three other cars in the garage. The car keys are on the wall in the kitchen. I'll see you later and please be careful," said Brittany as she leaned in and kissed Baby G passionately.

"Let me see your phone, bae," requested Baby G. Brittany handed him her phone, watched him log in a number. "Dat's my number, hit me when you on yo' way back."

"Okay," said Brittany as she turned to leave. "Oh, I almost forgot—here, babe." Brittany handed Baby G a thousand dollars. "That's for food or in case you want to purchase something while you're out. I'm gone! Bye love," said Brittany as she left.

****

Thirty Minutes Later

Baby G was sliding through the city streets of Killa Kounty in the new 760 Beema making calls. Even though Shantel didn't come to see him, he was glad she kept his phone bill paid. He was now on the phone with his childhood friend Scrab.

"So, you say you gotta play for me?" asked Scrab.

"Nall, nigga, I gotta play for us!" Baby G reiterated.

"Okay, shid, I'm on da three at Michelle spot, my nigga swang through."

"You might as well step out, I'm bendin' da block as we speak."

"A'ight, I'm on the porch, pull up."

Moments later, Baby G pulled into Michelle's driveway and hopped out. It was a few niggas and a couple of hood chicks posted up, gossiping about nothing.

"What's up, my nigga? You been missing in action, my nigga, I thought you was locked up or some shit," stated Scrab.

"Nall, fool, I just been out da way. What's good, doe? You ready?"

"Yeah, give me a minute. I gotta grab some shit right quick," said Scrab as he spent off and headed into the apartment.

"Damn, I ain't seen you in foreva and a day!" said Michelle approaching Baby G.

Michelle was half Jamaican and Haitian, and stunningly beautiful with a perfect, heart-shaped ass. She had been Baby G's lil fling before he went to prison. He'd turned her section 8 apartment into a Treehouse for his homies, trappin' out of it and storing guns.

"I'm good, baby girl? You been a'ight?"

"Yeah, I just been koolin'. You know how dis third life is, ain't no tellin' what you gon' wake up to. A beautiful morning or gun smoke. I'll tell you dis, though—I'll be good if you gave me a sample of dat good-good," said Michelle grabbing a handful of Baby G's dick.

"Fall back, ma," said Baby G pulling away from Michelle's python grip. "Be patient, good thangz come to those who wait."

"Uh...Uh...uh—I been waitin' long enough," stated Michelle, while having flashbacks of how Baby G beat her back in.

"What cha purse lookin' like?" asked Baby G, changing the subject.

"Shit, I'm fucked up right now, shit's hard."

Baby G went in his pocket and gave Michelle a hundred dollars. "Here put dis in ya purse. I might have a play for you in a few dayz. You still on dat or what?" asked Baby G referring to that gangsta shit.

"Ain't shit change, you know how I rock. Shid, just pull up on me. You know where I'm at," replied Michelle tucking the money in her bra.

188

"I'm feelin' dat," replied Baby G, as Scrab came out of the spot with a duffle.

"You ready?" asked Scrab.

Yeah, let's roll. A'ight, 'Chelle, I'ma fuck wit chu."

"Bye, Baby G."

Khufu

Chapter 64

Proper Preparation Prevents Prosecution

"Damn, my nigga, You slidin' pretty good, now?" asked Scrab admiring the inside of the Beema as they headed to their destination.

Baby G ignored the comment, as he glanced in the back seat. "What's in the duffle bag?"

"Oh, you already know. I hit me one, yesterday I hit dis kracka's house. He was in the military. Baby G, my nigga I'm talkin' 'bout John Wick shit! Big stupid artillery!" said Scrab getting more hyped by the second.

"What da ticket is?" asked Baby G. "Shid—for you, shoot me fifteen hunnid, dey yours!"

"I got eight hunnid on me right now. I'ma give you seven moe after we pull da drill," said Baby G diggin' in his pockets and handing Scrab the money.

"I call dat!" replied Scrab grabbing the money. "What da play is doe?"

"I got dis spot we finna run in. It should be a smash hit. Whateva we hit for, we bust down da middle."

"Already, my nigga!" Baby G turned off Oleander into a neighborhood called Robin Hood where a lot of youngsters ran wild causing all type of mischief. "Dis it right here, my nigga," said Baby G pulling in front of a nice home with a gate around it. "Check it, ain't nobody in there. When you get to the back of the house, it's the first window on the right, the lock is popped so the window is alwayz open."

"Hold up, you ain't coming with me?"

"Nall, don't trip doe! I can't have my shit parked outside, I'ma just bend da block. You'll be a'ight, my nigga. Da shit you lookin' fa is in the dryer. I already know how much it is, so don't cross me fool!"

Scrab exhaled, frustrated that he was diving head-first into the unknown. "A'ight, fuck it," said Scrab reaching into the back seat to retrieve a pistol from the duffle bag.

"Nall, you good, fool! You don't need a banga fa dis. It's sweet, ain't nobody in there. If you do get caught in there, dat's arm burglary, you don't need dat."

"Shid—if I get caught in dat bitch, I'ma shoot it out!"

"Man, get da fuck out and handle up. You wanna get paid or nah?"

"Aye, who da fuck you talkin' to like dat, my nigga? Watch how you talk to me, nigga, straight up!" yelled Scrab as he got out the car and headed to the back of the house.

Baby G pulled off in silence trying to gather his thoughts when his phone rang. "Yo!"

"Hi, baby. I was just calling to check up on you. Are you okay?"

"Yeah, bae, I'm good. What's up wit' you, doe? You a'ight? How many niggaz tried to get at my German boo?" teased Baby G.

"I'm fine, you know I can handle myself. I just have to stop by a few more places, then I'll be headed your way, baby face."

"A'ight, I should be home before you, Ma. I'll see you then, snuggle bunny."

Brittany laughed at the nickname Baby G just gave her. "Okay, baby, see you then."

"Yeah, yeah," replied Baby G and ended the call. "Dis nigga should be out by now," Baby G said to himself bending the corner, creeping up the block.

As he got closer, Scrab could be seen approaching the road. Baby G sped up and pulled beside Scrab unlocking the doors. Scrab hopped in with a grin on his face solidifying the lick was a success.

"Shid, let me see somethin'," demanded Baby G.

"We good," assured Scrap, removing the vacuum sealed money from up under his shirt.

"What type of nigga leave dis kind of money in a dryer?" asked Scrab.

"Dat was a transaction spot. Somebody was supposed to come pick dat money up, and leave da work," explained Baby G.

"Damn, dat's a hellava set up, my guy. So, where we gon' bust down at?" asked Scrab as Baby G turned down Avenue T.

"We almost there, my nigga, just put the money under the seat."

"Hell yeah, my nigga! I'ma buy a whole brick of molly," stated Scrab leaning over to put the money up under the passenger seat.

Blocka!

Baby G put a hole in the left side of Scrab's head, causing a mist of blood to spray about. As he slumped over on the passenger's floorboard, Scrab's leg jerked due to his nerves causing Baby G to put two more holes in his head.

Blocka! Blocka!

"Sorry my dog, but proper preparation prevents prosecution."

Baby G knew if he didn't kill Scrab it was a guarantee that he would have tried to murder him once they reached the bust down spot. Scrab was a vicious nigga like that and was known to cross the ones close to him. Baby G pulled on to Taylor's Creek ditch bank and backed in next to the pump house. Mango had put Baby G on this spot years ago. Late night, they would back in and fuck the oxygen out of some eaters they met at the Elk's Lounge. Baby G pulled Scrab from the car, took the eight hundred out of his pocket, then dragged him to the edge of the creek, kicking him down the ditch bank into the alligator infested water.

Khufu

Chapter 65

Baby Haitian

Baby G pulled into the car wash on 29th and spotted who he was looking for. He parked the Beema, hopped out with the money from the lick, and put it in the trunk.

"Aye, Baby Haitian, check it out!" yelled Baby G.

Baby Haitian was a hustler, he made a living washing and waxing cars all day.

"Baby G, long time no see. What up, killa?"

"Listen, I gotta mess for you to clean up. I'ma shoot 'chu three hunnid."

Baby Haitian already knew what Baby G meant by clean up. He'd been known to clean murder scenes after wet work. "Say none, I gotcha! Where we at wit' it?"

"The inside of dat Beema over there. How long you think it's gon' take you?"

"Give me thirty minutes, I'ma have you all da way right."

"Do you, my nigga. I'm finna step over here for a minute," said Baby G walking across the street to a tire shop.

When Baby G walked into the hanger, it was niggas shooting pool, shooting dice, and gambling on madden.

"Aye, what up? Dat nigga Po Boy in there?"

"Yeah, hold up," said one of the workers at the shop. "Aye, Po Boy!"

Moments later, Po Boy came out of the back eating a big ass turkey sandwich. He was a big, black ass nigga who looked like Gold Mouth from the movie Life.

"Damn, my nigga, get da mayo all off ya chin and shit!"

"Dis turkey good as a motherfucka!" Po Boy wiped his mouth and chin. "Da fuck is up doe? What blew you dis way?"

"I got Baby Haitian over there gettin' da Beema right. I'm tryin' to blow somethin'."

"Shid, I gotcha. What chu tryin' to do?"

"Let me get an eighth and a gram of molly."

"Give me a minute, I gotchu," said Po Boy, heading to the back.

Baby G Stepped outside and stretched when he noticed little specks of blood on his shirt.

"Damn!" said Baby G, as he took his shirt off and threw it in a dumpster on the side of the shop.

Now, with no shirt on, Baby G's physique showed, causing a traffic frenzy. Women hissed and blew their horns, but Baby G just nodded his head and headed back in the shop.

"Damn, nigga, I thought you had done skated on me—here." Po Boy handed Baby G an eighth of loud, and two grams of molly.

"Already!" said Baby G reaching into his pocket to pay Po Boy.

"Don't worry 'bout it, you good, homie. Just come back and fuck wit' me."

"I'm feelin' dat. You know I'm fuckin' wit' cha," stated Baby G, as he headed back across the street.

"As good as new, my nigga! Anytime you need me, you know where I'm at!" said Baby Haitian.

"Bet dat," replied Baby G, as he dug in his pocket and handed him three- hundred. Baby G got in the car and pulled off.

Chapter 66

Shit Finna Get Real Now

Baby G puffed a blunt of loud as he thumbed through the money he'd just hit for. After counting two hunnid bandz, he downed a shot of Remy causing the molly to kick in full effect. He stood up and paced back and forth, unable to keep still.

"Damn, I feel good as fuck," Baby G stated to himself as he exhaled and headed to the shower.

When Baby G entered the master bedroom's bathroom, he noticed that all the knobs were of antique gold, and the walls were all Calacatta Paonazzo marble. Taking off his clothes, Baby G stepped into the stand-up shower which was also marble, and saw that the shower was touch screen activated. He just started pressing buttons, causing the water to fall from the ceiling.

"Aahhh—shit! Damn, dis shit relaxin' as fuck." Baby GHe let the warm water ease the tension in his muscles.

He thought about the events that took place throughout the day and knew he might have pressure if somebody found out he fed Scrab to the gators. Being fresh out of the hospital after a near death experience, Baby G really didn't give a fuck about consequences. He was prepared to face them head on. He was feeling so good that he didn't even hear Brittany enter the bathroom.

"Baby G! What the fuck!"

Baby G looked up and saw Brittany standing in front of the shower but couldn't make out what she was saying. Her facial expression let him know that she'd seen all the money and guns on the kitchen table.

"Huh?" asked Baby G.

Brittany opened the shower door to convey what she had seen, but she was snatched into the shower. Before she could wrap her mind around what was taking place, Baby G was kissing all over her neck and sucking on her ears.

"Baby, why are you—sss—um. Baby, what's that in the kitchen?"

Baby G ignored her, ripping off her twenty-five hundred dollars Michael Kors dress. His aggressiveness turned her on as he placed tender kisses on succulent breasts and ripped her satin panties off.

"Baby G, sss—why?"

"Shut da fuck up," ordered Baby G, as he guided her to the wall, got on his knees and lifted one of her legs over his shoulder.

Knowing what was coming next, Brittany's breathing quickened with every second, anticipating his warm tongue. Baby G blew on her clit, licked it, then blew again.

"Yesss—Daddy—blow on my clit just like that aahhh!" Brittany moaned.

Using his left hand, Baby G grabbed her booty cheek, spread it, then used the middle finger of his right hand to put pressure on her asshole as he kissed, licked, and sucked on her clit relentlessly. This technique caused her to buck out of control. She grabbed the back of his head as she rolled her back and threw her pussy in his face.

"Aaahhh—yesss, Daddy! I'm cumming so fucking hard! Sss—aaahhh!" Brittany came all in Baby G's mouth while shaking violently.

After sucking everything her body dripped, he stood up. "Turn around and put'cha handz on the fuckin' wall!"

"Yes, Daddy—please fuck me now—please Daddy!" cried Brittany as she did as she was told.

Baby G entered her from behind, pushing all the way in. "You feel me?"

"Yes, Daddy, I feel you." Baby G grabbed her by the throat with his right hand, placed his left hand on her left breast, pinching her nipple as he stroked her viciously from behind. "Oh, my fucking God! Sss—ooohhh baby! Why are you so fucking hard?"

"Shut da fuck up!" Baby G's dominance sent Brittany over the edge, causing her to nut uncontrollably.

Baby G put both hands around her neck, as he slowed down his strokes and sucked on her ears. "Piccaso dis dick!" Baby G demanded as he slow stroked her long and deep. "Holy fucking shit! Daddy, I'm cumming—sss—aaahhhh!"

Brittany collapsed in the shower. Two orgasms and the steam from the shower had her exhausted. Baby G scooped her up and carried her to the bedroom. He laid her on her stomach. The molly had him in beast mode causing him to enter her from behind violently and punish her for three hours.

After licking her pussy clean, Baby G left her snoring, and headed back to the kitchen to put the money and guns up. Once he finished, he rolled up another blunt and just sat at the table in a daze and mumbled, "Shit finna get real now."

Khufu

Chapter 67

Booby Trap Tonight

"Baby, wake up, I need to talk to you." Brittany nudged Baby G. "Baby!"

"Huh, what'z up, bae?" Baby G wiped the corner of his eyes as he sat up. "What's going on?"

"Where did you get all that money?"

"Dat ain't nothin' to worry yo' self about, bae. I stopped by an old friend who owed me money before I got shot."

"And he gave you some guns?" asked Brittany.

"He didn't have all my money, so he threw in gunz. Don't trip, doe, I'ma get 'em out of here."

"You don't need to be driving around with all those weapons. What if you get pulled over? I have extra rooms you can put them in one of those."

"I already put 'em up."

"Baby G, I don't know what you are into, but you don't have to do that anymore. I'm willing to help you go legit."

"I appreciate you, bae. I really do, but I gotta get up some more money. Just give me a few more months I'ma go legit."

"From the looks of it, you already have enough to go legit."

"Not quite yet, snuggle bunny. Just give me a minute."

"Baby G, I hate that you are involved in underworld activities. I love you, so that means accepting everything that comes with you. I'm here for you if you need me," said Brittany kissing Baby G on the lips.

"Dat's deep, Ma. I respect and love you for dat. You need to know dat, I'll never put you in harmz way. You're safe wit' me, Ma. All I need is a few months to get right."

"Speaking of gettin' right," said Brittany as she got up and headed to her bedroom.

Baby G sat there perplexed until Brittany sashayed back in the living room with bags on top of bagz. "Here, baby, these are for you."

"What is it?"

"Just go in them and see." Baby G pulled the contents out of each bag and saw that they were all designer clothes and shoes.

"Damn, bae, you ain't have to do dat. I'm not on all dat flashy shit, ma."

"Well, in my eyes, you are a King, so you should dress as such. Don't be weird, babe, just wear the damn clothes."

"A'ight, I might throw a lil' somethin' on. Listen, you say you have a condo down in Pompano, right?"

"Yes, babe, for sure. Why?"

"Don't make any plans, you wit' me today."

"I'll follow you anywhere, babyface. Do you need me to do anything?"

"Yeah, pack a bag."

"I don't have to pack. I have everything that I need down there already."

"Okay, kool. Go shower and I'ma join you in a few minutes."

"Don't be long, Daddy." Brittany kissed Baby G, then pranced toward the bedroom completely naked.

"Damn, baby sexy as fuck," Baby G said to himself as he got up and headed out back.

Once outside, Baby G was engulfed with a marvelous stench of loud and the sounds of Gucci Mane.

"How you let a nigga in the fed out do you? How you let a nigga in the fedz out do you?"

Baby G walked up on Mango rapping along with Gucci Mane as he smoked a house blunt.

"Mango!" Baby G screamed over the loud music.

Mango turned down the music, then looked behind him. "What dey do, my dog?" said Mango while still bopping his head to the music.

"Nigga, you trippin! You out here wit' cha back to the fence— slippin'."

"Shid—I been seen you, bra. I ain't never slippin'," said Mango while brandishing a gold and black .40 caliber. "I keep 'em on me. What'z good, doe?" asked Mango as he passed Baby G the biggest blunt he'd ever seen.

"What dis is?"

"Be careful wit' dat, fuck round and cough up a lung or some shit."

"I need you to make dat call for me, I'm ready."

"You know I gotcha, but I'm sayin'—you gon' let da wind smoke all my shit? Hit dat shit, my nigga!" Mango always got excited when he had a potent strand of Kush.

"Calm down, my nigga," said Baby G as he hit the blunt one hard time and coughed viciously. The potency caused him to drool as he coughed clutching his chest.

"Aahhh man, give me my shit! Wit' dem virgin azz lungz! Give me my shit fa you fuck around and wet my shit up!"

"Nigga—fuck—you," Baby G manage to get out in between coughs.

"Go get 'cha some water or some shit. I'm finna make da call now. Give me a minute."

Still coughing Baby G headed to the bar, poured a shot, and downed it.

"Hey, babe! You took too long, I'm all done. Ready when you are, sweet face."

"Okay, go back in, I'll be in there in a few more minutes, bae.

"Okay, Daddy," said Brittany as she closed the door.

"Aye, Baby G, bra check it out!" yelled Mango.

Baby G downed another shot, then headed to the fence now feeling perfectly sedated from the Kush and Scotch.

"What da lick read?" asked Baby G.

"Everythang gucci, my dog. He says he gon' meet 'cha at the Booby Trap tonight."

"What time he gon' be there?"

"He alwayz in there, till dat bitch close."

"You ridin' wit' me?"

"Not dis time. I'ma catch you on the next one, I got too much shit going on right now."

"Dat's what'z up. You know I'ma straightin' you for the plug in."

"Don't trip, bih you my nigga. Gon' head and get down there before traffic get crazy. When you fall in there, most likely he on the top floor. He's bald, wit' a mouth full of gold. You'll know it's him kuz he looks like Blood Raw. They call him Aaron."

"A'igh't, bra, love. I'ma fuck wit' cha when I get back dis way."

"Already," said Mango.

Chapter 68

Ninety More Dayz

The C.O. opened the holding tank and called Mundo. "Mr. Moss you're up!" It was the same C.O. who broke up the fight Mundo had with Cherry.

Mundo grilled the C.O. showing all his gold teeth as he walked past him into the sally port. "Moss, what is your problem?"

"I'on got no rap fa you, Pig! Slave holdin' azz nigga! Just open the fuckin' doe!"

"I'll spray the shit out of your azz, boy! Who the hell you think you talking to?"

"Da fuck wrong wit' cha sprayerz? It's just me and you in here. I'll beat yo fuck azz, police azz nigga!"

The C.O. opened the door to medical to let him in. "Just gon' 'head, before you do something you're going to regret," the guard stated nervously.

"You a pussy!" Mundo replied as he walked into medical.

On his way in Mundo saw all the female inmates who told authorities that they were suicidal and were now in paper suits on suicidal watch. They were trying to get his attention by licking their tongues and pressing their breasts against the huge glass window of their cells. Mundo just ignored them and took a seat waiting to be called. He was so inflamed from the altercation with the guard, that he didn't even realize who he was sitting next to.

"Tyler, how are you doing today?" asked one of the nurses.

"I'm feeling okay, Ms. Tiffany."

Mundo turned to see who the nurse was speaking too. *Ol' shit, it's Tyler Hadley,* Mundo thought to himself.

He stared at the young white boy and wondered how he could slaughter both of his parents with a cliff hammer then throw a big azz party with their bodies in the back room.

"You a cold-blooded motherfucka," said Mundo.

Tyler just glanced at him, then went back to biting his nails without a care in the world.

"Moss!" called out one of the nurses.

"Right here," replied Mundo as he got up and walked into her office.

"How you doing today, Mr. Moss?"

"Just another day in Rock Road, can't complain."

"I know that's right. Have a seat, baby."

Ms. Nancy was a beautiful, heavy-set woman who always smelled of strawberries and kiwi. She wore tight scrubs, so when she was seated facing you, you were guaranteed camel toe action.

"You look nervous."

"I am."

"Well, if you wore protection, you wouldn't have anything to worry about. You got to strap it up, baby. A fine-looking young man such as yourself, shouldn't be playing Russian roulette with your sex organ."

"What the results say, Ms."

"You know we have counselling for this type of thing."

"So, you sayin' I'm fucked up?" asked Mundo as his heart rate picked up rapidly.

"Not at all, sweetie. You're negative as of now, but you need to come back in ninety days to be sure."

Mundo exhaled. "Damn, Ms. Nancy! It's too early for all that playing and shit."

"I'm trying to scare some shit into you. Not only do you need to practice safe sex, you need to stay out of these folks system. I'm tired of seeing my people come in and out of here. Now gone back to your cell and remember what I'm telling you."

"A'ight, Ms. Nancy, you still a trip doe!" Mundo stated as he got up and headed back to the waiting tank until a guard came to take him back to the hole.

Chapter 69

Police Azz Nigga!

Baby G hopped out of the Range Rover, dipped in Bally and knocked on Shantel's door.

"Come in," yelled Shantel.

Baby G entered the house looking like a million. "Um, what's up stranger?" asked Shantel as she eyed Baby G.

"What'z going on, baby momma? You showing pretty good dis morning. How far you is 'bout four—five months?"

"Baby G, you haven't called, came by to check on me or nothing. Just because you waltz in here swaggin' drippin' sauce don't mean nothin' dis way."

"Da fuck you mean? I'm here checkin' on yo crazy azz right now! You got my number, you kuda hit me"

"I got a doctor's appointment dis morning. You going with me?"

"See dat's why you shoulda called me. I'm finna shoot out of town for a couple dayz. Matter fact, here," Baby G said as he reached into his fitted jeans and gave Shantel a stack of money. "Dat's ten bandz. I know you still got the money I left you, just make sho my son gets the best of everythang."

"Baby G, what is you doing? You left me all the money you had. So, where'd you get dis money from? How you get here? Who you out there wit'?"

"All dat shit, ain't none of yo bidness. You and my son gon' be well taken care of. All dat other shit is frivolous."

"So, it ain't no moe you and me?"

"We gotta child together, it's gon' always be you and me. Just not on dat type of level. I'll be through in a few dayz to check on you. I'm gone," Baby G stated as he headed toward the door.

Shantel got up and hurried past him to see who he came with. As soon as she opened the door, she and Brittany locked eyes.

"Ooowww—bitch! You out there wit' a white girl?"

"You fuckin' right! Dat same white girl was there for me when

I was shot da fuck up in dat hospital. Don't brang yo' azz out here wit' all dat shit."

Shantel's eyes started to water, but she wiped them, exhaled, and held her head high. "You got dat," said Shantel.

Listen, call me if you need anythang."

"Alright," Shantel said in a whisper. "Before you leave, let me ask you somethin'."

"What'z good?"

"You never told me what happened, that night you got shot. I called C-Major's number. He told me you was wit' your sister after the show. So, what happened? Who shot ' cha?"

"I'm still lookin' into dat. When I get some answers, I'ma lace you up. A'ight?"

"Okay, Baby G, but somethin' feels off about the whole situation. Every time I call your sister, it goes straight to the voicemail."

"Don't stress yo' self about it. Look, I'm gone, call if you need me."

Back in the truck, Brittany stared at Baby G with anticipation. "Is everything okay, babe?"

"Yeah, bae, everythang good," replied Baby G, as his phone started ringing.

"Damn, I need somethin' to blow. Bae, slide down twenty ninth, right quick," requested Baby G, while answering his phone. "Yeah! Who dis?"

"What'z good wit 'cha? Dis Off Top."

"What up?"

"Nice to know you made it out dat situation. You know I wanted to come up there, but them people be watchin' shit like dat."

This nigga must don't know C.C. shot me, Baby G thought. "How you know I was released from the hospital?"

"The day before yesterday, Mango slid through and grabbed some shit from me. He laced me up. You know war and money don't mix, but if you know who did it, I'll shut down shop and suit up wit 'cha! I fucks wit 'cha, Baby G."

Baby G could hear the genuineness in Off Top's voice. "Dat's deep homie, but check it, I'll never let chu put everythang you built from the ground up in jeopardy. I haven't heard nothin' yet anyway, bra."

"Damn, dat's some wild shit. Aye, listen, I Know you just got out, but I need you."

"What'cha need, bra?"

"One of my spot's got hit. You heard anythang about it?"

"My feet ain't been planted long enough to hear nothin', but I can most definitely rattle a few treez and see what falls out of 'em."

"Yeah, do dat. If you find out before me, I got a whole yard on dat situation."

"I'm all da way on it," stated Baby G. "Already,"

"Damn, bae, you passed the tire shop. Pull in right here and turn around."

Brittany pulled in Dreamland Park and was about to reverse out, but Baby G stopped her.

"Hold up, bae!" Baby G hopped out of the Rover and pulled a 500 Smith & Wesson magnum with the cooling barrel from his designer jean.

The barrel was so long it seemed like it took ten seconds to pull it out.

"Yeah, police azz nigga!"

The youngin' tried to turn and get in his vehicle, but Baby G grabbed him by the shirt and gave him everything. Baby G was so close up on him that the victim's shirt caught on fire.

"Bitch azz nigga!" yelled Baby G, as he jumped back in the truck. "Drive bae, get on the turnpike."

"What the hell was that?" asked Brittany while leaving the scene.

"Just drive, bae, I'll explain later."

The youngin' that Baby G left hanging out of his car with holes in his back was Chris. Chris was the one in the car with Billy Da Kid. He was the witness in Mundo's discovery. Ten minutes later, they were on the turnpike riding in silence. Baby G was gazing out of the window collecting his thoughts while Brittany kept glancing at him with fear and admiration.

"What'z good, bae? You okay?" asked Baby G.

"Pull your dick out."

"Pull my dick out? You trippin, Ma."

Brittany reached over, unzipped his pants, and started fondling with his dick. She then put the truck on cruise control at 75 miles per hour.

"Grab the wheel," instructed Brittany.

Baby G did as he was told. "Bae, you crazy as fuck!"

Brittany ignored his comment and put his whole dick in her mouth. "Sss—shit!"

Baby G swerved in another lane, but quickly gained control of the vehicle. Brittany never looked up to see if everything was okay. In fact, the near-death experience only intensified the head she was giving.

She moaned, slurped, and sucked viciously driving Baby G crazy. "Ooowww—shit! Ssss, bae get dis fuckin' wheel," cried Baby G.

Brittany finally came up and grabbed the wheel. "Fine, cry baby. But I'm telling you now! When we get to the condo, your black azz is mine!"

Chapter 70

I'm Feelin' Yo Drip

Two and a half hours later, Brittany got off the turnpike on MLK. "Bae, when you get to the light make a right," stated Baby G.

"For what?" Brittany asked while turning on her right blinker.

"I gotta handle some bidness right quick. It'll only take a few minutes."

"And where is this place of bidness located?"

"Pull into Booby Trap."

"Your business, is in the strip club? Nice!"

"Come on, snuggle cheeks, It ain't nothin' like dat. I'ma be in and out."

"Alright, Baby G, don't have me out here all day," said Brittany as she pulled in the lot and found a parking space.

"Be right out, Ma." Baby G kissed her, then hopped out of the truck.

Before he entered the club, security checked him for weapons causing the wand to go off.

"Woe, my man, what is that? Lift your shirt for me."

Baby G lifted his shirt just above his Bally belt that had two metal B's on it. "Dat's just my belt, homie."

"You look kind of young, where is your ID?"

Baby G went in his pockets and handed him a hundred-dollar bill. "Alright, you good."

"A'ight," replied Baby G, as he slid in with the gun he'd just killed a man with. *Damn, I forgot to reload my shit,* thought Baby G, as he headed to the bar and got a hundred ones.

"You want anything else?" asked the bartender with lust in her eyes.

"Nall, I'm good, Ma." Baby G spun off and headed up stairs.

As soon as he reached the top, a man who fit Aaron's description was at the bar alone, enjoying a mid-day meal. "Damn, dat nigga do look like Blood Raw," said Baby G, to himself as he approached the scene.

"What up, big homie, you must be Aaron?"

"Dat be me," replied Aaron taking a bite of a T-Bone steak. "You, Baby G, huh?"

"In da flesh."

"You look young as hell. I'm surprised they let 'chu in dis bitch. How old you is?"

"Old enough to do bidness."

"*Old enough to do bidness*, huh?" repeated Aaron with a smile showing a mouth full of gold. "I hear dat, have a seat. You want food, a drink or some shit?"

"Nall, I'ma stand, I think better on my feet. I'm good on the food too."

"Look here, my nigga. All dat standin' round a nigga while I'm eatin', I ain't on dat. You gon' sit cha azz down, or you gon' get from 'round me. Whateva you choose is on you. Personally I'on give a fuck, but you gon' do somethin'!"

Baby G started to clutch his banga but remembered he didn't have any bullets left.

"Everythang a'ight over here?"

Baby G looked behind him and saw a nigga with long dreadz and a mouth full of gold standing 6'3 clutching a .40 caliber. It was Aaron's older brother Tank. He'd been in the cut getting a dance, watching from afar. Aaron's body language made him come check the temperature.

"Yeah, bra, we good. I got it," replied Aaron.

Tank stared Baby G down before heading back to the cut he was in. Baby G was heated and felt disrespected, but he took a seat. He didn't want to blow his chance with the plug.

"Talk to me, what 'chu tryin' to do?"

"Shid—I'm tryin' to grab three for ninety."

"You short six bandz. My shit go for thirty-two," stated Aaron sucking the steak juice from his fingers, then downing one of the many shots of Patron he had in front of him.

"Damn, my nigga, I done came all dis way. Then I gotta ride back wit' dat shit. You can't do no better than dat?"

Aaron downed another shot. "I tell you what. Since you a friend

212

of Mango, I'ma do somethin' for you. You know yo way around Pompano?"

"I get around, what'z up?"

"Meet me tomorrow, on Sixth Ave in da back."

"In da back?" questioned Baby G.

"Yeah, it's a dead end," replied Aaron looking Baby G dead in his eyes to see any signs of fear about the meeting place.

"I ain't trippin', shid. What time?"

"Be there round noon."

"I'll be there, noon sharp."

"What 'chu driving?" Baby G looked at Aaron like he was crazy. "You gotta let me know what 'chu pullin' up in, anybody can't just pull up in the back. Fuck around and get cha whole situation swiss cheesed up," explained Aaron.

"I overstand dat. I'm in a white rover."

"A'ight lil nigga, see you tomorrow."

Baby G got up to leave and headed toward the stairs when a stripper approached him.

"You leaving already, lil daddy? Let me get a dance before you leave,"

Baby G respected the hustle, so he went along with it. "Turn around and make dat azz clap for me."

The stripper was a pretty, high-yellow stallion named Yella Baby. She resembled Miami Tip from Love and Hip Hop, she was just thicker. Yella Baby turned around and clapped her ass delicately while Baby G went into his pocket and pulled out the one-hundred ones he'd gotten on his way in. He spread the money in his hand like a fan and slapped her ass aggressively with the whole hundred causing a mini rain shower. Baby G then walked off not caring about the dance, which only made Yella Baby more curious as to who he was.

"Wait!" yelled Yella Baby as she left the money on the floor to catch up with Baby G.

"What up?" asked Baby G.

"Why you leaving?"

"Bidness," replied Baby G.

"O—okay. What's your name?"

"Damn, Ms. lady, why you interrogating a nigga?"

"I ain't on nothin', I'm just feelin' yo drip," said Yella Baby referring to his swag.

"My name Baby G, Ma."

"Baby G, that's different—I like it. You mind if I get your number, Baby G?"

Baby G started to decline but realized he might be able to use her in the future. "Let me get yours," replied Baby G pulling out his phone and handing it to her.

She logged her number in and handed him back his phone. "It's up under Yella Baby, call me anytime."

"Already," stated Baby G, as he spun off and left her standing there.

Aaron had watched the whole episode unfold and was impressed how the youngster handled himself. He already put in his mind what he had in store for Baby G.

I got him, Aaron thought.

Chapter 71

Deeper Than What Meets the Eye

Baby G admired Brittany's condo In Palm Air. The walls were covered in wallpaper featuring Fellow Red Heads designed by Costanza Theodor-Brashi. A splashing 54 water chandelier by Tony Duquette hung from the ceiling over Vladimir Kagan sofas and Angelo Mangiarotti cocktail tables.

"Aaahh, yeah, Daddy! Smack my azz harder!" screamed Brittany while bent over the silver stone kitchen countertop.

Smack!

Brittany got louder with every smack Baby G delivered. She was trying her best to throw her azz back to meet Baby G thrust for thrust, but he started applying too much pressure, causing her to buckle against the counter tops.

"Nall, come here," said Baby G pulling her up by her hair while stroking with the intent to kill.

"Please don't stop," cried Brittany as she came all over him.

Baby G pulled out of her, grabbed a 1950s Cee Braakman's chair and took it to the living room. He then sat on the white alpaca carpet with his back against the white leather sofa and put the Braakman's chair in front of him.

"Come here," demanded Baby G.

Brittany did as she was instructed with confusion in her eyes.

"Sit in this chair," Baby G ordered.

After she sat down, he pulled the chair as close to his chest as he could, then spread her legs eagle. This position caused Brittany's vagina to sit directly in his face. Baby G went in for the kill, devouring her passion fruit for an hour straight. This was called *The Electric Chair*, due to all the shaking its victims did while cumming. Baby G had mastered this technique when he was sixteen.

"Okay, baby, fuck! I can't take anymore, please stop," cried Brittany while shaking furiously.

Baby G slid the chair back, got up and tried to pick her up, but she wasn't having it.

"Don't touch me!" Brittany cried while still shaking.

"You was talkin' all dat shit in da truck, now look at 'cha. Yeah, straight pressure!" Baby G boasted as he headed to the bathroom.

Moments later, he returned with a warm rag and cleaned Brittany up.

"You're such a sweetheart. I don't understand, why would someone try to kill you?"

"It's deeper than what meets the eye, baby girl."

"Baby girl? Excuse me, I'm nine years older than you."

"Yeah, but in my world you're just a baby."

"So, why don't you tell me all about it?"

Baby G picked her up, carried her to the bedroom and laid her down. He then turned on a French Ostrich egg lamp, lit an Ember candle and grabbed a bottle of oil.

"What are you doing?"

"Just chill, Ma," replied Baby G, as he began to massage her feet and give her his life story. He told her how he almost died being born a premature baby, and how the streets had raised him, due to his father being in prison and his mother working late nights. He even told her about how he found his first gun in the sixth grade on the way to his bus stop, and the first body he caught at sixteen. It had been a good night of grinding up until three in the morning, when a fiend approached him and asked for two-hundred worth of crack. Baby G was leery about serving the smoker, who was fidgety and kept looking around suspiciously rubbernecking.

"What up, man? You a'ight?" asked Baby G.

"Yeah, man, I'm good. I got the money right here," replied the smoker flashing the money quickly so Baby G couldn't see that it was only twenty dollars in fives.

As soon as Baby G dumped all the stones in his hand from the Garcia Vega tube, the smoker snatched a hand full and tried to run, but Baby G was on point and tripped him.

"Bitch!" Baby G yelled as he pulled a .38 from his right pocket and shot him in his ass.

"Okay, man, I'm sorry," pleaded the smoker.

Baby G just stood over him and shot him repeatedly. He was found at 5:30 a.m. by a civilian headed to work.

Baby G had never told anyone about this until now.

"Damn, baby, that's some heavy shit. So, why did you kill the guy in the park today?"

"He was a rat. It was either he died, or my lil brother get stuck with a life sentence."

Brittany sat there amazed at how he could just put his life on the line to free someone else. Baby G left out the notion, that the only reason he wanted his brother out of jail was so he could finish what he started and kill him.

"I love you," said Brittany, removing her feet from his grasp. She then faced him and placed sensual kisses on him from head to toe.

"I love you, too, Ma," replied Baby G, as he laid back and let Brittany give him everything he wanted.

Khufu

Chapter 72

Favor For a Favor

At 10:30 the next morning, Baby G got up showered, then got dipped in Versace and a pair of Jimmy Choo's. He put eighty thousand and a Glock 17 with an extension in a Louis Vuitton bag, grabbed the keys to the Rover and left Brittany sleeping peacefully in the bed. Pulling out of Palm Air, Baby G took Powerline to 15th Street, made a right and drove down to 6th Avenue. He saw what appeared to be hustlers posted at a corner store known as the BYU, so he pulled in and hopped out.

"Fie treez on deck!" yelled a young hustler name Frank. "Thirty-dollar half's!"

"Let me get one, bra," said Baby G, before walking into the store.

"I gotcha," replied Frank.

Baby G went in and bought two boxes of cigarillos and a Ying Ling. On his way out, Frank walked in the store, went in his boxers, and handed Baby G a half.

"You gon' do dis in here?" asked Baby G.

"Yeah, he straight, bra," replied Frank, referring to the owner.

"Thirty dollars, bra." Baby G handed him the money then slipped out the store.

Hopping back in the truck he saw that he had time to kill. He decided to sit at the store and roll a few blunts until it was time to meet Aaron. Before he knew it, he had blown two blunts while listening to Nipsey Hussle. Baby G backed out and headed down 6th Ave when his phone started ringing.

"What it is?" asked Baby G.

"What's going on? I'm just callin' to check dat situation. You ain't heard nothin' yet?" asked Off Top.

"Yeah, I was gon' pull up on you when I got back in town, but since you called I'ma lace you up. You seen da newz yesterday?"

"Yeah, I seen dat a nigga got smacked in Dreamland park."

"Dat was my lil' demonstration."

"Okay, say no moe. Come see me when you touch down."

"Already!"

"One!"

When Baby G reached the dead end, he saw a white Beema truck flashing its lights so he pulled in front of it and parked. He grabbed the Louie bag, hopped out and walked to the passenger's side. The Beema was heavily tinted, making it hard to see in. Baby G opened the door and hopped in.

"Baby G, what's up, lil homie? I see you found yo' way back here," stated Aaron. "No disrespect, my Cee, but let's get to it. What chu gon' let three go for?"

"You wanna get straight to it, huh? I tell you what, give me ninety dey yours."

"Where dey at?"

"Shid—I got'em back here," replied Aaron reaching in the back seat like he was grabbing something.

Baby G unzipped the bag and pulled out the Glock 17 and pointed it at Aaron. When Aaron turned around, he held nothing in his hands.

"Where it at!" yelled Baby G. Aaron just smiled showing all thirty-two teeth. "I knew you was gon' try some shit."

"Nigga you think dis shit a game!"

The whole time Baby G was in the truck, he never looked in the back seat. The weed had him slipping.

Click! Clack!

Baby G felt the steal being placed on the back of his head.

"You gots to be a silly nigga!" yelled a youngin' named Bullet from the back seat.

"Hold up, Bullet, don't hit him," ordered Aaron.

"Don't hit him! Nigga you trippin'!"

"Just put it down, Bullet, I got him."

"Fuck no!" screamed Bullet.

"Baby G, put it down, he ain't gon' hit 'cha, I promise you."

Baby G thought about his unborn child and all types of shit before he finally put the gun down.

"Bullet get out, let me holla at him."

220

"Man, what kinda shit you on? Fuck dis nigga!"

Aaron started the truck up and looked Bullet in his eyes. "Get out, I got it."

Bullet sucked his teeth, got out and slammed the door.

"Listen, I ain't let him kill you kuz I like you, lil nigga. You gotta lot of heart. You felt like I tried you yesterday at the club?" asked Aaron.

"You know, you tried me, bra."

Aaron laughed as he put the truck in drive and pulled off. "Maybe I did. The fact of the matter is, you owe me one, I spared yo' life."

"What 'chu hollin' 'bout?" asked Baby G. "Before you pulled up, a nigga called me sayin' he got five bricks for me. I personally feel like he don't deserve 'em. I want 'chu to watch my back while I do me."

"You kuda used Bullet for dat shit," stated Baby G.

"True, but you see dis here is a favor for a favor."

"What's in it for me?"

"We'll discuss dat after we handle up."

"Fuck it, say no moe."

"My man," stated Aaron as he headed to Deerfield.

Ten minutes later, Aaron got off on Hillsborough and pulled into a neighborhood called Airwoods. He then pulled into the driveway of a blue and white house.

"Get right, we here," said Aaron.

Baby G put the Glock 17 in the Louie bag, then hopped out behind Aaron. Aaron didn't even knock on the door, he just walked in so Baby G followed suit. When they walked in, a fat guy named Heavy was sitting at the kitchen table eating a big ass bowl of spaghetti next to five bricks.

"What up, A? Who dat is you got wit 'cha? You know I don't do bidness like dat," cried Heavy.

"Dat's my lil kuz'n, bitch he straight. I came to see what 'cha got for me."

"They right here. Give me thirty a piece since I fucks wit 'cha."

"Let me see what it's hittin' fa."

"The pots under the sink, and the baking soda in the fridge."

"A'ight, I got it," replied Aaron.

"You hungry, lil homie?" asked Heavy.

"Nall, big dog, I'm good," replied Baby G.

Aaron dropped seven grams and saw that it came back straight gator.

"Hell yeah! Bitch dis shit gon' have da trap booty shakin' God damn me!"

"You know my work," boasted Heavy.

Aaron grabbed a trash bag and loaded the five bricks in it. He even put the pot he just cooked in inside the bag too and headed out the door. Heavy got up, spilling his bowl of spaghetti to try and stop Aaron.

"Aaron, what 'chu doing? Where the money at?"

"Lil kuz got it, behind you."

Heavy looked back and caught three bullets to the face, killing him instantly. Baby G then took money from the dead man's pockets and stepped on him on the way out. Back in the truck, Aaron let it be known that he was impressed with Baby G's demonstration. He insisted that they work together in the future. Finally, back in Pompano, Aaron pulled into one of his spots and cut the truck off. It was a house across the street from where Baby G had parked the Rover.

"Listen, I see you a solid lil nigga, so dis what I'ma do for you. Just give me sixty for three, my nigga dey yours."

At first Baby G started to protest that they bust down all bricks, due to the fact that he'd killed a man. Once Baby G calculated in his head, and saw that Aaron was saving him thirty-six thousand, he decided to look at Heavy as a thirty-six thousand dollar hit.

"A'ight dat's a bet but check it. I need you to do somethin' for me."

"What 'chu need, lil homie?"

"Show me how to cook."

"Shid—dat ain't nothin' bitch I gotcha. When you want me to show you?"

"Like right, now."

"Come in I gotcha, but look, don't show nobody dis shit, especially not for free. Knowin' how to cook gon' put cha profits on a whole other level. Lil homie, you'll never be broke again."

"I hear you, my nigga," stated Baby G.

Khufu

Chapter 73

The Rest Is History

Back in Fort Pierce, Baby G was in a spot he'd rented that was directly above the Brown Store on 25th Street. He was standing over the stove with his phone clutched between his ear and shoulder, talking to Off Top as he poured water from the Pyrex bowl, then began beating the coke to a milky substance. Meek Millz played in the background as Baby G put on his performance,

Lean wit' it/rock wit' it/ throw some bake off in da pot wit' it/ microwave or we gone pot whip it.

"Yeah, bra, I just got a spot on top of the Brown store."

"How long you gon' be there? asked Off Top.

"Shid, I ain't going nowhere no time soon."

"A'ight, I'm on my way to go handle some bidness. I'ma stop by there on my way out, I got that for you."

"Already."

Baby G removed the pot and laid it flat on the counter to let the work lock and dry. He'd been over the stove since 10:00 a.m. turning every four ounces into eight cookies weighing twenty-five grams each, straight water weight. After whipping a whole brick, Baby G had seventy- two cookies laid out over the countertops and kitchen table. He even had them all in the window seals and his bedroom dressers.

It was now 8:30 p.m. and Baby G was exhausted. He stepped outside to smoke a blunt, and saw Off Top pulling in next to his new i8. After the incident at Dreamland Park, Brittany traded in her Rover and purchased Baby G an all-black i8. Off Top hopped out and swagged up the stairs with a duffle bag in hand.

"Baby G, what'z good, homie?" asked Off Top, handing Baby G the bag.

"Ain't shit, fam, you know, slow motion just tryin' to make it."

"Datz what it is, shid look like you tired as hell."

"Yeah, I just got off dat road, my nigga I'm finna lay it down."

"Who i8 dat is down there?"

"Dats an older chick I'm fuckin' wit'."

"Dat bitch clean. Listen doe, I appreciate dat lil' situation you took care of. I don't know how dat nigga knew 'bout dat spot. Who told you he was the one dat hit my shit?"

"Before I got on the highway, I stopped and grabbed some Molly and overheard some niggaz rappin' 'bout it. They was sayin' da nigga Chris had just left the spot braggin' 'bout a lick he hit in Robin Hood. So, when I left they spot, guess who I ran into at Dreamland Park? The rest is history."

"I still don't get how he knew 'bout dat spot doe."

"You gotta be cautious of who you keep around you, bra," stated Baby G, looking Off Top dead in his eyes.

"Yeah, you right. Good lookin' doe, my nigga, I'm gone. Go get 'chu some sleep."

"Already. If you need me, just hit me," stated Baby G as he headed back inside.

Baby G was so tired that he just put the bag of money on the floor and passed out on the living room couch with dope laid out everywhere.

Chapter 74

Choke Da City Out

The next morning, Baby G awoke to his phone ringing like crazy. Looking at the time, he saw that it was 12:45 p.m.

"Damnit, man, I overslept," said Baby G, as he answered his phone. "Yeah! Who dis?"

"Good morning, baby. How are you this morning?"

"What up, bae? I'm good, just gettin' up. You a'ight?"

"I'd be a lot better if you were here. How come you didn't make it home last night? Where are you?"

"How come I ain't make it home? Oh, we stay together now?"

"Baby G, don't play with me! Where are you?"

Baby G laughed before replying, "Ease up, lil baby. I told you I'm gettin' to da bidness."

"Where did you stay last night?"

"I gotta room, bae. I was tired after all dat rippin' and runnin'. Why you drillin' me? Come on, nah, is dis da type of shit I'ma be dealin' wit' fuckin' wit' you?"

"Not at all, honey. I was just worried about you."

"I'm good, Ma."

"So, will I be able to see you today?"

"Of course! As soon as I make a few moves, I'ma be in ya chest."

"Okay, baby, call me when you're done handling your bidness. I made plans for us so don't stand me up."

"What 'chu got going on?"

"Just call me when you're done, babe. I love you and be careful."

"Yeah, you too!"

Baby G got up, stretched, then lit a blunt he had in the ashtray from last night. He then looked around and saw all the dope he had scattered about.

"Damnit, man, ain't no lookin' back, bitch I'm finna choke da city out!"

Baby G's phone rang again, interrupting the calculation of his profit to come.

"Yeah, who dis?"

"Nigga, don't play wit' me! I just know you got my number saved up under *good pussy*!"

Baby G laughed at how goofy the caller was. "Shenida, what'z good, baby?"

"Nigga, how you let a nigga catch you out here dick dancin', put holez in ya azz, and you survive and don't call me? Matter fact, nigga where you at, I'm finna pull up?"

"Don't tell nobody where I'm at."

"You know better den dat. Now where you at?"

"I'm at the Brown Store. I grabbed an apartment on top."

"Okay, I'm finna pull up."

"Just come in, I'ma be in the shower."

"A'ight!"

Baby G grabbed all the dope that he had laying around, put them in styrofoam trays, then hopped in the shower. Ten minutes later, he wrapped a towel around him, stepped out of the bathroom and saw Shenida stretched out naked on his couch.

"Come on wit' da bull shit, Shenida!" Baby G lifted his hands in the air hopelessly.

"Nigga, you got me fucked up! You know what time it iz. Come get deep off in dis pussy. And what da fuck you got goin' on in here? What 'chu sellin',dinnerz?"

"Yeah, I got food for da streetz," replied Baby G dropping his towel walking toward Shenida.

"Yeah, dats right, come take dat frustration out on dis pussy, Daddy."

Baby G wasted no time getting deep off in her. For the next thirty minutes they had some of the roughest sex they'd ever had. It was then that Baby G realized how much he missed his ride or die.

Chapter 75

Till Death and Beyond

After putting Shenida in every position known to man, Baby G hopped back in the shower, then got saucy for the streets. Shenida had helped him load the trays in his i8, left her truck parked and hopped in with him. They were now bending through the city with a car full of cooked up dope.

"I like yo new whip, It fits you, Daddy."

"You think so?"

"Nigga stop playin, you know you killin' shit. Were we headed?"

"Just chill, Ma, you wit' me," stated Baby G, as he pulled into an apartment on 23rd and G and hopped out.

"What up, stranger?" asked Michelle. "Jamaican gal! What up wit' it?"

"One day at a time, you know how dis third shit is."

"You ready to get dis money or what?"

"Hell yeah, shid—what 'chu got for me?"

"Who dem lil niggaz iz across da street?"

"Oh, datz lil Mexico over there. Dem my lil homiez. Why, what'z good?"

"Come help me get dis shit out da car," demanded Baby G, as he opened the door and started unloading the trays of dope.

"You want me to sell food?" asked Michelle.

"Just help me take dis shit in da house. Shenida, baby, help me wit' dis shit."

Shenida did as she was told with a perplexed expression on her face. When they were finished, Baby G told Shenida to wait in the car. Once Shenida was out of the apartment, Baby G opened one of the trays.

"You know what dis is?" asked Baby G.

"Yeah, dats dat work."

"You think you can move it?"

"Of course!" replied Michelle.

"Good, you can put them lil niggaz across da street on. Listen, I'on play 'bout my fetti."

"Spare me dat, Baby G, I already know how you livin'. I got 'chu, baby."

"A'ight, so nothin' to talk about. If my paper come up short I'ma have to change yo form."

"*Form?* What 'chu mean change my form?"

"From physical to spiritual."

"I overstand fully, trust me. Damn!"

"Okay, dis what it iz. It's seventy-two cookies in deez trayz. They're a band apiece. You keep twelve thousand, just call me when you make sixty bandz."

"I'm kool wit' dat, but what'z good wit' dis?" asked Michelle grabbing a handful of Baby G's dick.

"Not right now, Chelle. I gotta move around a lil piece. Here log my number in yo' phone?"

Michelle sucked her teeth as she logged his number in. "When I move dis work for you, you gon' give me dat dick. I know dat much."

"Call me when you got my money, I'll give you a taste."

"I call dat," replied Michelle excitedly.

"I'm gone," stated Baby G, as he left Michelle with a whole brick of cooked up dope.

Back in the car, Baby G's thoughts were all over the place as he cruised through the city.

"Baby, who dat hoe was?" asked Shenida.

"Michelle, we used to get money together before I went to prison."

"What was in dem trayz?"

"Work."

"So, you put dat bitch on before me?"

"Chill out, Ma, you know I got 'chu. Matter fact, tomorrow I want 'chu to post in da cut and watch her spot. You know, just see how dis shit moving. You think you can handle dat?"

"Hell yeah, I'on trust dat hoe anyway." Baby G laughed at how overprotective Shenida was being.

He knew she meant well, and truth be told—it turned him on.
"Relax, Ma, we gon' get dis money together."
"I'm wit 'chu daddy, till death and beyond."

Khufu

Chapter 76

Uncle G

After dropping Shenida off, Baby G went to Lawnwood Elementary and picked up his nephews, Hezeron and Machi. It had been a while since he'd seen them, so he decided to surprise them and worry C.C. while he was at it.

"Uncle G, thank you for the pizza," Hezeron and Machi announced in unison.

"It's nothin! Y'all know Uncle G love y'all. What's up, doe? How dem grades lookin' in school?"

"I'm doing real good, Uncle G," stated Hezeron.

"Stop telling a story. Your teacher just called mama yesterday," said Machi.

"You a snitcher," declared Hezeron, pointing his pizza in Machi's face.

"Hey, Machi, we don't do no tellin' you hear me?"

"Yes, sir."

"Hezeron, you gotta be good in school. You might not like school, but 'chu gotta be good for yo' mama and make her happy. You never know when mama may leave."

"Yes, sir."

"Machi, you too, you hear me?"

"Yes, sir. I hear you, but my grades already good. I like school," admitted Machi.

"That's what's up! Keep at it," asserted Baby G, as he pulled in front of C.C.'s house and saw that she was outside on her porch.

C.C. tried to make out who was in the car, but the windows were five percent tinted. She clutched her pink Nina, prepared to squeeze if shit got crazy.

"When we gon' see you again, Uncle G?" asked Hezeron.

"Y'all gon' see me soon. Just be good in school a'ight?"

"Yes, sir," both brothers replied.

"Make sho y'all tell ya mama Uncle G said what up. Gon' ahead and get out, I love y'all."

"Love you, too," both brothers replied while grabbing their box of pizza and running to their mother.

"Mommy, mommy—look, we got pizza!" yelled Machi.

"Who picked y'all up from school? Who in dat car?" yelled C.C.

"Mommy that's, Uncle G," stated Hezeron.

"What? Y'all go in the house right now!"

"But mama!" cried Hezeron.

"Now!" C.C. screamed.

Machi and Hezeron did as they were told. Baby G pulled off in a slow creep taunting C.C. As soon as the boys were in the house, C.C. let off her whole clip, knocking out Baby G's back window. He laughed and got on the gas knowing that he was just toying with C.C. until he decided to kill her.

****

Baby G had just left the shop where he got his window repaired and was now headed to Hutcherson's Island to meet up with Brittany when his phone started ringing.

"Yeah, what up?"

"What'z good?" asked Shenida.

"I'm headed out da way, why?"

"I been layin' in da cut on dis hoe like you told me to."

"A'ight, what it look like?"

"Dis shit swangin! Taz ain't been beatin' da block at all. You want me to run down on her 'bout dat paper?"

"Nall, ma, give her a lil' moe time. You can get in da wind, I'ma hit chu in a few."

"Okay, G, be careful."

"Come on, ma, you know I'm off safety wit' it."

"Yo azz was off safety last time and look what happened."

"Oh, you gon' go there on me?"

"I love you, nigga! I gots to."

"I hear you and a nigga loves you, too. I got it—real shit."

"Okay, baby."

234

Chapter 77

Checkmate

Baby G pulled his i8 into the car's garage, cut the ignition and just laid his head back on the head rest. Being that he had so much going on, Baby G's thoughts were all over the place. After sitting for five minutes, he got out and went inside. Once he reached the kitchen, he saw that the table was laced with candles, salmon, and merlot.

"Damn, my lil German boo in here getting groovy for the kid," muttered Baby G to himself, rubbing his hands together as he proceeded down the hallway.

As he got closer to Brittany's bedroom, she could be heard talking to someone on the phone. Instead of making his presence known, Baby G eavesdropped on her conversation. After listening for ten minutes, he turned around and slid in the room where he kept his money and guns stashed. He counted his money, looked over his arsenal, then headed back to the kitchen table and poured a glass of wine. Taking small sips. While in deep thought his phone rang.

"Yeah, what up wit' it?" asked G.

"Baby G, baby, where you at?" questioned Michelle.

"I'm outta bounds, what's up?"

"Uhhh—when you get back in the city, pull up."

"Say less, Ma."

As soon as he hung up the phone, Brittany came walking in the kitchen with a look of perplexity.

"I thought I heard someone in here. How long have you been here?" she asked.

"Not long. How was yo day?"

"My day was okay. It would have been better if you were here. I've missed you, babe. Can't you tell?" stated Brittany, taking a seat across from Baby G.

"I'm digging dis lil setup you got going on."

"This is all for you, babe. I hope you're not allergic to seafood," stated Brittany while pouring a glass of wine.

"Listen, I need you to know dat you are appreciated for dis but let me ask you a question."

"Anything, babe."

"You ever played chess?"

"Of course, I love chess. I play it all the time on my phone. The queen is the most powerful piece on the board," exclaimed Brittany excitedly.

"Dat's true, but how do you know when the game is over?"

"When someone gets checkmated."

"You ain't never lied," stated G, as he lifted a .40 with a silencer on it.

Before Brittany's eyes could bulge to the fullest extent, Baby G put a hole right between them. A piece of the back of her head flew like JFK before her face dropped in the square plate of salmon and capers. Baby G had heard Brittany talking to her uncle, who was serving a life sentence for drug trafficking. She'd told her uncle about the money and guns that Baby G had in her house and about the murder he committed in Dreamland Park. Brittany desperately wanted a sentence reduction for her uncle and would line anybody up to get it. After hearing that, Baby G decided she had to go.

"Damn, snuggle bunny! I was low-key fucked up 'bout cha. Why you make me flush you? Now look at cha—face down in a fish dish," stated Baby G, as he tasted the salmon and washed it down with another glass of wine.

Once he was finished, he cleaned and wiped down everything he ever touched, then packed his money and guns. Baby G even cleaned her safe for a hundred bands and some jewelry. When he left, he was up two hundred plus.

Chapter 78

I'll Kill Ya in Dis Bitch!

"Who da fuck knockin' on my shit like they crazy?" yelled Michelle. "I said who?" Michelle stopped mid-sentence after snatching her front door open and seeing that it was Baby G.

"Da fuck you doin' all dat yelling for?" asked Baby G.

"Oh, hey, Baby G, baby. I thought you was one of dem cluckaz coming to beg for some dope. Come in, Daddy, get comfortable."

Baby G entered the apartment and made himself at home.

"You thirsty or anything?"

"Nall, I'm cool," stated Baby G, as he pulled out a pre-rolled blunt and lit it.

"Okay, give me a minute. I'll be back down," said Michelle as she slid up the stairs, leaving Baby G in deep thought.

He was thinking of how the ways of a woman are unknown when his phone rang from an unknown number.

"Who da fuck is dis?" asked Baby G, now buzzing from the weed.

"Listen, I'm only gon' tell you dis shit once. Stay da fuck away from my kids ole pussy ass nigga!" warned C.C.

"You know who phone you called," asked Baby G, as calm as a lake.

"You fuckin' right! Nigga, I know who da fuck I'm talking to. Like I said, stay da fuck away from my kids!"

Baby G laughed at his sister in amazement. "You calling me wit dem lil funky ass threats and shit. Bitch, you owe me some money for my window."

"I tell you what. Take five fangaz and get it out' cha ass! Fuck you mean, nigga? Matter fact when I see you it's on sight!" *Click.*

Baby G laughed unfazed as he continued to smoke his blunt.

"Baby G!" yelled Michelle.

"Yo?"

"Come holla at me for a second."

"Maaan, get my money up so I can get da fuck from round!"

stated Baby G, as he got up and made his way up the stairs.

Once Baby G reached Michelle's bedroom, he choked on the reefer smoke he'd just inhaled when he saw Michelle's lay out. She had spread all the money she owed him over her bed and was now butt booty naked with her legs spread like butter on toast.

"Dammit, man, fuck you got going on?" questioned Baby G with a smirk on his face.

"You told me to give you sixty bands, right?"

"I believe so."

"You a killa ana?"

"Sho' you right."

"Well, come get' cha money and kill dis pussy while you at it," taunted Michelle, as she played with her clit.

"Shid—bitch, you ain't sayin' shit vicious to a killa," replied Baby G, as he removed his pistol and placed it to the left of the bed.

He then removed a condom, took off his clothes and climbed in the bed. Baby G crawled up Michelle's body until he was straddling her chest.

"Bitch, I'ma teach you 'bout fuckin' wit' me."

"Um—teach me, Daddy," moaned Michelle.

Baby G grabbed her by her tracks and began fucking her face.

"Dats it, eat dat dick," demanded Baby G, while Michelle moaned and caught every inch he was throwing.

Three minutes later, Baby G snatched out of her mouth and started slapping her violently in her face and neck with his dick.

"Yesss—Daddy slap me wit' dat dick."

"Bitch, open yo' mouth and stick ya tongue out," instructed Baby G.

"Aaaahh!"

Baby G slapped and rubbed his dick on her tongue while still gripping the tracks in her head. Michelle's breathing quickened as she moaned and played with her clit.

"You couldn't just let me get my money and gon' 'bout my bidness, huh? Bitch, I'll kill ya in dis bitch!" yelled Baby G, as he jammed his dick back in her mouth, leaned forward in a push up position and started fucking her face mercilessly.

Michelle gagged, but never once stopped playing with her clit. In fact, she had already came twice.

"Ssss—shit!" yelled Baby G, as he snatched out of Michelle's mouth and painted her face with his kids.

He growled until every specimen in him was released. Before Baby G's arrival, Michelle was eating a bowl of Fruit Loops which was sitting on the dresser next to the bed. He grabbed the spoon, scraped the semen off Michelle's face and fed it to her. She moaned seductively while eating from the spoon, still playing with her clit.

"Dat's a good girl."

"Um—what' chu gon' give me for being a good girl, Daddy?"

Baby G got up, pulled her to the edge of the bed and flipped her on her stomach.

"Dat's what da fuck I'm talking 'bout, take dis pussy!" cried Michelle as she put a mean arch in her back.

Baby G put on a condom and slid right into her wetness.

"Sss—whooo—yes!" moaned Michelle.

"Damn, dis pussy warm as fuck!" stated Baby G, grabbing both of her soft cheeks, and long stroked her violently, causing her ass to shake reverberantly.

"Shit yeah! Fuck dis pussy, Daddy," pronounced Michelle through clenched teeth.

Baby G grabbed his pistol and slapped her on her ass every three strokes, causing Michelle to holler sounds of pleasure and pain while throwing her ass back thrust for thrust.

"Bitch, look at me," demanded Baby G.

When Michelle turned to look at him, he stopped stroking her and put the silencer in her mouth.

"Suck it!" Baby G ordered, moving the barrel in and out of her mouth.

When he felt like it was lubricated enough, he spread her ass cheeks, spit in her asshole, and proceeded to fuck her with the silencer. Michelle was so turned on that she held her own ass open so she could feel everything. Baby G slow-stroked her pussy as he moved the silencer in and out of her ass driving Michelle bananas.

"Aaahh—shit! Sss—Baby G—damn! Shh—dats it, nigga,

fuck dat ass!" He stopped fucking her and was now playing with her clit while jamming the silencer in and out of her ass relentlessly.

"Bitch, I'll kill ya in here!" stated Baby G. "Ooohhh—my—fuckin' God! Sss—goodness!" screamed Michelle as she came from her ass and pussy simultaneously.

She was still shaking when Baby G flipped her on her back.

"Clean dis shit off my gun!" demanded Baby G, forcing Michelle to suck the silencer clean.

Once satisfied, Baby G pulled Michelle to the edge of the bed, spreading her eagle. After playing with her clit with the head of his dick, he entered her, giving her everything he had for thirty minutes straight, leaving her in a comatose-like state.

"Bitch, I told ya 'bout fuckin' with me! Now look at' cha, I done put dat ass in a coma!" boasted Baby G, as he cleaned all the money off the bed and got in the wind.

Chapter 79

We Going to War

Mundo was in deep thought as a guard escorted him to his attorney visit. He'd fired his lawyer and was now about to do the same to his public defender. Mundo had no idea that his previous attorney had already contacted Yana and gave her half the retainer back. Yana hired a new attorney out of Tampa, Florida whose track record was impeccable. Once they reached the Sally port, a guard signed Mundo in and told him that his lawyer was already present. The guard uncuffed him and instructed him to go to room five. When Mundo entered the room, he saw a preppy, middle-aged, white man who had a mean suave to him.

"Hi, how are you today, Mr. Moss?"

"Other than facing life in prison, I'm cool," replied Mundo.

"Well, that's why I'm here, Mr. Moss. I'm Mark O'Brien, your new attorney and let me tell you, I feel like we can win this thing. I've been informed that the state's witness has passed?" Mundo smiled wickedly.

"Is dat right?" asked Mundo.

"To my knowledge, yes, he was gunned down weeks ago. Now, I must tell you that the state has come down from fifteen to ten years. With me putting that out there. My next question to you is what is it you want to do?"

"Shid—with all due respect, Mr. O'Brien—dead men can't talk. I'ma suit up! I wanna go to war!"

"That's exactly what I wanted to hear. I'll contact the state and let them know that I'm moving to get the charges dropped or set a date for trial. Any more questions, Mr. Moss?"

"Not at all."

"Alright," said O'Brien standing to shake Mundo's hand, "I look forward to getting you home to your family soon."

As Mundo departed with his lawyer, it dawned on him why Baby G had gone to get his discovery from their mother.

"Dis nigga thinks he slick," Mundo muttered to himself, "I got something for dat ass doe."

Chapter 80

See Me in Thirty Days

Baby G called Shenida over to his apartment and showed her how to cook up dope. After fucking up an ounce that Baby G brought back to life, Shenida had mastered the art of cooking crack. She was instructed to drop the work off to Michelle once she was done. Shenida tried protesting it, but once Baby G bent her over the couch, she caved. Baby G left her at the apartment and was now walking into Hip Hop fashion with the jewelry he took from Brittany. Hip Hop Fashion was a clothing and jewelry store owned by an Arab named Zack. Zack took everything from guns to jewelry. When G walked in Zack was engaging in an argument with a hood rat.

"Aaahh—what da fuck ever, Zack! You know you want dis pussy you Iraqi mothafucka!"

"No, no, no! American woman—too many dicks! Arabian woman—one dick!"

"Fuck you, Zack!" yelled the hood rat before storming out of the store.

"Damn, Zack, you sho'll know how to treat da bitches, huh?" clowned Baby G.

"These American women are crazy!" Baby G, my friend, what do I owe the pleasure?"

"You already know I'm 'bout dat check," stated Baby G placing a bag on the counter.

Zack spread a velvet cloth on the counter so he could examine the diamonds for cut, clarity, color, and carats. After meticulously viewing the jewelry through a jewelers loom, Zack made Baby G an offer.

"I'll give you one hundred thousand cash, right now."

"Nall, dat shit worth three hunnid easy!"

"Yeah, but this shit is hot, Baby G. I think one hundred is more than reasonable."

"You know what, you right, let me get my shit. I'm finna roll out."

"No wait! Okay, buddy! What do you feel is reasonable?"

"Listen, keep da ice. I want some custom made shit in exchange. I want a Cuban with a charm dat says Baby G. Make sho my shit weigh a thousand grams and I want a Cuban bracelet and pinky ring. Make sho it got ice all through it."

"Okay, my friend. For you, no problem. Come see me in sixty days."

"Already!" replied Baby G.

Three Weeks Later

"Who is it?" yelled Michelle as she pranced down the steps and peeped out of her blinds.

What the fuck? thought Michelle as she opened her front door.

She recognized the woman from a couple of weeks ago when Baby G came by and dropped some work off.

"May I help you?"

"You sure can. I'm here for dat check," announced Shenida, bombarding her way into Michelle's apartment, slightly bumping her.

"Bitch! You must be some kinda crazy walkin' in my shit like you just like dat! Talking 'bout you came for a check!" yelled Michelle rolling her neck and talking with her hands.

Shenida just smirked. "Listen, it's been three weeks since I dropped dat work off. Baby G sent me to collect and drop moe work off."

The sound of moe dope caused Michelle's attitude to lighten up.

"Well, why you ain't just say dat shit, girl? Where da work at?"

"It's in da car I gotta count dat paper first before I give you dat work."

"Hold up and give me a minute," Michelle exclaimed, running upstairs, and returning moments later with a Walmart bag.

"Here, dat's eighty-two bands. Sixty for Baby G and the other twenty-four is for a brick. Tell Baby G I'ma shoot him eight thousand on the back in, plus the money for whatever he front me."

"I'ma tell'em. Listen doe, da work gotta be cooked up cuz Baby G ain't have enough time to cook it."

"Damn, I guess I'ma just have to sell soft then cuz I don't know how to cook no damn crack," Michelle admitted, drawing laughter from Shenida.

"Shid—if you got some baking soda, I'll cook most of it up for ya."

"I got some of dat shit in da fridge. I don't know if it's enough cuz I be brushin' my teeth wit' it."

"Let me see?" asked Shenida.

"I wanna see you cook dis shit up so I can learn, girl. Come on." Shenida followed Michelle in the kitchen and stood behind her as she bent over for the baking soda.

"Damn, bitch, where da food at?"

"Girl, I was just finna go shopping before you came. Here, is dis enough baking soda?"

"Put it on the counter and hand me one of dem wine coolers, bitch."

"I only got two left, but' chu can get one," said Michelle, bending over to get a wine cooler.

Boc!

Shenida put a hole in Michelle's head the size of a hockey puck, leaving her slumped over in the fridge.

"Next time watch who you callin' a bitch! Oh, I'm trippin—won't be a next, huh? Po ass hoe!"

Khufu

Chapter 81

I'm Trippin

Baby G stood at Shantel's door after knocking for five minutes. As soon as he turned to leave, she opened the door.

"Wassup, baby daddy?" asked Shantel, rubbing her stomach.

Baby G ignored her, pulled out his banger and walked past her.

"Boy, what da hell you trippin off?"

Baby G maneuvered through the house like swat checking every room. After clearing the whole house, he approached Shantel.

"What da fuck took you so long to open da door!" he yelled.

"Nigga, I'm five months pregnant! I was in there sleep. What' chu think I'ma have a nigga up in here while I'm carrying yo' child, so you can kill me? I thought you had more respect for me then dat. You can let' cha self out, thank you!" cried Shantel as her eyes started to water.

Baby G sat the same gun that he killed Brittany with on the living room table, then turned and grabbed Shantel holding her tight.

"I'm sorry, Ma. You right—I'm trippin' like a mothafucka. Deez streets got a nigga a lil' 'noid. I'm sorry for how I been treatin' you lately. If you say the reason for you not coming to see me in the hospital was because you ain't wanna stress the baby out—I'ma go for dat. I need you to know dat I'ma make sho you and my son Gucci. As for me staying out late, you gon' have to deal wit' dat. It's gone be some nights I might not even come home. Ma, you know how I'm livin.'"

"So, you tellin' me dat—it's me and you again?" asked Shantel excitedly.

"It's gon' always be me and you. Don't neva forget dat."

"Thank you, Jesus, Mary and da billy goat!"

"I'on think dat's how dat bible shit go."

"Boy, whateva! I been round dis bitch goin' crazy wit' out' chu! Nigga, I'm horny as hell. I need some dick like right now!"

"Calm down, I got' chu. Come on," instructed Baby G, as he

led her to the bedroom.

After rubbing her stomach and feet, Baby G turned Shantel on her side and slow-fucked her to sleep. Even though it felt good to be back home, Baby G felt guilty about the chaos he was about to embark on while waiting for his child's birth. But Baby G knew he had to restore order out of chaos.

****

"Moss, get ready, you have a visit!" yelled a male guard.

"What da fuck?" Mundo muttered to himself as he got up to do his hygiene.

There were no visits on Friday, so Mundo was confused as to why he was called for a visit. Ten minutes later, the guard opened the flap so Mundo could cuff up. Once he was cuffed, the guard radioed central to pop the cell door.

"Man, when y'all gon' let me back in population?" asked Mundo.

"I don't know, Moss. They're saying that you're unfit for population. You've been in two altercations in a short span of time, and one involved a stabbing. After this visit, I don't think they will let you out anyway."

"What' chu mean?" questioned Mundo, perplexed.

"This is a special visit, Moss."

"What kind of special visit? It's the feds or some shit?"

"No, it's not the feds. It's a visit in the chapel."

Mundo stopped walking and stared at the guard.

"Man don't tell me somebody done died. I can't take dat shit right now," exclaimed Mundo, throwing his hands in the air.

"I believe so, Moss."

"Man, just take me back to my cell."

"We're already here, Moss, you might as well get it over with now, man."

Mundo's heart rate increased as he thought of the worst. He took a deep breath, exhaled, and continued down the hallway until they reached the chapel. The guard removed the cuffs from

Mundo's wrists and wished him good luck. As soon as Mundo entered the chapel, he saw his sister C.C. talking to the chaplain. Mundo approached and asked what was going on.

"Mr. Moss, it's come to my attention that it's been a death in your family. I'm going to let you have a moment with your sister. If you desire prayer or counseling afterward, inform me. I'm sorry for your loss," expressed the chaplain before walking off.

"Sis, who died?"

"Boy, ain't nobody died. I made dat shit up so I can talk to you face to face. You know they be recording them other visits and we damn sho can't talk over the phone."

"Damn, you had me spooked a lil' piece. Dat shit was swift doe."

"You lookin' good, bro. Yo' hair done got long and yo' skin glowing."

"Man, fuck all dat! What up?"

"Well, anyways, you heard 'bout dat nigga Chris?"

"Yeah, my lawyer told me somebody smoked his boots."

"So, you should be coming home, soon, right?"

"Yeah, I'm going to trial if they don't drop charges. No prints, no face, no witness, no case. Listen, sis, you remember when Baby G went and got my discovery from mama?"

"Yeah, what about it?"

"He wanted to know who da rat was so he can kill him to free me. He tryin' to free me, so he can kill me. Dat nigga on some other shit. Baby G must have forgot I'ma killa, too."

"I don't think he forgot, bro. Me personally, I don't think he gives a fuck. You gotta be careful when you come home bro. I'ma ride wit' chu doe, bro, you know dat," expressed C.C.

"I hear you, sis, but it's some shit I ain't tell ya."

"Like what?"

"Remember when Baby G got shot?"

"Duhh, I'm da one who shot him remember?"

"Nall, I'm talking 'bout da time he got hit up on twenty third Street."

"Oh, yeah, I remember dat. What about it?"

"I was da one who hit' him up, sis."

"Is you fuckin' serious?" C.C. asked, eyes wide.

"I'm serious as a life sentence. I wet dat boy all over a misunderstanding, then told him dat C did it."

"What fuckin' misunderstanding? And why in da hell would you tell Baby G that Cee shot him? I'm confused." C.C. was totally frustrated.

"Cee was fuckin' Yana and I thought Baby G was, too. So, I played dem against each other. It is what it is, sis."

"It is what it is? Nigga, you trippin! I done shot dis man the fuck up over nothin'—my own brother! You gotta help me make dis shit right with Baby G."

Mundo stood up and headed toward the door.

"Aye, guard, get me the fuck from round here!" Mundo turned to face C.C. before leaving, "I can't help you wit' dis, sis. I'm all da way in wit dis shit. See you on da other side," he stated as he left to go back to the hole.

Chapter 82

Cook Dat Last Brick Up

"Hold up, wait a minute. Run dat shit by me again. You did what?"

"Nigga, you heard me! I said I had to smoke dat pussy ass hoe!" yelled Shenida while placing the bag of money on the kitchen counter.

"I had a nice lil' operation running on dat side of town. Da fuck you had to kill her for?"

"When I went to collect, da hoe played, so I did me! I'on like how you giving me third degree over dis off brand ass hoe. Nigga, I been down wit' chu since day one! Ain't no way in hell you was supposed to put dat hoe in position before me and I'm rockin wit' chu one hunnid," cried Shenida beating on her chest. "Nigga, you got me fucked up!" Shenida's eyes were now full of tears and falling freely.

Baby G knew she was right. On top of that, Michelle's apartment was the last place Scrab was seen with Baby G before he dumped him in Taylor's Creek. Shenida just killed a problem that he would have had to fix later.

"Damn, ma, come here," said Baby G, wrapping his arms tightly around Shenida. He had never seen her cry and was thrown off by this sensitive side of her.

"I'm sorry, Ma. Don't ever feel like I'on love you. I appreciate you, Ma. I was just tryin' to lock dat part of town down, but shit, fuck dat hoe. If dis what you really want, you got it, Ma. Now dry dem tears and get' cha ass in there and cook dat last brick up," demanded G, squeezing her soft ass, and kissing her in the mouth.

"Okay, Daddy. On some real shit doe, if I knew dis all it took I woulda been smoked dat pussy ass hoe!"

****

Baby G tried calling Aaron again, but all he got was the voicemail. It had been a few weeks since he'd hit for three bricks down in Pompano and he was trying to re-up.

Man, fuck dis shit. I'ma just take me a nigga shit, thought Baby G, as he slid through the city and turned up the volume on Nipsey Hussle.

I'm prolific/So gifted/I'm da type dat's gone go get it, no kiddin/Breakin down a swisher, front of yo building/Sittin on da steps, feelin no feelings/Last night it was a cold killin/You gotta keep da devil in his hole nigga/But you know how it goes nigga/I'm frontline every time it's on nigga.

Baby G was caught up in the allure of Nipsey's poetic vernacular when his phone vibrated. He'd missed a call from Off Top. Curious as to what the call was about, Baby G called him back. Top picked up on the third ring.

"G, what it do?"

"You already know, one moment at a time—slow motion."

"I hear dat, but check it, I need ya," exclaimed Off Top.

"Say da word!"

"Shid, you feel like going on one?"

"Affirmative! Drop da location, you'll smell me in a minute."

"Already!" replied Off Top.

Five minutes later, Baby G was pulling into J-n-J's Liquor store. He stopped at the service window and purchased a fifth of Remy and a box of swisher kings. After grabbing what he needed, Baby G pulled off and backed in next to Off Top's CL 550. Baby G wasn't sure if he could fully trust Off Top due to the toxic circumstances that enveloped him. So, he cocked his banga, tucked it and hopped out watching everything. When Baby G hopped in the whip, Off Top was blowin' high grade as usual.

"How you feeling?" asked Off Top as he attempted to pass Baby G the blunt.

"I'm good. On dat smoke. But, to answer yo' question, shid—I feel like fucking some shit ova."

"Say no more. You know a nigga named Face?"

"Yeah, I used to grab from him back in da days."

"Yo' past dealings wit' him, is dat gon' be a problem?"

"Fuck no! What da ticket is?"

"I got thirty for ya and you keep everything you run down on when you hit him."

"Say less. Give me a few days, I'ma pull up on ya."

"Aye, Baby G, before you leave, I wanna ask you some shit."

Baby G low key clutched his banga, ready to hit Top if he did or said anything crazy.

"Yeah, what up?" asked Baby G.

"You ever found out who hit' chu?"

"You know I heard a few whispers, but I ain't acted on nem yet. I'm just laying right now, ya heard."

"Dat's what's up. What about Mundo? Yo' sister told me a nigga kidnapped him and left him for dead."

"Yeah, I heard he let a nigga catch him slippin'. He should be a'ight doe, he bout to jump in a few. We'll get to da bottom of it when he touches down."

"Already! You good on weaponry?" asked Top.

"Always, good lookin' doe. I'm finna get in da wind big homie. You gon' smell me when it's done."

"Fasho!"

"Already!"

Khufu

Chapter 83
Lay On Nem

Baby G grabbed an empty milk jug and urinated in it. He refused to leave or exit his vehicle for anything. He had been laying on Face's trap house since daybreak, snorting and smoking dirties back-to-back. It had been months since he indulged in coke, so he was geekin for real, high as hell, but on point. Looking through a pair of binoculars he noticed that Face had four young niggas working out of his yard. All of them had bulges on their hips, solidifying that they were strapped. Face appeared to be in a wheelchair and rolled out on the front porch occasionally to survey the scene.

An hour later, Face rolled out to his '78 Impala and had his youngins help him in the car. Baby G started his whip and pulled behind Face staying at a safe distance. Ten minutes later, Face pulled into a nice estate as a young, beautiful, yellow tenderoni pranced out of the front door with the baddest walk she could muster. She grabbed Face's wheelchair from the back seat and helped him out of the car.

Awkward couple, Baby G thought as he pulled off at a slow creep.

"I gotcha, playboy," muttered Baby G to himself.

****

A week later, Baby G and Shenida sat at the living room table and counted everything he'd accumulated since his release from Townsend Medical Center. When they finished counting, Baby G was four-hundred and eighty-two bands up.

"Baby G, Daddy—like—I'm so fucking proud of you. You ain't letting nothin' stop you from running it up. I love how you just ten toes down, two middle fangaz up with dis shit," expressed Shenida.

"I can dig it. Check it doe, I need you to pull up on Floyd for me."

"Floyd who?" asked Shenida

"Floyd rooming housing on twenty-third and D."

"Okay, Daddy, but what for?"

"I want dat building. When you pull up on' nem take a hunnid bands for dat property."

"How you know he gon' go for it?"

"Cuz he got gambling debts and if he don't—you make sho he do."

"Okay, Daddy, I got' chu. So, what about da dope I just cooked up?"

"We gon' sit on it for a minute. Listen, I need you to come back to da spot after you holla at Floyd. Hold shit down till I get back," stated Baby G before sliding in his room.

Shenida rolled a blunt, sparked it and fell into deep thought about what was to come. Moments later, Baby G returned dressed in a UPS uniform causing Shenida to choke on the smoke she'd just inhaled.

"Boy! What da hell you got going on? You got a job?"

"You can say dat. Here, deez my car keys. Let me use yo truck for today."

"They on da kitchen counter, daddy."

"When you leave put dat money up and make sho you lock up. I'm gone."

"I gotcha, boo. Just stay on point and make sho you make it back to me cuz I know you ain't going nowhere to work for no white folks," pronounced Shenida.

"You just make sho you get dat building and be butt booty naked when I fall back in dis bitch. A nigga loves you, doe."

"Love you too, baby."

****

Baby G pulled up to Face's trap in a minivan he'd stolen and put UPS magnets on the side. He then hopped out with a box and a clipboard and approached the gate. One of the youngins walked toward the gate with a dubious look.

"I got a package for Mr. Fabian," announced Baby G.

"Aye! Go get Face, he got a package!" screamed the youngin to his comrade.

"Where da fuck yo truck at?" asked the youngin.

"They let us use our own whips now lil homie. Dis dat new shit."

"Let em in, lil one," screamed Face from the porch.

Lil' one opened the gate then went back to his post.

"A package for me, huh? Where the UPS truck at?" questioned Face.

"I was just telling lil homie they let us use our own vehicles for small packages."

"Come on in playa, put it on the table."

Baby G followed Face into the house and could smell the stench of high grade instantly.

"You can sit the box on this table right here, my dog." When Baby G placed the box on the table Face tried to grab it.

"Slow up, big dog! You gotta sign dis shit first," stated Baby G handing Face a clip board. *Dis nigga dumb as hell,* thought Baby G.

Everybody knows that packages get signed electronically these days and here was Face signing for something he knew nothing about. Greed will get a nigga every time. Baby G pondered pulling a SIG 9mm with a silencer on it.

"Bitch ass nigga. You know you wasn't expecting no package." Baby G slapped Face in the mouth with his pistol, knocking several teeth out. Before Face could scream, Baby G hit him again, this time knocking him out of his wheelchair. He then placed his hand over Face's mouth and jammed the silencer in his eye.

"Fuck nigga, shut up. You say anything I'ma send yo' ass to da other side. Nigga you straight?"

Face shook his head with tears in his eyes. The blood that was now seeping through Baby G's hands pissed him off. He snapped, rubbing it all over Face's face violently.

"A'ight nigga I smell it. I'ma ask you one time. Where it at?"

"It's in the kitchen under the sink. Lil homie don't kill me—I got a baby on the way."

"Oh, word?"

"Dat's my word, lil homie."

"Damn, I got one on the way, too. I can dig it," asserted Baby G, as he hit Face three times directly in the forehead. "Sorry, partna, it's a check on yo head."

Baby G grabbed a duffle bag out of the box that he made Face sign for and headed to the kitchen. After taking thirty pounds, he slid out the back door and ran into a Presa Canarias. Without hesitation, he fired two shots in the beautiful dog's massive head, killing him instantly. Never sympathetic about collateral damage, Baby G kept it pushing, leaping over the back gate after throwing the bag over. Moments later, he hopped in Shenida's truck that he had left running and headed to the north side of town.

A half a mile before his destination, Baby G switched clothing, reloaded his gun and proceeded on what he had set out to do. Less than five minutes he was maneuvering through a neighborhood that contained nice houses. Once he found the one he was looking for he pulled into the driveway, left the truck running and hopped out with a package. Trying to be inconspicuous as possible, Baby G pulled his hat lower as he approached the door and rang the doorbell.

"Coming, hold on," said a voice behind the door.

"Damn, dis bitch sound familiar," muttered Baby G.

Seconds later, the door opened and what Baby G gazed at startled and excited him at the same time. Nevertheless, he kept his composure—shid—he had a job to do.

"How you doing, Ms. Lady? I got edible arrangements from a Mr. Fabian."

"Edible arrangements? Dis nigga trippin', I guess, bring em in and put em on the table. And why the hell you got dat hat so down low? Pull dat shit up so I can see dem eyes," said the woman letting Baby G in and shutting the door behind her.

Baby G sat the arrangements on the living room table, pulled his hat up and turned around.

"Oh, my God! I know you, um—you um—Baby G, right?"

"In da flesh. What dey do, Yella Baby?"

"Why you never called me? So, this yo job?"

"Well, I arrange and rearrange shit. So, you can say dat. Listen,

258

Ma, I hate to fuck yo day up, but you know what dis is," stated Baby G, pulling his banga and holding it by his side. "I'm only gon' ask you one time, ma. Where it at?"

To his surprise Yella Baby didn't panic or scream. If she was terrified, she concealed it well, which he found attractive and intriguing.

"See, if you would have called me, we coulda been set dis play up. I'on care nothing 'bout dis nigga. Follow me, the money back here in his lil' man cave and shit."

"Bitch, hold up!" demanded Baby G aggressively. "Who else in here?"

"Nobody, just me, lil daddy."

"Alright na! If you flaggin I'ma smoke yo big, fine, thick ass in here. Let's get it," commanded Baby G, slapping Yella Baby on her ass with his pistol.

"Um," she moaned as she led the way.

Baby G watched as her ass moved with pizazz to a rhythm in harmony with the vibrations of the universe. When he had run into Yella Baby in the club, he never paid attention to how well put together she was. She had a low cut like Anita Baker and was tatted from head to toe. Nine years older than Baby G, Yella knew what it took to capture a man's attention and she did just that while turning her head to the side, watching him watch her from her peripheral.

"Yeah, I see you. You a bad bitch, but dat shit don't mean a fucking thing right, now. You play wit' me bitch I'ma kill ya."

"I understand fully. I'm just tryna show a lil civility."

"All you gotta do is show me da money. Anything else is just an impediment," exclaimed Baby G, pointing the pistol at Yella.

Yella bit her bottom lip and continued to make her ass clap as she entered a room that appeared to be Face's man cave. Right on her trail, Baby G entered the room behind her and noticed that Face was a diehard Miami fan. The paintings on the walls, the pool table, the carpet, and bar stools were all Miami Dolphins. Baby G followed Yella behind the bar and watched her squat down to open a safe.

"Da fuck is up wit dis nigga?" asked Baby G.

"What chu mean?"

"Don't he know da Dolphins ain't worth a fuck?"

"Yeah, he knows. He's just a diehard fan. Every game he bet big on da dolphins," replied Yella opening the safe.

"Watch out," stated Baby G, pointing the pistol at Yella's face. He removed the money from the safe and placed it on the bar. "Da fuck is dis? Dis like fifteen bands! Where da fuck da real money at?"

"Dat's all he had in there. He keeps most of his money in banks dat he washed through his lil bidnesses. If he had dat type of money in here I woulda been got his ass. I told you, I don't care nothing 'bout dis nigga. Shid, you might as well let me come with you."

"My pops once told me dat you leave a hoe how you meet a hoe."

"And what is dat supposed to mean?"

"It means, if you'll do dis shit to him, you damn sho don't have a problem fucking me over."

Fop!

Baby G hit Yella right between her eyes, dropping her dead. He cuffed the money and got in the wind, leaving Yella with her eyes open and her soul behind her.

Chapter 84

Hold Da Spot Down

After trying on his jewels, Baby G put them back in their cases and left Hip Hop Fashion. Zack knew the jewelry was worth more than what he'd got them for. So, he threw in a gold red faced Rolex, cluttered with stones. Baby G was now headed to 23rd and Ave. D to check out the spot he had Shenida purchase from Floyd. His stepfather, D-Dog had been working on it for the past week and now he was almost finished. All the walls were knocked down, making it one big room with two stoves and a service window. The only door was in the front that could only be opened by being buzzed in.

"D-Dizzle off da mothafucking bone grissle! Da fuck is up?"

"Baby G, what's happenin', home skillet? What it do, baby?"

"Shid, whateva necessary to make tomorrow better then yesterday. I see you got dis bitch looking trap ready."

"You know how D-Dizzle roll, baby. A few more days and we'll be ready to rock."

"Music to my ears. Here," said Baby G pulling twenty blue faces from his pocket and handing them to his stepfather. "I'ma shoot you da rest when you finish," stated Baby G.

"I ain't tripping, I'm chillin," replied D-Dog, stuffing the money in his pocket.

"I gotta move around, hold da spot down for me."

"You know I got' chu, baby."

"Already!"

Khufu

Chapter 85

Wham Whamz

Mundo dialed Yana's number and glanced at Jerry Springer as he waited for her answer. He was now back in general population after doing ninety days in the hole.

"Hello! Yeah, dis me," Mundo said.

"Hey, baby! Why you just now calling me?" asked Yana.

"I been in da hole and shit."

"Yeah, but don't they let you use the phone back there?"

"I ain't feel like talking to nobody."

"So, you feel like talking now?"

"What kinda question is dat? I'm on da phone ain't I?"

"Okay, Mundo, I'm not tryna argue wit' chu. I miss you, we miss you."

"How da baby doin?"

"We fine. I just seen the doctor yesterday, I'm four months."

"Damn, I can't wait to get out dis shit."

"I seen dat boy on da news. He got killed. They gotta let' chu outta there, bae."

"Yeah, my lawyer working on it. I know they gon' drag me man. Deez crackas play dirty in St. Lucie County. They'll drag you da whole five years, then offer you time served. You tell' em no drop da charges or you gon' run it, they'll take you to trial, convict you wit' no evidence and make you fight it on appeal!"

"Well, dat's why you gotta lawyer, baby. It's gone be okay, baby. We gon' get through dis together."

"Yeah, you right. Look, I know I be trippin' and shit, but a nigga love you doe."

"Who is dis? Stop playing and put Mundo back on da phone."

"Cut it out, you know dis me."

"I'm just saying, Mundo don't talk like dat. You feeling okay?"

Mundo managed to laugh through the frustration. "Come on Yana, you know a nigga love you."

"I love you too, boy."

"Look, I'ma call you tonight. I'm finna take a shower."

"Okay, call back for real now, Mundo. I love you."

"Already."

As soon as Mundo hung up the phone a guard entered the dorm and started mail call.

"Moss, you got mail!" Mundo approached the guard and showed him his wrist band. "Moss, you related to Randy Moss?"

"Nall, man, just let me get my mail."

"A'ight playa, calm down and head back to yo' rack or something for I spray yo ass."

"Imagine dat," replied Mundo, snatching his post card from the guard's hand and heading back to his cell.

He laid in his rack and read his mail.

Dear Frenemy,

How dem walls looking to you? Dey talkin' to you yet? What about dat shower in the day room, you lovin' dat? What about dat third world country food? Tasty, huh? It'll all be over soon lil' nigga—and don't thank God. Nigga, you know who to praise. I'm out here waitin' on you like da first and da third, ya heard? Oh, yeah, check yo' account. Wham Whamz on me nigga!

Disrespectfully Submitted,
King Baby G

Mundo threw the post card in his bin and slid it under his rack. He then laid back and gazed at the ceiling in deep thought. Moments later, he found himself laughing and amused with Baby G's creative enigma.

"Tssskkk—dis green ass nigga a trip," Mundo muttered before closing his eyes to get some rest.

Chapter 86

Dark Web

"Where we headed?" Shenida asked Baby G.

"I'm finna pull up on one of my guys 'bout some bidness real quick. Dat's cool?"

"Baby G, stop playing wit' me. You know I'll follow you anywhere."

"I know it. Look, I appreciate you steppin' down on Floyd bout dat building for me. I'ma turn it into a seafood shack as a front, but I'ma be moving work, too," Baby G stated, pulling into C-Major's driveway. "Get out, I want chu to meet somebody in case something ever happens to me."

"Stop saying shit like dat, Baby G."

"I'm just being realistic, Shenida. Ain't no happy ending wit' dis shit. All I can do is make sho' my people straight before I blow rec."

"You looking out for yo' people, I overstand dat. But I know plenty of street niggas who made it out. We just gotta go legit."

"I got some shit lined up. Now, get cho ass out da car."

After banging on the door like an unpaid rent man, C-Major opened the door in a rage.

"Who the fuck! Baby G? Aww man, bro!" C-Major grabbed Baby G and started jumping up and down like a kid who missed his father.

"A'ight man shit! Calm down a lil' piece—ease up."

"My bad, bro. I'm just happy to see you. I tried to come and see you, but they told me family only. I thought you were a veggie, bro. They said you got hit in the head."

"You know my bob and weave game stupid. I seen dat shit coming, ain't nothing but a lil graze."

"You're fucking crazy, bro. Dat's why I love you, man."

"Already! Check it, doe, dis my rib right here, Shenida. She on everything I'm on."

"Nice to meet chu, Shenida. I'm C-Major."

"Likewise," replied Shenida.

"Come on in, bro, let's talk about why you're here."

"Yeah, let's do dat," asserted Baby G as he entered the double wide trailer with Shenida behind him.

"Can I get chu guys a drink or something?"

"Yeah, you got liquor?" asked Baby G.

"Of course, I got Bourbon and Vodka."

"Po, two Vodkas, bra, straight."

"Coming right up. So, uhh—what happened when you left the show, bro?"

"Shid—some niggas pulled up and snatched me out at the light," lied Baby G.

"What did they do to your sister?"

"She pulled off after they snatched me."

"Damn, bro, you shoulda left with me," pronounced C-Major passing Baby G and Shenida their drinks.

"It's all good. From da looks of it I'm hard to kill," Baby G clowned while downing his cup.

"Okay, then, what's up? What do you wanna do?" questioned C-Major.

"I need some work like yesterday."

"Well, I don't have any coke, but I got a helluva connect on molly," said Major.

"What da ticket is?"

"For you, bro, just give me ten racks and I'll give you the keys to a whole new world."

"What chu mean?"

"I got a plug, twelve hundred a brick, straight from China, bro! I been fucking with that dark web shit, bro. It comes in the mail and I have a pickup guy. Just leave me the money for your order and the fee for my pickup guy. When they land I'll call you."

"So, for a one-time fee of ten bands you gon' order for me whenever?"

"As long as you pay the pickup fee, I got chu, bro."

"I call dat! Shenida, baby, go get my bag out da car."

"Okay, Daddy," Shenida remarked in a seductive manner,

feeling a buzz from the Vodka.

"She seems cool," stated C-Major.

"Yeah, man, dat's my nigga fa real. She overstands dat I'm da Vanguard of dis shit ya know. She trusts my judgement wholeheartedly wit' outta doubt."

"That's what's up. So, how's the wife?"

"Who, baby mama? She good."

"Baby mama?" asked C-Major as Shenida walked back in with the money.

"Yeah, I got a youngin on the way."

"Congrats, bro! Let's celebrate with a line of coke, bro!"

"Not right, now, fam," stated Baby G, grabbing the bag from Shenida.

"So, what's da fee for the pickup guy?"

"Two hundred dollars a brick."

Baby G counted out the money and handed it to Major.

"A'ight, dis eighty bands. Ten for you, ten for ya pick up guy and sixty for fifty bricks. Keep me out da mix bra fa real. If he gets bagged I'm in da clear. If you mention my name, everything around you getting crushed!"

"Damn, bro, I can't believe you just threatened me, let alone assume I would put you in harm's way. Didn't I move that coke for you so you wouldn't catch a fed case?"

"Yeah, you right, bra, I'm tripping."

"Come on, bro—this is me! If he flips, I'll have every motherfucker around him killed. Speaking of killing, I got something for you," stated C-Major leaving the living room and returning with a box.

"Fuck is dat?" asked Baby G.

"Just open it, bro."

"I got it," said Shenida, getting up to open the box. "Hell yeah!" screamed Shenida excitedly while pulling a tommy gun from the box. "It's two of them."

"C-Major—bra—what da fuck?"

"Consider it an early birthday gift, bro. I got 'em for the low off the dark web."

"Bra! Do you know how many niggas you just killed?"

"Whatever, bro, do your thing."

"Bet dat up, fam, for real. Listen, I'ma do something for my birthday at the Elk's. I want chu to put together a promo video telling dem when and where. Use some of my music videos and all ladies get in and drink free."

"I got chu, bro."

"Why da Elk's? Dat's a hole in da wall and it's too risky. It's in da heart of da city, in da middle of a war zone," stressed Shenida.

"I know, Ma, but dat's where I need to be."

"For what?"

"Advertisement!"

Chapter 87

Why You Crying?

C.C. sat curled up on her sectional couch smoking a blunt of birthday cake, while strolling down Facebook. She'd seen the promo video C-Major did for Baby G's birthday bash and fell into a slight state of depression. Seeing Baby G do what he does best only made her reminisce of her times in the studio with him. C.C. thought of all the times Baby G would be a good listener when she needed an ear. Tears fell from her eyes as the guilt settled in of her choosing sides without proper investigation. She wanted so badly to explain her bad judgement to Baby G but knew talking without bloodshed was nonnegotiable with Baby G at this moment.

"Mommy, why you crying?" asked Machi and Hezeron, startling C.C.

"I'm not crying," lied C.C.

"Yes, you are," said Hezeron, wiping her tears away.

"Mommy, I miss Uncle G," asserted Machi.

"Yeah, Mommy me too," remarked Hezeron.

"I miss him, too," she admitted.

"Then why did you shoot at him, Mommy?" questioned Machi.

"I didn't shoot at him."

"Yes, you did Mommy. We was looking out the window," replied Hezeron.

"I thought he was somebody else. I didn't mean to."

"Well, Mommy, we told you Uncle Baby G brought us the pizza," said Machi.

"Y'all go lay down. Get out my face, I'ma call y'all when dinner ready!" yelled C.C.

"If I were you, Mommy, I would call Uncle G and say I'm sorry," cried Hezeron on the way to his room.

Moments later, Off Top walked through the hallway and into the living room.

"What the kids talking 'bout?" asked Off Top.

"I'on know what dem kids talking 'bout. You hungry?" she

asked, trying to change the subject.

"Nall, I gotta run somewhere right quick. What dey mean you shot at Baby G, doe?"

"Bae, it's nothing, dey heard wrong. I was supposed to meet Baby G at the shootin' range, but I stood him up. Dat's all, bae, it ain't nothing," she lied.

"You a'ight?"

"Yeah, bae, I'm good, go handle yo bidness."

"Oh, so—now you kicking me out? Dis shit crazy. It looks like you been crying. What up?"

"I said ain't shit wrong wit' me! God—lee, man!" yelled C.C. out of frustration.

"Oh, yeah? Dat's what we doing? A'ight, den, shid fuck it!" stated Off Top slamming the door behind him.

C.C. just continued to puff her pain away as tears fell more rapidly than before. It hurt her to know that she had just done to her kids and their father what she had never done before and that's lie.

****

Baby G turned the knob slowly and opened the back door to the project apartment. It was dark, all except for a light from a laptop screen. As he slipped into the apartment, sounds of a porno could clearly be heard. Baby G drew his red hawk 44 Ruger, crept up on his prey who was sitting with his back turned and placed the barrel on the back of his head.

"Drop da lotion, bitch ass nigga!" yelled Baby G with a smirk on his face.

"Ohhh—shit! Oh, shit—shit man, don't kill me. I ain't got shit."

"Shut da fuck up freak nigga! Yousa mad, wild, freak nigga!" yelled Baby G, as he backed up and turned the living room light on. "Nigga, pull yo' pants up and turn yo' fuck ass round," demanded Baby G.

"A'ight man, don't shoot," pleaded the victim, as he put the laptop down, pulled his pants up and turned around letting off two shots from a snub nose .38. Baby G already knew the victim had gotten low ducking the shots.

"It's me, Billy, don't shoot! I was just fucking wit' cha, bra," yelled Baby G, now stretched out on the floor laughing hard as shit. "Dis me, G—don't shoot," Baby G managed to get out in between laughs.

Billy walked and stood over Baby G to make sure it was really him.

"Baby G? Is you fucking serious? I thought you was in a coma or some shit. Da fuck you doing in my shit, wit' dat big raggedy ass pistol? Let me help you up."

"Nigga, don't fucking touch me! Go wash yo' fucking hands," stated Baby G, getting up and regaining his composure.

After washing his hands, Billy returned, now laughing about the situation. "Aye, man, don't tell nobody 'bout dis shit," pleaded Billy.

"Be easy, freak nigga. Everybody watches porn."

"It's good to see you, doe. A nigga ain't seen you since we flipped big Gene fat ass."

"Well, if you done whacking off, I came to get' cha. I need you to ride wit' me."

"A'ight, shid—I'm ready. Let me reload my shit first."

"Aye, man, leave dat fuck ass pea shooter here. I'ma be in the car."

"All I need is a Revolver, I'on need thirty shots," Billy muttered as he reloaded his .38 and left his apartment.

Khufu

Chapter 88

A Fucking Monopolist

Baby G slid down Avenue Q as he laced Billy Boy up on what he had planned.

"Damn, dis bitch clean as fuck! You grabbed dis fresh out da hospital?" asked Billy.

"You can't be ridin' better than dis if you keep it real wit'cha people dem."

"My people who?" asked Billy.

"Me, silly nigga! Come on, Billy, man. I need you to stay o-fifty."

"What's dat?"

"Damnit, man, on point, Billy. I need you to pay attention. If you don't, you gon' fuck around and get' cha self killed. Now, if you do the right thing you gon' make a lot of paper. Billy, I fuck wit' cha, but if you get jammed and you mention me—I'ma kill everything you love," expressed Baby G, looking Billy Boy dead in his eyes.

"Quit sizing my shit, bra! Nigga, I'm rock solid from da projects, to da prison, to da fucking grave!"

"Nigga, watch yo' tone in my shit. You might fuck around and upset old dirty silver," remarked Baby G, holding up his banga.

"Man, you need to take Clint Eastwood back his shit. Dat big rusty ass pistol." Billy's dinginess caused Baby G to laugh. "All bullshit aside, doe, I got' cha, my nigga. I'm wit' chu all da way," stated Billy.

"I hear you," replied Baby G, making a right on 13th Street.

"Da fuck you doing over here?"

"I'm just bending blocks, relax. Matter fact, I see something," said Baby G, pulling into a project complex known as the L.P. or the Lil Projects.

Baby G spotted an old friend that he did time with. They were from opposite sides but made a pact that they would continue their friendship, even though their homies didn't approve of it.

"Stay in da car. If shit go to looking crazy, do you."

"Say less," assured Billy, pulling his lil .38.

Baby G hopped out of his i8 in a red Ferrari shirt, black Ferrari jeans and a pair of exclusive all red wicker Air Forces.

"Mane man. What dey do, Oliver?" asked Baby G as he approached Oliver and dapped him up.

"Baby G, what's going on, my nigga? I see you flamed up like a mothafucka now."

"You know I gotta stay dripping."

"Okay, drip on playa," stated Oliver looking over his shoulder seeing his lil homies approaching on the creep.

He waved them off, letting them know to stand down, then continued his conversation with Baby G.

"So, what brings you to this dark side of town?" questioned Oliver.

"Shid, I was just bending through the city. I seen you and figured I'd scream at' cha."

"I respect dat. Shid, I just been cooling you know, getting to this paper. Look like you been doing the same."

"Yeah, speaking of getting to da paper, I got something I think you'll vibe with."

"Anything dealing with money, I can most def vibe with."

"Shoot me da math, I'ma pull up on ya in a couple days," asserted Baby G.

"Say no more," remarked Oliver.

After exchanging numbers, Baby G hopped back in his whip and pulled off.

"You a'ight?" Baby G asked Billy.

"Yeah, I thought I was gon' have to flip one of dem niggas."

"They was just doing what they was supposed to do. It's all good."

"I don't even like this side of town," noted Billy.

"Yeah, I know. It's like a whole different type of world on this side of town. The air tastes different and all," added Baby G.

"Then why the fuck was you just hollering at a nigga from the tray?"

"Cuz I'ma fucking monopolist. We from dat same gang culture, we just live by two different philosophies. Being the real niggas dat we are, we can put our differences to the side and get rich."

"I can dig it," asserted Billy.

"As you should." Baby G's phone rang displaying Shenida's number.

"What's good, baby girl?"

"Hey, G baby, everything's in motion," said Shenida.

"Did you put da LLC in the name I told you to?"

"Yeah, Patty's Seafood. I found a cook and a plug on seafood. I paid D-Dog the rest of his money too."

"A nigga like me appreciate you, doe."

"*Appreciate me?* Dat's all?"

"You know a nigga love you girl."

"Shid, I'm on my Drake shit. I'm gon' need you to say something, baby," she sang.

"You a trip. So, who is da cook?"

"I didn't know if you would approve, but I gave D-Dog the job."

"Damn, I forgot dat nigga can cook. He family, so he good."

"You gon' serve out da spot or you gon' find somebody else?"

"Yeah, I'ma let Billy do it."

"Billy who?" asked Shenida.

"Billy Boy, who else?"

"Come on now, G. You know all dat boy cheese ain't on his cracker!"

"Bye, Shenida!"

"What dat be 'bout?" asked Billy.

"I'ma holla at' chu later 'bout it."

"What da fuck is an LLC?"

"Limited Liability Corporation," stated Baby G, pulling into Billy's driveway.

"So, when we gon' get to da money?" asked Billy.

"Next time I pull up on ya, I'ma have something for ya."

"Already."

Khufu

Chapter 89

Dis Shit Crazy

After dropping Billy off, Baby G stopped by the liquor store then went by the tire shop and grabbed some molly and loud. He kicked it with Po Boy and discussed a few numbers on work then departed across the street to the carwash and backed in. Baby G hated the taste of molly but loved how it made him feel. He ate a gram then drowned it with Remy and sparked a blunt as he waited on some money to pull up. Ten minutes later, Baby G was feeling the effects of the molly as he listened to Nipsey Hussle talk that shit.

Royalties, publishing plus I own my masters/I be damn if I slave for some white cracker/I been mapping this out, I hit da heist backwards/Hopping out da '85 in Reebok Classics.

Baby G was zoned out until a red 2020 Kia pulled up. Moments later, a lil tenderoni hopped out, standing five feet in a tight ass Fashion Nova sweat suit.

"Damn, bae look like Natural Nikkie from Love and Hip-Hop Miami," Baby G stated to himself. "Oooweee, look at dat lil fat pussy," muttered Baby G, hopping out of his car to approach the young woman.

He could clearly see a dude on the passenger side but ignored him. Baby G figured that if a man would sit in the car while his woman washed it he was not a man at all. In fact, in his mind he was pussy.

She saw Baby G approaching and even though her dude was in the car, she liked what she saw. Without words Baby G walked right up to her, lifted her chin and kissed her in the mouth, sparing no tongue.

"Uh-uhhh, boy! What is you doing? My dude in the car, you tripping."

"Am I?" asked Baby G, then he looked into the Kia and waved at her dude.

The guy got out of the car but didn't approach. Another sign of weakness.

"Bra, dat's my baby mama. What the fuck you got going on?"

"Aye check dis out, playboy. Gone ahead and get back in da car while I holla at Miss Lady." The look in Baby G's eyes and the bulge on his hip made the guy hesitate.

"Man, this shit crazy."

"I know it. It be like that sometimes. You'll be a'ight, just gon' get cha ass back in the car where it's safe," noted Baby G.

After watching Baby G demonstrate, her pussy was now wet as a jellyfish.

"Oh, my God, you is really crazy. Who are you?"

"I'm, Baby G, baby. What's yo name?"

"I'm Unita."

"Unita, I like dat," said Baby G, licking his lips tweaking on the molly.

"You said yo' name is Baby G? Ain't chu throwing a birthday bash at the Elk's lounge?"

"Yeah, dat's me. Fuck all dat doe, let me take you out to eat."

"My nigga is right there!"

"So, what dat mean? What chu don't like food?"

"Yeah, but I'on know. You just too much," exclaimed Unita.

"Where you stay, I'ma pull up and get chu."

"I'm on thirty-third off of Louisiana, apartment twenty-seven."

"A'ight, lil mama. I'm in ya chest in about an hour," declared Baby G, then headed back to his whip.

As soon as he reached his vehicle. Off Top pulled up right beside him and got out with a brown paper bag.

"What's good, big homie?" asked Baby G, as he embraced Off Top.

"Ain't nothing you know, getting to the money. Dat's thirty, all blue faces," stated Off Top handing Baby G the bag.

"Already!"

"Look like you feeling good, my boy," Off Top implied, showing all twenty gold teeth.

"Yeah, I'm jigging a lil piece," admitted Baby G.

"Ain't nothing wrong with it. Listen, let me ask you something. When the last time you talked to your sister?"

"It's been a few weeks, why? She missing or some shit?"

"Nall, I was just asking. Ain't nothing. Look I'm finna move around and make a few plays," pronounced Off Top.

"Already. Hit me if you need me, bra."

"No questions," replied Off Top.

****

The sun had just settled on the West side of the city when Baby G arrived at his apartment on top of the brown store. He went in, put the money up, grabbed some coke and rubbers then headed out. Normally, the molly had Baby G on point, but the thought of sucking Unita's lil fat pussy had his mind's eye clouded. As soon as Baby G came off the last step, a man slipped from behind the dumpster pointing a long nose .22 at his face.

"You know what dis is, young blood, don't make me change you."

Baby G cursed himself for slipping, knowing that it was a blind side by the steps. The more the perpetrator advanced, Baby G started to put a name to the face. It was an old head named Steel Wheel who used to be posted at Veron Dixon when Baby G was pitching small time crack. Baby G's hesitation angered Steel Wheel, causing him to swipe the pistol across Baby G's face, scraping him above the right eye. Baby G fell to the ground and curled up.

"I ain't gon' ask you again, young blood."

"A'ight, man, be cool. Dis shit ain't nothing, you can get it," pleaded Baby G.

Steel Wheel stood over Baby G with murder in his eyes when noise came from under the steps, startling Steel and causing him to look away briefly.

Boc!

Baby G blew a chunk out the side of Steel's face and rolled over before his body could fall on him. The noise under the steps was a smoker named Foots. The Arab store owners always ran him off, but tonight Baby G was glad they didn't. Baby G ran to Foots, reached in his pocket and handed him a fist full of hundreds.

"Bet dat up, Foots. You ain't seen shit ya hear me?"

"You damn right, I ain't seen shit, nephew," replied Foots, as he tucked the money and got ghost.

Moments later, the owner of the store ran out with a .357 pointed at Baby G.

"Hold it, motherfucker!" screamed Wolly.

"Whoa, dis me, ock! Don't shoot me, G."

"What the fuck happened, buddy? Who is that on the ground?"

"Some old nigga tried to rob me. I had to hit him ock, my bad, man."

"Damnit, Baby G! This is my place of business. Go ahead, I got it, buddy. Hurry up now, go!"

"Good looking, ock," replied Baby G, as he hopped in his whip and crept off.

Chapter 90

Rules of Engagement

"Damn, old head almost had me," Baby G pronounced to himself, as he moved through traffic, smoking a Newport laced with coke.

Baby G never served out of the apartment, so he wondered what made him a target. Maybe it was dis fucking car, he thought as he glanced in the rearview mirror and noticed the blood splattered on his face and head. Laughing to himself, Baby G pulled his shirt off and wiped his face as he thought of how a smoker had just saved his life. Pulling another drag from his cigarette, Baby G's phone rang, displaying an unknown number.

"Who da fuck is dis?" yelled G.

"Dis me, we need to talk."

"Me who?"

"Dis me, yo' sister C.C. Can we please talk?"

Baby G laughed. "Oh, so now you wanna talk? What chu wanna talk about, huh? What chu—what'chu want me to come check ya tires again?"

"Baby G, bra I didn't know. I'm sorry."

"Dis shit wild! Now you sorry? You know what? Da shit dat hurt the most, is dat you chose sides!"

Baby G hung up on C.C. and was now pulling into Shenida's new home on 29th and Avenue E. He smoked another cigarette as he thought about the conversation he just had with his sister. He loved her but knew that sometimes love can get you killed. He lived by the rules of engagement and C.C. had already engaged. Baby G was all in. The front door opened and Shenida stood in the doorway parrot toed. She had on some red satin Prada shorts and top, displaying heavy camel toe and cleavage.

"You coming in or what?" asked Shenida. Baby G hopped out and patted Shenida on her pussy before walking in. "Don't start nothing if you ain't gon' fuck nothing," she stated.

"I got clothes over here?"

"Yeah, why?"

"I just had to hit a nigga. I need to clean up."

"The towels and wash rags in the hallway closet," said Shenida, as she finished rolling her blunt and sparked it. She then sashayed down the hallway into the bathroom with Baby G. "So, what's up, baby, what happened?" she asked, grabbing a sponge to wash his back.

"I slid to da spot to put some money up. When I came out a nigga came from behind the dumpster. Da nigga had me to, Ma. Mothafuckin' Foots was under the stairs and shit. He must have rolled over on dat cardboard or some shit, I'on know. But whatever he did caused da nigga to look away. I guess you know."

"He dead?" asked Shenida.

"Is yo pussy fat?"

"Hell yeah, he's dead as fuck," laughed Shenida.

"Wolly took care of da situation, doe. Don't go over there for a few days, let shit cool off."

"Ain't no traffic coming dat way. He must have seen you hop outta dat damn i8. Dat's why you need me with you at all times, Daddy."

"I got this shit," assured Baby G.

"A'ight, I hear you. I'ma get rid of deez clothes and put some fresh ones out for you. Where da banga at?"

"It's in my jeans."

"I'ma pull another one out for you and get rid of dis one. You gotta vest over here, too. Make sho you put it on."

"Dat's why I love you, ma."

"Love you too, Daddy."

Chapter 91

Catch Me in Traffic

Baby G pulled into the apartment complex on 33rd, parked and left the car running. He poured a cup, ate some molly and rolled a blunt.

"Play Rockstar by Da Baby," he spoke into his bluetooth, then put flame to the blunt and vibed to the music, feeling every word Da Baby was spittin'.

Brand new Lamborghini fuck a cop car/Pistol in my lap like I'ma cop/Have you ever met a real nigga rock star?

Dis ain't no guitar bitch dis a Glock

The molly mixed with what Da Baby was saying had Baby G ready to kill again. He cocked his Glock 17, killed the engine and hopped out. It was a few niggas hanging out who stopped all goofing off when they saw Baby G approach in all-black. A few of them even clutched but Baby G was unfazed. He was God amongst men. Baby G looked them all in the eyes as he floated right past them and headed up the stairs. When he reached apartment 27, Unita's baby daddy was outside sitting in a chair. Baby G ignored him and knocked on the door.

"Bra, is you serious? What the fuck is you doing?" asked Anthony.

"Da fuck it looks like, nigga! I'm doing me," stated Baby G, when the door to the apartment opened.

"Oh, my God. I didn't believe you was coming for real," said Unita.

"Believe it, baby girl. You ready?"

"Mannn, dis shit crazy," cried Anthony, as he kept rubbing his hands over his face as if he would wake up from the nightmare he was living.

"I thought you was playing, so I went ahead and cooked."

"I'on play games, Ma. So, you gon' invite me in or what?"

"Come on in, I guess."

"A'ight, playboy, I'ma holla at cha. Burn up!" demanded Baby G.

"Man, this where I live. Where I'm supposed to go?" cried Anthony.

"You'll think of something."

"Man, this shit crazy! Bra, can I at least get a cigarette?"

Baby G went in his pocket and gave Anthony two cigarettes, intentionally forgetting to tell him that they were laced with coke.

"Thanks, bra," stated Anthony.

"Nall, thank you," replied Baby G, as he entered the apartment and locked the door behind him.

When Baby G turned around Unita was standing there with her hands on her hips in a T-shirt that sat right above her camel toe.

"Are you hungry?" asked Unita.

Baby G walked up on her and kissed her in the mouth.

"You taste good."

"You think so?" Unita asked, leaning in for another kiss.

Baby G cuffed her bite sized cheeks and lifted her in the air. When Unita wrapped her legs around Baby G he could feel the heat from her throbbing pussy as they continued to kiss passionately like they'd known each other for years. Baby G carried her to the kitchen, knocked everything off the table and laid her on it.

"What da hell's going on in there?" yelled Anthony from outside.

The sounds of broken dishes caused him to peek through the window, but he couldn't see into the kitchen. Baby G ripped Unita's panties off and almost lost his mind at what lay before him. Unita had the prettiest pussy he'd ever seen. It was pleasantly plump, cleaned shaven with the cutest clit ever. Unita even had a beauty mark on her right coochie lip that he found profoundly attractive. He grabbed her legs and pinned her knees to her chest. This position caused her pussy to protrude outwardly, exciting Baby G all the more. He sucked her right lip where the beauty mark was, then slid to her clit.

"Sss—ohh—" she moaned, arching her back.

Baby G tongue kissed, sucked and licked on Unita's clit relentlessly. He pulled back and stared at the pussy amazed at how pretty and tasteful it was, then attacked again.

284

"Ohh—yes—shh—shit!" screamed Unita.

"Umm-hmm!" boasted Baby G, as he flattened his tongue out and moved it over her clit slowly from right to left, up and down in a circular motion.

This technique caused Unita to rotate her hips slowly, throwing her pussy in Baby G's face. He cuffed her whole vagina with his mouth, blew softly over her clit and began to hum. Unita bucked as a mini spurt shot into Baby G's mouth. After tasting and swallowing her nectar, Baby G could tell she ate a lot of fruit.

"Please fuck me now. Fuck me right now, baby. Please, put dat dick in me," pleaded Unita, as she rose up and started pulling on his pants.

Baby G grabbed her aggressively under her chin and put two fingers in her mouth forcing her to suck them. He then forced her to lay back down on the table.

"Take your shirt off," demanded Baby G.

Unita complied, then started playing with her clit. Baby G removed his black Versace T-shirt and bulletproof vest. He placed his Glock on the counter and stepped out of his Versace sweatpants and briefs.

Damn, this nigga hood as fuck, thought Unita, cumming for the second time.

Baby G walked around the table and grabbed her under her armpits, pulling her towards him. The only thing that hung over the table was Unita's head and neck. Baby G grabbed his dick and rubbed pre-cum all over her lips and face.

"Um, Daddy, put it in my mouth!"

Baby G grabbed her by the neck, cutting her air and words short, then pushing every inch in her mouth. To his surprise, she had no gag reflex. Unita moaned and massaged his balls as he slow-stroked her mouth.

"Shhhhitt, dat's right-sss-eat dat dick up!" commanded Baby G, slightly weak in the knees.

Unita moaned louder as she grabbed Baby G by the back of his thighs and pulled him toward her mouth, encouraging him to speed it up. Baby G obliged and turned it all the way up, fucking her face

285

rapidly as he cuffed her perfect sized breasts while pinching her nipples.

"Sss—awww—shit! Fffuck! You an animal," declared Baby G, after cumming in her mouth.

Baby G snatched out of her mouth, walked around the table, and pulled her to the edge.

"You finna beat dis pussy ain't you, Daddy?"

Baby G pushed down in Unita slowly. She was so wet, warm and tight that Baby G had to snatch out of her to keep from cumming. He beat the top of her clit with his dick briefly, then slid back in.

"Damn dis pussy wet!" moaned Baby G.

"Dis yo pussy, Daddy," cried Unita.

Baby G grabbed her right leg, pushed it toward her left one, turning her sideways so her walls were now clamping around him tighter. He grabbed her neck with his left hand and her shoulder with his right and proceeded to power fuck Unita violently.

"Aahhh—ssshit! Fuck me, nigga! Yesss!" she moaned, as she came back-to-back.

Baby G stopped mid-stroke, opened her legs, and cuffed under her thighs. "Put cha arms around my neck," commanded Baby G.

"Yes, Daddy," replied Unita.

Baby G lifted her off the table and carried her to the living room where Anthony had a clear view. Baby G stood in the middle of the living room and bounced Unita chaotically up and down on his dick. Anthony watched in disbelief with tears in his eyes as the mother of his child screamed another man's name in pure bliss.

"Whooo—yeaaaa—ssss-haaaa-fuck!" cried Unita.

Baby G slowed down, now bouncing her at a steady pace, moving in and out of her in deep circles.

"Oooweee—daddy—yesss—throw dat dick, daddy!"

Baby G stopped, then laid Unita on the floor. She grabbed her legs and put them behind her head, driving Baby G insane.

"Oh shit," pronounced Baby G, getting into the push up position and pushing deep down inside her.

"Sss-haaa-fuck me," cried Unita.

286

She was so wet that Anthony could hear her pussy smacking from outside. Baby G was now giving her all he had, trying to throw his back out in the process.

"Whoooa—okay—sss—okay, daddy," cried Unita.

"Okay what?"

"I feel you, daddy—please! Ffffuckkkk—Daddy don't-sss-don't stop, daddy!"

"Who da fuck yo', daddy?"

"Shii—sss—you—my—ssss—you my daddy!"

"What's daddy's name?"

"Baby Geeeee!"

"Say fuck dat nigga!"

"Ssss-whooo-fuck'em daddy!"

"Fuck who bitch?"

"Anthony! Sss-whoooo, God, fuck dat nigga-ohh—sshitt!" screamed Unita as she orgasmed and shook perpetually.

She squirted and contracted her vagina walls around Baby G, forcing him to cum right behind her. Baby G laid on Unita to catch his breath, while she placed kisses on his neck and ear. She then turned him over and began to clean all of her juices off his dick.

"Unita!" yelled Anthony from outside.

She ignored him and continued to clean Baby G with her mouth. Unita had some of the best pussy and mouth he ever had, but he knew he couldn't afford to fall weak for a chick who'd just put her baby's father out for a dose of real nigga dick. Baby G pushed her to the side and slid in the kitchen to get dressed. She followed behind him firing question after question.

"So, when I'ma see you again," she cried.

"You got a nigga, baby girl."

"That ain't stop you from fucking da shit outta me doe."

"Come on, now, you a bad lil' bitch. You know I had to see what dat pussy do."

"I just felt like we had a connection," pleaded Unita.

"Yeah, we do. Sexually, nothing more," assured Baby G.

"Come on, now Baby G, you was kissing me passionately and shit and you fucked me raw. What da fuck was all that?"

"Da heat of da moment type shit. You know how dat shit go. Speaking of fucking you raw if you gave me some shit I'ma kill you. Yo' soft ass nigga and yo' baby!" threatened Baby G, as he headed toward the door.

"Nigga, you got me fucked up. This pussy A1."

"Yeah, a'ight."

"Fa real, when can I see you?" cried Unita one last time.

"Catch me in traffic," asserted Baby G, before walking out of the apartment.

Chapter 92

Get Da Fuck Outta Here!

Off Top sat in his Benz and smoked a blunt of moon rock as he replayed the conversations that he had with C.C. and Baby G. Something didn't smell right, and he hated being perplexed.

"Dis shit don't make no sense," Off Top muttered, as he stepped out of his car and leaned against it still smoking. Trying to get the full effect of the high grade, Off Top took a deep pull from the blunt and started to cough uncontrollably. He hunched over drooling and spitting when something caught his eye.

"Da fuck?" questioned Off Top, as he picked up seven shell casings and headed in the house. C.C. was at the dining room table, scrolling Facebook when he came in.

"Hey, bae, you hungry?" asked C.C.

"Nall I'm good," he replied, sitting at the table still smoking his blunt.

C.C. looked up and noticed him gazing at her strangely.

"What's up, bae?"

"I'on know shid—you tell me."

"What chu talking 'bout?" she asked.

"I saw Baby G earlier today."

"Okay, and?"

"He told me he ain't talked to you in weeks. So, my question to you is, why the fuck you lied about y'all going to da shooting range?"

"I didn't lie to you, bae. You know Baby G be on all dem drugs. He be forgetting shit," proclaimed C.C.

"Before I left, I heard Machi ask you why you shot at Baby G?"

"You know dem kids be—" Before she could finish her lie, he laid the shell casings on the table.

"So, what da fuck is dis? When we start lying to each other? And why the fuck was you shooting at Baby G? Dat's yo' fucking brother!"

Tears fell down her face as her bottom lip quivered. "I gotta tell you something, bae, but dis stays between us."

"I'm listening."

"First, I'm sorry for lying to you. You know I would never lie to you unless I had to. I didn't wanna involve you in my bullshit."

"What bullshit? You don't do shit, but cook, clean and count money. What is you talking about?"

"I shot Baby G. I'm the one who put him in the hospital."

"Get da fuck outta here!" yelled Off Top.

"Will you just listen and stop talking please?"

Once he saw that she was serious, he calmed down and listened. She broke everything down about her, Yana, Cee, Mundo, and Baby G leaving out no details. When she was finished explaining, he stared at her with mixed emotions.

"So, you telling me the mother of my kids is some type of fucking assassin?"

"I'm not no damn assassin, but I do know how to bust my shit. Shid, you the one who bought me the gun!" she pronounced, wiping the tears from her eyes.

"Yeah, but I ain't think yo' ass was gon' be playing proud Mary and shit, putting holes all in ya brother. I been doing bidness with Baby G lately. If he didn't fuck with me like he do? He coulda exed me out to get back at chu. You ain't have no bidness getting in dat beef. This shit puts me in a fucked up position."

"I'm sorry, bae."

"You gotta make shit right wit' cha brothers."

"I tried to call Baby G and talk to him. He ain't got no rap, he wants me dead."

"Nall you ain't doing no dying. I'll kill him myself before dat happens. Trust me, if he wanted you dead, you woulda been dead by now."

"Why you say dat?"

"Just think about it. He's making good money with me. Plus, he loves Hezeron and Machi. All dat picking them up from school and catching you at ya mama's house is just mind games. He just fucking wit' chu, bae."

"Mannn—I'on know about all dat," replied C.C.

****

Shantel sat up and ate vanilla ice cream and a pickle while Baby G rubbed her belly. He hadn't been home in three weeks, but Shantel was still happy to see him. They had been having sex three days straight and Baby G couldn't get enough of that pregnant pussy. At one point, Shantel thought she was going into labor three months early.

"You know you done missed all my doctor appointments Baby G."

"I know, bae, I'm sorry. When da next one?"

"Tomorrow at nine-thirty. We get to see what we having."

"You already know, we having a lil G, baby."

"So, I saw on Facebook you having a lil birthday bash," she stated, changing the subject.

"Yeah, I'ma go hang out a lil' piece."

"You ever found out who shot cha?"

"Nall, I ain't heard nothing," he lied.

"You sure you wanna have a party not knowing who shot cha?"

"I'll be a'ight, bae, don't trip."

"I'ma put some life insurance on yo' ass, cuz you out here reckless."

"Dat might be a good idea," he implied.

Before Shantel could share more of her thoughts his phone rang.

"Awww—here we go," cried Shantel.

"I ain't going nowhere, bae," Baby G assured. "Yeah, what up?"

"Bro, this Major."

"What's up wit' it?"

"Everything is everything, bro."

"A'ight, I'ma send people through."

"I'm here, bro, fuck with me."

"Already!"

Baby G dialed Shenida's number and she picked up on the second ring.

"What's up, baby?"

"Aye, go grab dat from my white boy and put dat up."

"Okay, daddy, I went by the spot and the Arab Wolly told me to tell you everything's good."

"Oh, yeah? Shid—gon' ahead and put D-Dog on dem pots and open up."

"I hear you."

"Listen, I thought about what chu said about Billy. I ain't gone let him serve out da spot, I'ma put him on something else. As for that last thing you cooked up, go 'head and do you."

"Okay. What chu doing right now? I miss you, Daddy."

"I'm with baby mama, catch me later."

"I'm finna swing through. Come outside and let me eat dat dick up real quick."

Baby G hung up on Shenida and found Shantel staring at him.

"Who was dat?" questioned Shantel.

"Dat was my bidness partner. We opening a seafood shack, Patty's Seafood."

"You named it after yo' mama?"

"Yeah, I ain't tell her yet doe."

"You be having so much shit going on and don't be telling me shit," cried Shantel.

"I know, baby, I'm sorry. I'ma do better," assured Baby G, opening Shantel's legs and latching on her clit.

It had been a while since Shantel had some head, so she was going bananas gripping the sheets, biting a pillow and calling on a higher power through clenched teeth.

"Yesss!" she moaned, as she came back-to-back.

Baby G had mastered a technique to where he could lick and suck the clit at the same time, and he was applying it to Shantel relentlessly. Shantel came so many times that she started hyperventilating.

"Sss—why you—sss—oww—why you be keeping this from meeee?"

Chapter 93

Ride With Me

C.C. rented a Chevy Malibu and had the windows tinted by Baby Haitian on 29th at the carwash. She was bending through the city, smoking girl scout cookies, vibing to Megan the Stallion.

Acting-stupid-what's happenin
What's happenin? I'ma savage!

She turned the music down as she pulled into Yana's new home and blew the horn. Moments later, Yana came to the door in a yellow sundress, standing five months pregnant.

"Who dat is?" Yana yelled with her hands on her hips.

C.C. cracked her window to show her face, then let it back up. Once Yana was standing at her window, C.C. cracked it again and told Yana to come ride with her.

"Hold up. Let me go lock my house up," Yana stated, then spun around to go lock up.

C.C. was still smoking when Yana plopped down on the passenger seat.

"You want me to put dis out?" asked C.C.

"Hell nall, girl. I can't smoke, but I love the smell of me some weed. Blow some in my face," implied Yana.

"Girl, you a trip," C.C. said, after blowing smoke in Yana's face.

"Who all this food for?"

"I bought us some subway and shit. We finna go to the pier and watch the waterfall on Taylor's Creek. I got a lot on my mind, girl, I just need some peace. I'm finna smoke my lil weed, listen to the waterfall and eat my damn food."

"Hell yeah, shid—I can use some solace and tranquility. I been stressed out over yo brother."

"He won't be in there much longer, girl, relax," pronounced C.C., pulling up close to the gate that sat at the pier.

"I hope so, girl. I'm horny as hell," replied Yana, while helping C.C. get the food out of the car.

After walking down a few steps, they walked out to the edge of the pier and had a seat, dangling their feet. C.C. lit another blunt, while Yana violated her turkey sub.

"Damn that water is dark as hell. If I fell in there, I'll probably die of a damn heart attack from being so damn scared," said Yana.

"Shit, me too. You see dat sign say five hundred feet, swim at ya own risk? I betcha all kinda shit in there," C.C. added, blowing smoke out of her nose.

Yana took a big sip from her pink lemonade and sat it back down. Moments later, she held her throat and looked at C.C. as she began to choke up spurts of blood.

"Girl, what da hell wrong wit' chu?" C.C. stood and patted Yana on the back. "You okay?" asked C.C., as she looked around, then kicked Yana off the pier into the murky, alligator and snake infested water.

Yana couldn't swim and on top of that she was five months pregnant. C.C. watched her flop around unable to scream due to the crushed glass that C.C. had mixed in her drink. Once she finally went under, C.C. grabbed all evidence and left the scene. Back in the car, she smoked her blunt as tears fell from her eyes. C.C. loved Yana, but she felt as if Yana was the main cause of her brothers beefing. On top of that, C.C. knew that the baby wasn't Mundo's it was Cee's.

****

Baby G had been at the doctor's office all morning with Shantel and was elated that he was having a little boy. After singing *I told you so* to Shantel all the way home, he dropped her off and headed to his apartment on top of the brown store. While weaving through traffic, he pulled out his phone and called Shenida.

"Hello."

"What's good, baby girl?"

"Hey, bae, I'm just moving around, getting rid of dis shit. What's good wit' chu?"

"I just found out I'm having a baby boy, Ma."

"Congrats, baby, I'm happy for you," stated Shenida.

"Already. Check it doe, I'm headed to da spot. Where you put dat at?"

"Everything is duffled up on the bed, Daddy."

"Already. I'ma hit' chu later, love you."

"Love you too, baby."

Baby G pulled in the back of the brown store and hopped out. On his way up to his apartment he viewed the stained blood of a man who had tried to take his life. A man who would have killed him had it not been for a smoker. The thought of it made him think of Foots. Baby G slid into his apartment and got trap ready. After taking a hot shower, he got dipped in Armani Exchange from head to toe, grabbed three duffle bags and loaded them in his whip.

"Hey, Baby G, buddy. How are you?" asked Wolly in a strong Arabian accent, startling Baby G causing him to reach for his banga.

"Whoa, don't shoot Baby G, buddy. It's me Wolly."

"Damn, what up with it, Wolly?"

"I should be asking you the same. How have you been sleeping? Are you okay?" asked Wolly concerned.

"Yeah, I'm good. Dat wasn't my first time changing a nigga form. Listen, I appreciate what chu did for me Wolly for real," expressed Baby G, going in his pocket to pay Wolly for his good deed.

"Put that money back in your pocket. Your money's no good with me. My father and your grandfather good friends."

"Oh, yeah, how good?"

"Conversation for later, buddy, okay. Just keep safe my friend."

"A'ight, Wolly, I respect dat, but I'm pullin' back up on you 'bout dat," Baby G declared getting in the car.

"Okay, buddy," replied Wolly, waving before heading back inside his store.

Khufu

Chapter 94

Dis Bidness

Baby G pulled in front of Billy's apartment and dialed his number.

"Yeah!" Billy screamed through the phone.

"Fuck you screaming fa? Nigga, come outside," instructed Baby G.

Moments later, Billy came outside and got in the passenger's seat.

"What it do?" asked Billy.

Baby G looked Billy in his face and noticed he'd gotten 666 tattooed on his forehead and a pyramid on his left cheek.

"Aye, Billy—my dude. You know I'm on dat sinister shit, but my nigga what da fuck?"

"You know what it is, my nigga. Straight beast mode," confirmed Billy.

"Oh, yeah? Animal beast type shit, huh?"

"Yeah, dis how I'm coming!"

"Oh, okay. Shid, so I'on even need guns no moe. I can just pull up on some niggas wit' chu and let chu post up with dat on yo' face. Dem niggas ain't gon' want no smoke," Baby G clowned laughing hard while clutching his stomach. "What chu supposed to be? DC Young Fly or some shit?"

"What chu a fucking comedian now?" questioned Billy, slightly angered.

"Let me ask you something. You ever hit a nigga's shit?" asked Baby G.

"What chu mean?" Billy asked, confused.

"You ever front rowed a nigga's mama? I'm talking about standing over a nigga after you hit him and watching his whole facial expression change when life leaves his body. I'm asking you if you ever killed a nigga before?"

"Come on, my nigga. Dis killa county, da fuck kinda question is dat?"

"Well, I wanna be the first to tell you. If you ever go in front of a judge with dat shit on yo' face boy, you fucked over. I'm talking mashed taters and baked beans. Dem crackers gon' make a meal out cha ass!" Baby G stated, laughing harder than before.

"Man, why you call me out here? Cut da bullshit, my nigga," said Billy. "A'ight man, check it. You scared to trap out of yo' apartment?"

"Fuck no! Nigga, I'm with da shits!"

"Good." Baby G grabbed a duffle bag from the back seat and handed it to Billy. "Listen, it's thirty pounds of wedding cake in there. I'm giving dem to you for two thousand a piece. You can move em for twenty-five or better. Just give me fifty bands, bra. Can you handle dat?"

"Yeah bih, I got chu. I'ma have da whole projects swanging!"

"A'ight, my nigga, I'ma scream at cha in a few days. One more thing before you leave doe. If you play with my money you gon' be the next nigga I stand over. You already know I'on give no fucks about dat shit you done tatted on yo' face. Dis bidness!"

****

Shenida had been making moves all over the city since sunrise. It was a little over twelve in the afternoon when she pulled into Orangewood. Orangewood is an apartment complex at the end of 29th Street, one way in and one way out. A soon as she parked her truck, Pink Lip Joe approached and got in on the passenger side. Everybody called him Pink Lip Joe because he was born with pink lips that looked as if they'd been burned. His unusual look didn't hurt his chances with the ladies. In fact, it only made Joe hustle harder, which is what attracted most women. He had a mouth full of gold and a few whips with all the works. Unfortunately, Shenida wasn't impressed with his hustle or tricked out cars. She knew the sick twisted methods he used to trick young hood rats out of their panties.

"What's up, Shenida?" asked Joe. "You already know what time it is."

"Damn, loosen up, baby girl. I'm just speaking to you. By the way, you looking real snackish and shit. I'm feeling dat lace front."

"And you looking real furtive and shit. I ain't feeling dat," she stated.

"Furtive? Da fuck dat mean?" Joe asked, perplexed.

"Fuck all dat. Nigga, I got fifteen cookies left, you grabbing one or nall?"

"Strictly bidness, huh? Shid, you gon' let me get em for five hunnid a piece?"

"Not today. Dey a stack a piece, now you copping or not?" Shenida was aggravated.

"Yeah, let me get em," he replied, reaching in his pockets and handing Shenida fifteen thousand.

After putting the money in her Prada bag, she handed Joe the Styrofoam trays.

"What chu bought a nigga something to eat? I knew you was feeling my drip," proclaimed Joe, licking his pink lips.

"Nigga, dat's work. It's five cookies in each tray. In a few days I'ma have pure molly on deck. Hit me if you trying to do something."

"Shid, I'm trying to do something to you. What's up? Let a nigga suck on dat lil fat pussy," asserted Joe, licking his lips again.

"Listen, errbody know Shenida ain't turning down no head, but da way yo' lips set up I'ma gon' head and pass on dat, cat daddy. Fuck with me if you tryna grab some molly doe."

"You talking real crazy, Ma. Talking about how my lips set up. Girl deez lips work! Da hell you talking about? I see what type of time you on, so I'ma gon' and get out cha way. I'ma hit chu when I'm ready. Now stay safe out 'chere, Ma," Joe stated, opening the door to exit.

"You mean off safety," replied Shenida, pulling a FN 9mm from her Prada bag, letting Joe get a glimpse before closing the door.

Khufu

Chapter 95

Bidness over Bullshit

After leaving Billy's apartment Baby G picked his mother up and headed to Patty's Seafood. Baby G's mother had no idea about the seafood restaurant he had put in her name.

"So, what's been going on? I haven't seen you around in a while," implied Patty.

"I just been moving around a lil piece. You know how dat go ma."

"You can't sit still for nothing. God lee boy! Somebody just tried to kill you. That don't scare you none?"

"I'm a'ight, Ma. I can't die but once. Don't worry yo' self, I got me," assured Baby G.

"Okay, I hear you. I just want chu to be careful cuz deez niggas will kill you for anything around here."

"I hear you, Ma."

"A'ight. I like yo' car. What chu doing to get a car like dis?"

"Ma, you asking too many questions," he pronounced, pulling into the restaurant.

"Boy, I'm yo mama! I can ask you what I want. What chu talking about?" Patty looked up and saw her name on the restaurant.

"Oh, somebody done opened a seafood place with my name on it. That's crazy. I should sue they butts!"

"How you gon' sue yo' self?" asked Baby G getting out of the car.

Patty got out behind him clutching an old ass Guess purse. "Boy what chu talking about sue myself?"

D-Dog had already saw Baby G pull up, so he buzzed the front door open. Baby G walked in and dapped his stepfather up.

"What's good, D-Dog? You got it smelling good as a pair of Doja Cat panties in dis mothafucka!"

"You know how I get down, baby," bragged D-Dog.

"What chu doing in these people restaurant cooking?" asked Patty.

"Oh, you ain't told her yet?" D-Dog asked Baby G.

"Told me what?" questioned Patty, looking back and forth at Baby G and D-Dog.

"Mama, dis yo restaurant. I bought it for you."

"Boy stop playing with me. I told you about lying to yo' mama."

"I ain't never lied to you about nothing. Dis yo shit fa real, mama."

Patty looked at D-Dog for confirmation.

"It's yours for real, Patty, he ain't lying to you," assured D-Dog.

Patty looked at Baby G with wide eyes. "Boy, how can you afford to buy me a restaurant?"

"Mama, just say thank you. I got bidness to handle."

Patty looked Baby G in his eyes, hugged his neck and told him she loved him. She then turned around and punched D-Dog in the arm for not telling her.

"I'ma kick yo butt," she said to her husband playfully.

Baby G stepped outside and waited for Oliver to pull up. Before picking up his mother he called Oliver and told him to meet him on 23rd and Avenue D at the new seafood spot. At first Oliver was in a dubious state of mind about the meeting place, but Baby G assured his safety.

Moments later, Oliver pulled up in a Buick LeSabre with no tint. Baby G saw that he had two of his shooters in the back seat and a pretty redbone in the passenger seat. Oliver hopped out in a blue Adidas suit with some cocaine white shell toes and approached Baby G dapping him up.

"What dey do? I see you on yo' loc shit?" teased Baby G.

"Come on, now. You know I gotta stay trayed up. Blue is the true, baby," stated Oliver, as he looked around in a paranoid manner.

"I see you kinda 'noid, so I'ma speed dis up," Baby G asserted, opening his back door.

"Baby G!" yelled Patty, walking out to his car.

"What chu out here doing?"

"Oliver dis my nosy mama. Mama, dis Oliver."

"Nice to meet you ma'am."

"You too, Oliver. Now answer my question, boy. What chu out here doing?"

"My dog just came by to get him a seafood platter, Mama. Go get him one for me and double bag it for me please."

Patty looked at Baby G with a *I don't know what you really doing face*, then turned to go do as she was asked.

"Mom dukes seem cool," said Oliver.

"You mean nosy as hell."

"She just being caring, my nigga. Dat's what mothers do."

"I hear you. Check it doe, I'ma shoot you ten bricks of pure molly. I want eighty-five hunnid a piece. Dat's eighty-five bands. You can move dem shits for ten flat, cuff fifteen hunid a brick, dat's fifteen bands. Or you can tax niggas, I'on give a fuck. Just have my end right and we good. You cool with dat?"

"Cool beans, baby. I got you! You know I'ma hustler."

Moments later, Patty came out with Oliver's platter double bagged.

"Here you go, Oliver."

"Thank you, ma'am."

"Where my money at, boy?" questioned Patty.

Baby G laughed at his mother.

"He already paid me, Ma, I got it. Gone head, Mama, I'ma bring da money in there."

"Okay, bye Oliver, come again."

"Thank you, ma'am," Oliver replied before Patty went back inside.

"Give me dat extra bag she brought out here."

"Here," said Oliver, handing Baby G the extra bag and watching him load it with bricks of molly.

"Here be safe out there," encouraged Baby G.

"Always, homie. I'ma hit chu when I'm ready," replied Oliver, hopping in his whip and pulling off.

As soon as he pulled off, a cream-colored Delta '88 with a red top pulled up. A youngin hopped out with a medallion around his neck and rings on every finger. He also had a .40 Caliber with a dick on it, *street term for extended clip*. It was Pony Boy, who was four years younger than Baby G. He was a young hustler who preferred money over beef but would show his teeth when necessary.

"Baby G, my nigga. What da fuck you doing rapping with dem niggas from da tray? You got dem niggas posted on da three like shit sweet! My nigga, what's up?"

"First off, my nigga, put dat fucking gun up! My fucking moms in their nigga! Second, I'm 'bout bidness over bullshit any day. We getting money together."

"You eatin' with dem loc ass niggas?" yelled Pony Boy.

"Hell yeah. Dey money green, too. Me and you can get dis money, too, if you get past dat geographical street shit. Lil nigga, you can't tell me why y'all beefing. You know why? Cuz you wasn't even born when dis dumb ass beef started."

"Man, fuck all dat! What's up with dis *get money* shit you hollering about?"

"Look, lil nigga, I'ma front you ten bricks of molly, just bring me five bands a piece," pronounced Baby G.

"Shid, you ain't gotta front me shit," replied Pony Boy, going to his car and returning with a Chanel bag.

Pony Boy counted fifty thousand and handed it to Baby G.

"Come on, man, you know I do dis shit. I ain't got time to be owing a nigga shit!"

"I respect dat," replied Baby G, loading the molly in Pony Boy's Chanel bag.

"Fuck with me, lil homie."

"Dis where you at?" asked Pony Boy.

"If you see my whip, pull up. Dis my mama seafood spot."

"Say no more, big homie."

"Already!" replied Baby G.

Chapter 96

House of Meats

Four days later, Baby G was at the House of Meats with his mother getting food for her restaurant. Baby G strolled down Facebook while his mother loaded a cart and went on about how much she loved her new restaurant and how fast the food was selling out. Caught up on the hype surrounding his party, Baby G wasn't paying attention to what was in front of him and bumped into someone.

"Damn, my bad, Ma," explained Baby G.

When the young woman turned around Baby G saw that it was Unita.

"Well, I'll be damn. It's Mr. Hit and Run," stated Unita.

"Who is she?" asked Patty.

"Just a friend, Ma."

"She cute. How you doing, I'm Patty, his mama."

"Hey, Ms. Patty, I'm Unita. It's nice to meet chu. Y'all look like twins."

"I know, chile. People be thinking we sister and brother," added Patty.

"Cut it out, Ma."

"He trying to run me off, girl. Nice to meet you, Unita. I got a seafood spot on twenty third and Avenue D. You can stop by anytime."

"Okay, Ms. Patty. I'll be through there to see what you tasting like."

"Alright, I'ma hold you to that," replied Patty, strolling off.

"I like Ms. Patty. She just might be my new ma-in-law."

"Not a chance! Dat lil pussy got some power, but it ain't packing dat many watts," declared Baby G.

"Is dat right?" asked Unita standing parrot toed in a Chanel bodysuit.

Unita's pussy sat so perfectly in her body suit that it gave Baby G chill bumps, causing the hair to stand up on his arms and neck.

"Dat's what cha mouth say, but ya mind and dat bulge in yo'

pants saying some other shit," implied Unita, massaging Baby G's dick through his designer jeans. "When you gon' stand up in dis pussy again? She misses you so fucking much," moaned Unita, grabbing Baby G's hand and placing it on her meaty pussy. "You feel da heat venting off dis pussy?"

Baby G was low key fucked up about Unita but vowed never to fall for a woman of her caliber. He refused to love what made him weak.

"Listen, Unita, I fucks with cha but I'm on some other shit, right now. When I get time to play, I'll come jump up and down in dat stuff."

"What other shit you on?" she asked.

"I just want da money."

"What's wrong with me getting money wit' chu? What chu think I'm green or something?"

"Nall, it ain't dat. I just don't wanna have to kill you and dat po broke ass nigga 'bout my shit."

"You ain't gotta worry about dat nigga. I put him out the same night you climbed in dis pussy. I ain't gon' play wit' chu Baby G. I know about you and yo brother, the streets talk."

"A'ight, ma. I'ma bless you when I pull up, be ready."

"Okay, baby, I'ma be waiting now."

"I gotcha, dat's my word," promised Baby G, as he hugged her.

Squeezing her drug store cotton soft booty cheeks. He then left to catch up to his mother who was pushing her cart out of the store. Baby G took the cart from his mother and pushed it to the trunk of her 2020 Jeep Cherokee.

"That girl seems nice. Where did you meet her?" asked Patty, popping her trunk.

"At a carwash," replied Baby G, while loading the groceries in the trunk.

"Boy, don't put nothing on top of my eggs. You gon' break them," cried Patty as she leaned in to reposition her bags of food.

As soon as Baby G turned around to grab another bag a youngin walked by exposing a .380, showing all thirty-two gold teeth. He was shaking his head up and down, sending a clear message that the only reason Baby G wasn't filled with holes was because he was with his mother. As Baby G locked eyes with the youngin, he recognized that it was Lil One.

Lil One was the youngin who opened the gate for Baby G right before he robbed and killed Face. Baby G respected Lil One for giving him a pass because he was with his mother. If the tables were turned, without a doubt, Baby G woulda left Lil One and his mother slumped face down in a trunk full of groceries.

On the way back to Patty's Seafood, Baby G's mind was on murder. He couldn't believe he had been caught slipping again. Since he was only making a quick run with his mother, he had decided to leave his gun in his car.

"Boy, what's wrong wit' chu?" asked Patty.

"Ain't nothing wrong, Ma, I'm cool."

"You lying, I can see it all over your face. Now tell me what's wrong."

"Nothing, Ma, I just forgot I had to do something," replied Baby G trying to sound convincing.

"If you say so," stated Patty, cutting her eye at Baby G. "Oh, yeah, I forgot to tell you they found yo' brother's baby mama in Taylor's Creek over there behind Paradise Park. They say she must of fell in."

"You talking about Yana?"

"Yeah, that's her. I know yo' brother probably going crazy."

"Damn, dat's crazy, Ma. Da hell she doing at Taylor's Creek by herself?"

"Her neighbor said somebody picked her up in a Malibu and never came back."

"Sound like a murder to me," exclaimed Baby G, as they pulled into the restaurant. "A'ight, Ma, I gotta go handle something. I'ma catch you later, I love you."

"Okay! Love you, too, boy. Be careful out here."

"Already, Ma," replied Baby G, then hopped out and got in his i8.

Khufu

Chapter 97

Gotcha Ass Now!

After putting two dollars in the coin machine, C.C. grabbed her eight quarters and walked back to her car. She grabbed all the Mickey D's trash from the back seat that Hezeron and Machi left.

"I'ma beat dey ass soon as I get home," she announced to herself.

She removed the rugs from the back of her car and banged them against the brick wall on the side of Amoco. Then she put fifty cents in the vacuum machine and started vacuuming the back of her car. While cleaning, she zoned out and started thinking about what she was going to cook for dinner when something slapped her hard on her ass.

Instead of getting out of the car, she just turned her head to the side to see who would disrespect her like that. To an unexpected surprise it was Baby G. Her eyes widened as she tried to crawl across the back seat, but to no avail.

Boc!

Baby G shot her in her ass, causing her to clutch her ass cheek and scream for help.

"Bitch, ain't nobody stupid enough to come over here and help you," stated Baby G.

"Bra, I'm sorry man. I ain't know, please," she cried, as she tried to crawl out the other side of the car again. "Nooo, just listen to me, bro."

Baby G ignored her pleas and turned her over. "Yeah, bitch, I gotcha ass now!" declared Baby G, pointing a big ass .45 caliber in her face, and squeezing one off.

Boc!

C.C. sat up swinging at the air, sweating and screaming until she opened her eyes and realized it was all a dream.

"Girl, what da hell wrong wit' chu?" Off Top asked, staring at her from the other side of the bed, while smoking a blunt.

"Nothing, I'm alright," lied C.C., trying to downplay the

situation.

"Nothing my ass. What chu was screaming no please for?"

"Boy, I told you it ain't nothing. Man, leave it alone."

"Yo' lil bad ass seeing shit in ya sleep, huh? Dat's what yo' ass get for trying to play Hana and shit," clowned Off Top.

"Man, I ain't got time for this shit," said C.C., getting up to use the restroom.

"Oh, hell nall, you done pissed da damn bed up."

"Fuck you!"

"Yeah, a'ight. Getcha pissy ass out here and wash deez damn sheets."

C.C. ignored him as she sat on the toilet, heart still racing from the nightmare she just had. "Damn, I gotta pull up on Baby G," she muttered, as she buried her face in her hands.

****

It had been a good week for Billy. He had moved twenty-seven pounds and had someone on the way for the last three. Hyped up about moving the weed so quickly, he called Baby G to let him know.

"Yeah, talk to me," exclaimed Baby G.

"My nigga don't never disrespect my hustle. Dat shit gon', pull up on me pronto," implied Billy proudly.

"Say no more. I'm in ya chest in a minute," replied Baby G.

Billy grabbed a bottle of Vodka and took a shot straight from the bottle, then there was a knock at the door.

"Yeah, hold up," screamed Billy, taking another shot before opening the door.

"Damn, what took you so long to open da door. What chu in here playing with ya self?" proclaimed Koko.

Koko was an around the way girl who was a little friendly with her pussy. In high school she was one of the baddest bitches in the city. She favored Mary J. Blige with long natural hair and a stripper body, but the elements of the underworld had eaten her alive and now she looked like, *Mary May Die*. She belonged to the streets now. Koko had promised Billy a shot of ass earlier that day after he pulled out all his money and paid for her food at the Chinese rice hut.

"Don't try me like dat. I'm in some different pussy every night," lied Billy.

"Is dat, right? Well, I hope you ready to get in dis one," conveyed Koko, walking past Billy making her ass clap with every step.

Billy was up under such hypnosis, captured by the hypnotic ways of a woman's ass that he didn't even see the gunman behind him.

Crack!

The gunman hit Billy in the back of his head, knocking him down. Before the gunman could close the door good, Koko was already going into Billy's pockets.

"Damn, hoe, hold da fuck up. Go look around for the work or something. I got dis."

"Nigga, we busting down everything anyway," Koko declared, stormin' off to go check the rest of the apartment.

Billy gained consciousness back and turned over to see who had hit him.

"Fifty?" asked Billy, surprised.

"In real life, ana? And I'm bare faced, so you already know what da lick read. You like flashing money in front of deez hoes, huh? Turn yo' bitch ass over."

Billy turned on his stomach while Fifty went through his pockets, only to find nothing.

"Where it at, bitch ass nigga!"

"You better kill me, soft ass nigga! You know you ain't living like dat," proclaimed Billy.

Fifty kicked Billy in his ass, then put his rusty .38 to the back of his head and counted down from three.

"Three—two—"

"I found it! I found da weed," yelled Koko excitedly.

"Bitch, shh, shut da fuck up. You talking all loud and shit," stated Fifty.

"My bad," Koko replied, whispering.

"Three—two—"

"A'ight man, it's in da back," indicated Billy.

"Get up, nigga, take me to it."

Billy got up and walked slowly to the back of the apartment. He couldn't believe he was about to die for thinking with his lil head. Koko was right behind Fifty, adrenaline pumping and pussy juices flowing. Real street shit always turned her on. She was known for setting a few niggas up that ended in death.

Once Billy got to the back room, he went to a hamper that held his dirty clothes and started pulling them out.

"Nigga hurry da fuck up!" urged Fifty.

"Fuck you, pussy!" replied Billy.

Fifty blacked out and started pistol whipping Billy viciously.

"Fuck his ass up!" Koko cheered from behind.

Crack!

Baby G hit Koko so hard that he knocked a piece of her earlobe off, dropping her instantly. Fifty was so caught up in beating Billy that he didn't even hear Koko drop behind him. While he was in mid swing, Baby G wacked him in the right hemisphere of his brain, dropping him next to Koko.

"Get up, Billy, tighten up!"

The sound of Baby G's voice brought Billy back to life. He sprang up and went to work on Fifty immediately, taking his own gun and beating the meat off his head. Right when Billy stood up and pointed at Fifty's head, Baby G stopped him.

"Hold up, Billy. Go turn the music on and bring me the broom," demanded Baby G.

Billy kicked Koko in the face and spit on her before walking out.

"Y'all almost had y'all one, huh? I respect game, ain't nothing wrong with it. You probably shoulda locked da door doe. Dat was dumb," explained Baby G.

Billy walked back in and handed Baby G the broom.

"Pull dem panties off, hoe!" Recognizing who Baby G was, Koko did as she was told. "Hoe you wanna be 'bout it, 'bout it, huh?

Here! And bitch you better fuck it like you love it, or I'ma leave yo shit all over deez project floors!"

Koko wasted no time pushing a quarter of the broom down in her deepness. She bit her bottom lip and moaned while grinding her hips as if death wasn't imminent.

"Damn!" yelled Billy, while pointing the .38 at Fifty and looking at Koko massaging his manhood.

Boc!

Boc!

Boc!

Baby G put three holes in Koko's face.

"You a sick ass nigga! Da fuck wrong wit' chu?" asked Baby G.

"Nigga, how am I sick? You da one made da hoe fuck da broom," stated Billy, standing over Fifty.

"Nigga, I should stick dat same broom in yo' ass!" Billy told Fifty.

"You gotta real nigga fucked up! Tender dick ass nigga!" yelled Fifty.

Boc!

Boc!

Boc!

Boc!

Boc!

Billy pumped five holes into Fifty with his own gun.

"Bet dat up, Baby G. Bitch, I owe you my life."

"You good, just watch how you move from now on. Where my money at doe?"

"I got chu, right here," replied Billy, pulling a Wal-Mart bag from the hamper.

"You gotcha cut already?"

"Yeah, I got it."

"Good! Cuz you paying for da clean up."

"What clean up?"

Baby G ignored Billy and dialed Baby Haitian's number. He picked up on the first ring.

"What's hood, fam? Dis Baby G, I got something for you."
"What it lookin' like?"
"Filthy! I got two for you."
"Drop da location, goon."
"Already!" replied Baby G.

Chapter 98

Dumb Nigga!

Baby G had just picked up some money from Oliver and dropped him off ten more bricks of molly. He was now headed to meet Shenida at the spot when he got a call from his mother.

"What's up, Ma? How you feeling?"

"Hey! I'm alright, what chu doing?"

"I'm just moving around a lil' bit. Why, what's up?"

"I need you to do something for me. Yo' cousin just got here from Kentucky and he need a ride from the bus station."

"Who J.J.?"

"Yeah, he already here. He just called me."

"A'ight, I'm on my way now."

"Oh, yeah, I forgot to tell you. Yo—"

Baby G hung up before Patty could finish her sentence. He made a right on 13ᵗʰ and Okeechobee and took it all the way out until reaching the bus station. J.J. was a high yellow nigga, standing 5'4 with green eyes. Everybody told him that he resembled Steph Curry. He was a real lady's man, but would suit up and go to war about his cousins. Baby G pulled up on him and blew the horn. Patty had already told him what Baby G was driving, so he approached the car, opened the back door and put his duffle bag in the back seat. He then got in the front seat and gave Baby G a half ass handshake.

"What's up, lil nigga? Dem Kentucky niggas done ran yo ass from up there, huh," joked Baby G.

"You got me fucked up! Them niggas up thurr know my work," assured J.J.

Baby G laughed at J.J.'s country grammar, but J.J. ain't find shit funny. In fact, for the next five minutes it was an awkward silence. Once they reached Angle Road, J.J. busted up the silence with a statement that Baby G wasn't expecting.

"You know that shit you did to Mundo was fucked up! Dat's your fucking brother," exclaimed J.J., with a mug on his face.

Baby G knew something was off about J.J.'s energy. Now he

knew why. He didn't respond to J.J.'s statement right away. He remained silent, waiting on the perfect moment. As soon as J.J. turned his head to gaze out the window, Baby G pulled his banga and pressed J.J.'s face to the window with brute force.

"Aye, man, what chu—"

"Shut da fuck up, country ass nigga! You know stupidity can getcha ass killed fucking with me? Huh? Now whoever told you dat ain't tell you dat I'll burn yo' dumb ass and hug ya mama at cha grave. Huh, nigga! Get cho' bitch ass out my shit! Hurry up for I fuck around and kill ya on G.P."

"A'ight, man, just let me get my bag."

"Dat's my shit now, dumb ass nigga!"

J.J. got out of the car, visibly shaking from fear and anger and just stood there while Baby G pulled off with everything he came with.

****

After dropping two bricks of molly on Unita Baby G parked his car on Avenue S at one of his lady friends that he grew up with named Lanetta. Lanetta favored Zoe Zaldana from the movie Colombiana. She was real down to earth and street smart, which was why Baby G loved her company. They were now smoking a blunt and catching up on old times.

"So, what's been up, Baby G? What blew you this way?"

"I just been cooling. Shid—I was in the area, so I pulled up on you. I know you gon' let me do dat," said Baby G.

"No question! You know you my nigga, Baby G. You also know I'm not stupid, so what's up?" asked Lanetta.

"What chu mean?"

"You show up out of the blue, dipped in all black and shit! Come on, man. What's up?"

Baby G's phone vibrated, letting him know that he had a text message. After reading it he got up to leave.

"You good on dat blunt, Ma. I'm out."

"You up to something. Just make sure you stop back by," stated

Lanetta.

Baby G kissed her on the forehead and got in the wind. Behind her apartment was a trail that led to more apartments on Avenue T. Baby G took the trail and cut through the apartments until he reached a rundown motel that everybody went to when they were on the run. He jumped the six-foot brick wall that surrounded the motel and headed to the room that Shenida rented with a fake I.D. Baby G drew his FN 509 that held seventeen shots and cracked the room door. Once he saw that everything was going to plan, he crept in and had a seat next to the bed. Shenida was riding youngin's face, smothering him to the point where he didn't even hear Baby G enter the room.

"Sss—fuck, yeah. Suck da nut out dis pussy," moaned Shenida as she rotated her hips and squeezed her pussy muscles.

Once she finished cumming she continued to gyrate her hips until she felt her bladder fill with urine and let her rip. She urinated in the youngin's mouth until he finally realized it was piss and pushed her off his face. He attempted to grab his gun off the table with intentions of pistol whipping her, but Baby G's FN pointed in his face through a monkey wrench in his plans. Youngin was so in shock that he couldn't even scream. His eyes just bulged as if he'd hit a dime rock dropped in ammonia.

"Lil One, boy what dey do? You a hard nigga to track down. I'ma give it to you. You move kinda nice, but all dat shit don't matter now. All I had to do was dangle some pussy on a string and presto—I got'cha lil horny ass," boasted Baby G.

"I shoulda killed yo' ass at the meat house," conveyed Lil One.

"I concur," said Baby G, throwing Shenida a zip tie. "Tie dat nigga hands behind his back."

"Gone ahead and turn over, lil daddy," instructed Shenida.

Lil One did as he was told with the goofiest look on his face. He couldn't believe he had been caught slipping.

"Don't feel no type of way, lil daddy. For what it's worth, dat lil head was fire!" proclaimed Shenida while going in his pockets and removing a small bankroll and a phone.

"Fuck you, slimy ass hoe!" asserted Lil One.

"If Baby G would have waited any longer, I probably woulda fucked you," she admitted.

"Get dressed and wipe dis room down," ordered Baby G. "I respect you giving me a pass when I was with my mom dukes. I'ma keep it fifty twenties wit' chu doe. If it was me, I woulda hit you and mom dukes, but dat's just me. I do have somewhat of a heart. Dat's why I made sho you at least got to smell some pussy before I kill you."

"My nigga, I ain't got no rap for you! Stop playing deez lil hoe ass games and do you. You a killa or nah? Da fuck you waiting on?" replied Lil One.

"I'm done, Daddy," said Shenida.

"I hear you, lil nigga, but dat lil speech ain't swaying shit dis way," stated Baby G, using his shirt to open the door. "Let's move! Take him to the back of the motel," demanded Baby G.

Once they reached the back of the motel, Baby G ordered Shenida to pull Lil One's pants to his ankles.

"Come on, man. All dis ain't called for," cried Lil One.

"Turn yo lil fuck ass around and get on yo' knees," instructed Baby G.

Lil One complied to Baby G's order, while Shenida lusted over Baby G's vernacular and sinister demeanor.

"You wanna pray or some shit before I hit' cha?"

"Yeah, man, let me—"

Boc!

Baby G hit Lil One in the back of his head, then stood over him and put the remaining sixteen in his ass and back. Baby G wanted to make sure Lil One was found execution style. Pulling his pants to his knees was a humiliation tactic Baby G had learned from the OG's that walked before him. Baby G helped Shenida over the brick wall, then followed suit behind her. He then took her through the trail that led back to Lanettals apartment where he parked his car. They hopped in his i8 and peeled out.

Chapter 99

Lighten Up

Baby G had been swerving through the city making plays with Shenida right behind him in her Infiniti truck. He had sold Pink Lip Joe ten bricks of molly earlier on the strength of Shenida and was now down to eight bricks. Baby G took a pull from a cigarette laced with coke as he came to a stop sign on 23rd and Avenue E.

Before pulling off he noted that he'd dropped ashes on his designer sweats and attempted to brush them off, knocking his pistol off his lap in the process.

"Damnit, man!" yelled Baby G, putting his car in park.

He slid his seat back and reached for the gun that was now behind the pedals. While reaching for the gun, a '98 Toyota pulled in front of him, blocking him off. A shooter then hopped out of the back seat dumping multiple rounds in Baby G's windshield. After realizing that he was getting hit at, Baby G decided to stay low. He didn't know what direction the shots were coming from, so he didn't attempt to get a shot off.

A second shooter hopped out the driver's side and started shooting, walking his way around the car to fill Baby G's door with holes, but was caught off guard by Shenida hopping out with two .38 Quad Glocks. Shenida let both guns go, hitting the shooter that hopped out of the back seat and forcing the driver to retreat to his car and pull off, leaving his shooter.

"Baby, tighten up!" yelled Shenida, as she walked up and stood over the shooter.

Baby G came from up under the dashboard, opened the door and hopped out, clutching as onlookers watched in shock. When Baby G stood over the wounded man, he couldn't believe his eyes.

"Ain't dis some shit! Nigga, dis the reason you came down here?" asked Baby G.

"G baby, you know dis lil nigga?" questioned Shenida.

Boc!

Baby G hit J.J. in the side of his head, killing him instantly.

"Yeah, Ma, dis lil nigga my cousin."

"Oh, dat make sense."

"What chu mean?" asked Baby G.

"Cuz, da driver was yo' brother. What don't make sense is why da fuck they shooting at you?"

****

Baby G parked his whip behind Shenida's house and put a car cover over it. He gave Shenida the whole rundown about his family feud as she laid on his chest.

"Damn, bae, why you ain't tell me dis shit when you first got out da hospital? You supposed to keep me on point about shit like dat," stated Shenida.

"Yeah, I know, Ma. I just didn't want chu in da middle of my family beef."

"I hear you, but I ain't feeling dat shit. You already know I'on give a fuck about dat being yo family. My loyalty is with you!" proclaimed Shenida, sitting up to look Baby G in his eyes.

"You right. From now on I'ma keep you on point. No matter what, Ma. It won't happen again. You know a nigga loves you forever."

"I love you, too, baby."

"Speaking of family. How yo daughter doing?" asked Baby G.

"She good, I got her staying with my sister while I run dis bag up."

"Dat's real. If she needs anything you know where da money at." Baby G ran his hands through Shenida's hair.

"It's okay. I got a lil something saved up, but you are appreciated," replied Shenida, leaning in to kiss him.

She then crawled on top of him with intentions of riding him into pure bliss, but his phone rang.

"Cut dat shit off. It's been a minute since we had us some alone time," she cried.

"Hold up dis my mama. Let me take dis one call, then it's you and me," promised Baby G. "Yeah, Ma. What's up?"

"You hard to kill, ana?"

Baby G took the phone from his ear to make sure it was his mother's number.

"Who da fuck is dis?" he questioned.

"Nigga you know death when you hear it! It's only a matter of time, bitch ass nigga!"

"What chu doing playing on mama phone, po ass nigga? You seen what happened to J.J. Next time squeeze right, lil nigga," advised Baby G.

"I know you killed Yana, too, nigga!"

"Nigga, I ain't kill dat bitch."

"Yeah, whateva. Tell Shenida she food, too. You already know how I'm coming!" *Click.*

"Who was dat, Daddy?" asked Shenida.

"My lil brother, Mundo."

****

Patty was sitting on her porch, writing down numbers from a dream book to play Lotto with when Baby G pulled up in Shenida's Infiniti truck. He hopped out aggressively with Shenida right behind him, both carrying the Tommy guns that C-Major gave them.

"What's up, Ma? My brother here?" asked Baby G.

"You just missed him about five minutes ago."

"What's he driving?"

"I took him to get a what chu ma call it. Ah—Benz truck," stated Patty, still oblivious to what was going on. "Why y'all got dem big behind guns out in the open like dat?"

"I heard what happened to J.J., Ma. I'm trying to find da niggas who did it," lied Baby G.

"Yeah, dat' was messed up man. Dat boy wasn't even here a whole two days and got killed. I had to call his mama and tell her son that her son died. She was just a hollering and screaming," explained Patty.

"Don't trip, Ma. I'ma get dem niggas!"

"Who dat girl wit' chu?"

"Dat's my ride or die, Ma."

"Hi Ms. Patty, nice to meet you," greeted Shenida.

"Hey, how you doing? Well, be careful is all I'ma tell you. I ain't going to no jail to visit nobody! If you get killed, I'ma come pay my respects. Now it's on you, I done told you," asserted Patty.

"I respect dat, Ma. You know I love you, but you know how I'm living."

Patty took a deep breath and exhaled. She knew Baby G was gonna do him no matter the odds.

"Okay, son, I love you."

Chapter 100

Say His Name

Mundo bent through the city in his new white-on-white G-Wagon 550 bumping Casanova. He periodically took sips from a bottle of Remy and bobbed his head chaotically to the violent influencing music.

I'ma catch a body if I pop da trunk
I'ma catch a body if I pop da trunk
I swear to God
Dis ain't What'cha really want

He had never been the type to do drugs, but he had reached his apex on life's unapologetic wickedness. The weight of the world was crushing him, and he vowed to crush everything in his path along with him. Mundo was riding around snorting grade A coke, with a .40 Caliber on his lap and a choppa on the passenger seat. He was so high that he didn't notice Detective Peer following him.

Detective Peer had been on Mundo's trail since his release. He even watched the whole scene play out with Baby G and Mundo on 23rd that left J.J. dead. He decided not to pursue them, so he could have something over their heads. He would soon give them the ultimatum to move his drugs or face murder charges.

Mundo made a right on 20th Street and Avenue D, creeping past a run-down hotel called Reno's. Once he reached 20th and Canel he made a left on to a dirt road and pulled over to take another bump of cocaine. Detective Peer pulled behind him but didn't cut his lights on. Instead, he exited his vehicle and crept up to Mundo's window tapping on it with a flashlight.

"Hey, step outta the ca—"

Boc!

The tap on the window startled Mundo causing him to reach for his gun and squeeze with no hesitation, shooting through his window.

"Da fuck!" yelled Mundo, opening his door and hopping out.

As he stood over the body, he realized that it was Detective

Peer. Detective Peer had a vest on, but the force from the projectile put him on his ass, knocking the wind out of him.

"Detective Peer? Da fuck you doing? You following a nigga? You ain't even cut ya lights on. What chu was finna kill a nigga? Oh, you thought you had a free pick, huh?" Mundo asked with a smirk on his face and coke on his nose. He stood over Detective Peer and pointed his .40 in his face. "George Floyd! Say his name!" demanded Mundo.

"Put the gun down, Moss," implied Detective Peer.

"Pussy cracka say his name!"

"George Floyd, George Floyd, don't shoot! Please!" begged Detective Peer.

Mundo put the rest of his clip into Detective Peer's face, then hopped back in his G-wagon and left the scene unnoticed.

****

Baby G stood over the stove scrambling cheesy eggs after fucking Shantel. Cheesy eggs were something he enjoyed after a nice slice of pussy.

"Baby G!" yelled Shantel.

"Yeah, what up I'm cooking."

"Just come here real quick, bae. Hurry up," she yelled.

Baby G took the pot off the stove and continued to stir the eggs as he walked into the bedroom.

"What up, bae?"

"Look at da news, bae. Ain't that the detective that came by the house looking for you about that triple murder?"

Baby G gazed at the TV and recognized the photos that were being flashed across the screen.

"Yeah, dat's his bitch ass. Turn it up."

Shantel did as she was told. Breaking news—just hours ago, Detective Peer was found brutally gunned down on 20th Street and Canal. An urban area known for drug dealing and gang violence. Detective Peer didn't radio anything in, and it appears to officials that he never turned on his lights. There was no footage on the dash cam and no suspects have been apprehended thus far. The St. Lucie Sheriff Department is offering a fifty-thousand-dollar reward for any information leading to an arrest.

"Damn! Somebody finally got his bitch ass. Whoever did it must have been a nigga with nothing to lose."

"You know dem crackers gonna be beating the streets heavy behind that detective getting killed. I think you need to slow down on whatever you doing until shit cool down," pronounced Shantel.

"I ain't moving nothing, but I do need you to do something for me, doe."

"What, Baby G?"

"I need you to sign for me a Benz Sprinter for my party. One of dem big shits."

"I thought you said you wasn't doing nothing Baby G."

"I said I wasn't moving nothing. I'm still throwing my party."

"I'ma do it. I ain't gone even argue wit' chu. I'ma do it tomorrow."

Khufu

Chapter 101

Birthday Bash

Baby G, Shenida and Billy Boy relaxed in the Benz Sprinter parked behind the Elk's lounge in front of the back entrance, as the crowd grew by the minute. Instead of snorting coke or eating molly, Baby G just settled for blowing wedding cake kush and Remy. He had on all his new jewels and was dipped in a ten thousand dollar all red cashmere linen suit, with thousand-dollar Loro Piana Calfskin loafers.

Shenida rocked a red, lace front and was elegantly wrapped in a thirty-five hundred-dollar red Michael Kors dress with slits so deep on both sides that when she was seated you could see everything, but her passion fruit. Her finger and toenails were painted black with red tips, complementing her black-red bottom six-inch heels. She even had a small Michael Kors purse that concealed her compact Nina.

Billy was dressed in all black True Religion from head to toe with a creamy peanut butter colored FN on his waist. Billy Boy hated Shenida's guts but he couldn't keep his eyes off her.

"Damn, Shenida, you looking good as fuck, no bullshit!" complimented Billy.

"Yeah, you looking like a real queen, ma," added Baby G.

"Thank you, Daddy. Billy, I appreciate the compliment, but you can get the thought of how good dis pussy is out cha mind."

"See, a nigga can't even be nice to you. I was just complimenting yo' lil stank ass," cried Billy.

"And I told you I appreciate it, but the next time you call me out my name I'ma heat dat ass up," stated Shenida.

"You ain't da only one strapped," declared Billy, tapping his waist.

"You ain't gone fuck with her," assured Baby G.

"What y'all supposed to be a couple or some shit?" asked Billy.

"Fuck with her and find out," said Baby G.

"Dis shit crazy," whined Billy.

"Yeah, I know it," replied Baby G.

"Y'all chill out with dat shit! Y'all here to have a good time," proclaimed D-Dog, as he passed a blunt from the drivers' seat.

D-Dog was Baby G's driver for the night and he took the job serious.

"It's all good D-Dog," asserted Baby G.

Moments later, security knocked on the door letting them know that their table was ready.

"A'ight let's roll out," commanded Baby G.

"I'ma be right here when y'all come out," stated D-Dog.

****

All eyes were on the trio as they fell in the club through the back door. Straight ahead was a section roped off for them with a table that contained ten bottles of Remy. To the left were stairs that led to the stage and D.J. booth.

"Awww shit, the birthday boy is in da building with his team. Baby G baby what's happenin? Happy twentieth birthday, my nigga! I fucks with dis nigga, man!" screamed D.J. One Lakh.

Shenida and Billy stayed at the base of the stairs, while Baby G walked on stage and grabbed the mic.

"Everybody who came to fuck with me, I'm fucking with you! I see a lot of bad bitches in here tonight. All drinks are free for the ladies. If you eat molly, come see me at my table. It's all on me!" Baby G left the stage and headed to his table with Shenida and Billy behind him.

"Aye, Big Rude, let' em in five at a time," said Baby G, going into his pocket handing the security guard a hundred dollars.

Once Baby G was seated, he reached into his designer briefs and pulled out a crown royal bag that contained two hundred and fifty-two grams of molly. He then handed it to Billy Boy.

"What da fuck is dis?" questioned Billy.

"Dat's molly. Just pass it out when dey come to da table," instructed Baby G.

"Man, I ain't come here for dis! I'm just tryna relax and blow dis good."

"Just give it to da hoes, bra."

Billy was about to continue his protest until he saw how jazzy the women were that lined up for molly.

"Damn, you eat molly?"

"Yeah, I do my thang on the weekend," stated the Irene the Dream look alike.

"I tell you what. Come pop one of deez bottles and have a seat. You with me tonight," asserted Billy, pulling out a seat for her.

"G baby, you wearing dat Cuban. It looks good on you. I'm getting so fucking wet just looking at chu," admitted Shenida while massaging Baby G's dick through his linen slacks.

"As you should," replied Baby G, grabbing Shenida and pulling her closer to him. "You smelling good enough to eat," implied Baby G, sliding his hand under her dress and playing with her clit from the back.

She then stood over him and pulled his slacks down enough to pull his dick out and eased down on him slowly.

"Fffuck," moaned Baby G, as he slid deep up in her.

She wrapped her arms around his neck and whispered in his ear.

"So, I'm bae now?" she asked, as she began to rock slowly back and forth on Baby G.

"Sss—oh—shit! You been bae. Damn—sss—fuck! You gone always be bae," moaned Baby G, as he rubbed his hands up her back and dug his nails in her skin slightly and scratched her back, as he brought his hands back down her back, letting her know how good she felt.

"I love you so much, Daddy," Shenida moaned, kissing him passionately while rolling her back and grinding on him slowly.

"Man, y'all tripping," noted Billy.

Women watched as they stood in line for molly, but Baby G and Shenida didn't care. They were making love in the club. After relieving their pressure, they just sat there loving on each other until a young woman stood behind Shenida and cleared her throat.

Shenida stood up, put Baby G's dick back in his slacks, then turned to see who had ruined their moment.

"Hoe, da molly line over there!" yelled Shenida.

"Bitch, I'on want no motherfucking molly. I need to holla at Baby G, so excuse yo self," replied Unita.

Shenida attempted to rush her, but Baby G grabbed her.

"Chill, Ma, I got it," said Baby G.

"Dat's right tame ya lil hoe!" yelled Unita.

"Who da fuck is dis hoe, Baby G?" asked Shenida.

"Calm down, she just wanna buy some work," he lied.

"Well, why she acting like y'all done had dealings before?"

"I fucked da hoe a long time ago," he lied again. "Let me just see what she tryna grab."

"I'm cool," assured Shenida, sitting her purse down.

When Baby G turned to face Unita she threw the money that she owed him in his face, scattering money everywhere. Again, Shenida tried to intervene, but he stopped her.

"Just pick da money up, I got it," conveyed Baby G.

It took everything in Shenida to obey Baby G's command, but she did.

Baby G walked up on Unita and put his hands around her neck, applying enough pressure to scare the shit out of her.

"Do I look like da type of nigga you can disrespect, huh?" Unita wanted to answer him so badly, but she couldn't breathe.

She clawed at G's arms and hands, but to no avail.

"Yeah, hoe! You gone die tonight, bitch," taunted Shenida, as she stood on the side of Baby G.

"Baby G, chill out! Don't kill da hoe, you gon' fuck up da party," noted Billy Boy.

As soon as Baby G let Unita go, Shenida hit her twice in the face, knocking her down. Before security could pick her up, Shenida kicked her in the face.

"Come on now, that's enough," cried security, as he picked Unita up and carried her out of the club.

"How much money dat was?" asked Baby G.

"I'on know, I didn't count it."

"Sit cha ass down and count dat shit," instructed Baby G, while grabbing a bottle of Remy.

"Birthday boy! God damn, my nigga, check it out."

Baby G looked up and saw Mango and Off Top at the velvet rope.

"Big Rude, let 'em in!"

Once they were let in, they greeted Baby G with all love.

"Happy birthday, my nigga," stated Off Top, handing Baby G a wad of money. "Dat's about five bands, you know a lil change to hang out with."

"Love, bra," replied Baby G.

"I ain't got no money for ya ass, just straight gas!" clowned Mango, as he fired up a blunt.

"I ain't come here to hang out. I just wanted to show my face and give you dat, I'm out."

"Fasho, big homie. I respect dat," replied Baby G, dapping Off Top up before he left.

"Here, baby, fifteen thousand. I'll be back, I gotta go to the ladies room," said Shenida.

"Damn, my nigga. I'm saying doe, who da lil hoe was who threw da money in ya face? Dat lil bitch sexy ass fuck!" implied Mango.

"Dat wasn't nothing, but a headache. What's good wit' chu, doe? Da feds still on ya trail?" Baby G asked Mango, before taking a shot from the Remy bottle.

"Hell yeah. They let my girl out on an ankle monitor till she goes to court. I'ma just stay elusive until the statute of limitations on dat shit run out."

"Nigga, ain't no statute of limitation for murder. Even if it was, the feds don't give a fuck, 'bout laws and rules. Dey play how dey wanna," informed Baby G, passing Mango the bottle in return for the blunt.

"Well, fuck it. When dey come I'ma be ready."

"I hear you."

"I see you in here with Shenida. Dat's Billy over there too, right?"

"Yeah, dat's my team."

"Already, shid get dat money."

"Aye, I been trying to call Aaron, but dat nigga shit go straight to voicemail. Ever since I slid from Pompano I ain't been able to reach em."

"Shid, bra fucked up in da feds. Somebody killed his lil homie and he lost it. Aaron facing like four bodies."

"Damn, shit real," expressed Baby G.

Shenida returned from the ladies room and sat next to Baby G.

"Damn, Ma, what chu was in there shitting?" joked Baby G.

"Don't play with me. I had to clean dis pussy."

"What dey do, Shenida?" asked Mango.

"What's up, bra?"

Baby G was about to take a pull from the blunt when he saw a nigga standing five feet from the velvet rope in a hoodie, just watching him. Baby G zoned out, not hearing Mango or Shenida. The more he focused, the more the mysterious man's face appeared.

"I'm finna go holla at Billy Boy," conveyed Mango, as he got up to walk around the table.

Everything seemed to slow down in Baby G's mind, reminding him of the scene from Above the Rim, when Bugaloo caught Tupac slippin' in the club.

"What's—wrong—Daddy?" Shenida's voice even seemed to slow down in Baby G's mind.

Shenida followed his eyes and finally saw what he saw. She reached for her Nina but was too slow on the draw.

Boc!
Boc!
Boc!

Mundo fired three shots, causing a panic in the club. He then blended with the crowd as they made their way toward the exit. Shenida and Billy returned fire, but only hit innocent bystanders. Mundo had slithered out untouched. When the smoke cleared, Baby G was on his knees cradling Mango. Mundo had hit Mango with all three shots in his side, dropping him rigorously. Baby G knew those bullets were meant for him, but he also knew that collateral damage came with war. Mango couldn't even get a word out. He was coughing up blood every time he tried to breathe.

"Baby G,—we gotta go now!" urged Shenida.

Baby G pulled Mango close and whispered in his ear. "My nigga, I'on know if it's life after death, but if it is—I promise you I'ma send dat nigga to you and when he get there you better handle ya fucking bidness. I love you, my nigga."

Billy snatched Baby G up and they slid out the back door where D-Dog was waiting.

Khufu

Chapter 102

A Man Dies How He Lives

The next night Shenida drove the car that they had rented from a smoker indignantly under the Florida moon while Baby G and Billy stalked the scenery. They rode though the whole Sunland Gardens, street for street, looking for Mundo but it seemed as if he waded into the abyss without a trace.

"Damn, man. Dat's fucked up what happened to Mango," expressed Shenida.

"Yeah, dat was my nigga. He just got caught up in da mix, but you know—a man dies how he lives? He at peace now. Death is easy, da shit we doing now is da hard part," philosophized Baby G.

"What we doing now?" questioned Billy, perplexed.

"We living, Billy," answered Baby G.

"I'on get it."

"Neva mind, Billy."

"So, who was dat shooting at us anyway?" asked Billy.

"Some lil nigga I shot at before," lied Baby G, not wanting Billy in his family bidness.

"Damn, you shoulda killed dat nigga," added Billy.

"G Baby, we slid through da whole city. Dis nigga laying low as fuck. I'm tired, bae, let's turn it in for da night," whined Shenida.

Before Baby G could answer his phone rang. "Run it."

"Baby G, dis Oliver! Come getcha money and bring me ten more, bra."

"I only got eight left and I want the money up front for dem."

"Shid, that ain't a problem. Money on deck, my nigga."

"I'm in da wind right now."

"Fasho, just pull up in the L.P. I'm here."

"Already!"

"Aye, I'ma drop y'all off. I gotta go bust a play up."

"Nall, we coming wit' chu," Shenida insisted.

"Nall, I need some time alone anyway. I'll be a'ight," assured Baby G.

"Be careful, my nigga. Ya know dem niggas on da tray cutthroat," warned Billy.

"Come on, man, you know I'm off safety with it. I'm good."

****

Baby G didn't want to provoke any tension or paranoia amongst Oliver's lil hittas, so he parked the murder bucket and jumped in his i8. When he pulled in, Oliver was leaning on a 2020 Audi truck smoking a cigarette. Baby G grabbed his thousand-dollar Mansur Gavril calf backpack and hopped out with his .40 caliber in hand.

"What's happenin, bra?" asked Baby G.

"Shid, I'm cooling, but um, why you hop out with dat shit in ya hand like it's pressure? Put dat shit up. You with me," stated Oliver.

"I hear you, but it's late and dark as fuck over here. I feel better with my shit out. So, we gon' do bidness or nall?"

"I guess dat's understandable. Come on in, man. The money in da spot."

Baby G followed behind Oliver with his senses on high alert. Something felt off to Baby G because it was so quiet—a little too quiet for comfort. Baby G was about to tell Oliver that he'll wait by his car when he heard movement in some bushes ahead of him to his left. Out of pure instinct Baby G let off four shots. All four shots had miraculously hit a target. Baby G walked up on the youngin who was groaning in pain and hit him in his head.

Seconds later, the sounds of multiple pistols being cocked pierced the airwaves. When Baby G looked up, he was surrounded by young hittas.

"If you asked me, looks like we got a deadly situation on our hand," announced Oliver.

"Damn, my nigga. I thought we had an understanding," said Baby G.

"We did! But you told me I had to pay you up front for deez," replied Oliver, taking the backpack and gun from Baby G. "I got five kids from five different women. Plus, I got expensive habits. You seen dat Audi truck out there? You see all these young wolves around me? I gotta feed 'em too my nigga."

"All you had to do was tell me dat like a man and I woulda blessed you, my nigga," asserted Baby G.

"I wasn't taking no chances, homie. Now listen. You done killed one of my youngins, but I'ma let chu go. Shid, he was a fucking rat, anyway. I'ma let chu make it cuz I like you, homie. Y'all clean dis shit up," ordered Oliver. The youngins drug the body out of sight. "Gone 'head and get from around here," stated Oliver.

Right then and there Baby G realized that Oliver had no idea who he was fucking with. Baby G said nothing as he headed back to his car.

You should have killed me, silly nigga, he thought as he got in his car and left with murder on his mind.

Khufu

Chapter 103

Built for Dis

Baby G knew all he had to do was grab the tommy guns that C-Major gave him and take Shenida with him to go air Oliver and his whole set. In his mind, that was too easy. He wanted them to suffer, he wanted to inflict pain on them slowly. Instead, he called Shenida on his way to the jetty and told her to meet him out there.

Twenty minutes later, Shenida walked to the end of the paved road that extends a few hundred feet into the ocean and found Baby G in a pensive state of mind.

"What's up, daddy?" asked Shenida, wrapping her arms around him.

"Look at dis view, ma. When you stand out here the stars almost seem to be in arms reach."

"It's a helluva view."

"It's so peaceful, ya know?"

"Are you okay?"

"I'm cool, I just got a lot of shit coming at me at one time."

"You built for dis type of pressure, bae. Make a diamond outta dat shit. So, how did shit go when you went to handle bidness?"

Baby G looked at her and shook his head. "You give a weak man some strength and he becomes addicted," proclaimed Baby G.

"So, what chu wanna do, Daddy?"

"I got a project I'ma need you to help facilitate."

"It's whateva for my nigga," said Shenida.

Baby G kissed Shenida passionately, then dialed C-Major's number. He picked up on the first ring.

"What's good, bro?" asked C-Major excitedly.

"Listen, I need you to put in a special order for me."

"Come on over, bro, I'm here," said C-Major.

"Already!"

****

It was an exhilarating Saturday. The sun was covered by the clouds, causing a cool breeze, putting everybody in good spirits. It was a homie day at the 13th Street park, so all the young and old killers came out to bask in the glory of their reputations. The hustlers brought out their tricked-out cars and the thotties were choosing, wearing next to nothing. While Oliver and his youngins were sectioned off in their own area of the parking lot, Baby G and Billy Boy were behind tint, eagerly waiting to emulate Al Capone's Valentine's Day massacre bloodshed.

"I told you you shoulda let us go with cha to drop dat pack off. You done blessed dis nigga and look, he turned around and snaked ya," asserted Billy.

"You know whatever a man does in da end is what he intended to do all along. The nature of the universe is what goes around comes around. We here to deliver dat come around," philosophized Baby G.

"Oh, so now you Aristotle?" clowned Billy.

"Nall, silly nigga. I'ma descendant of the ones who taught him!"

"And who was dat?" questioned Billy.

"I'm through rapping. Stay on point," advised Baby G, taking another bump of coke.

Shenida maneuvered through the cesspool of animals until she reached Oliver. Baby G made sure she was dipped in gold to give off the persona of a trap queen. Her hair and nails were on point and the red, tight, sweat suit she wore with no panties even had the women gawking. Heavy camel toe action was irrepressible. Shenida stood parrot toed in a pair of all red Jordan 11s and gave Oliver the *I wanna fuck you* look.

"Damn, miss lady! You fine as aged wine, but what's up with all dat red, lil mama? What chu a Red Ruby or some shit?" asked Oliver.

"What if I was? You gon' let a lil red stop you from bagging a bad bitch?"

"Shid, you might be poison. Dat look like da type of pussy dat niggas go to war over," proclaimed Oliver.

"Anyways, you look like you about money so what's up?" asked Shenida.

"What chu mean, lil mama?" Shenida pulled a vacuum sealed pack of pills from her sweat jacket.

"I got a thousand pills for a thousand dollars."

"Dat's a mighty sweet deal. What dem is?"

"Dis da new wave, fresh off da press. Deez silverbacks, five times more potent than monkeys. Ain't nobody got deez. You'll be da only one with em," asserted Shenida.

"Five times more potent, huh?" asked Oliver.

"Yeah, you gon' have to tell yo customers to pop half first."

"Pop half? Lil mama we pill popping animals over here. Yeah, let me take deez off ya hands," replied Oliver, going in his True Religions and handing Shenida a thousand dollars. "All blue scrips, baby."

"I see dat. You might as well log my number in," advised Shenida.

Oliver handed Shenida his iPhone, while eyeing her camel toe.

"What's yo name, ma?"

"Karma," replied Shenida, while logging in a fake number and handing Oliver back his phone.

When he reached for the phone, she grabbed his hand and rubbed it on her fat pussy.

"Oh, my lamb! Lil mama, why dat thang so warm like dat?"

"Call me in a lil bit, I'll let you see why," asserted Shenida, then strolled off making sure to slang her lil soft booty cheeks truculently.

Khufu

Chapter 104

Ambivalence

Baby G and Billy were in the back seat behind a tent, still self-medicating when Shenida returned to the driver's seat.

"Here," said Shenida, handing the thousand dollars to Baby G.

"Nall dat's all you, Ma. Yo' performance was invigorating."

"Inviga, who?" asked Billy.

"Billy, you so dingy. Thank you, Baby G."

"Look, he passing dem pills out to the whole park. Come on, let's go switch cars real quick," instructed Baby G.

He didn't want to be seen hopping out of the same car that Shenida pulled up in. After switching cars and pulling back on the scene, Baby G saw that the ninety percent Fentanyl that was pressed in the pills were taking effect. Bodies were sprawled out all over the park in the weirdest positions. Baby G pulled his red ski mask down and grabbed his tommy gun. Seeing that it was time, Billy did the same.

"Let's rock," stated Baby G, hopping out of the car.

The ones who didn't pop the pills, which was a hand full, ran when they saw Baby G and Billy ski masked up, with big ass guns. Billy was waiting on Baby G's order to start lighting shit up, but he never gave it. Instead, he walked right up on Oliver who was bending down trying to revive his older brother with words.

"Come on, bra, don't leave me like dis. I need you my nigga. Mama already left me, my nigga you can't leave me out here," cried Oliver, while shaking uncontrollably.

"Man, dat nigga ass dead! Gone let him go, my nigga," stated Baby G coldly.

Oliver turned around and saw two masked men dipped in red. Seeing the red, Oliver automatically thought of Karma. The name that Shenida had given him. He knew then that it was a set up. Baby G lifted his mask to let Oliver see his killer, before transcending into the unknown. When Oliver saw Baby G's face, he just turned back around and kept cradling his brother. He already knew what time it was and was prepared to die like he lived.

"You know, I believe a man dies when he no longer wanna live. I'm here to do nature's will."

Baby G nodded his head, signaling Billy to wet him.

Billy lifted the tommy and blew Oliver's head off his shoulders. Baby G then went into his pockets and took the pills and a bankroll. On the way back to the car Billy and Baby G shot up lifeless bodies on g.p. Billy stopped once he saw a beautiful young woman stretched out with her four-year-old son trying to wake her up. When Baby G walked up, he saw the tears falling freely from Billy's eyes.

"I'm saying, like, I'ma have to leave you out here with her or what?" asked Baby G.

Billy didn't respond. Instead, he just walked away. Baby G squatted next to the child and lifted his mask.

"What's up, lil homie?"

"Hey, my mommy take da medicine and now her sleeping. Mommy, get up!"

"You wanna go to sleep with mommy?" asked Baby G.

The child shook his head up and down. Baby G went in the pack and gave the kid a pill.

"Eat dis and you'll go to sleep with mommy."

After watching him eat the pill, Baby G went back to the car. Billy was now crying more frantically, on the verge of hyperventilating. Baby G even heard a few sniffles coming from the front seat. Shenida knew Baby G was a wicked nigga, but now she knew she was dealing with a whole different type of entity. An evil that was inconceivable. The ride home was silent and full of ambivalence.

****

"Oooh, yeaahhh! Sss—dat's it, get dis pussy! Sss-damn, dat's my spot, nigga! Ahh! Sss—oh, Baby G !" moaned Unita.

"Bitch! What da fuck you called me?" asked Mundo, with a screw face.

344

"Oh, I'm so sorry! I didn't mean to—let's just keep going please," she whined, while rotating her hips.

Dis pussy ass hoe, thought Mundo.

He grabbed her legs and flipped her on her stomach. The rubber that he did have on, he snatched off, then entered her aggressively from behind with no compassion. While Unita cried out symphonies of bliss, Mundo grabbed his .40 off the bed and slapped Unita in the back of her head, knocking her out cold. He continued to fuck her unconscious body for at least two minutes.

"Yeah, bitch, look at cha dumb ass now." Mundo pulled out of her pussy and entered her ass, viciously. The pain from his insertion woke her up like a hit of smelling sauce.

"Oh, God! What chu doing to me?" yelled Unita.

"I'm killing yo fuck ass slowly," admitted Mundo.

Unita had never been anal fucked before, so the pain was unbearable. She bled and shitted all over Mundo but he gave no fucks. He was menacingly depraved on a war path. He snatched his shitty covered dick out of her ass and pushed it back in her pussy, contaminating her with her own fecal matter.

"Get off me!" she cried.

He pinned her head to the mattress with his .40 and kept fucking until he came, leaving his every specimen in her womb. He then pulled out of her and wiped his dick with her sheets.

"I'ma get my people to fuck yo ass up!" she screamed with tears in her eyes.

"Imagine dat," replied Mundo, while getting dressed.

"Why would you do me like dat? What da fuck is wrong wit' chu?" asked Unita, tears still falling rapidly from her eyes.

Now fully dressed, Mundo pointed his pistol in her face. "Bitch how da fuck you know Baby G?"

She knew that something was seriously wrong with Mundo, so she answered quickly.

"I met him at the carwash. We fucked one time, then after dat we did bidness."

"What kinda bidness?"

"He fronted me two bricks of molly," she conveyed through

tears.

"Call him and get him over here."

"He don't fuck with me no more like dat."

"Bitch, I said call him!"

She grabbed her phone and dialed Baby G's number,but was forwarded to the voicemail.

"He not picking up. You ain't gon' kill me, is you?"

"I already did," stated Mundo before leaving.

Before he was released, he took another AIDS test, and it came back positive. He didn't give a fuck about nothing no more. While Mundo was long gone, Unita was curled up in her bed in a fetal position trying to figure out what he meant by his last comment. One thing for certain, she would be finding out sooner than later.

Chapter 105

Face Yo Demons

Baby G had finally gotten his i8 out of the body shop that was now candy red. He had been at Shenida's ever since he picked it up. Shenida lit a blunt and passed it to him and continued to lay and rub on his chest.

"Daddy, you, okay?"

"Yeah, I'm good. Why, wassup?"

"You know I love you more than any nigga I've ever fucked with, right?"

"I love you too, Ma, but wassup?"

"Baby G, you don't think you went too far at the park?"

"I did what I did," he replied, blowing smoke out of his nose.

"You coulda just left him. Somebody woulda found him," replied Shenida, sitting up to look him in his eyes.

"Dey was gonna send him through the system. Kids be getting raped in dem foster homes. If he was lucky, he might have been adopted by some freaky as white folks and turned into a sex slave or domestic servant. I did him a favor," stated Baby G with no emotion.

"You do know I have a daughter, so dis is a sensitive ass subject for me," she exclaimed while tearing up.

"If it's so sensitive, then why da fuck is you talking about it?"

"I just wanted to know what da fuck you were thinking dat's all."

"Look, you already know a nigga would never hurt you or yo daughter. I love you. You on da right side of da gun, baby girl. Chill out!"

"And if I wasn't?"

"You already know da answer to dat."

"You know I'm riding wit'chu. I've loved you since I was thirteen but dis shit you got going on wit' cha people done turned you into some other shit," Shenida said.

"Man, I ain't trying to hear dat shit."

"I know, but you gotta face yo' demons or they gon' follow you to the grave."

"Here you go with dis spookism shit! Aye, I'ma leave you to it, my nigga. Hit me up when you remember dat deez mothafuckas tried to kill me first."

"Dat lil boy ain't have shit to do with dat."

"You da one who helped me kill his mama! You remember dat?" Shenida just put her head down in silence. "My nigga, I'm out!" yelled Baby G, as he got dressed and left Shenida's house.

****

"All you fuck niggas lay down, right now! Side by side, on ya stomach! Oh, you think dis a—"

Boc!

"You think dis shit a fucking game?" yelled Mundo, putting a hole in the head of a youngin' who was moving too slow.

Mundo had drove past a dope hole on 9th Street and saw a crowd of niggas playing dominoes, shooting dice and selling dope. He saw that everybody was so oblivious to the treachery that came with being in a dope hole and said fuck it.

"Shut da fuck up! I'on wanna hear shit! Put ya hands on da back of ya head wit' cha face in da dirt! Yeaaahhh, I done caught ya fuck niggas out' chere dick dancing," stated Mundo, as he went down the line taking money and jewelry.

When Mundo got to the last youngin' he saw that the jewelry he was wearing was fake and killed him.

"Urban appeal jewelry wearing ass nigga! Damn. A'ight, none of you niggas strapped? Mama, dey sweet," clowned Mundo, kicking a bucket over and grabbing the nine ounces that were under it. "Y'all fuck niggas see I'm bare face. Nigga, dis Mundo. Y'all done heard da name before. Dis da face to go with it! I ain't ducking nothing, I'm in dis white G-Wagon, spinning all day bitch ass niggas!" yelled Mundo, backpedaling to his truck. He hopped in and left the scene.

****

After picking up another fifty bricks of molly from C-Major, Baby G stopped by Mango's mother's house and gave her twenty thousand for his burial. He was now posted in front of his mother's restaurant getting the bricks off. Pink Lip Joe and Pony Boy had already come through and grabbed ten a piece, then a childhood friend from the projects named Rabbit also stopped by and grabbed ten. Rabbit was just stopping by to check out the restaurant and ended up buying bricks. Baby G's day was starting out productive, but due to the world that he was creating around him, he knew the energy could change at any moment.

"Baby G, you want something to eat?" asked Patty.

"Yeah, Ma, bring me some shrimp, sausage and boiled eggs please."

"Okay, give me a minute," replied Patty, turning to go inside her restaurant.

Moments later a '75 Impala pulled in next to Baby G, causing him to grab his carbine and step out with it in hand. When the driver hopped out Baby G relaxed and sat back in his car. His passenger door opened, and Billy hopped in.

"Nigga, my shit glass house! I know you see it was me. What' chu hoppin' out with dat big ass gun for?" questioned Billy.

"I'm saying like, what chu call yo' self checking me about dat? You feeling something behind me jumping out with my shit?" replied Baby G aggressively.

"Nall I'm just saying. I know you know dat was me," explained Billy.

"And what, nigga?"

"Man, I see you on bullshit today," asserted Billy.

"Here Baby G, here go yo food," said Patty.

"Thanks, Ma."

"How you doing today, Ms. Patty?" asked Billy.

"I'm good. You hungry?"

"No thank you. I'm good, Ms. Patty."

"Okay. Baby G, I'm in here if you need me."

"A'ight, Ma, love you."

"Love you, too, boy," replied Patty, then went inside.

"What's good doe? You like my new slider?" asked Billy.

"Yeah, you tight work. I know you about broke after buying dat."

"I still got a couple dollars."

"Man, look in the back seat and grab ten of them thangs. Just bring me fifty bands and you good," proclaimed Baby G.

"Man, you a trip! First, you wanna shoot a nigga, now you dropping ten bricks on a nigga," cried Billy.

"Man, just get da shit and slide. I gotta handle some shit. Get at me whenever you get at me, ain't no rush."

"I got chu, my nigga. One hunnid," solidified Billy.

"Already!"

Chapter 106

All Sixty

Mundo was coked up rolling through the projects sipping white Remy out of the bottle when his phone started ringing. When he saw who the caller was, he smiled wickedly. It was Unita. Two days later, after Mundo had his way with her she called and asked him if he could dominate her again, which he obliged. Thinking it was a set up, he went heavily armed with a vest and two twin .40's, but when he went it was just her.

"Yeah, what da fuck is up?"

"Hey, Mundo. You think you can maybe come see me tonight?" asked Unita.

"Shid, bitch I'on know about all dat."

"Well, whenever you get a chance or some free time, can you please come see me?"

"You want dis dick in ya ass?"

"Yes."

"You wanna suck da blood and shit off dis dick after I pull it out'cha ass?"

"Yes, please."

"Oh, you a nasty bitch!" Mundo put the phone down and took a bump of coke, then picked the phone back up. "Yeah, bitch, you still there?"

"Yes, I'm here."

Mundo passed by this vehicle and saw a familiar face.

"Aye, hoe call me later."

He pulled in a driveway and made a U-turn, creeping up the block. He then grabbed both forties with extensions, let the passenger window down and pulled up next to the Impala. The driver was so into his phone call that he didn't even notice Mundo on the side of him. Mundo put his truck in park and blew the horn. He wanted his victim to see his killer before death. As soon as Billy looked up, Mundo lifted both forties and let off every shot he had, all sixty. He then got in the wind. Billy was left dead in his Chevy, unrecognizable with ten bricks in the back seat.

****

Traffic was heavy at Patty's Seafood and the women that were in and out were as radiant as the Florida sun. Baby G admired them from afar. He had too much on his mind to be making new companions. He continued to enjoy his seafood platter when a tinted-up Benz pulled in front of his i8. Using greasy hands, Baby G grabbed his carbine again and started to hop out, but saw that it was just Off Top. Off Top opened Baby G's passenger door and got in.

"What's good, bra?" asked Off Top.

"Shid, cooling. What up?" replied Baby G, still gripping his carbine.

"I'on know if you done heard, but the dude I saw you with in da club just got hit up," conveyed Off Top.

"Who Billy?"

"Yeah, dat's who they saying got hit up in the projects."

"Impossible! Billy just left from up here, bra."

"He just bought an Impala, right? I'm telling you, dat's him. Dey found ten bricks of molly in da backseat and all," pronounced Off Top.

Baby G just shook his head and gazed out the window.

"Dey say it was a white G-Wagon," added Off Top.

Baby G looked Off Top in his eyes and could tell that he knew who did it.

"Listen, I know you probably don't wanna hear dis shit, right now, but ya sister told me everything."

"Stay outta family bidness, bra," warned Baby G.

"Come on now, Baby G. You know you gonna have to kill me too, my nigga."

"I play chess, homie. I been calculated dat move."

"What da fuck you gon' tell yo' nephews? How da fuck you gon' look dem and yo mama in da eyes?"

"Cross dat ocean when I get to it."

"I know dis shit sounds crazy, but ya sister loves you, my nigga."

"Fuck all dat! Get out my car with dat shit!"

"Yeah, well, ya mama right there. I know you ain't gon' kill her in front of ya mama nigga. Listen, just listen to what she gotta say. If you ain't feeling what she talking about then kill her," stated Off Top, as he got out of the car and waved C.C. out of the Benz.

As soon as Baby G saw C.C. his adrenaline shot to one hundred. He zoned out and lifted his carbine but put it back down when he heard Off Top say his mother's name.

"Hey, Ms. Patty! How my mother-in-law doing?" asked Off Top on purpose. He knew Baby G wouldn't kill her in front of his mother.

"I'm doing good. Come here let me talk to you," said Patty.

C.C. got in the passenger's seat with tears in her eyes and saw that Baby G had the carbine pointed at her. He looked her in her teary eyes with pure murder on his mind.

"Run ya mouth," he demanded.

Khufu

Chapter 107

Pain Breeds Evolution

Shenida accompanied Baby G at Billy Boy's funeral in a red Prada dress, Dior lenses and a pair of red embellished Sophia Webster heels. She even had a red, mini Fendi Baguette bag that concealed her Nina in case shit got real at the graveyard. Baby G sported a red Louie suit, red lens Louie frames to match his red face Rolex and a pair of twelve-thousand-dollar Donhill leather zip boots. He also had a Louis body holster that held two FN's.

"Rest in power, my nigga. I gotcha," promised Baby G, as he threw a red rose on Billy's casket.

"You okay?" asked Shenida, rubbing his back.

"Yeah, I'm good. Dat lil nigga been dropping dat pain on me lately. I got something for dat ass, doe. Pain breeds evolution. It's all on how you perceive it," asserted Baby G, then his phone rang.

"You know I'm wit' cha no matter what," replied Shenida.

"Yeah, I know, Ma. Hello? Yeah, wassup, bae? A'ight I'm on da way. Come on, Shenida."

"Where we headed?"

"Shantel going in labor, we gotta get to da hospital."

****

Shenida waited in the lobby while Baby G took the elevator to the third floor. When the doors opened, he walked to the front desk where a Spanish woman worked.

"Excuse me, miss, can you tell me what room Shantel Sheffield is in?"

"Yes, she's going into labor like, right now. She's in room three-o-two, hurry."

Baby G rushed to the delivery room, heart pounding and blood pumping anticipating that feeling of being a father. As soon as he crossed the threshold, the doctor was pulling his son from Shantel's womb.

After cleaning the after birth from his nose, the doctor thought Baby G's son wasn't breathing until he let out a little noise. He found it strange that the baby wasn't screaming and crying.

"You want to cut the cord?" the doctor asked.

"Indeed," replied Baby G, stepping up to cut the cord.

"Is this your first one?"

"Yeah."

After wiping him clean the doctor handed the baby boy to Baby G instead of Shantel. He was light-skinned and weighed eight pounds with a head full of hair.

"I didn't think you was gonna make it," said Shantel.

"Come on, ma, you know I be ready late," replied Baby G, locking eyes with his son. "Thank you for giving me a son."

"You're welcome, but can I hold him now? Dang!"

After passing Shantel the baby, Baby G was approached by a nurse.

"Excuse me, Sir, are you the father?"

"Unless you know something I don't," he joked.

"Boy stop playing," cried Shantel.

"This is his birth certificate. If you would just sign right here." Baby G signed the certificate and then stood by Shantel's side and watched her in adulation.

"What? Why you looking at me like dat?" she asked.

"Admiration. It takes a lot to go through what you just went through. Witnessing yo strength got me wanting to fuck da shit out cha."

"Boy, you crazy."

"I ain't bullshitting," asserted Baby G going to the other side of the bed. "Come on, turn on yo side. Toot dat shit up."

"Boy you know we can't do shit for a while. Stop acting so goofy."

He leaned in to kiss her and then his phone rang.

"Hello!"

"She had the baby, yet?" asked Shenida.

"Yeah, beautiful boy, eight pounds."

"I'm happy for you. I'm finna go check on my daughter. Call

you later."

"A'ight. Thank you for being here for me and stay off safety."

"Always. Oh, yeah, what's yo son's name?"

"Khafre Le Grand Moss!"

Khufu

Chapter 108

Let Me Get Dat

Unita held both of her legs behind her head while Mundo had both of his hands around her neck going in and out of her relentlessly. She could barely breathe, but had a fetish for asphyxiation, so she enjoyed every minute of it. Right before she could no longer breathe, Mundo removed his hands, got into a push up position and gave her everything he had. Fighting to regain consciousness while having her spot hit caused Unita to squirt intensely all over him.

"Oh, my God!" yelled Unita as she shook in glorious pleasure.

"Dat's it, bitch. Wet me up with dis pussy," replied Mundo.

As soon as he was about to cum, he was snatched out of the pussy by his dreads.

"What da fu—"

Fop!

Baby G wrapped his hands in Mundo's dreads and beat him in his head with the pistol.

"Yeaahhhh—nigga!"

Fop!

"Dis position brings back memories?"

Fop!

"You killed—"

Fop!

"Two of my—"

Fop!

"Fucking niggas!"

Fop! Fop! Fop!

Baby G let Mundo go and backed up off him.

When Mundo got his head back right, he looked up and saw Shenida pointing a gun at him.

"Nigga, I'on see dat shit!" stated Mundo, spitting blood from his mouth. "I'm dead anyway bitch ass nigga! Yeah, I killed Billy. Ain't mean to kill Mango but fuck it! He was wit' cha, so he got what I gave! You killed Yana bitch ass nigga!" screamed Mundo walking towards Baby G.

"I ain't kill ya bitch!" conveyed Baby G raising his FN.

"Whatever, nigga! Put da gun down! I'll beat yo' fuck ass!"

"Dat's what you want?" asked G.

"Fuck yeah! Let me get dat tough, ass nigga!" pronounced Mundo.

Baby G threw his gun down behind him.

"What chu doing? Kill his ass," cried Unita.

Baby G waved at Shenida to put the gun down.

"Come on, nigga," stated Baby G.

Mundo engaged, but was yanked by his dreads again.

Boc!

Mundo dropped dead, but some of his dreads and the meat from his head were still in C.C.'s hand.

"Ahhhh!" cried C.C., dropping the rest of Mundo's head on the floor.

Shenida then raised her gun and fired four shots.

Boc!

Boc!

Boc!

Boc!

"Pussy ass hoe!" yelled Shenida, killing Unita and leaving her dead in her own blood and pussy juices.

C.C. walked up to Baby G with tears in her eyes and hugged him as tight as she could.

"I love you, big bra."

Baby G kissed C.C. on her forehead.

"Love you too, sis."

****

Ten Years Later

Baby G and Shantel were in the kitchen making steak and salad when their son, Khafre ran in the house frantically screaming for Baby G.

"Daddy, daddy!" he cried.

Baby G put down the steak knife and ran into the living room.

"What's going on?" asked Baby G.

"Daddy, that man hit me."

"What man?"

"The man next door. His son tried to take my tablet so I hit him in the head with a bottle. He bleeding real bad, daddy. I didn't mean to," cried Khafre.

"Listen, you did the right thing, you hear me?"

"Yes, sir."

"Stop all dat damn crying and come on."

"Yes, sir," replied Khafre, as he followed his father.

Baby G walked to the house next door and knocked on the door.

Moments later a woman came to the door.

"May I help you?"

"Yeah, may I please speak to the man of the house."

"Just a minute. Eugene! Somebody at the door for you!"

Eugene came to the door with his belly hanging over his pants.

"Dis him?" asked Baby G.

"Yes, sir," assured Khafre.

Baby G pulled a high point 9mm from his designer jeans and shot Eugene between his eyes, killing him instantly.

"Come on, son," ordered Baby G, as he turned to leave.

Once he reached his house, he handed Shantel the gun.

"Hurry up, go throw dis shit in Taylor's Creek."

"What did you do?" whined Shantel.

"Now!" yelled G.

Shantel grabbed the gun and put it in her purse and left.

"Khafre, listen to me. Don't ever let nobody hurt you or yo mama! You do whatever you gotta do to protect what you love you hear me?"

"Yes, Daddy, I hear you."

"What did I say?"

"Protect what I love," said Khafre.

"Promise me!"

"I promise, Daddy!"

"Some people gonna come take me away. I'ma be gone for a while, but I'll be back. I need you to be the man of the house."

"Okay, Daddy. Why are they coming to get you? Is it because you killed that man?"

"Yeah, do you understand why I killed him?"

"To protect what you love."

"And who do I love?"

"Me and mommy."

"Dat's right. Always remember daddy loves you."

"I love you, too, Daddy," replied Khafre with tears in his eyes.

Moments later, Shantel stormed in the house and wrapped her arms around Baby G's neck.

"The police are outside, bae. They got they guns out and everything," cried Shantel.

"Mr. Moss! Come out with your hands up!" demanded the police.

"Bae, go in my phone and call Shenida. Tell her what happened, and she gon' make dis disappear," he said.

"Who da fuck is Shenida?"

Baby G hugged his son one last time.

"I love you, son."

"Love you, too, Daddy."

"Listen Shantel, it ain't like dat," stated Baby G, while heading for the door.

"Then who is she?"

"My killa," asserted Baby G, before walking out the door.

"Get on the fucking ground!"

To Be Continued...
Killa Kounty 2
Coming Soon

Submission Guideline

Submit the first three chapters of your completed manuscript to ldpsubmissions@gmail.com, subject line: Your book's title. The manuscript must be in a .doc file and sent as an attachment. Document should be in Times New Roman, double spaced and in size 12 font. Also, provide your synopsis and full contact information. If sending multiple submissions, they must each be in a separate email.

Have a story but no way to send it electronically? You can still submit to LDP/Ca$h Presents. Send in the first three chapters, written or typed, of your completed manuscript to:

LDP: Submissions Dept
Po Box 944
Stockbridge, Ga 30281

DO NOT send original manuscript. Must be a duplicate.

Provide your synopsis and a cover letter containing your full contact information.

Thanks for considering LDP and Ca$h Presents.

BOW DOWN TO MY GANGSTA

By **Ca$h**

TORN BETWEEN TWO

By **Coffee**

BLOOD OF A BOSS **VI**

SHADOWS OF THE GAME II

TRAP BASTARD II

By **Askari**

LOYAL TO THE GAME **IV**

By **T.J. & Jelissa**

IF LOVING YOU IS WRONG... **III**

By **Jelissa**

TRUE SAVAGE **VIII**

MIDNIGHT CARTEL IV

DOPE BOY MAGIC IV

CITY OF KINGZ III

By **Chris Green**

BLAST FOR ME **III**

A SAVAGE DOPEBOY III

CUTTHROAT MAFIA III

DUFFLE BAG CARTEL VI

HEARTLESS GOON VI

By **Ghost**

A HUSTLER'S DECEIT III

KILL ZONE **II**

BAE BELONGS TO ME III

A DOPE BOY'S QUEEN III

By **Aryanna**

Killa Kounty

COKE KINGS V

KING OF THE TRAP III

By **T.J. Edwards**

GORILLAZ IN THE BAY V

3X KRAZY III

De'Kari

THE STREETS ARE CALLING II

Duquie Wilson

KINGPIN KILLAZ IV

STREET KINGS III

PAID IN BLOOD III

CARTEL KILLAZ IV

DOPE GODS III

Hood Rich

SINS OF A HUSTLA II

ASAD

KINGZ OF THE GAME VI

Playa Ray

SLAUGHTER GANG IV

RUTHLESS HEART IV

By Willie Slaughter

FUK SHYT II

By Blakk Diamond

TRAP QUEEN

RICH $AVAGE II

By Troublesome

YAYO V

GHOST MOB II

Stilloan Robinson

CREAM III

Khufu

By Yolanda Moore
SON OF A DOPE FIEND III
HEAVEN GOT A GHETTO II
By Renta
FOREVER GANGSTA II
GLOCKS ON SATIN SHEETS III
By Adrian Dulan
LOYALTY AIN'T PROMISED III
By Keith Williams
THE PRICE YOU PAY FOR LOVE III
By Destiny Skai
I'M NOTHING WITHOUT HIS LOVE II
SINS OF A THUG II
TO THE THUG I LOVED BEFORE II
By Monet Dragun
LIFE OF A SAVAGE IV
MURDA SEASON IV
GANGLAND CARTEL IV
CHI'RAQ GANGSTAS IV
KILLERS ON ELM STREET IV
JACK BOYZ N DA BRONX III
A DOPEBOY'S DREAM II
By **Romell Tukes**
QUIET MONEY IV
EXTENDED CLIP III
THUG LIFE IV
By **Trai'Quan**
THE STREETS MADE ME III
By **Larry D. Wright**

Killa Kounty

Khufu

368

Killa Kounty

COKE KINGS I II III IV

BORN HEARTLESS I II III IV

KING OF THE TRAP I II

By **T.J. Edwards**

IF LOVING HIM IS WRONG...I & II

LOVE ME EVEN WHEN IT HURTS I II III

By **Jelissa**

WHEN THE STREETS CLAP BACK I & II III

THE HEART OF A SAVAGE I II III

By **Jibril Williams**

A DISTINGUISHED THUG STOLE MY HEART I II & III

LOVE SHOULDN'T HURT I II III IV

RENEGADE BOYS I II III IV

PAID IN KARMA I II III

SAVAGE STORMS I II

By **Meesha**

A GANGSTER'S CODE I &, II III

A GANGSTER'S SYN I II III

THE SAVAGE LIFE I II III

CHAINED TO THE STREETS I II III

BLOOD ON THE MONEY I II III

By J-Blunt

PUSH IT TO THE LIMIT

By **Bre' Hayes**

BLOOD OF A BOSS **I, II, III, IV, V**

SHADOWS OF THE GAME

TRAP BASTARD

By **Askari**

THE STREETS BLEED MURDER **I, II & III**

THE HEART OF A GANGSTA I II& III

Khufu

Killa Kounty

MIDNIGHT CARTEL I II III

CITY OF KINGZ I II

By **Chris Green**

A DOPEBOY'S PRAYER

By **Eddie "Wolf" Lee**

THE KING CARTEL **I, II & III**

By **Frank Gresham**

THESE NIGGAS AIN'T LOYAL **I, II & III**

By **Nikki Tee**

GANGSTA SHYT **I II &III**

By **CATO**

THE ULTIMATE BETRAYAL

By **Phoenix**

BOSS'N UP **I , II & III**

By **Royal Nicole**

I LOVE YOU TO DEATH

By Destiny J

I RIDE FOR MY HITTA

I STILL RIDE FOR MY HITTA

By **Misty Holt**

LOVE & CHASIN' PAPER

By **Qay Crockett**

TO DIE IN VAIN

SINS OF A HUSTLA

By **ASAD**

BROOKLYN HUSTLAZ

By **Boogsy Morina**

BROOKLYN ON LOCK I & II

By **Sonovia**

GANGSTA CITY

Khufu

Killa Kounty

Elijah R. Freeman
GOD BLESS THE TRAPPERS I, II, III
THESE SCANDALOUS STREETS I, II, III
FEAR MY GANGSTA I, II, III IV, V
THESE STREETS DON'T LOVE NOBODY I, II
BURY ME A G I, II, III, IV, V
A GANGSTA'S EMPIRE I, II, III, IV
THE DOPEMAN'S BODYGAURD I II
THE REALEST KILLAZ I II III
THE LAST OF THE OGS I II
Tranay Adams
THE STREETS ARE CALLING
Duquie Wilson
MARRIED TO A BOSS... I II III
By Destiny Skai & Chris Green
KINGZ OF THE GAME I II III IV V
Playa Ray
SLAUGHTER GANG I II III
RUTHLESS HEART I II III
By Willie Slaughter
FUK SHYT
By Blakk Diamond
DON'T F#CK WITH MY HEART I II
By Linnea
ADDICTED TO THE DRAMA I II III
IN THE ARM OF HIS BOSS II
By Jamila
YAYO I II III IV
A SHOOTER'S AMBITION I II
BRED IN THE GAME

373

Khufu

374

Killa Kounty

JACK BOYZ N DA BRONX I II

A DOPEBOY'S DREAM

By **Romell Tukes**

LOYALTY AIN'T PROMISED I II

By Keith Williams

QUIET MONEY I II III

THUG LIFE I II III

EXTENDED CLIP I II

By **Trai'Quan**

THE STREETS MADE ME I II

By **Larry D. Wright**

THE ULTIMATE SACRIFICE I, II, III, IV, V, VI

KHADIFI

IF YOU CROSS ME ONCE

ANGEL I II

IN THE BLINK OF AN EYE

By **Anthony Fields**

THE LIFE OF A HOOD STAR

By Ca$h & Rashia Wilson

THE STREETS WILL NEVER CLOSE

By K'ajji

CREAM I II

By Yolanda Moore

NIGHTMARES OF A HUSTLA I II III

By King Dream

CONCRETE KILLA I II

By Kingpen

HARD AND RUTHLESS I II

MOB TOWN 251

By Von Diesel

Khufu

GHOST MOB II

Stilloan Robinson

MOB TIES I II

By SayNoMore

BODYMORE MURDERLAND I II III

By Delmont Player

FOR THE LOVE OF A BOSS

By C. D. Blue

MOBBED UP

By King Rio

KILLA KOUNTY

By Khufu

Killa Kounty

BOOKS BY LDP'S CEO, CA$H

TRUST IN NO MAN

TRUST IN NO MAN 2

TRUST IN NO MAN 3

BONDED BY BLOOD

SHORTY GOT A THUG

THUGS CRY

THUGS CRY 2

THUGS CRY 3

TRUST NO BITCH

TRUST NO BITCH 2

TRUST NO BITCH 3

TIL MY CASKET DROPS

RESTRAINING ORDER

RESTRAINING ORDER 2

IN LOVE WITH A CONVICT

LIFE OF A HOOD STAR

Khufu

CPSIA information can be obtained
at www.ICGtesting.com
Printed in the USA
LVHW082128010921
696580LV00013BA/1226